Critical acclaim for Ian Rankin

'Rankin's ability to create a credible character, delivering convincing dialogue to complement sinister and hard-hitting plots set against vividly detailed atmosphere, is simply awesome' *Time Out*

'Rankin is streets ahead in the British police procedural writing field . . . our top crime writer'
Independent on Sunday

'His ear for dialogue is as sharp as a switchblade. This is, quite simply, crime writing of the highest order'

Daily Express

'Rankin writes laconic, sophisticated, well-paced thrillers' *Scotsman*

'Ian Rankin bridges the gulf between the straight novel and the mystery with enviable ease'
Allan Massie

'First-rate crime fiction with a fierce realism'
Sunday Telegraph

'Rankin uses his laconic prose as a literary paint stripper, scouring away pretensions to reveal the unwholesome reality beneath' *Independent*

'His fiction buzzes with energy . . . Essentially, he is a romantic storyteller in the tradition of Robert Louis Stevenson . . . His prose is as vivid and terse as the next man's, yet its flexibility and rhythm give it a potential for lyrical expression which is distinctively Rankin's own' *Scotland on Sunday*

By Ian Rankin

The Inspector Rebus series
Knots & Crosses
Hide & Seek
Tooth & Nail
Strip Jack
The Black Book
Mortal Causes
Let It Bleed
Black & Blue
The Hanging Garden
Death Is Not The End (*novella*)
Dead Souls
Set in Darkness
The Falls
Resurrection Men
A Question of Blood
Fleshmarket Close

Other novels
The Flood
Watchman
Westwind

Writing as Jack Harvey
Witch Hunt
Bleeding Hearts
Blood Hunt

Short stories
A Good Hanging and Other Stories
Beggars Banquet

Omnibus editions
Rebus: The Early Years
(Knots & Crosses, Hide & Seek, Tooth & Nail)
Rebus: The St Leonard's Years
(Strip Jack, The Black Book, Mortal Causes)
Rebus: The Lost Years
(Let It Bleed, Black & Blue, The Hanging Garden)
Rebus: Capital Crimes (Dead Souls, Set in Darkness, The Falls)

All Ian Rankin's titles are available on audio. Also available:
Jackie Leven Said by Ian Rankin and Jackie Leven.

Born in the Kingdom of Fife in 1960, Ian Rankin graduated from the University of Edinburgh and has since been employed as grape-picker, swineherd, taxman, alcohol researcher, hi-fi journalist and punk musician. His first Rebus novel, *Knots & Crosses*, was published in 1987 and the Rebus books have now been translated into 26 languages. Ian Rankin has been elected a Hawthornden Fellow, and is a past winner of the prestigious Chandler-Fulbright Award, as well as two CWA short-story 'Daggers' and the 1997 CWA Macallan Gold Dagger for Fiction for *Black & Blue*, which was also shortlisted for the Mystery Writers of America 'Edgar' award for Best Novel. *Black & Blue*, *The Hanging Garden*, *Dead Souls* and *Mortal Causes* have been televised on ITV, starring John Hannah as Inspector Rebus. *Dead Souls*, the tenth novel in the series, was shortlisted for the CWA Gold Dagger Award in 1999. An Alumnus of the Year at Edinburgh University, he has also been awarded four honorary doctorates, from the University of Abertay Dundee in 1999, from the University of St Andrews in 2001, in 2003 from the University of Edinburgh and in 2005 from the Open University. In 2002 Ian Rankin was awarded an OBE for services to literature. In 2004 *Resurrection Men* won the Edgar Award for Best Novel. In 2005 *Fleshmarket Close* won the Crime Thriller of the Year award at the British Book Awards. Ian is the winner of the Crime Writers' Association Diamond Dagger 2005. In 2005 he was also awarded the Grand Prix du Littérature Policier (France), the Deutsche Krimi Prize (Germany) and the Icons of Scotland award. He lives in Edinburgh with his wife and two sons. Visit his website at www.ianrankin.net.

Ian Rankin

Resurrection Men

ORION

An Orion paperback

First published in Great Britain in 2001
by Orion
This paperback edition published in 2002
by Orion Books Ltd,
Orion House, 5 Upper St Martin's Lane
London WC2H 9EA

Reissued 2005

10

A CIP catalogue record for this book is available
from the British Library.

ISBN 0 75287 721 6

Printed and bound in Great Britain by
Clays Ltd, St Ives plc

'All men have secrets . . .'
(The Smiths, 'What Difference Does It Make?')

Durate et vosmet rebus servate secundis
(*Aeneid*, I, 207)

INTRODUCTION

For my previous novel, *The Falls*, I'd had to do some research into the infamous Edinburgh killers Burke and Hare, who dispatched seventeen victims in a single year, selling the corpses to local surgeons for dissection under the pretext of having freshly disinterred them. There was a roaring trade in body-snatching at the time, as the only specimens medical students were allowed to practise on were those of executed criminals – and there just weren't enough going around to satisfy the demands of the city's burgeoning medical school.

Of course, Burke and Hare were not body-snatchers: they just pretended to be. But the fear among Edinburgh's citizens was very real. On the fourth floor of the Museum of Scotland sits a 'mort safe', this being a heavy iron box which would be placed over a coffin until the body within had had time to decompose past the point of serving any use to grave-robbers and their clients. For the same reason, watchtowers exist at the corners of several local cemeteries (the most obvious is on Lothian Road, opposite the Caledonian Hotel). Guards would be paid to take a night shift in these, warning off and chasing away the 'human hyenas'. Various terms were used for the grave-robbers themselves, including sack-em-up men and – quite obviously my favourite – resurrection men.

So it was that, part-way through my research for *The Falls*, I had already found the title of my next Rebus adventure. And a plot was not long in joining it, thanks to a review of *The Falls* in a Sunday newspaper. The review had been penned by the city's Chief Constable. He was flattering in his praise – saying at one point that he wished he had one, just *one*, officer like Rebus on his force – but he felt the need to add one final caveat: if Rebus drank as much and smoked as much and had the lifestyle he so obviously did, then in real life he would probably be sent back to police college. I decided to contact the Chief Constable.

'It's a deal,' I told him. 'You fix it for me to visit the Scottish Police College at Tulliallan, and I'll send Rebus there in his next book.'

The Rebus novels, after all, had by now earned a reputation for realism. But serving officers had occasionally wondered why Rebus never made mention of Tulliallan. He would have trained there, and throughout his professional career he would have returned there to hone various skills and learn new tricks. I needed to know how the place worked, and now, with the Chief Constable's blessing, I was going to be given the opportunity.

The recruits weren't told who I was, and didn't know what to make of me. I wasn't in uniform, so was probably 'brass' of some kind, even if I didn't dress or act the part. To be on the safe side, they saluted me at every opportunity. I heard about the physical demands of the training – an assault course more or less ringed the college – and of the mental challenges on offer (such as thinking up ingenious ways to earn money for charity, including the parachute jump scene which eventually made it into *Resurrection Men* verbatim). I also sat in on a training session for new detectives: a group of three or four would be given a case to work on, their actions and decisions monitored by video cameras as they formed themselves into a team, interviewed 'suspects' (members of the training staff) and were sent anonymous calls (also from the training staff) offering them a mixture of clues and red herrings. It was while watching this process that I began to see my story beginning to emerge. The resurrection men of the title would be guys like Rebus, men who had broken the rules too often and weren't team players. Cops made cynical about the job, overweight and out of condition. For them, Tulliallan offered a final chance for resurrection.

I say that the Rebus novels had up to this point gained a reputation for a certain level of realism, yet curiously I had not set foot in Rebus's flat until the year 2000. Back in 1985, I'd been a student, sharing a ground-floor flat in Arden Street. I'd stared from my window towards the tenement across the street, let my eyes drift upwards a couple of storeys, and decided that Rebus should live there. But it wasn't until Melvyn Bragg's *South Bank Show* came to Edinburgh to make a film about me that I was persuaded to enter Rebus's stairwell, climb those two flights and knock on his door. He wasn't there, of course; the door was opened by a German lecturer. But it did mean that when the time came to write *Resurrection Men*, I could for the first time describe with confidence the stairwell, with its 'patterned wall-tiles and mosaic floor'. And when Rebus's fellow 'resurrection men' return with him to the flat after a night's boozing, I move them through the interior with that same confidence, having examined its layout for myself.

Not that books have to be 'true' necessarily; all they have to be is realistic. I felt few qualms, for example, about inventing a wholly fictitious Jack Vettriano painting – though I did make a preparatory phone call to the artist, just to make sure he was comfortable with the notion. Like me, he's from Fife – I didn't want him angry. The Vettriano is a clue in the murder of an art dealer, a case the newly promoted Siobhan is working on. I felt it was time Siobhan took at least one step up the ladder. Rebus has been around for more than a dozen novels, and managed only one promotion in all that time. (Again, for purposes of realism: precious few detectives past the rank of inspector get to travel any distance from their desks and meeting rooms.) Siobhan may be a very different beast to Rebus, but when he does retire she'll be quietly capable of filling his shoes as a DI.

In April 1998, I had travelled to New York for the annual 'Edgar' Awards, which are presented by the Mystery Writers of America organisation. My novel *Black & Blue* had been shortlisted in the 'Best Novel' category. It didn't win; James Lee Burke did. (He told me, years later, that he remembered my magnanimity that night. According to his version, I'd approached him afterwards and shaken him by the hand. I can't believe I did that; I think his memory deceives him.) In 2004 I made the same transatlantic trip. On 27 April I'd finished the first draft of *Fleshmarket Close*. Next day was my birthday, and on the 29th I flew to New York. This time I did not go home empty-handed: *Resurrection Men* won Best Novel.

Which means it's probably pretty good. But as usual I'll let you, the reader, decide.

May 2005

1

'Then why are you here?'

'Depends what you mean,' Rebus said.

'Mean?' The woman frowned behind her glasses.

'Mean by "here",' he explained. 'Here in this room? Here in this career? Here on the planet?'

She smiled. Her name was Andrea Thomson. She wasn't a doctor – she'd made that clear at their first meeting. Nor was she a 'shrink' or a 'therapist'. 'Career Analysis' was what it had said on Rebus's daily sheet.

2.30–3.15: Career Analysis, Rm 3.16.

With *Ms* Thomson. Which had become Andrea at the moment of introduction. Which was yesterday, Tuesday. A 'get to know' session, she'd called it.

She was in her late thirties, short and large-hipped. Her hair was a thick mop of blond with some darker streaks showing through. Her teeth were slightly oversized. She was self-employed, didn't work for the police full-time.

'Do any of us?' Rebus had asked yesterday. She'd looked a bit puzzled. 'I mean, do any of us work full-time . . . that's why we're here, isn't it?' He'd waved a hand in the direction of the closed door. 'We're not pulling our weight. We need a smack on the wrists.'

'Is that what you think you need, Detective Inspector?'

He'd wagged a finger. 'Keep calling me that and I'll keep calling you "Doc".'

'I'm not a doctor,' she'd said. 'Nor am I a shrink, a therapist, or any other word you've probably been thinking in connection with me.'

'Then what are you?'

1

'I deal with Career Analysis.'

Rebus had snorted. 'Then you should be wearing a seat-belt.'

She'd stared at him. 'Am I in for a bumpy ride?'

'You could say that, seeing how my *career*, as you call it, has just careered out of control.'

So much for yesterday.

Now she wanted to know about his feelings. How did he feel about being a detective?

'I like it.'

'Which parts?'

'All of me.' Fixing her with a smile.

She smiled back. 'I meant—'

'I know what you meant.' He looked around the room. It was small, utilitarian. Two chrome-framed chairs either side of a teak-veneered desk. The chairs were covered in some lime-coloured material. Nothing on the desk itself but her A4-sized lined pad and her pen. There was a heavy-looking satchel in the corner; Rebus wondered if his file was in there. A clock on the wall, calendar below it. The calendar had come from the local fire brigade. A length of net curtaining across the window.

It wasn't her room. It was a room she could use on those occasions when her services were required. Not quite the same thing.

'I like my job,' he said at last, folding his arms. Then, wondering if she'd read anything into the action – defensiveness, say – he unfolded them again. Couldn't seem to find anything to do with them except bunch his fists into his jacket pockets. 'I like every aspect of it, right down to the added paperwork each time the office runs out of staples for the staple-gun.'

'Then why did you blow up at Detective Chief Superintendent Templer?'

'I don't know.'

'She thinks maybe it has something to do with professional jealousy.'

2

The laugh burst from him. 'She said that?'

'You don't agree?'

'Of course not.'

'You've known her some years, haven't you?'

'More than I care to count.'

'And she's always been senior to you?'

'It's never bothered me, if that's what you're thinking.'

'It's only recently that she's become your commanding officer.'

'So?'

'You've been at DI level for quite some time. No thoughts of improvement?' She caught his look. 'Maybe "improvement" is the wrong word. You've not wanted promotion?'

'No.'

'Why not?'

'Might be I'm afraid of responsibility.'

She stared at him. 'That smacks of a prepared answer.'

'Be prepared, that's my motto.'

'Oh, you were a Boy Scout?'

'No,' he said. She stayed quiet, picking up her pen and studying it. It was one of those cheap yellow Bics. 'Look,' he said into the silence, 'I've got no quarrel with Gill Templer. Good luck to her as a DCS. It's not a job I could do. I like being where I am.' He glanced up. 'Which doesn't mean here in this room, it means out on the street, solving crimes. The reason I lost it is . . . well, the way the whole inquiry's being handled.'

'You must have had similar feelings before in the middle of a case?' She had taken her glasses off so she could rub the reddened skin either side of her nose.

'Many a time,' he admitted.

She slid the glasses back on. 'But this is the first time you've thrown a mug?'

'I wasn't aiming for her.'

'She had to duck. A full mug, too.'

'Ever tasted cop-shop tea?'

3

She smiled again. 'So you've no problem then?'

'None.' He folded his arms in what he hoped was a sign of confidence.

'Then why are you here?'

Time up, Rebus walked back along the corridor and straight into the men's toilets, where he splashed water on his face, dried off with a paper towel. Watched himself in the mirror above the sink as he pulled a cigarette from his packet and lit it, blowing the smoke ceilingwards.

One of the lavatories flushed; a door clicked its lock off. Jazz McCullough came out.

'Thought that might be you,' he said, turning on the tap.

'How could you tell?'

'One long sigh followed by the lighting of a cigarette. Had to be a shrink session finishing.'

'She's not a shrink.'

'Size of her, she looks like she's shrunk.' McCullough reached for a towel. Tossed it in the bin when he'd finished. Straightened his tie. His real name was James, but those who knew him seemed never to call him that. He was Jamesy, or more often Jazz. Tall, mid-forties, cropped black hair with just a few touches of grey at the temples. He was thin. Patted his stomach now, just above the belt, as if to emphasise his lack of a gut. Rebus could barely see his own belt, even in the mirror.

Jazz didn't smoke. Had a family back home in Broughty Ferry: wife and two sons about his only topic of conversation. Examining himself in the mirror, he tucked a stray hair back behind one ear.

'What the hell are we doing here, John?'

'Andrea was just asking me the same thing.'

'That's because she knows it's a waste of time. Thing is, we're paying her wages.'

'We're doing some good then.'

4

Jazz glanced at him. 'You dog! You think you're in there!'

Rebus winced. 'Give me a break. All I meant was . . .' But what was the point? Jazz was already laughing. He slapped Rebus on the shoulder.

'Back into the fray,' he said, pulling open the door. 'Three thirty, "Dealing with the Public".'

It was their third day at Tulliallan: the Scottish Police College. The place was mostly full of recent recruits, learning their lessons before being allowed out on to public streets. But there were other officers there, older and wiser. They were on refresher courses, or learning new skills.

And then there were the Resurrection Men.

The college was based at Tulliallan Castle, not in itself a castle but a mock-baronial home to which had been added a series of modern buildings, connected by corridors. The whole edifice sat in huge leafy grounds on the outskirts of the village of Kincardine, to the northern side of the Firth of Forth, almost equidistant between Glasgow and Edinburgh. It could have been mistaken for a university campus, and to some extent that was its function. You came here to learn.

Or, in Rebus's case, as punishment.

There were four other officers in the seminar room when Rebus and McCullough arrived. 'The Wild Bunch', DI Francis Gray had called them, first time they'd been gathered together. A couple of faces Rebus knew – DS Stu Sutherland from Livingston; DI Tam Barclay from Falkirk. Gray himself was from Glasgow, and Jazz worked out of Dundee, while the final member of the party, DC Allan Ward, was based in Dumfries. 'A gathering of nations,' as Gray had put it. But to Rebus they acted more like spokesmen for their tribes, sharing the same language but with different outlooks. They were wary of each other. It was especially awkward with officers from the same

5

region. Rebus and Sutherland were both Lothian and Borders, but the town of Livingston was F Division, known to anyone in Edinburgh as 'F Troop'. Sutherland was just waiting for Rebus to say something to the others, something disparaging. He had the look of a haunted man.

The six men shared only one characteristic: they were at Tulliallan because they'd failed in some way. Mostly it was an issue with authority. Much of their free time the previous two days had been spent sharing war stories. Rebus's tale was milder than most. If a young officer, fresh out of uniform, had made the mistakes they had made, he or she would probably not have been given the Tulliallan life-line. But these were lifers, men who'd been in the force an average of twenty years. Most were nearing the point where they could leave on full pension. Tulliallan was their last-chance saloon. They were here to atone, to be resurrected.

As Rebus and McCullough took their seats, a uniformed officer walked in and marched briskly to the head of the oval table where his chair was waiting. He was in his mid-fifties and was here to remind them of their obligation to the public at large. He was here to train them to mind their Ps and Qs.

Five minutes into the lecture, Rebus let his eyes and mind drift out of focus. He was back on the Marber case . . .

Edward Marber had been an Edinburgh art and antique dealer. Past tense, because Marber was now dead, blud-geoned outside his home by assailant or assailants unknown. The weapon had not yet been found. A brick or rock was the best guess offered by the city pathologist, Professor Gates, who had been called to the scene for a PLE: Pronouncement of Life Extinct. Brain haemorrhage brought on by the blow. Marber had died on the steps of his Duddingston Village home, front-door keys in his hand. He had been dropped off by taxi after the private viewing night of his latest exhibition: New Scottish Colourists. Marber owned two small, exclusive galleries in the New Town, plus antique shops in Dundas Street, Glasgow and Perth. Rebus had asked someone why Perth, rather than oil-rich Aberdeen.

'Because Perthshire's where the wealth goes to play.'

The taxi-driver had been interviewed. Marber didn't drive, but his house was at the end of an eighty-metre driveway, the gates to which had been open. The taxi had pulled up at the door, activating a halogen light to one side of the steps. Marber had paid and tipped, asking for a receipt, and the taxi-driver had U-turned away, not bothering to look in his mirror.

'I didn't see a thing,' he'd told the police.

The taxi receipt had been found in Marber's pocket, along with a list of the sales he'd made that evening, totalling just over £16,000. His cut, Rebus learned, would have been twenty per cent, £3,200. Not a bad night's work.

It was morning before the body was found by the postman. Professor Gates had given an estimated time of death of between nine and eleven the previous evening. The taxi had picked Marber up from his gallery at eight thirty, so must have dropped him home around eight forty-five, a time the driver accepted with a shrug.

The immediate police instinct had screamed robbery, but problems and niggles soon became apparent. Would someone have clobbered the victim with the taxi still in sight, the scene lit by halogen? It seemed unlikely, and yet by the time the taxi turned out of the driveway, Marber should have been safely on the other side of his door. And though Marber's pockets had been turned out, cash and credit cards evidently taken, the attacker had failed to use the keys to unlock the front door and trawl the house itself. Scared off perhaps, but it still didn't make sense.

Muggings tended to be spontaneous. You were attacked on the street, maybe just after using a cash machine. The mugger didn't hang around your door waiting for you to come home. Marber's house was relatively isolated: Duddingston Village was a wealthy enclave on the edge of Edinburgh, semi-rural, with the mass of Arthur's Seat as its neighbour. The houses hid behind walls, quiet and secure. Anyone approaching Marber's home on foot would have triggered the same halogen security light. They would then have had to hide – in the undergrowth, say, or behind one of the trees. After a couple of minutes, the lamp's timer would finish its cycle and go off. But any movement would trigger the sensor once again.

The Scene of Crime officers had looked for possible hiding places, finding several. But no traces of anyone, no footprints or fibres.

Another scenario, proposed by DCS Gill Templer:

'Say the assailant was already inside the house. Heard the door being unlocked and ran towards it. Smashed the victim on the head and ran.'

But the house was high-tech: alarms and sensors everywhere. There was no sign of a break-in, no indication that anything was missing. Marber's best friend, another art dealer called Cynthia Bessant, had toured the house and pronounced that she could see nothing missing or out of place, except that much of the deceased's art collection had been removed from the walls and, each painting neatly packaged in bubble-wrap, was stacked against the wall in the dining room. Bessant had been unable to offer an explanation.

'Perhaps he was about to re-frame them, or move them to different rooms. One *does* get tired of the same paintings in the same spots . . .'

She'd toured every room, paying particular attention to Marber's bedroom, not having seen inside it before. She called it his 'inner sanctum'.

The victim himself had never been married, and was quickly assumed by the investigating officers to have been gay.

'Eddie's sexuality,' Cynthia Bessant had said, 'can have no bearing on this case.'

But that would be something for the inquiry to decide.

Rebus had felt himself side-lined in the investigation, working the telephones mostly. Cold calls to friends and associates. The same questions eliciting almost identical responses. The bubble-wrapped paintings had been checked for fingerprints, from which it became apparent that Marber himself had packaged them up. Still no one – neither his secretary nor his friends – could give an explanation.

Then, towards the end of one briefing, Rebus had picked up a mug of tea – someone else's tea, milky grey – and hurled it in the general direction of Gill Templer.

The briefing had started much as any other, Rebus washing down three aspirin caplets with his morning latte. The coffee came in a cardboard beaker. It was from a concession on the corner of The Meadows. Usually his first and last decent cup of the day.

'Bit too much to drink last night?' DS Siobhan Clarke had asked. She'd run her eyes over him: same suit, shirt and tie as the day before. Probably wondering if he'd bothered to take any of it off between times. The morning shave erratic, a lazy run-over with an electric. Hair that needed washing and cutting.

She'd seen just what Rebus had wanted her to see.

'And a good morning to you too, Siobhan,' he'd muttered to himself, crushing the empty beaker.

Usually he stood towards the back of the room at briefings, but today he was nearer the front. Sat there at a desk, rubbing his forehead, loosening his shoulders, as Gill Templer spelt out the day's mission.

More door-to-door; more interviews; more phone calls.

His fingers were around the mug by now. He didn't know whose it was, the glaze cold to the touch – could even have been left from the day before. The room was stifling and already smelt of sweat.

'More bloody phone calls,' he found himself saying, loud enough to be heard at the front. Templer looked up.

'Something to say, John?'

'No, no . . . nothing.'

Her back straightening. 'Only if you've anything to add – maybe one of your famous deductions – I'm all ears.'

'With respect, ma'am, you're not all ears – you're all talk.' Noises around him: gasps and looks. Rebus rising slowly to his feet.

'We're getting nowhere fast.' His voice was loud. 'There's nobody left to talk to, and nothing worth them saying!'

The blood had risen to Templer's cheeks. The sheet of paper she was holding – the day's duties – had become a cylinder which her fingers threatened to crush.

'Well, I'm sure we can all learn something from *you*, DI Rebus.' Not 'John' any more. Her voice rising to match his. Her eyes scanned the room: thirteen officers, not quite the full complement. Templer was working under pressure: much of it fiscal. Each investigation had a ticket attached to it, a costing she daren't overstep. Then there were the illnesses and holidays, the latecomers . . . 'Maybe you'd like to come up here,' she was saying, 'and give us the benefit of your thoughts on the subject of just exactly *how* we should be proceeding with this inquiry.' She stretched an arm out, as if to introduce him to an audience. 'Ladies and gentlemen . . .'

Which was the moment he chose to throw the mug. It travelled in a lazy arc, spinning as it went, dispensing cold tea. Templer ducked instinctively, though the mug would have sailed over her head in any case. It hit the back wall just above floor level, bouncing off and failing to break. There was silence in the room as people rose to their feet, checking their clothes for spillage.

Rebus sat down then, one finger punching the desk as if trying to find the rewind on life's remote control.

*

'DI Rebus?' The uniform was talking to him.

'Yes, sir?'

'Glad you've decided to join us.' Smiles all around the table. How much had he missed? He didn't dare look at his watch.

'Sorry about that, sir.'

'I was asking if you'd be our member of the public.' Nodding to the opposite side of the table to Rebus. 'DI Gray will be the officer. And you, DI Rebus, will be coming into the station with what could turn out to be some vital information pertaining to a case.' The teacher paused. 'Or you could be a crank.' Laughter from a couple of the men. Francis Gray was beaming at Rebus, nodding encouragement.

'Whenever you're ready, DI Gray.'

Gray leaned forward on the table. 'So, Mrs Ditchwater, you say you saw something that night?'

The laughter was louder. The teacher waved them quiet. 'Let's try to keep this serious, shall we?'

Gray nodded, turned his eyes to Rebus again. 'You definitely saw something?'

'Yes,' Rebus announced, coarsening his voice. 'I saw the whole thing, Officer.'

'Though you've been registered blind these past eleven years?'

Gales of laughter in the room, the teacher thumping the table-top, trying to restore order. Gray sitting back, joining the laughter, winking across at Rebus, whose shoulders were rocking.

Francis Gray was fighting hard against resurrection.

'I thought I was going to wet myself,' Tam Barclay said, lowering the tray of glasses on to the table. They were in the larger of Kincardine's two pubs, lessons finished for the day. Six of them forming a tight circle: Rebus, Francis Gray, Jazz McCullough, plus Tam Barclay, Stu Sutherland and Allan Ward. At thirty-four, Ward was the youngest of the group and the lowest-ranking officer on the course. He had a tough, spoilt look to him. Maybe it came from working in the south-west.

Five pints, one cola: McCullough was driving home afterwards, wanted to see his wife and kids.

'I do my damnedest to *avoid* mine,' Gray had said.

'No joking,' Barclay said, squeezing into his seat, 'near wet myself.' Grinning at Gray. '"Blind these past eleven years".'

Gray picked up his pint, raised it. 'Here's tae us, wha's like us?'

'Nobody,' Rebus commented. 'Or they'd be stuck on this damned course.'

'Just got to grin and bear it,' Barclay said. He was late thirties, thickening around the waist. Salt-and-pepper hair brushed back from the forehead. Rebus knew him from a couple of cases: Falkirk and Edinburgh were only thirty minutes apart.

'I wonder if Wee Andrea grins when she bares it,' Stu Sutherland said.

'No sexism, please.' Francis Gray was wagging a finger.

'Besides,' McCullough added, 'we don't want to stoke John's fantasies.'

Gray raised an eyebrow. 'That right, John? Got the hots for your counsellor? Better watch, you might make Allan jealous.'

Allan Ward looked up from the cigarette he was lighting, just glowered.

'That your sheep-frightening look, Allan?' Gray said. 'Not much to do down in Dumfries, is there, except round up the usual ewes?'

More laughter. It wasn't that Francis Gray had made himself the centre of attention; it seemed to happen naturally. He'd been first into his seat, and the others had congregated around him, Rebus sitting directly opposite. Gray was a big man, and the years told on his face. And because he said everything with a smile, a wink or a glint

12

in his eye, he got away with it. Rebus hadn't heard anyone making a joke about Gray himself yet, though they'd all been his target. It was as if he were challenging them, testing them. The way they took his comments would tell him everything he needed to know about them. Rebus wondered how the big man would react to a jibe or joke directed against him.

Maybe he'd have to find out.

McCullough's mobile sounded, and he got up, moving away.

'His wife, odds-on,' Gray stated. He was halfway down his pint of lager. Didn't smoke, told Rebus he'd given up a decade back. The two of them had been outside during a break, Rebus offering the packet. Ward and Barclay smoked too. Three out of six: it meant Rebus could feel comfortable lighting up.

'She's keeping tabs on him?' Stu Sutherland was saying.

'Proof of a deep and loving relationship,' Gray commented, tipping the glass to his mouth again. He was one of those drinkers, you never saw them swallow: it was as if they could hold their throat open and just pour the stuff down.

'You two know each other?' Sutherland asked. Gray glanced over his shoulder to where McCullough was standing, his head bowed towards the mobile phone.

'I know the type,' was all Gray said by way of answer.

Rebus knew better. He rose to his feet. 'Same again?'

Two lagers, three IPAs. On his way to the bar, Rebus pointed towards McCullough, who shook his head. He still had most of his cola, didn't want another. Rebus heard the words 'I'll be on the road in ten minutes . . .' Yes, he was on the phone to his wife. Rebus had a call he wanted to make too. Jean was probably finishing work right around now. Rush hour, the journey from the museum to her home in Portobello might take half an hour.

The barman knew the order: this was their third round of the evening. The previous two nights, they'd stuck to the college premises. First night, Gray had produced a good bottle of malt, and they'd sat in the common room, getting to know each other. Tuesday, they'd met in the college's own bar for an after-dinner session, McCullough sticking to soft drinks and then heading out for his car.

But at lunchtime today, Tam Barclay had mentioned a bar in the village, good rep.

'No trouble with the locals,' was the way he'd put it. So here they were. The barman looked comfortable, which told Rebus he'd dealt with intakes from the college before. He was efficient, not over-friendly. Midweek, only half a dozen regulars in the place. Three at one table, two at one end of the bar, another standing alone next to Rebus. The man turned to him.

'Up at the cop school, are you?'

Rebus nodded.

'Bit old for recruits.'

Rebus glanced at the man. He was tall, completely bald, his head shining. Grey moustache, eyes which seemed to be retracting into the skull. He was drinking a bottle of beer with what looked like a dark rum in the glass next to it.

'Force is desperate these days,' Rebus explained. 'Next thing, they'll be press-ganging.'

The man smiled. 'I think you're having me on.'

Rebus shrugged. 'We're here on a refresher course,' he admitted.

'Teaching old dogs new tricks, eh?' The man lifted his beer.

'Get you one?' Rebus offered. The man shook his head. So Rebus paid the barman and, deciding against a tray, hoisted three of the pints, making a triangle of them between his hands. Went to the table, came back for the last two, including his own. Thinking: best not leave it too late to phone Jean. He didn't want her to hear him drunk. Not that he was planning on getting drunk, but you could never tell . . .

14

'This you celebrating the end of the course?' the man asked.

'Just the beginning,' Rebus told him.

St Leonard's police station was mid-evening quiet. There were prisoners in the holding cells waiting for next morning's court appearance, and two teenagers being booked for shoplifting. Upstairs, the CID offices were almost empty. The Marber inquiry had wound down for the day, and only Siobhan Clarke was left, in front of a computer, staring at a screen-saver in the form of a banner message: WHAT WILL SIOBHAN DO WITHOUT HER SUGAR DADDY? She didn't know who had written it: one of the team, having a bit of a laugh. She surmised it referred to John Rebus, but couldn't quite work out the meaning. Did the author know what a sugar daddy was? Or did it just mean that Rebus looked after her, watched out for her? She was annoyed to find herself so irritated by the message.

She went into the screen-saver options and clicked on 'banner', erased the present message and replaced it with one of her own: I KNOW WHO YOU ARE, SUCKER. Then she checked a couple of other terminals, but their screen-savers were asteroids and wavy lines. When the phone on her desk started ringing, she considered not answering. Probably another crank wanting to confess, or ready with spurious information. A respectable middle-aged gent had called yesterday and accused his upstairs neighbours of the crime. Turned out they were students, played their music too loud and too often. The man had been warned that wasting police time was a serious matter.

'Mind you,' one of the uniforms had commented afterwards, 'if I'd to listen to Slipknot all day, I'd probably do worse.'

Siobhan sat down in front of her computer, lifted the receiver.

'CID, DS Clarke speaking.'

'One thing they teach at Tulliallan,' the voice said, 'is the importance of the quick pick-up.'

She smiled. 'I prefer to be wooed.'

'A quick pick-up,' Rebus explained, 'means picking up the phone within half a dozen rings.'

'How did you know I was here?'

'I didn't. Tried your flat first, got the answering machine.'

'And somehow sensed I wasn't out on the town?' She settled back in her chair. 'Sounds like you're in a bar.'

'In beautiful downtown Kincardine.'

'And yet you've dragged yourself from your pint to call me?'

'I called Jean first. Had a spare twenty-pence piece . . .'

'I'm flattered. A whole twenty pee?' She listened to him snort.

'So . . . how's it going?' he asked.

'Never mind that, how's Tulliallan?'

'As some of the teachers would say, we have a new tricks–old dog interface scenario.'

She laughed. 'They don't talk like that, do they?'

'Some of them do. We're being taught crime *management* and victim *empathy response*.'

'And yet you still have time for a drink?'

Silence on the line; she wondered if she'd touched a nerve.

'How do you know I'm not on fresh orange?' he said at last.

'I just do.'

'Go on then, impress me with your detective skills.'

'It's just that your voice gets slightly nasal.'

'After how many?'

'I'll guess four.'

'The girl's a marvel.' The pips started sounding. 'Hang on,' he said, putting in more money.

'Another spare twenty pee?'

'A fifty, actually. Which gives you plenty of time to update me on Marber.'

'Well, it's all been very quiet since the coffee incident.'

'I think it was tea.'

'Whatever it was, the stain's not budging. For what it's worth, I think they over-reacted, sending you into purdah.'

'I'm wasting money here.'

She sighed, sat forward. The screen-saver had just kicked in: I KNOW WHO YOU ARE, SUCKER scrolling right to left across the screen. 'We're still looking at friends and associates. Couple of interesting stories: an artist Marber had fallings-out with. Not unusual in the business, apparently, but this came to blows. Turns out the artist is one of these New Scottish Colourists, and leaving him out of the exhibition was a definite snub.'

'Maybe he whacked Marber with his easel.'

'Maybe.'

'And the second story?'

'That one I've been saving up to tell you. Did you ever see the guest list for the preview?'

'Yes.'

'Turns out not everyone who turned up was on the list. What we had were people who'd signed Marber's guest book. But now we've printed off a list of the people who actually got invites. Some of them were at the exhibition, hadn't bothered to RSVP or sign the book.'

'This artist was one of them?' Rebus guessed.

'God, no. But a certain M. G. Cafferty was.'

She heard Rebus whistle. Morris Gerald Cafferty – Big Ger, to those in the know – was the east coast's biggest gangster, or the biggest one they knew about. Cafferty and Rebus went back a long way.

'Big Ger a patron of the arts?' Rebus mused.

'He collects paintings, apparently.'

'What he doesn't do is smack people over the head on their doorsteps.'

'I bow to your superior knowledge.'

There was a pause on the line. 'How's Gill doing?'

'Much better since you left. Is she going to take it any further?'

'Not if I finish this course – that was the deal. How about the L-plate?'

Siobhan smiled. By L-plate Rebus meant the latest addition to CID, a detective constable called Davie Hynds. 'He's quiet, studious, industrious,' she recited. 'Not your type at all.'

'But is he any good?'

'Don't worry, I'll slap him into shape.'

'That's one of the prerogatives, now you've been promoted.'

The pips were sounding again. 'Do I get to go now?'

'A concise and helpful report, DS Clarke. Seven out of ten.'

'Only seven?'

'I'm deducting three for sarcasm. You need to address this attitudinal problem of yours, or—'

The sudden hum on the line told her his time was up. It was taking some getting used to, being addressed as 'DS'. She sometimes still introduced herself as Detective Constable Clarke, forgetting that the recent round of promotions had been kind to her. Could jealousy be behind the message on her screen? Silvers and Hood had stayed the same rank – as had most of the rest of CID.

'Narrowing the field nicely, girl,' she told herself, reaching for her coat.

Back at the table, Barclay lifted a mobile phone and told Rebus he could have borrowed it.

'Thanks, Tam. I've actually got one.'

'Are the batteries flat?'

Rebus lifted his glass, shook his head slowly.

'I think,' Francis Gray said, 'John just prefers things done the old-fashioned way. Isn't that right, John?'

Rebus shrugged, tipped the glass to his lips. Above the rim, he could see the bald man standing sideways on to the bar, watching the group intently . . .

2

'Good morning, gentlemen!' the voice boomed, entering the room.

Six of them already seated at the same oval table. A dozen or more box-files at one end, the end where the teacher would sit.

9.15–12.45: Case Management, DCI (ret'd) Tennant.

'I trust we're all feeling bright as buttons. No thumping heads or churning stomachs to report!' Another box-file was slammed down on to the table. Tennant dragged his chair out, causing its feet to grate against the floor. Rebus was concentrating on the grain of the table's wood, trying to keep it in focus. When he did finally look up, he blinked. It was the bald guy from the bar, dressed now in an immaculate chalk-stripe suit, white shirt and navy-blue tie. His eyes seemed little pin-pricks of devilment as they alighted on every member of the previous night's drinking party.

'I want all those cobwebs blown away, gentlemen,' he said, slapping his hand down on one of the files. Dust rose from it, hanging in a beam of light which was streaking through the window behind him, its sole purpose to fry the eyeballs of last night's drinkers. Allan Ward, who'd hardly said three words in the bar, but who'd moved quickly from pints to shots of straight tequila, was now sporting a pair of blue-tinted wraparound sunglasses, and looked like he should be on the ski-slopes rather than stuck in this airless room. He'd smoked a cigarette with Rebus outside after breakfast, hadn't said a thing. But then Rebus hadn't felt much like talking either.

'Never trust a man when you can't see his eyes!' Tennant barked. Ward turned his head slowly towards him. Tennant didn't add anything, just waited him out. Ward reached into his pocket, brought out a pouch and slipped the sunglasses into it.

'That's better, DC Ward,' Tennant said. There were a couple of surprised looks around the table. 'Oh yes, I know all your names. Know what that's called? It's called preparation. No case can succeed without it. You need to know who and what you're dealing with. Wouldn't you agree, DI Gray?'

'Absolutely, sir.'

'No use jumping to conclusions, is there?'

The look Gray gave Tennant, Rebus knew Tennant had struck a chord. He was showing that he *had* done his research: not just names, but everything else in their files.

'No, sir,' Gray said coldly.

There was a knock at the door. It opened, and two men started carrying in what looked like a series of large collages. It took only a moment for Rebus to realise what they were: the Wall of Death. Photographs, charts, news cuttings . . . the sort of stuff you pinned to the walls of an inquiry room. The material was mounted on sheets of cork boarding, and the men placed these against the walls of the room. When they'd finished, Tennant thanked them and told them to close the door when they left. Then he got up and walked around the table.

'Case management, gentlemen. Well, you're old pros, aren't you? You know how to manage a murder inquiry. No new tricks to be learned?' Rebus remembered Tennant's words to him last night at the bar: he'd been on a fishing expedition, wondering how much Rebus would say . . . 'That's why I'm not going to bother with new tricks. Instead, how about sharpening up the old ones, eh? Some of you will know about this part of the course. I've heard it called "Resurrection". We give you an old case, something dormant, unsolved, and we ask you to take another look. We *require* you to work as a team. Remember how that used to be? Once upon a time you were all team players. These days you think you know better.' He was spitting out the words now, circling the table. 'Maybe you don't *believe* any more. Well, believe this: for me, you'll work together as a team. For me,' he paused, 'and for the poor bloody victim.' He was back at his end of the table, opening a file, bringing out a series of glossy photographs. Rebus was remembering RSMs he'd known in his army days. He was wondering if Tennant had served in the forces.

'You'll remember your CID training here, how we put you in teams we called "syndicates" and gave you a case to work on. You were videotaped . . .' Tennant pointed upwards. Cameras were watching from the corners of the room. 'There'd be a whole squad of us watching and listening in another room, feeding you tidbits of information, seeing what you'd do with it.' He paused. 'That won't happen here. This is just you lot . . . and *me*. If I tape you, it's for my own satisfaction.' As he started his walk around the table again, he deposited one print in front of each man.

'Take a look. His name is Eric Lomax.' Rebus knew the name. His heart missed a beat. 'Beaten to death with something resembling a baseball bat or pool cue. Hit with such force that splinters of wood were embedded in the skull.' The photo landed in front of Rebus. It showed the body at the scene of crime, an alleyway illuminated by the photographer's flash, raindrops falling into puddles. Rebus touched the photo but didn't pick it up, afraid that his hand might tremble. *Of all the unsolveds still mouldering in their boxes and storerooms, why did it have to be this one?* He focused on Tennant, seeking a clue.

'Eric Lomax,' Tennant was saying, 'died in the centre of our biggest, ugliest city on a busy Friday night. Last seen a bit the worse for wear, leaving his usual pub. About five hundred yards from this alley. The alley itself used by ladies of the night for knee-tremblers and God knows what else. If any of them stumbled across the body, they didn't come forward at the time. A punter on his way home phoned it in. We've still got the tapes of his call.' Tennant paused. He was back at the head of the table, and this time he sat down.

'All this was six years ago: October 1995. Glasgow CID handled the original investigation, but came to a slow stop.' Gray had looked up. Tennant nodded towards him. 'Yes, DI Gray, I appreciate that you were part of that inquiry. It doesn't make any difference.' Now his eyes scanned the table, fixing each man in turn. But Rebus's gaze had shifted to Francis Gray. Gray had worked the Lomax case . . .

'I don't know any more about this case than you do, gentlemen,' Tennant was telling them. 'By the end of the morning, you should know more than me. We've got a session each day, and if some of you want to continue in the evening after your other classes, you won't find me complaining. The door will always be open. We're going to sift the paperwork, study the transcripts, see if anything was missed. We're not looking for cock-ups: as I say, I've no idea what we're going to find in these boxes.' He patted one of the files. 'But for ourselves, and Eric Lomax's family, we're going to have a bloody good go at finding his killer.'

'Which do you want me to be: good cop or bad cop?'

'What?' Siobhan was busy looking for a parking spot, didn't think she'd quite heard him.

'Good cop, bad cop,' DC Davie Hynds repeated. 'Which one am I?'

'Jesus, Davie, we just go in and ask our questions. Is that Fiesta pulling out, do you think?' Siobhan braked, flashed her lights. The Fiesta moved from its kerbside spot. 'Hallelujah,' Siobhan said. They were at the north end of the New Town, just off Raeburn Place. Narrow streets

23

lined with cars. The houses were known as 'colonies': split into upper and lower halves, exterior stone stairs giving the only clue that these weren't normal terraces. Siobhan stopped again just in front of the space, preparing to reverse into it, then saw that the car behind was nosing in, stealing *her* precious parking place.

'What the—' She sounded her horn, but the driver was ignoring her. The rear end of his car was jutting out into the street, but he seemed happy enough, was reaching over to the passenger seat to pick up some papers. 'Look at this sod!' Siobhan said. Then she undid her seat-belt and got out of the car, Hynds following.

He watched her tap on the driver's window. The man pushed open his door, getting out.

'Yes?' he said.

'I was backing in here,' Siobhan told him, pointing to her own car.

'So?'

'So I'd like you to shift.'

The man pressed the button on his ignition key, locking all the doors. 'Sorry,' he said, 'but I'm in a hurry, and possession *is* nine tenths of the law.'

'That may be so,' Siobhan was opening her warrant card, holding it up before him, 'but I happen to be the other tenth, and right now that's the part that matters.'

The man looked at the card, then at Siobhan's face. There was a dull clunk as the car's locks sprang open again. The man got in and started his ignition.

'Stand there,' Siobhan told Hynds, gesturing to the spot the man's car was leaving. 'Don't want any other bugger trying that trick.'

Hynds nodded, watched her making for her own car. 'I think this means I'm the good guy,' he said, but not loud enough for her to hear.

Malcolm Neilson lived in one of the upper colonies. He answered the door wearing what looked like pyjama trousers – baggy, with vertical pink and grey stripes – and a fisherman's thick pullover. He was barefoot and sported wild, frazzled hair, as if he'd only recently disconnected himself from the mains. The hair was greying, the face round and unshaven.

'Mr Neilson?' Siobhan asked, opening her warrant card again. 'I'm DS Clarke, this is DC Hynds. We spoke on the phone.'

Neilson leaned out from his doorway, as if to look up and down the street. 'You better come in then,' he said, closing the door quickly after them. The interior was cramped: living room with a tiny kitchen off, plus maybe two bedrooms maximum. In the narrow hallway, a ladder led up through a trap-door into the loft.

'Is that where you . . . ?'

'My studio, yes.' He glanced in Siobhan's general direction. 'Out of bounds to visitors.'

He led them into the chaotic living room. It was split-level: sofa and stereo speakers down below, dining table above. Magazines were strewn around the floor, most with pictures and pages torn from them. Album sleeves, books, maps, empty wine bottles with the labels peeled off. They had to be careful where they put their feet.

'Come in if you can get in,' the artist said. He seemed nervous, shy, never meeting his visitors' eyes. He smeared an arm along the sofa, clearing its contents on to the floor. 'Sit down, please.'

They sat. Neilson seemed content to crouch in front of them, sandwiched by the loudspeakers.

'Mr Neilson,' Siobhan began, 'as I said on the phone, it's just a few questions about your relationship with Edward Marber.'

'We didn't *have* a relationship,' the artist snapped.

'How do you mean?'

'I mean we didn't speak, didn't communicate.'

'You'd had a falling-out?'

'The man rips off his customers and his artists both!

How is it possible to have a *relationship* under those circumstances?'

'Just to remind you that Mr Marber's dead,' Siobhan said quietly. The artist's eyes almost met hers for an instant.

'What do you mean?'

'It's just that you talk about him in the present tense.'

'Oh, I see.' He grew thoughtful. Siobhan could hear his breathing; it was loud and hoarse. She wondered if he might be asthmatic.

'Do you have any proof?' she asked at last.

'That he was a cheat?' Neilson considered this, then shook his head. 'It's enough that I know it.'

From the corner of her eye, Siobhan noticed that Hynds had taken out his notebook and was busy with his pen. The doorbell rang and Neilson bounded to his feet with a muttered apology. When he'd gone, Siobhan turned to Hynds.

'Not even the offer of a cuppa. What are you writing?'

He showed her. It was just a series of squiggles. She looked at him for an explanation.

'Concentrates the mind wonderfully if they think everything they say is likely to be recorded.'

'Learn that in college?'

He shook his head. 'All those years in uniform, boss. You learn a thing or two.'

'Don't call me boss,' she said, watching as Neilson led another visitor into the room. Her eyes widened. It was the parking-space thief.

'This is my . . . um . . .' Neilson was attempting introductions.

'I'm Malcolm's solicitor,' the man said, managing a thin smile.

Siobhan took a moment to recover. 'Mr Neilson,' she said, trying for eye contact, 'this was meant to be a casual chat. There was no need for . . .'

'Nice to formalise things though, don't you find?' The

solicitor stepped through the debris. 'My name's Allison, by the way.'

'And your surname, sir?' Hynds enquired blithely. In the fraction of a second it took the solicitor to recover, Siobhan could have hugged her colleague.

'William Allison.' He handed a business card to Siobhan.

She didn't so much as glance at it, just handed it straight to Hynds. 'Mr Allison,' she said quietly, 'all we're doing here is asking a few routine questions concerning the relationship – professional and personal – which may have existed between Mr Neilson and Edward Marber. It would have taken about ten minutes and that would have been the end of it.' She got to her feet, aware that Hynds was following suit: a quick learner, she liked that. 'But since you want to formalise things, I think we'll continue this discussion down at the station.'

The solicitor straightened his back. 'Come on now, no need for—'

She ignored him. 'Mr Neilson, I assume you'll want to travel with your lawyer?' She stared at his bare feet. 'Shoes might be an idea.'

Neilson looked at Allison. 'I'm in the middle of—'

Allison cut him off. 'Is this because of what happened outside?'

Siobhan held his gaze without blinking. 'No, sir. It's because I'm wondering why your client felt the need of your services.'

'I believe it's everyone's right to—'

Neilson was tugging at Allison's sleeve. 'Bill, I'm in the middle of something, I don't want to spend half the day in a police cell.'

'The interview rooms at St Leonard's are quite cosy actually,' Hynds informed the artist. Then he made a show of studying his watch. 'Of course, this time of day . . . it's going to take us a while to get through the traffic.'

'And back again afterwards,' Siobhan added. 'Plus the

27

waiting time if a room's not available . . .' She smiled at the solicitor. 'Still, makes things nice and formal, just the way you want them.'

Neilson held up a hand. 'Just a minute, please.' He was leading the solicitor out into the hallway. Siobhan turned to Hynds and beamed. 'One–nil to us,' she said.

'But is the referee ready to blow?'

She shrugged a reply, slid her hands into her jacket pockets. She'd seen messier rooms; couldn't help wondering if it were part of an act – the eccentric artist. The kitchen was just behind the dining table and looked clean and tidy. But then maybe Neilson just didn't use it very much . . .

They heard the front door close. Neilson shambled back into the room, head bowed. 'Bill's decided . . . um, that is . . .'

'Fine,' Siobhan said, settling once again on the sofa. 'Well, Mr Neilson, sooner we get started and all that, eh?'

The artist crouched down between the speakers. They were big and old; wood-veneered sides and brown foam grilles. Hynds sat down, notebook in hand. Siobhan caught Neilson's eye at last and offered her most reassuring smile.

'So,' she said, 'just why exactly *did* you feel the need to have a solicitor present, Mr Neilson?'

'I just . . . I thought it was the done thing.'

'Not unless you're a suspect.' She let this sink in, Neilson muttered something that sounded like an apology.

Sitting back in the sofa, beginning to relax, Siobhan started the interview proper.

They both got cups of hot brown liquid from the machine. Hynds grimaced as he took his first sip.

'Couldn't we all chip in for a coffee-maker?' he asked.

'It's been tried before.'

'And?'

'And we started arguing about whose turn it was to buy

the coffee. There's a kettle in one of the offices. You can bring your own mug and stuff, but take my advice: keep everything locked up, or it'll go walkies.'

He stared at the plastic beaker. 'Easier to use the machine,' he mumbled.

'Exactly.' She pushed open the door to the murder room.

'So whose mug did DI Rebus throw?' Hynds asked.

'Nobody knows,' she admitted. 'Seems it's been here since they built this place. Could even be that the builders left it.'

'No wonder he got kicked into touch then.' She looked at him for an explanation. 'Attempted destruction of a historical artefact.'

She smiled, made for her desk. Someone had borrowed her chair – again. Looking around, the nearest spare was Rebus's. He'd taken it from the Farmer's office when the old DCS had retired. That no one had touched it was testament to Rebus's reputation, which didn't stop her pushing it across the floor and making herself comfortable.

Her computer screen was blank. She hit a key, bringing it back to life. A new screen-saver was flickering across her vision. PROVE IT THEN – POINT ME OUT. She looked up from the screen, scanning the room. Two primary targets: DC Grant Hood and DS George 'Hi-Ho' Silvers. They had their heads together, standing by the far wall. Maybe they were discussing the following week's rota, swapping assignments. Grant Hood had had a thing about her not that long back. She thought she'd managed to damp those flames without making an enemy of him. But he did like his boxes of tricks: computers; video games; digital cameras. It would be just his style to start sending her messages.

Hi-Ho Silvers was different. He liked his practical jokes, had made her his victim before. And though he was married, he had a reputation. He'd propositioned Siobhan half a dozen times over the past few years – she could always depend on him for some lurid suggestion at the Christmas party. But she wasn't sure he'd know how to change a screen-saver. He could barely change misspelled words when he was typing his reports.

Other candidates . . . ? DC Phyllida Hawes, on secondment from Gayfield Square . . . newly promoted Detective Chief Inspector Bill Pryde . . . Neither of them seemed to fit the bill. When Grant Hood turned his head in her direction, she pointed at him. He frowned, shrugged his shoulders as if to ask what she wanted. She indicated her computer screen, then wagged her finger. He broke off his conversation with Silvers and started towards her. Siobhan tapped a key, so that the screen-saver disappeared, replaced with a fresh page from the word-processing software.

'Got a problem?' Hood asked.

She shook her head slowly. 'I thought I had. The screen-saver . . .'

'What about it?' He was at her shoulder now, studying the screen.

'It was slow to shift.'

'Could be your memory,' he said.

'Nothing wrong with my memory, Grant.'

'I mean the memory on the hard disk. If it's filling up, everything slows down.'

She knew as much but pretended she didn't. 'Oh, right.'

'I'll check it, if you like. Only take two ticks.'

'Wouldn't want to keep you from your little chit-chat.'

Hood looked over to where George Silvers was now perusing the Wall of Death: a montage of photos and documents relating to the case, stuck to the far wall with Blu-Tac.

'Hi-Ho's turned malingering into an art form,' Hood said quietly. 'He's been over there half the day, says he's trying to get a "feel" for events.'

'Rebus does the same thing,' she stated. Hood looked at her.

'Hi-Ho's no John Rebus. All George Silvers wants is a quiet life until his pension maxes out.'

'Whereas?'

'Whereas Rebus will be lucky to still be around to collect his.'

'Is this a private confab, or can anyone join in?' Davie Hynds was standing not three feet away, hands in trouser pockets to indicate that he was at a loose end.

Grant Hood straightened up, slapped a hand on to Hynds's shoulder. 'And how's the new boy shaping up, DS Clarke?'

'So far, so good.'

Hood whistled, making a show of reappraising Hynds. 'That's high marks, coming from DS Clarke, Davie. You've obviously wangled your way into her affections.' With an exaggerated wink, he moved off, heading once more for the Wall of Death.

Hynds took a step towards Siobhan's desk. 'Is there some history between you two?'

'Why do you say that?'

'DC Hood obviously doesn't like me.'

'It'll take a while, that's all.'

'But am I right? Is there a history?'

She shook her head slowly, keeping her eyes on his. 'You reckon yourself a bit of an expert, don't you, Davie?'

'How do you mean?'

'As an amateur psychologist.'

'I wouldn't say—'

She was resting against the back of Rebus's chair. 'Let's give you a test: what did you make of Malcolm Neilson?'

Hynds folded his arms. 'I thought we'd covered this.'

By which he meant their conversation as Siobhan drove them from Neilson's home back to St Leonard's. They hadn't learned very much from the meeting, Neilson admitting it was no secret he wasn't on speaking terms

31

with the art dealer. He'd further admitted being annoyed that he'd suddenly been excluded from the New Colourists.

'That bugger Hastie couldn't paint a living room wall, and as for Celine Blacker . . .'

'I quite like Joe Drummond though,' Hynds had interrupted. Siobhan had given him a warning look, but Neilson wasn't listening anyway.

'Celine's not even her real name,' he was saying.

In the car, Siobhan had asked if Hynds knew anything about painting.

'I did read up on the Colourists a bit,' he'd admitted. 'Case like this, thought it might come in handy . . .'

Now, he rested his knuckles against the edge of Siobhan's desk, leaning in towards her. 'He's not got much of an alibi,' he stated.

'But did he act like a man who might need one?'

Hynds considered this. 'He called his lawyer . . .'

'Yes, but that was a moment's panic. Once we actually got talking, didn't you think he relaxed?'

'He was pretty confident.'

Siobhan, gazing into the middle-distance, found herself locking eyes with George Silvers. She pointed to her computer screen, then wagged the finger at him. He ignored her, went back to his pretence of studying the wall.

Detective Chief Superintendent Gill Templer was suddenly standing in the doorway.

'Noise Abatement Society been leafleting again?' she bellowed. 'A quiet office is one that isn't working hard enough.' She narrowed in on Silvers. 'Think you're going to solve the case by osmosis, George?' There were smiles, but no laughter. The officers were trying to look busy but focused.

Templer was heading relentlessly for Siobhan's desk. 'How did you get on with the artist?' she asked, her voice dropping several decibels.

'Says he was in a few pubs that evening, ma'am. Got a takeaway and went home to listen to Wagner.'

'*Tristan und Isolde,*' Hynds confided. Then, when Templer turned her laser glare on him, he blurted out that Neilson had wanted a solicitor present at the interview.

'Did he now?' The beams switched to Siobhan.

'It'll go in my report, ma'am.'

'But you didn't think it worth mentioning?'

The side of Hynds's neck was reddening as he realised he'd dropped Siobhan in it.

'We don't think it really means anything . . .' His voice fell away as he found himself the centre of attention again.

'That's your judgement, is it? Well, I can see I'm completely surplus to requirements. DC Hynds,' Templer announced to the room, 'thinks he's competent to make all the decisions around here.'

Hynds tried for a smile, failed.

'But just in case he's wrong . . .' Templer was moving towards the doorway again, gesturing into the corridor. 'Seeing how we're down a DI, the Big House have let us borrow one of theirs.'

Siobhan sucked air between her teeth as a body and face she recognised walked into the room.

'DI Derek Linford,' Templer stated by way of introduction. 'Some of you may already know him.' Her eyes turned towards Hi-Ho Silvers. 'George, you've been staring at that wall long enough. Maybe you can bring Derek up to speed on the case, eh?'

With that, Templer left the room. Linford looked around, then walked stiffly towards George Silvers, shaking the proffered hand.

'Christ,' Hynds was saying in an undertone, 'I felt like I was on her petri dish for a minute back there . . .' Then he noticed Siobhan's face. 'What is it?'

'What you were saying before . . . about Grant and me.' She nodded her head in Linford's direction.

'Oh,' Davie Hynds said. Then: 'Fancy another coffee?'

Out at the machine she gave him an edited version of events, telling him that she'd gone out with Linford on a couple of occasions, but leaving out the fact that Linford had started spying on her. She added that there was bad blood between Linford and Rebus, too, with the former blaming the latter for a severe beating he'd been given.

'You mean DI Rebus beat him up?'

Siobhan shook her head. 'But Linford blames him all the same.'

Hynds gave a low whistle. He seemed about to say something, but now Linford himself was walking down the corridor, sorting out some loose coins in his hand.

'Change for fifty pee?' he asked. Hynds immediately reached into his own pocket, allowing Linford and Siobhan to share a look.

'How are you, Siobhan?'

'Fine, Derek. How are you?'

'Better.' He nodded slowly. 'Thanks for asking.' Hynds was slotting coins home, refusing Linford's offer of the fifty-pence piece.

'Was it tea or coffee you were after?'

'I think I'm capable of pushing the button myself,' Linford told him. Hynds realised he was trying too hard, took half a step back.

'Besides,' Linford added, 'knowing this machine, it hardly makes any difference.' He managed a smile, but it didn't quite reach his eyes.

'Why him?' Siobhan asked.

She was in DCS Templer's office. Gill Templer had just come off the phone and was scribbling a note in the margin of a typewritten sheet.

'Why not?'

It struck Siobhan that Templer hadn't been Chief Super back then. She didn't know the full story.

'There's . . .' She found herself echoing Hynds's word:

'history.' Templer glanced up. 'Between DI Linford and DI Rebus,' Siobhan went on.

'But DI Rebus is no longer part of this team.' Templer lifted the sheet of paper as if to read it.

'I know that, ma'am.'

Templer peered at her. 'Then what's the problem?'

Siobhan took the whole office in with a sweep of her eyes. Window and filing cabinets, potted plant, a couple of family photographs. She wanted it. She wanted some day to be sitting where Gill Templer was.

Which meant not giving up her secrets.

Which meant seeming strong, not rocking the boat.

'Nothing, ma'am.' She turned towards the door, reached out for the handle.

'Siobhan.' The voice was more human. 'I respect your loyalty to DI Rebus, but that doesn't mean it's necessarily a good thing.'

Siobhan nodded, keeping her face to the door. When her boss's phone rang again, she made what she felt was a dignified exit. Back in the murder room, she checked her screen-saver. No one had tampered with it. Then she had a thought, and walked the short distance back across the corridor, knocking on the door, putting her head around without waiting. Templer put a hand across the receiver's mouthpiece.

'What is it?' she asked, her voice once again iron.

'Cafferty,' Siobhan said simply. 'I want to be the one who interviews him.'

Rebus was slowly circling the long oval table. Night had fallen, but the slat-blinds remained open. The table was strewn with stuff from the box-files. What it lacked as yet was some order. Rebus didn't think it was his job to impose order, yet that was what he was doing. He knew that come the morning, the rest of the team might want to rearrange everything, but at least he'd have tried.

Interview transcripts, reports from the door-to-door

enquiries, medical and pathology, forensics and Scene of Crime . . . There was a lot of background on the victim, as was to be expected: how could they hope to solve the crime until they had a motive? The area's prostitutes had been reluctant to come forward. No one had claimed Eric Lomax as a client. It didn't help that there had been a series of murders of Glasgow prostitutes and that the police had been accused of not caring. Nor did it help that Lomax – known to his associates as Rico – had operated on the fringes of the city's criminal community.

In short, Rico Lomax was a low-life. And even on this morning's evidence, Rebus could see that some of the officers on the original inquiry had felt that all his demise did was erase another name from the game. One or two of the Resurrection Men had mooted similar feelings.

'Why give us a scumbag to work on?' Stu Sutherland had asked. 'Give us a case we *want* to see solved.'

Which remark had earned him a roasting from DCI Tennant. They had to want to see all their cases solved. Rebus had watched Tennant throughout, wondering why the Lomax case had been chosen. Could it be random chance, or something altogether more threatening?

There was a box of newspapers from the time. A lot of interest had been shown in them, not least because they brought back memories. Rebus sat himself down now and leafed through a couple. The official opening of the Skye Road Bridge . . . Raith Rovers in the UEFA Cup . . . a bantamweight boxer killed in the ring in Glasgow . . .

'Old news,' a voice intoned. Rebus looked up. Francis Gray was standing in the open doorway, feet apart, hands in pockets.

'Thought you were down the pub,' Rebus said.

Gray sniffed as he came in, rubbed a hand across his nose. 'We just ended up discussing all this.' He tapped one of the empty box-files. 'The lads are on their way over, but looks like you beat us all to it.'

'It was all right when it was just tests and lectures,'

Rebus said, leaning back in his chair so he could stretch his spine.

Gray nodded. 'But now there's something for us to take seriously, eh?' He pulled out the chair next to Rebus's, sat down and concentrated on the open newspaper. 'But you seem to be taking it more seriously than most.'

'I just got here first, that's all.'

'That's what I mean.' Gray still wasn't looking at him. He wet a thumb and turned back a page. 'You've got a bit of a rep, haven't you, John? Sometimes you get *too* involved.'

'Oh aye? And you're here for always toeing the line?'

Gray allowed himself a smile. Rebus could smell beer and nicotine from his clothes. 'We've all crossed the line sometime, haven't we? It happens to good cops as well as bad. Maybe you could even say it's what makes the good cops *good*.'

Rebus studied the side of Gray's head. Gray was at Tulliallan because he'd disobeyed one order too many from a senior officer. Then again, as Gray had said: 'My boss was, is, and will forever be a complete and utter arsehole.' A pause. 'With respect.' That final phrase had cracked the table up. The problem with most of the Resurrection Men was, they didn't respect those above them in the pecking order, didn't trust them to do a good job, make the right decision. Gray's 'Wild Bunch' would only be returned to duty when they'd learned to accept and respond to the hierarchy.

'See,' Gray was saying now, 'give me a boss like DCI Tennant any day of the week. Guy like that's going to call a spade a shovel. You know where you stand with him. He's old school.'

Rebus was nodding. 'At least he's going to give you a bollocking to your face.'

'And not go shafting you from behind.' Now Gray found himself at the newspaper's front page. He held it up for Rebus to see: *Rosyth Bid Brings Hope of 5,000 Jobs . . .* 'Yet we're still here,' Gray said quietly. 'We haven't quit and they haven't made us. Why do you think that is?'

'We'd cause too much trouble?' Rebus guessed.

Gray shook his head. 'It's because deep down they understand something. They know that they need us more than we need them.' Now he turned to match Rebus's gaze, seemed to be waiting for Rebus to say something in reply. But there were voices in the corridor, and then faces in the doorway. Four of them, toting a couple of carrier-bags from which were produced tins of beer and lager and a bottle of cheap whisky. Gray rose to his feet, quickly took over.

'DC Ward, you're in charge of finding us some mugs or glasses. DS Sutherland, might as well shut the blinds, eh? DI Rebus here has already got the ball rolling. Who knows, maybe we'll wrap this up tonight and put Archie Tennant's gas at a peep . . .'

They knew they wouldn't, but that didn't stop them trying, starting with a brainstorming session that went all the better for the loosening effects of the alcohol. Some of the theories were wild, and got wilder, but there were nuggets among the dross. Tam Barclay made a list. As Rebus had suspected would happen, the separate clusters of paperwork on the table soon collided, restoring chaos to the whole. He didn't say anything.

'Rico Lomax wasn't expecting anything,' Jazz McCullough stated at one point.

'How do you reckon?'

'Wary men tend to change their routine, but here's Rico, cool as you like, at his usual spot in his usual bar on the same night as always.'

There were nods of agreement. Their thinking had been: some gangland falling-out, an organised hit.

'We all spoke to our grasses at the time,' Francis Gray added. 'A lot of pieces of silver crossed a good many undeserving palms. Result: sweet FA.'

'Doesn't mean there wasn't a contract on him,' Allan Ward said.

'Still with us, Allan?' Gray said, sounding surprised. 'Is it not time you were tucked up in bed with your teddy?'

'Tell me, Francis, do you buy your one-liners wholesale? Only they're well past their sell-by.'

There was laughter at this, and a few fingers pointed at Gray, as if to say: *The lad got you, Francis! He definitely got you!*

Rebus watched Gray's mouth twist itself into a smile so thin it could have graced a catwalk.

'I can see this is going to be a long night,' Jazz McCullough said, bringing them back to earth.

After a can of beer, Rebus excused himself to visit the toilet. It was at the end of the corridor and down a flight of stairs. As he left the room, he could hear Stu Sutherland repeating one of the earlier theories:

'Rico was freelance, right? As in not affiliated to any gang in particular. And one of the things he was good at, if the rumours are true, was getting the various soldiers off the battlefield when things got too hot . . .'

Rebus knew what Sutherland was talking about. If someone did a hit, or got into any other trouble which necessitated them getting out of town for a while, it was Rico's job to find a safe haven. He had contacts everywhere: council flats, holiday homes, caravan sites. From Caithness to the border, the Western Isles to East Lothian. Caravans on the east coast were a speciality: Rico had cousins who ran half a dozen separate sites. Sutherland wanted to know who'd been hiding out at the time Rico had been hit. Could one of the safe houses have been breached, a visit with a baseball bat Rico's punishment? Or had someone been trying to find out a location from him?

It wasn't a bad notion. What troubled Rebus was how, six years on, they'd go about finding out. By the stairwell, he saw a shadowy figure heading down. Cleaner, he thought. But the cleaners had been round earlier. He started to descend, but then thought better of it. Walked the length of the opposite corridor: there was another set of stairs down at its end. Now he was on the ground floor. He walked on tiptoe back towards the central stairwell, keeping in against the wall. Pushed open the glass doors and surprised the figure who was skulking there.

'Evening, sir.'

DCI Archibald Tennant spun round. 'Oh, it's you.'

'Spying on us, sir?'

Rebus could see Tennant considering his options.

'I'd probably do the same thing,' Rebus said into the silence, 'under the circumstances.'

Tennant tilted his head upwards. 'How many are in there?'

'All of us.'

'McCullough's not bunked off home?'

'Not tonight.'

'In that case, I *am* impressed.'

'Why don't you join us, sir? Couple of cans of beer left . . .'

Tennant made a show of checking his watch, wrinkled his nose. 'Time I was turning in,' he said. 'I'd appreciate it if you didn't . . .'

'Mention bumping into you? Wouldn't that be going against the team ethos, sir?' Beginning to smile, enjoying Tennant's discomfort.

'Just this once, DI Rebus, maybe you could play the outsider.'

'Step out of character, you mean?'

This elicited a smile from the older man. 'Tell you what, I'll leave it to your judgement, shall I?' He turned and pushed his way out of the college's main doors. The path outside was well lit, and Rebus watched him all the way, then stepped beneath the staircase, where the public telephones were.

His call was answered at the fifth ring. Rebus kept his eyes on the stairs, ready to hang up if anyone came down.

'It's me,' he said into the receiver. 'I need a meet.' He listened for a moment. 'Sooner if you can manage it. What about this weekend? It's nothing to do with you-know-what.' He paused. 'Well, maybe it is. I don't know.' He nodded as he learned that the weekend was out of the question. After listening to a few more words, Rebus hung up and pushed open the door to the toilets. Stood there at the sink, running the water. It was less than a minute before someone else came in. Allan Ward offered a grunt before making for one of the cubicles. Rebus heard the door lock, Ward loosen his trouser-belt.

'Waste of time and brain-cells,' Ward's voice bounced off the ceiling. 'Complete and utter waste of manpower.'

'I get the feeling DCI Tennant has failed to sway you?' Rebus called.

'Fucking waste of time.'

Taking this as a yes, Rebus left Ward to his business.

3

Friday morning, they were back on the Lomax case. Tennant had asked for a progress report. Several pairs of eyes had gone to Francis Gray, but Gray himself stared levelly at Rebus.

'John's put in more hours than any of us,' he said. 'Go on, John, tell the man what we've found.'

Rebus took a sip of coffee first, gathering his thoughts. 'Mostly what we've got is conjecture, not much of it new. The feeling is, someone was waiting for the victim. They knew where he'd be, what time he'd be there. Thing is, that alley was used by the working girls, yet none of them saw anyone hanging around.'

'Not the world's most reliable witnesses, are they?' Tennant interrupted.

Rebus looked at him. 'They don't always want to come forward, if that's what you mean.'

Tennant shrugged by way of an answer. He was circling the table. Rebus wondered if he'd noticed that there were fewer hangovers this morning. Sure, some of them still looked like their faces had been drawn by kids armed with crayons, but Allan Ward had no need of his designer sunglasses, and Stu Sutherland's eyes were dark-ringed but not bloodshot.

'You think it's a gang thing?' Tennant asked.

'That's our favoured explanation, same as it was with the original inquiry team.'

'But . . . ?' Tennant was facing Rebus from the other side of the table.

'But,' Rebus obliged, 'there are problems. If it was a

gang hit, how come no one seemed to know? The CID in Glasgow have their informers, but nobody'd heard anything. A wall of silence is one thing, but there's usually a crack somewhere, sometime down the road.'

'And what do you glean from that?'

It was Rebus's turn to shrug. 'Nothing. It's just a bit odd, that's all.'

'What about Lomax's friends and associates?'

'They make the Wild Bunch look like the Seven Dwarves.' There were a couple of snorts from the table. 'Mr Lomax's widow, Fenella, was an early suspect. Rumour was, she'd been playing around behind hubby's back. Couldn't prove anything, and she wasn't about to tell us.'

Francis Gray pulled his shoulders back. 'She's since hitched her wagon to Chib Kelly.'

'He sounds delightful,' Tennant said.

'Chib owns a couple of pubs in Govan, so he's used to being behind bars.'

'Do I take it that's where he is now?'

Gray nodded. 'A wee stretch in Barlinnie: reset of stolen goods. His pubs do more business than most branches of Curry's. Fenella won't be pining – plenty men in Govan know what she likes for breakfast . . .'

Tennant nodded thoughtfully. 'DI Barclay, you don't look happy.'

Barclay folded his arms. 'I'm fine, sir.'

'Sure?'

Barclay unfolded the arms again, while attempting to find space beneath the table to cross his legs. 'It's just that this is the first we've heard of it.'

'Heard of Mrs Lomax and Chib Kelly?' Tennant waited until Barclay had nodded, then turned his attention to Gray.

'Well, DI Gray? Isn't this supposed to be a team effort?'

Francis Gray made a point of not looking at Barclay. 'Didn't think it pertinent, sir. There's nothing to show that

Fenella and Chib knew one another when Rico was around.'

Tennant pushed out his lips. 'Satisfied, DI Barclay?'

'I suppose so, sir.'

'What about the rest of you? Was DI Gray right to hold back on you?'

'I can't see that it did any harm,' Jazz McCullough said, to nods of agreement.

'Any chance we can question Mrs Lomax?' Allan Ward piped up.

Tennant was standing right behind him. 'I don't think so.'

'Not much chance of us getting a result then, is there?'

Tennant leaned down over Ward's shoulder. 'I didn't think results were your forte, DC Ward.'

'What's that supposed to mean?' Ward was beginning to rise to his feet, but Tennant slapped a restraining hand on the back of his neck.

'Sit down and I'll tell you.' When Ward was seated again, Tennant left his hand where it was for a few seconds, then moved away, once more circling the table. 'This case might be dormant, but it's not extinct. You prove to me that you need to check on something, maybe interview someone, and I'll fix it up. But I will need to be persuaded. In the past, DC Ward, you've been a mite overenthusiastic as far as interview technique is involved.'

'That was a piece of lying junkie scum,' Ward spat.

'And since his complaint was not upheld, we must naturally concede that you did nothing wrong.' Though Tennant beamed a smile in Ward's direction, Rebus had seldom seen a face look less amused. Then Tennant clapped his hands together. 'To work, gentlemen! Today I'd like to see you get through the interview transcripts. Work in pairs if it makes it easier.' He pointed to where a clean white marker-board had been placed against the wall. 'I want the path of the original inquiry laid out for me, along with comments and criticisms. Anything they

44

missed, all the side roads, especially ones you feel they should maybe have ventured down a little further.' As Stu Sutherland let out a perceptible groan, Tennant fixed him with a stare. 'Anyone who doesn't see the point of this can head back downstairs.' He checked his watch. 'The uniformed recruits will be starting their three-mile run in the next quarter of an hour. Plenty of time to change into your vest and shorts, DS Sutherland.'

'I'm fine, sir,' Sutherland said, making a show of patting his stomach. 'Bit of indigestion, that's all.'

Tennant glowered at him, then left the room. Slowly, the six men turned back into a team again, sharing out the piles of paperwork. Rebus noticed that Tam Barclay kept his head down, keen to avoid eye contact with Francis Gray. Gray was working with Jazz McCullough. At one point, Rebus thought he heard Gray say, 'Know what "Barclays" is rhyming slang for down south?' but McCullough didn't take the bait.

After almost an hour had passed, Stu Sutherland closed another file and slapped it down on to the pile in front of him, then got up to stretch his legs and back. He was over by the window when he turned to face the room.

'We're wasting our time,' he said. 'The one thing we need is the one thing we'll never get.'

'And what's that, Sherlock?' Allan Ward asked.

'The names of whoever it was Rico was hiding in his various caravans and safe houses at the time he got whacked.'

'Why would they have anything to do with it?' McCullough asked quietly.

'Stands to reason. Rico helped gangsters disappear – if someone wanted to find one of them, he'd have to go through Rico.'

'And before they got round to asking the whereabouts, they decided to smash his brains in?' McCullough was smiling.

'Maybe they underestimated how hard they'd hit

him . . .' Sutherland stretched out his arms, looking for someone to back him up.

'Or maybe he'd already told them,' Tam Barclay added.

'Just came out with it, did he?' Francis Gray growled.

'Threatened with a baseball bat, maybe that's just what he did,' Rebus said, trying to direct Gray's flak away from Barclay. 'I haven't seen anything in here' – he jabbed a report – 'saying Rico wouldn't give in to threats and intimidation. Could be he gave up the name, thinking it would save his neck.'

'What name?' Gray asked. 'Anyone turn up dead about the same time?' He looked around the table, but received only a few shrugs for his trouble. 'We don't even know he was protecting anyone back then.'

'The very point I was trying to make,' Stu Sutherland said quietly.

'If Rico's job was helping people disappear,' Tam Barclay said, 'and someone got to them, chances are they just stayed disappeared permanently. Meaning we've hit a brick wall.'

'You put your feet up if you want to,' Gray said, stabbing a finger in Barclay's direction. 'It's not like we're hanging on your every brilliant deduction.'

'At least I don't hide information from the group.'

'Difference is, in the big bad city we actually do stuff like this all day. What keeps you busy in Falkirk, Barclay – having a quick chug with the lavvy door locked? Or maybe you like to live dangerously, keep it open while you're on the job?'

'You're full of it, aren't you?'

'That's right, champ, I am. While you, on the other hand, are practically *drained*.'

There was a moment's silence, then Allan Ward started laughing, joined by Stu Sutherland. Tam Barclay's face darkened, and Rebus knew what was going to happen. Barclay leapt from his chair, sending it flying back. He had one knee up on the table and was readying to launch himself across it, straight at Francis Gray. Rebus reached out an arm to stop him, giving Stu Sutherland time to lunge forward and hold him in a bear hug. Gray just sat back, smirking, pen tapping against the table-top. Allan Ward was slapping his hand against his thigh, as if he had a front-row seat at Barnum and Bailey. It took them a while to notice that the door was open, and Andrea Thomson was standing there. She folded her arms slowly as something like order was restored to the room. Rebus was reminded of a classroom settling at the approach of authority.

Difference was, these were men in their thirties, forties and fifties; men with mortgages and families; men with careers.

Rebus didn't doubt that there had been enough to analyse in that momentary scene to keep Thomson busy for the next few months.

And she was looking at him.

'Phone call for DI Rebus,' she said.

'I won't ask,' she said, 'what was going on back there.'

They were walking along the corridor towards her office. 'That's probably wise,' he told her.

'I don't know how the call ended up coming through to my phone. I thought it was easier just to come and fetch you . . .'

'Thanks.' Rebus was watching the way her body moved, shifting from side to side as she walked. It reminded him of a very awkward person trying to do the twist. Maybe she'd been born with some slight spinal deformity; maybe a car crash in her teens . . .

'What is it?'

He pulled his eyes back, but too late. 'You walk funny,' he stated.

She looked at him. 'I hadn't noticed. Thanks for pointing it out.' She opened her door. The phone was off the hook, lying on the desk. Rebus picked it up.

'Hello?'

In his ear, he heard the hum of the open line. He caught her eye and shrugged. 'Must have got fed up,' he said.

She took the receiver from him, listened for herself, then dropped it back into its cradle.

'Who did they say they were?' Rebus asked.

'They didn't.'

'Was it an external call?'

She shrugged.

'So what exactly *did* they say?'

'Just that they wanted to talk to DI Rebus. I said you were along the corridor, and they asked if . . . no . . .' She shook her head, concentrating. 'I offered to get you.'

'And they didn't give a name?' Rebus had settled into the chair behind the desk – *her* chair.

'I'm not an answering machine!'

Rebus smiled. 'I'm just teasing. Whoever it was, they'll call back.' At which point the phone rang again. Rebus held his hand out, palm facing her. 'Just like that,' he said. He reached for the receiver, but she got to it first, her look telling him that this was still her office.

'Andrea Thomson,' she said into the phone. 'Career Analysis.' Then she listened for a moment, before conceding that the call was for him.

Rebus took the receiver. 'DI Rebus,' he said.

'I had a careers adviser at school,' the voice said. 'He dashed all my dreams.'

Rebus had placed the voice. 'Don't tell me,' he said. 'You weren't tough enough to make it as a ballet dancer?'

'I could dance all over you, my friend.'

'Promises, promises. What the hell are you doing spoiling my holiday, Claverhouse?' Andrea Thomson raised an eyebrow at the word 'holiday'. Rebus responded with a wink. Deprived of her chair, she'd slid one buttock up on to the desk.

'I heard you'd offered your chief super a cuppa.'

'And you called for a quick gloat?'

'Not a bit of it. Much though it pains me to say it, we just might require your services.'

Rebus stood up slowly, taking the phone with him. 'Is this a wind-up?'

'I wish it was.'

Seeing her chance, Andrea Thomson had reclaimed her empty chair. Rebus walked around her, still holding the phone in one hand, receiver in the other.

'I'm stuck out here,' he said. 'I don't see how I can . . .'

'Might help if we tell you what we want.'

'We?'

'Me and Ormiston. I'm calling from the car.'

'And where's the car exactly?'

'Visitors' car park. So get your raggedy arse down here pronto.'

Claverhouse and Ormiston had worked in the past for the Scottish Crime Squad, Number 2 Branch, based at the Big House – otherwise known as Lothian and Borders Police HQ. The SCS dealt with big cases: drug-dealing, conspiracies and cover-ups, crimes at the highest level. Rebus knew both men of old. Only now the SCS had been swallowed up by the Drug Enforcement Agency, taking Claverhouse and Ormiston with it. They were in the car park all right, and easily identified: Ormiston in the driver's seat of an old black taxi-cab, Claverhouse playing passenger in the back. Rebus got in beside him.

'What the hell's this?'

'Great for undercover work,' Claverhouse said, patting the door-frame. 'Nobody bats an eye at a black cab.'

'They do when it's in the middle of the bloody countryside.'

Claverhouse conceded as much with a slight angling of his head. 'But then we're not on surveillance, are we?'

Rebus had to agree that he had a point. He lit himself a cigarette, ignoring the No Smoking signs and Ormiston's wilful winding-down of the front windows. Claverhouse had recently been promoted to detective inspector, and Ormiston detective sergeant. They made for an odd pairing – Claverhouse tall and thin, almost skeletal, his figure accentuated by jackets which he usually kept buttoned; Ormiston shorter and stockier, oily black hair ending almost in ringlets, giving him the appearance of a Roman emperor. Claverhouse did most of the talking, reducing Ormiston to a role of brooding menace.

But Claverhouse was the one to watch.

'How's Tulliallan treating you, John?' he asked now. The use of his first name seemed portentous to Rebus.

'It's fine.' Rebus slid his own window down, flicked out some ash.

'Which other bad boys have they cornered this time round?'

'Stu Sutherland and Tam Barclay . . . Jazz McCullough . . . Francis Gray . . .'

'That's about as motley as a crew could come.'

'I seem to fit right in.'

'There's a surprise,' Ormiston snorted.

'No tip for you, driver,' Rebus said, flicking his nails against the plexiglass screen which separated him from Ormiston.

'Speaking of which,' Claverhouse said. It was a signal. Ormiston turned the ignition, crunched into first gear and started off.

Rebus turned to Claverhouse. 'Where are we going?'

'We're just having a chat, that's all.'

'I'll get detention for this.'

Claverhouse smiled. 'I've had a word with your head-master. He said it would be okay.' He leaned back in the seat. The cab clanked and rattled, doors juddering. Rebus could feel each spring beneath the frayed leather seat-cover.

'I hope you've got breakdown insurance,' Rebus complained.

'I'm always covered, John, you know that.' They were leaving the college grounds, turning left towards the Kincardine Bridge. Claverhouse turned to face the window, taking in the view. 'It's about your friend Cafferty,' he said.

Rebus bristled. 'He's not my friend.'

Claverhouse had spotted a thread on the leg of his trousers. He picked it up now, as though it were more pertinent than Rebus's denial. 'Actually, it's not Big Ger so much as his chief of staff.'

Rebus frowned. 'The Weasel?' He caught Ormiston watching him in the rear-view, thought he could make out a certain reticence, mixed with excitement. The pair of them believed they were on to something. Whatever it was, they needed Rebus's help, but weren't sure they could trust him. Rebus himself knew the rumours: that he was too close to Cafferty, that they were too much alike in so many ways.

'The Weasel never seems to put a foot wrong,' Claverhouse continued. 'When Cafferty went away, that should have been the end of him in Edinburgh.'

Rebus nodded slowly: during Cafferty's time in jail, the Weasel had kept his city warm for him.

'Just wondering,' Claverhouse mused, 'if, with Cafferty back behind the wheel, our friend the Weasel maybe feels a bit aggrieved. From driver's seat to back seat, so to speak.'

'Some people prefer to be chauffeured. You won't get to Cafferty through the Weasel.'

Ormiston noisily cleared his nostrils, the sound of a snuffling bull. 'Maybe aye, maybe no,' he said.

Claverhouse didn't say anything, just held his body very still. Even so, his partner seemed to get the message. Rebus doubted he'd hear another word from Ormiston until Claverhouse gave the nod.

'Can't be done,' Rebus felt it necessary to stress.

Now Claverhouse turned his head and fixed him with a

stare. 'We've got some leverage. The Weasel's son's been a bit naughty.'

'I didn't even know he had one.'

Claverhouse blinked slowly in lieu of nodding: it took less energy. 'His name's Aly.'

'What's he done?'

'Started a little business of his own: Morningside speed predominantly, but also a bit of Billy Whizz and wacky baccy.'

'You've charged him?' Rebus asked. They'd left the bridge far behind and were on the M9, heading east. The oil refinery at Grangemouth would be off to their left in the next few minutes.

'That depends,' Claverhouse was saying by way of an answer.

It was like a Polaroid developing in front of him – Rebus saw the full picture now. 'You'll do a trade with the Weasel?'

'That's what we're hoping.'

Rebus was thoughtful. 'He still won't go for it.'

'Then Aly's going down. Could be a long one, too.'

Rebus looked at him. 'How much stuff did you catch him with?'

'We thought it would be best if we showed you.'

Which was just what they did.

West Edinburgh, a commercial estate just off Gorgie Road. The place had seen better days. Rebus got the idea the only growth industry would be in security – protecting vacated premises from vandalism and arson. The warehouse was ringed by a chain-link fence, twenty-four-hour guard detail on the gate. Rebus had been there before, years back: a weapons haul in the back of a truck. The truck inside the warehouse this time round didn't look so different, except that it had been stripped, many of its component parts laid out in order on the concrete floor. Doors and panels had been unbolted and unscrewed. All the wheels had been jacked up and removed, their tyres taken off. A couple of boxes provided a makeshift step. Rebus climbed up and peered inside the cab. The seats weren't there, and the flooring had been sliced away to reveal a secret compartment, now empty. Rebus climbed down again and walked around the back of the lorry to where the haul now lay, the whole lot displayed on a length of light-blue tarpaulin. Not all the packages had been opened as yet. A chemist – one of the forensics crew from the labs at Howdenhall – was working with test-tubes and solutions. He'd dispensed with the white coat and was dressed for the cold in a bright-red ski jacket and woollen tammy. He'd labelled about half the clear-wrapped packets. There were maybe fifty left to go through . . .

Nearby, Ormiston was snuffling again. Rebus turned to Claverhouse, who was warming his hands by blowing on them. 'Better watch Ormy doesn't get too close to the drugs. He could end up hoovering the lot.'

Claverhouse smiled. Ormiston muttered something Rebus didn't catch.

'It looks like a fair haul,' Rebus commented. 'Who grassed him up?'

'Nobody. We got a lucky break, that's all. Knew Aly had been doing a bit of dealing.'

'You'd no idea he was shifting quantities like this?'

'Not a scooby.'

Rebus looked around. It was much more than a fair haul, they all knew it. Bulk like this, it was a PR coup. Yet there was nobody here but himself, the two SDEA men and the chemist. Drug runs from the Continent were usually a job for Customs and Excise . . .

'It's above board,' Claverhouse said, reading Rebus's face. 'Carswell gave us the nod.'

Carswell was the Assistant Chief Constable. Rebus had had run-ins with the ACC before.

'Does he know about me?' he asked.

'Not yet.'

'Let's see if I've got this. You stopped a lorry, found a heap of illegal substances. It's enough to put the Weasel's son away for ten years . . .' He broke off. 'How does the Weasel's son tie in exactly?'

'Aly's a lorry-driver. Long-distance a speciality.'

'You were tailing him?'

'We just had an inkling. Arsehole was smoking a joint in a lay-by when we stopped him.'

'No Customs involvement?'

Claverhouse shook his head slowly. 'Stopped him on spec. Docket showed he'd been delivering computer printers to Hatfield, bringing back a load of software and computer games.' Claverhouse nodded towards the far corner of the warehouse, where half a dozen pallets sat. 'Aly started shitting it the minute we introduced ourselves . . .'

Rebus watched the chemist pouring himself some tea from a flask. 'And you want me to do what exactly? Talk to his dad, see if I can fix a deal?'

'You know the Weasel better than we do. Maybe he'll listen to you. Just two fathers having a little chat . . .'

Rebus stared at Claverhouse, wondering how much the man knew. A little while back, when Rebus's daughter had been put in a wheelchair, the Weasel had found the culprit, handed him over to Rebus in a warehouse not unlike this one . . .

'Can't do any harm, can it?' Claverhouse's voice was a soft echo, bouncing off the corrugated walls.

'He won't shop Cafferty,' Rebus said quietly. But his own words lacked the power to resonate like Claverhouse's.

4

Lateral thinking.

It had been Davie Hynds's idea. Interviewing the deceased's friends and business acquaintances was all well and good, but sometimes you got a clearer picture by going elsewhere.

'Another art dealer, I mean,' he'd said.

So Siobhan and Hynds found themselves in a small gallery owned by Dominic Mann. It was located in the city's west end, just off Queensferry Street, and Mann hadn't been there long.

'Soon as I saw the place, I knew it was a good location.'

Siobhan glanced out of the window. 'Bit of a backwater for shops,' she mused. Offices to one side, a solicitor's to the other.

'Not a bit of it,' Mann snapped. 'Vettriano used to live quite near here. Maybe his luck will rub off on me.'

Siobhan was looking puzzled, so Hynds stepped in. 'I like his stuff. Self-taught, too.'

'Some of the galleries don't like him – jealous if you ask me. But as I always say, you can't argue with success. I'd have represented him like a shot.'

Siobhan had turned her attention to a nearby painting. It was bright orange, titled 'Incorporation', and priced at a very reasonable £8,975, which was just a shade more than her car had cost. 'How about Malcolm Neilson?'

Mann rolled his eyes. He was in his mid-forties, with bottle-blond hair and a tight little two-piece suit in a colour Siobhan would have called puce. Green slip-on shoes and a pale green T-shirt. The west end was probably the only safe place for him. 'Malcolm is a nightmare to work with. He doesn't understand words like "co-operation" and "restraint".'

'You've represented him then?'

'Only the once. A mixed show. Eleven artists, and Malcolm quite ruined the private view, pointing out imagined defects to the clients.'

'Does anyone represent him now?'

'Probably. He still sells overseas. I imagine there's someone somewhere taking their cut.'

'Ever come across a collector called Cafferty?' Siobhan asked innocently.

Mann angled his head thoughtfully. 'Local, is he?'

'Fairly.'

'Only he sounds Irish, and I have a few enthusiastic clients in the Dublin area.'

'Edinburgh-based.'

'In that case, I can't say I've had the pleasure. Would he be interested in joining my mailing list?'

Hynds, who had been flicking through a catalogue, closed it. 'I'm sorry if this sounds callous, sir, but would Edward Marber's demise benefit other art dealers in the city?'

'How so?'

'Well, his clients will have to go somewhere . . .'

'I see what you mean.'

Siobhan locked eyes with Hynds. They could almost hear the working of Dominic Mann's brain as the simple truth of this hit home. He'd probably be busy late into the evening, enlarging his mailing list.

'Every cloud,' he said at last, not bothering to finish the sentence.

'Do you know the art dealer Cynthia Bessant?' Siobhan asked.

'My dear, everyone knows Madam Cyn.'

'She seems to have been Mr Marber's closest friend.'

Dominic Mann appeared to pout. 'That *could* be true, I suppose.'

'You don't sound too sure, sir.'

'Well, it's true they were great friends . . .'

Siobhan's eyes narrowed. There was something Mann wasn't saying, something he wanted to have prised out of him. Suddenly he clapped his hands.

'Does Cynthia inherit?'

'I wouldn't know, sir.' But she did know: Marber's will left portions of his estate to various charities and friends – including Cynthia Bessant – and the residue to a sister and two nephews in Australia. The sister had been contacted, but had said that it would be difficult for her to come to Scotland, leaving Marber's solicitor and accountant to deal with everything. Siobhan was hoping they'd charge well for their services.

'I suppose Cyn deserves it more than most,' Mann was musing. 'Sometimes Eddie treated her like his bloody servant.' He looked at Siobhan, then at Hynds. 'I'm not one to speak ill of the dead, but Eddie wasn't the easiest friend anyone could have. The occasional tantrum or rudeness.'

'But people put up with it?' The question came from Hynds.

'Oh, he was charming, too, and he could be generous.'

'Mr Mann,' Siobhan said, 'did Mr Marber have any *close* friends? Closer than Ms Bessant, I mean.'

Mann's eyes twinkled. 'You mean lovers?'

Siobhan nodded slowly. This was what Mann had wanted to be asked. His whole body seemed to writhe with pleasure.

'Well, Eddie's tastes . . .'

'I think we can guess at Mr Marber's proclivities,' Hynds interrupted, aiming for levity. Siobhan fixed him with a stare: *No guesses*, she wanted to hiss.

Mann was looking at Hynds too. He held his hands

57

against his cheekbones. 'My God,' he gasped, 'you think Eddie was gay, don't you?'

Hynds's face sagged. 'Well, wasn't he?'

The art dealer forced a smile. 'My dear, wouldn't I have *known* if he was?'

Now Hynds looked to Siobhan.

'We got the impression from Ms Bessant . . .'

'I don't call her Madame Cyn for nothing,' Mann said. He'd stepped forward to straighten one of the paintings. 'She was always good at protecting Eddie.'

'Protecting him from what?' Siobhan asked.

'From the world . . . from prying eyes . . .' He looked around, as though the gallery were filled with potential eavesdroppers, then leaned in towards Siobhan. 'Rumour was, Eddie only liked short-term relationships. You know, with *professional* women.'

Hynds opened his mouth, ready with a question.

'I think,' Siobhan told him, 'Mr Mann means prostitutes.'

Mann started nodding, moistening the corners of his mouth with his tongue. The secret was out, and he couldn't have been more thrilled . . .

'I'll do it,' the Weasel said.

He was a small gaunt man, always dressed just this side of ragged. On the street, he'd be taken for a transient, someone not worth bothering or bothering about. This was his skill. Chauffeured Jaguars took him around the city, doing Big Ger Cafferty's work. But as soon as he stepped from them, he got in character again and became as conspicuous as a piece of litter.

Normally, he worked out of Cafferty's cab-hire office, but Rebus knew they couldn't meet there. He'd called from his mobile, asked to speak with the Weasel. 'Just tell him it's John from the warehouse.'

They'd arranged to meet on the towpath of the Union Canal, half a mile from the cab office. It was a route Rebus hadn't taken in many a year. He could smell yeast from the local brewery. Birds were paddling in the canal's oily water. Coots? Moorhens? He'd never been good with names.

'Ever do any ornithology?' he asked the Weasel.

'I was only in hospital once, appendicitis.'

'It means bird-watching,' Rebus said, though he suspected the Weasel knew this as well as he did, the two-short-planks routine part of his image, inviting the unwary to underestimate him.

'Oh aye,' he said now, nodding. Then: 'Tell them I'll do it.'

'I haven't told you what they want.'

'I *know* what they want.'

Rebus looked at him. 'Cafferty'll have you killed.'

'If he can, yes, I don't doubt it.'

'You and Aly must be pretty close.'

'His mum died when he was twelve. Shouldn't happen to someone that young.' The way he was staring out over the narrow, debris-strewn stretch of water, he might have been a tourist in Venice. A bicycle came towards them along the path, the rider nodding a greeting as they made room for her to pass.

At twelve, Rebus's own daughter had been living with her mother, the marriage over.

'I always did the best I could,' the Weasel was saying. There was no emotion in the voice, but Rebus didn't think the man was acting any longer.

'Did you know he was dealing?'

'Course not. I'd have stopped him otherwise.'

'Bit hypocritical in the circs?'

'Fuck you, Rebus.'

'I mean, least you could have done was give him a job in the firm. Your boss has always got a vacancy for a pusher.'

'Aly doesn't know about me and Mr Cafferty,' the Weasel hissed.

'No?' Rebus smiled without humour. 'Big Ger's not going to be too happy, is he? Either way you're shafted.' He nodded to himself. If the Weasel grassed up his boss, he was dead meat. But when Cafferty found out that his most trusted servant's son had been dealing on *his* turf . . . well, the Weasel was a marked man either way. 'I wouldn't like to be there,' Rebus went on, lighting a cigarette. He crushed the empty packet and tossed it on to the ground, then toed it into the canal.

The Weasel looked at it, then crouched down and fished it out, slipping it still wet into a greasy coat-pocket. 'I always seem to be picking up other people's shite,' he said.

Rebus knew what he meant: he meant Sammy in her wheelchair, the hit-and-run driver . . .

'I don't owe you anything,' Rebus said quietly.

'Don't fret, that's not the way I work.'

Rebus stared at him. Whenever he'd met the Weasel in the past he'd seen . . . what exactly? Cafferty's henchman, a piece of low-life – someone who served a certain function in the big picture, fixed, unchanging. But now he was being offered glimpses of the father, the human being. Until today, he hadn't even known the Weasel had a son. Now he knew the man had lost a wife, raised the kid himself through the difficult teenage years. In the distance, a pair of swans were busy preening themselves. There'd always been swans on the canal. Story was, the pollution kept killing them, and the brewery kept replacing them so no one would be any the wiser. They were only ever apparently changeless.

'Let's go get a drink,' Rebus said.

The Diggers wasn't really called the Diggers. Its given name was the Athletic Arms, but because of its proximity to a cemetery, the name had stuck. The place took pride in its beer, a polished brass advert for the nearby brewery. Initially, the barman had looked on the Weasel's request as a joke, but when Rebus shrugged he went and filled the order anyway.

'Pint of Eighty and a Campari soda,' the barman said now, placing the drinks before them. The Campari sported a little paper umbrella and glacé cherry.

'Trying to be funny, son?' the Weasel said, fishing both out and depositing them in the ashtray. A second later, the rescued cigarette packet joined them there.

They found a quiet corner and sat down. Rebus took two long gulps from his glass and licked foam from his top lip. 'You're really going to do it?'

'It's family, Rebus. You'd do anything for your family, right?'

'Maybe.'

'Mind you, you put your own brother away, didn't you?'

Rebus glanced towards him. 'He put himself away.'

The Weasel just shrugged. 'Whatever you say.' They concentrated on their drinks for half a minute, Rebus thinking of his brother Michael, who'd been a small-time dealer. He was clean now, had been for a while . . . The Weasel spoke first. 'Aly's been a bloody fool. Doesn't mean I won't stand by him.' He lowered his head, pinched the bridge of his nose. Rebus heard him mutter something that sounded like 'Christ'. He remembered the way he'd felt when he'd seen his daughter Sammy in the hospital, hooked up to machines, her body broken like a puppet's.

'You all right?' he asked.

Head still down, the Weasel nodded. The crown of his head was bald, the flesh pink and flaky. Rebus noticed that the man's fingers were curled, almost like an arthritic's. He had barely touched his drink, while Rebus was finishing his.

'I'll get us another,' he said.

The Weasel looked up, eyes reddened so that more than ever he resembled the animal which had given him his nickname. 'My shout,' he said determinedly.

'It's okay,' Rebus assured him.

But the Weasel was shaking his head. 'That's not the way I work, Rebus.' And he got up, kept his back straight as he walked to the bar. He came back with a pint, handed it over.

'Cheers,' Rebus said.

'Good health.' The Weasel sat down again, took another sip of his drink. 'What do you suppose they want from me anyway, these friends of yours?'

'I wouldn't exactly call them friends.'

'I'm assuming the next step is a meeting between me and them?'

Rebus nodded. 'They'll want you to feed them everything you can get on Cafferty.'

'Why? What good will it do them? The man's got cancer. That's why they let him out of the Bar-L in the first place.'

'All Cafferty's got are some doctored X-rays. Build up a case against him, and we can ask for a new set of tests. When they show up negative, he goes back inside again.'

'And suddenly there's no crime in Edinburgh? No drugs on the street, no money-lending . . . ?' The Weasel offered a weak smile. 'You know better than that.'

Rebus didn't say anything, concentrated on his beer instead. He knew the Weasel was right. He licked more foam from his lip and made up his mind. 'Look,' he said, 'I've been thinking . . .' The Weasel looked at him, eyes suddenly interested. 'The thing is . . .' Rebus shifted in his seat, as if trying to get comfortable. 'I'm not sure you need to do anything right now.'

'How do you mean?'

'I mean you shouldn't agree to anything, not straight-away. Aly needs a lawyer, and that lawyer can start asking questions.'

The Weasel's eyes widened. 'What sort of questions?'

'The way the drugs boys found the lorry and searched it . . . it might not have been entirely above board. They've kept the whole thing quiet from the likes of Customs and Excise. Could be there's some technicality somewhere . . .' Rebus held up his hands at the look of hope which had bloomed on the Weasel's face. 'I'm not saying there is, mind.'

'Of course not.'

'I can't say one way or the other.'

'Understood.' The Weasel rubbed his chin, nails rasping over the bristles. 'If I go to a lawyer, how do I stop Big Ger finding out?'

'It can be kept quiet; I doubt the SDEA will want to make a noise.'

The Weasel had brought his face a little closer to Rebus's, as if they were conspirators. 'But if they ever got a whiff that you'd said anything . . . ?'

Rebus leaned back. 'And what exactly have I said?'

A smile spread across the Weasel's face. 'Nothing, Mr Rebus. Nothing whatsoever.' He reached out a hand. Rebus took it, felt soft pressure as the two men shook. They didn't say anything, but the eye contact was enough.

Claverhouse's words: *Just two fathers having a little chat . . .*

Claverhouse and Ormiston dropped him off at Tulliallan. There hadn't been much conversation on the trip back.

Rebus: 'I don't think he's up for it.'

Claverhouse: 'Then his son's going to jail.'

It was a point Claverhouse reiterated angrily and often, until Rebus reminded him that he was trying to convince the wrong man.

'Maybe *I'll* talk to him,' Claverhouse had said. 'Me and Ormie, maybe we could be more persuasive.'

'Maybe you could.'

When Ormiston pulled on the handbrake, it sounded like a trap-door opening. Rebus got out and walked across the car park, listening to the cab moving away. When he stepped into the college, he headed straight for the bar. Work had finished for the day.

'Did I miss anything?' he asked the circle of officers.

'A lecture on the importance of exercise,' Jazz McCullough replied. 'It helps work off feelings of aggression and frustration.'

'Which is why you're all doing some circuit training?' Rebus pointed at the group and made a stirring motion, ready to take their drinks orders. Stu Sutherland was, as usual, the first to reply. He was a brawny, red-faced son of a Highlander, with thick black hair and slow, careful movements. Determined to hang in until pension time, he'd long since grown tired of the job – and wasn't afraid to admit as much.

'I'll do my share,' he'd told the group. 'Nobody can complain about me not doing my share.' The extent of this 'share' had never really been explained, and no one had bothered to ask. It was easier just to ignore Stu, which was probably the way he liked it, too . . .

'Nice big whisky,' he said now, handing Rebus his empty glass. Having ascertained the rest of the order, Rebus went up to the bar, where the barman had already starting pouring. The group were sharing some joke when Francis Gray put his head round the door. Rebus was ready to add to the order, but Gray spotted him and shook his head, then pointed back into the hallway before disappearing. Rebus paid for the drinks, handed them out and then walked to the door. Francis Gray was waiting for him.

'Let's go walkies,' Gray said, sliding his hands into his pockets. Rebus followed him down the corridor and up a flight of stairs. They ended up in a sub post office. It was a pretty accurate mock-up of the real thing, with a range of shelves filled with newspapers and magazines, packets and boxes, and the glass-fronted wall of the post office itself. They used it for hostage exercises and arrest procedures.

'What's up?' Rebus asked.

'See this morning, Barclay having a go at me for keeping information back?'

'Not still eating you, is it?'

'Credit me with some sense. No, it's something I've found.'

'Something about Barclay?'

Gray just looked at him, picked up one of the magazines. It was three months out of date. He tossed it back down.

'Francis, I've a drink waiting for me. I'd like to get back before it evaporates . . .'

Gray slid a hand from his pocket. It was holding a folded sheet of paper.

'What's this?' Rebus asked.

'You tell me.'

Rebus took the sheet and unfolded it. It was a short, typewritten report, detailing a visit to Edinburgh by two CID officers from the Rico Lomax inquiry. They'd been sent to track down 'a known associate', Richard Diamond, but had spent a fruitless few days in the capital. By the last sentence of the report, the author's feelings had got the better of him, and he proffered 'grateful thanks to our colleague, DI John Rebus (St Leonard's CID), for endeavours on our behalf which can only be described as stinting in the extreme'.

'Maybe he meant "unstinting",' Rebus said blithely, making to hand the sheet back. Gray kept his hands in his pockets.

'Thought you might want to keep it.'

'Why?'

'So no one else finds it and starts to wonder, like me, why you didn't say anything.'

'About what?'

'About being involved in the original inquiry.'

'What's to tell? A couple of lazy bastards from Glasgow, all they wanted was to know the good boozers. Headed

back after a couple of days and had to write something.'
Rebus shrugged.

'Doesn't explain why you didn't bring it up. But maybe
it *does* explain why you were so keen to sift through all the
paperwork before the rest of us had a chance.'

'Meaning what?'

'Meaning maybe you wanted to make sure your name
wasn't there . . .'

Rebus just shook his head slowly, as if dealing with a
stubborn child.

'Where did you disappear to today?' Gray asked.

'A wild-goose chase.'

Gray waited a few seconds, but could see he wasn't
going to get any more. He took the sheet from Rebus and
started folding it. 'So, do I slip this back into the case-
notes?'

'I think you better.'

'I'm not so sure. This Richard Diamond, he ever turn up
again?'

'I don't know.'

'If he's back in circulation, he's someone we should be
talking to, isn't he?'

'Could be.' Rebus was studying the sheet, watching the
way Gray was sliding his fingers along its sharp edges. He
reached out his own hand and took it, folded it into his
pocket. Gray gave a little smile.

'You were a late entrant to our little gang, weren't you,
John? The sheet they sent me with all our names on it . . .
yours wasn't there.'

'My chief wanted rid of me in a hurry.'

Gray smiled again. 'It's just coincidence then: Tennant
coming up with a case that both you and me worked?'

Rebus shrugged. 'How can it be anything else?'

Gray looked thoughtful. He gave one of the cereal boxes
a shake. It was empty, as he'd expected. 'Story is, only
reason you're still on the force is that you know where the
bodies are buried.'

'Any bodies in particular?' Rebus asked.

'Now how would I know a thing like that?'

It was Rebus's turn to smile. 'Francis,' he said, 'I even have the photographs.' And with a wink, he turned back and headed for the bar.

5

Cynthia Bessant's flat comprised the entire top floor of a bonded warehouse conversion near Leith Links. One huge room took up most of the space. There was a cathedral ceiling with large skylights. An enormous painting dominated the main wall. It was maybe twenty feet high and six wide, an airbrushed spectrum of colours. Looking around, Siobhan noted that it was the only painting on display. There were no books in the room, no TV or hi-fi. Two of the facing walls comprised sliding windows, giving views down on to Leith docks and west towards the city. Cynthia Bessant was in the kitchen area, pouring herself a glass of wine. Neither officer had accepted the invitation to join her. Davie Hynds sat in the centre of a white sofa meant to accommodate a football team. He was making a show of studying his notebook; Siobhan hoped he wasn't going to sulk. They'd had words on the stairwell, starting when Hynds had mentioned his relief that Marber hadn't been, in his words, 'an arse-bandit'.

'What the hell difference does it make?' Siobhan had snapped.

'I just . . . I prefer it, that's all.'

'Prefer what?'

'That he wasn't an—'

'Don't.' Siobhan had raised her hand. 'Don't say it again.'

'What?'

'Davie, let's just drop this.'

'You're the one who started it.'

'And I'm finishing it, okay?'

'Look, Siobhan, it's not that I'm—'

'It's finished, Davie, *okay?*'

'Fine by me,' he'd grunted.

And now he sat with his nose in his notebook, taking in nothing.

Cynthia Bessant sauntered over to the sofa and joined him there, proffering a smile. She took a slug from her glass, swallowed and exhaled.

'Much better,' she said.

'Hard day?' Siobhan asked, deciding at last to sit down on one of the matching chairs.

Bessant started counting off on her fingers. 'The taxman, the VAT man, three exhibitions to organise, a greedy ex-husband and a nineteen-year-old son who's suddenly decided he can paint.' She peered over the rim of her glass, not at Siobhan but at Hynds. 'Is that enough to be going on with?'

'Plenty, I'd have said,' Hynds agreed, his face breaking into a smile as he suddenly realised he was being flirted with. He glanced towards Siobhan to gauge her annoyance.

'Not forgetting Mr Marber's death,' Siobhan said.

Bessant's face creased in pain. 'God, yes.' The woman's reactions were slightly exaggerated. Siobhan was wondering if art dealers always put on a performance.

'You live by yourself?' Hynds was asking Bessant now.

'When I so choose,' she replied, dredging up a smile.

'Well, we're grateful you put aside some time to talk to us.'

'Not at all.'

'It's just that we have a few more questions,' Siobhan said. 'To do with Mr Marber's private life.'

'Oh?'

'Could you tell us how often he resorted to prostitutes, Mrs Bessant?'

Siobhan thought she could see the woman flinch.

Hynds glared at her. His eyes seemed to say, *Don't use her to get at me.* But now Bessant was speaking.

'Eddie didn't "resort to" anything.'

'Well, how would you put it?'

There were tears in Bessant's eyes, but she straightened her back, trying for resilience.

'It was how Eddie chose to order his life. Relationships always got messy, that's what he said . . .' She seemed about to say more, but stopped herself.

'So did he cruise Coburg Street or what?'

She looked at Siobhan in mild distaste, and Siobhan felt a little of her own hostility ebb away. Hynds's eyes were still on her, but she refused to meet them.

'He used a sauna,' Bessant said quietly.

'Regularly?'

'As often as he needed. We weren't *quite* so close that he felt he had to share every detail.'

'Did he shop around?'

Bessant took a deep breath, then sighed. She remembered she was holding a glass of wine and tipped it to her mouth, swallowed.

'Best way to get through this is to tell us everything, Cynthia,' Hynds said quietly.

'But Eddie was always so . . . so *private* in that way . . .'

'I understand. You're not breaking any confidences, you know.'

'Aren't I?' She was looking at him.

He shook his head. 'You're helping us try to find whoever killed him.'

She thought about this, nodded her head slowly. The tears had cleared from her eyes. She blinked a couple of times, focusing on Hynds. For a moment, Siobhan thought they were going to hold hands.

'There's a place not too far from here. Whenever Eddie dropped in, I knew he was either on his way there, or on his way home.' Siobhan wanted to ask if she could tell the difference, but she stayed silent. 'It's up a lane off Commercial Street.'

'Do you know what it's called?' Hynds asked.

She shook her head.

'Don't worry,' Siobhan said, 'we can find it.'

'I just want to protect his name,' Bessant said imploringly. 'You do understand?' Hynds nodded slowly.

Siobhan was rising to her feet. 'If it has no bearing on the case, I can't see a problem.'

'Thank you,' Cynthia Bessant said quietly.

She insisted on seeing them to the door. Hynds asked if she'd be okay.

'Don't worry about me,' she said, touching his arm. Then, with the door open, she shook his hand. Siobhan stood just over the threshold, wondering whether to stretch out her own hand, but Bessant had turned back into the room. Davie Hynds pulled the door closed.

'Think she'll be all right?' he asked as they descended the echoing stairs. The walls were brick, painted pale yellow. The steps themselves were metal, vibrating tinnily. 'Bloody creepy place to live.'

'Check on her later, if you like.' Siobhan paused. 'Once you're off duty.'

'This is a new side of you I'm seeing,' Hynds said.

'Stick around,' she told him. 'I've got more sides than John Rebus's record collection.'

'Meaning he's got a lot of records?'

'More than a few,' Siobhan admitted.

Back on the street, she sought out a newsagent's and bought an evening paper, opened it at the classifieds.

'Buying or selling?' Hynds asked. She stabbed her finger at a list headed 'Saunas', then ran the same finger down the page, checking addresses. 'Paradiso,' she said. 'VIP suites, TV and on-street parking.'

Hynds looked: the address seemed right. It was two minutes away by car. 'We're not going there?' he asked.

'Too right we are.'

'Shouldn't we give them some warning?'

'Don't be soft; it'll be fun.'

The look on Hynds's face told her he didn't quite believe this.

The 'commercial' aspect of Commercial Street had long ago withered, but there were signs of rejuvenation. Civil servants now had a sparkling glass edifice to call home at Victoria Quay. Small restaurants had appeared – though some had already been forced to close – catering to suits and expense accounts. Further along the road, the Queen's old yacht *Britannia* attracted tour parties, and a huge new redevelopment was pencilled in for the surrounding industrial wasteland. Siobhan guessed that Cynthia Bessant had bought her warehouse conversion in the hope of being one of the early settlers in what would become Edinburgh's equivalent of London's Docklands. It was entirely possible that the placement of the Sauna Paradiso was no accident either. It seemed, to Siobhan's thinking, that it was placed halfway between the money and the working girls in Coburg Street. The working girls kept their prices low, but attracted the dregs. Sauna Paradiso was after the more upmarket punter. Its frontage had been boarded over and painted a Mediterranean blue, with palm trees and surf prominent. The VIP suites were again advertised. It had probably been a shop of some kind at one time. Now, it was an anonymous door with a square of one-way mirrored glass in its centre. Siobhan pressed the buzzer and waited.

'Yes?' came a voice.

'Lothian and Borders CID,' Siobhan called out. 'Any chance of a word?'

There was a pause before the door opened. Inside, the cramped space was mostly taken up with armchairs. Men had been sitting there, dressed in blue towelling robes. Nice touch, Siobhan thought: the blue matched the paintwork. The TV was on, showing a sports network.

Some of the men had been drinking coffee and soft drinks. Now they were on the move, heading for a doorway at the back where Siobhan guessed their clothes were hanging up.

Just to the side of the front door was a reception desk, a young man seated on the stool behind it.

'Evening,' she said, showing him her warrant card. Hynds had his open, too, but his eyes were elsewhere, scoping the room.

'Is there any problem?' the young man asked. He was skinny, wore his dark hair back in a ponytail. There was a ledger book in front of him, but it was closed now, a pen sticking out of it.

Siobhan brought out a photo of Edward Marber. It was recent: taken on the night he'd died. He was in his gallery, a sheen of sweat on his face. A nice big smile for the camera, a man with not a care in the world and about two hours to live.

'You probably don't go in for second names around here,' Siobhan said. 'He might've called himself Edward or Eddie.'

'Oh?'

'We know he was a customer.'

'Do you now?' The young man glanced at the picture. 'And what's he done?'

'Someone killed him.'

The young man's eyes were on Hynds, who was over at the back doorway.

'Did they now?' he said, his mind elsewhere.

Siobhan decided enough was enough. 'Okay, you're not telling me anything. That means I have to talk to all the girls, find out who knew him. You better call your boss and tell him the place is shutting down for the night.'

She had his attention now. 'This is my place,' he said.

She smiled. 'Sure it is. Every inch of you's a born entrepreneur.'

He just looked at her. She held the photograph in front

73

of his nose. 'Take another look,' she said. A couple of the sauna's customers, dressed now, brushed past, averting their eyes as they escaped to the outside world. A woman's face appeared at the back doorway, then another.

'What's going on, Ricky?'

The young man shook his head at them, then met Siobhan's gaze. 'I might have seen him,' he admitted. 'But that could just be because his face was in the paper.'

'It was,' Siobhan agreed, nodding.

'I mean, we get a lot of faces in here.'

'And you take down their details?' Siobhan was looking at the ledger.

'Just the first name, plus the girl's.'

'How does it work, Ricky? Punters sit in here, choose a girl . . . ?'

Ricky nodded. 'What goes on once they're in a suite is their business. Maybe they just want a back-rub and a bit of chat.'

'How often did he come in?' Siobhan was still holding up the photograph.

'Couldn't tell you.'

'More than once?'

The doorbell rang. Ricky ignored it. He'd missed his morning shave; started rubbing the back of his hand against his chin. More men, carrying their jackets, shoes not quite laced, were making to exit. As they pulled open the door, the clients outside – a couple of drunken businessmen – stumbled in.

'Laura on tonight?' one of them asked. He noticed Siobhan and proffered a smile, his eyes running the length of her. The phone started ringing.

'Ricky will be with you in a minute, gentlemen,' Siobhan said coldly, 'as soon as he's finished helping me with my enquiries.'

'Christ,' the man hissed. His friend had flopped into a

74

chair, was asking where 'the burdz' were. The first man hauled him back to his feet.

'Polis, Charlie,' was the explanation.

'Come back in ten minutes!' Ricky called out, but Siobhan doubted the men would be back, not for a while.

'I seem to be bad for business,' Siobhan said with a smile.

Hynds appeared at the inner doorway. 'It's a bloody maze back there. Stairs and doors and I don't know what. There's even a sauna, would you believe. How are we doing?'

'Ricky here was just about to tell me if Mr Marber was a regular.'

Hynds nodded, reached over and picked up the still-ringing phone. 'Sauna Paradiso, DC Hynds speaking.' He waited, then looked at the receiver. 'Hung up,' he said with a shrug.

'Look, he came in a few times,' Ricky burst out. 'I'm not always on shift, you know.'

'Daytime or evenings?'

'Evenings, I think.'

'What did he call himself?'

Ricky shook his head. 'Eddie, maybe.'

Hynds had a question. 'Did he take a shine to any one girl in particular?'

Ricky shook his head again. Another phone was sounding: the theme to *Mission: Impossible.* It was Ricky's mobile. He unclipped it from his trouser-belt, held it to his ear.

'Hello?' He listened for a few moments, his back straightening. 'It's under control,' he said. Then he looked up at Siobhan. 'Still here, yes.'

Siobhan knew: it was the owner of the sauna. Maybe one of the girls had called him. She held out a hand.

'She wants to talk to you,' Ricky said, then he listened again and shook his head, eyes still on Siobhan. 'Do I need to show them the books?' He blurted this out, as Hynds started prising a hand beneath the ledger. Ricky's free hand came down and stopped him.

'I said I can handle it,' Ricky said more firmly, before terminating the call. His face had hardened.

'I've told you what I know,' he said, clipping the phone back on his belt, his free hand still resting on the closed ledger.

'Mind if I talk to the girls?' Siobhan asked.

'Be my guest,' Ricky said, his face breaking into a smile.

When Siobhan stepped over the threshold, she knew the place was empty. She saw shower cubicles, lockers, a wooden coffin of a sauna. Stairs down to the rooms where the girls worked. No windows: the downstairs was below ground level. She peered into one room. It smelt perfumed. There was a deep bath in one corner; lots of mirrors. The lighting was almost nonexistent. Sounds of grunts and moans – a TV high up on one wall, playing a hard-core video. Back out in the corridor, she noticed a curtain at the far end. Walked towards it and pulled it open. A door. Emergency exit. It led out into a narrow alley. The girls were gone.

'Done a runner,' Hynds confirmed. 'So what do we do now?'

'We could charge him with possession of illegal videos.'

'We could,' Hynds acknowledged. He glanced at his watch. 'Or we could call it a day.'

Siobhan started climbing the narrow stairs. The sauna's phone was ringing again. Ricky was about to answer, but thought better of it when he saw Siobhan.

'Who's your boss?' she asked.

'Solicitor's on his way,' Ricky told her.

'Good,' she said, making for the exit. 'I hope he charges through the nose.'

The Resurrection Men had moved from the bar to the break-out area, and from alcohol to soft drinks. A lot of the probationers at Tulliallan would be staying through the weekend, but those who were allowed would be heading home. Jazz McCullough and Allan Ward had left already, Ward complaining of the long drive ahead. The others were trying to rouse themselves, or maybe it was that there was nothing about the weekend that they couldn't live without. The break-out area was an open lounge of leather chairs and sofas, just outside the lecture theatre. Rebus had known men get too comfortable there and end up falling asleep, waking stiffly next morning.

'Got plans, John?' Francis Gray asked.

Rebus shrugged. Jean was off to a family wedding south of the border. She'd asked if he wanted to go, but he'd declined.

'How about you?' he asked.

'I've been away five days. Pound to a penny things have started to break, drip or leak.'

'You're a bit of a DIY man then?'

'Christ, no. Why do you think things go wrong in the first place?'

There was tired laughter at this. Five days they'd been at Tulliallan. They felt like they knew each other.

'Suppose I'll go watch my team tomorrow,' Tam Barclay said.

'Who's that? Falkirk?'

Barclay nodded.

'Need to get yourself a proper grown-up team,' Gray commented.

'Would that be one from Glasgow, Francis?'

'Where else?'

Rebus got to his feet. 'Well, I'll see you all first thing Monday morning . . .'

'Unless we see you first,' Gray answered with a wink.

Rebus went to his room to pack a few things. The room itself was a comfortable box with en suite bathroom, better than many a hotel he'd stayed in. Only the CID were assured single rooms. A lot of probationers were doubling up, such were their numbers. Rebus's mobile was where he'd left it, charging at one of the wall-points. He poured himself a small Laphroaig from his secret stash and switched on the radio, tuning it to some station with pulsing dance music.

Then he picked up his mobile and punched in some numbers.

'It's me,' he said, keeping his voice low. 'How come I haven't heard from you?' He listened as the person at the other end complained about the lateness of the hour. When Rebus said nothing to this, the person then asked where he was.

'In my room. That's just the radio you can hear. When do we get to meet?'

'Monday,' the voice said.

'Where and how?'

'Leave that to me. Any luck so far?'

'That's not what I want to talk about.'

There was silence on the line. Then: 'Monday.' And this time the phone's back-lit screen told him the connection had ended. He re-tuned the radio, switched it off, making sure the alarm function wasn't set. He had his bag open, but suddenly wondered what the rush was. There was nothing awaiting him in Edinburgh but an empty flat. He picked up his going-away present from Jean – a portable CD player. She'd added some CDs, too: Steely Dan, Morphine, Neil Young . . . He'd brought a few others: Van Morrison, John Martyn. He fixed the headphones on and pushed the start button. The swelling opening of 'Solid Air' filled his head, pushing out everything else. He leaned back against the pillow. Decided the song was definitely on the shortlist for his funeral.

Knew he should write the shortlist down. After all, you never could tell.

Siobhan answered her door. It was late, but she was expecting company. Eric Bain always called first, to make sure it was all right. It usually was. Bain worked at Police

HQ, the 'Big House'. He specialised in computer crime. The two had become good friends – nothing more than that. They talked on the phone; sometimes ended up at one another's flat, sharing late-night milky coffee and stories.

'You're out,' Bain called through from the kitchen. Out of decaf, he meant. Siobhan was back in the living room, putting some music on: Oldsolar, a recent purchase – good late-night music.

'Middle cupboard, top shelf,' she called.

'Got it.'

Eric – the officers at Fettes called him 'Brains' – had told Siobhan early on that his favourite film was *When Harry Met Sally*. Letting her know where he stood, and that if she wanted things to go any further, the first move would have to come from her.

Of course, none of their colleagues believed it. Eric's car had been spotted parked outside at midnight, and next morning both police stations had been buzzing. It didn't bother her; didn't seem to bother Eric. He was coming into the living room now, carrying a tray containing cafetière, a jug of steamed milk, two mugs. He set it down on her coffee table, next to some notes she'd been writing.

'Been busy?' he asked.

'Just the usual.' She noticed the grin on his face. 'What is it?'

He shook his head, but she dug her biro into his ribs.

'It's your cupboards,' he confessed.

'My what?'

'Your cupboards. All the tins and jars . . .'

'Yes?'

'They're arranged with the labels facing out.'

'So?'

'It just spooks me, that's all.' He wandered over to her CD rack, pulled a disc out at random, opened its case. 'See?'

'What?'

'You put your CDs back in the case so they're the right way up.' He snapped the case shut, opened another.

'It makes them easier to read,' Siobhan said.

'Not many people do it.'

'I'm not like other people.'

'That's right.' He kneeled in front of the tray, pushed down on the cafetière's plunger. 'You're more organised.'

'That's right.'

'A lot more organised.'

She nodded, then jabbed him with her pen again. He chuckled, poured milk into her mug.

'Just an observation,' he said, adding coffee to both mugs, handing hers over.

'I get enough grief at the office, Mr Bain,' Siobhan told him.

'You working this weekend?'

'No.'

'Got plans?' He slurped from his mug, angled his head to read her notes. 'You were at the Paradiso?'

A little vertical frown appeared between her eyes. 'You know the place?'

'Only by reputation. It changed hands about six months back.'

'Did it?'

'Used to be owned by Tojo McNair. He has a couple of the bars down Leith.'

'Salubrious establishments, no doubt.'

'Sticky carpets and weak beer. What was the Paradiso like?'

She considered the question. 'Not as seedy as I'd expected.'

'Better than having the girls walking the streets?'

She thought this over, too, before nodding agreement. There was a plan afoot to zone off part of Leith, turn it into a safe area for streetwalkers. But the first choice had been an industrial estate, badly lit and the scene of an attack a few years before. So now it was back to the drawing board . . .

Siobhan tucked her feet beneath her on the sofa; Eric slumped in the chair opposite.

'Who's on the hi-fi?' he asked.

She ignored this and asked her own question instead. 'Who owns the Paradiso nowadays?'

'Well . . . that all depends.'

'On what?'

He patted the side of his nose with his index finger.

'Do I have to thrash an answer out of you?' Siobhan asked, smiling above the rim of her mug.

'I bet you'd do it, too.' But he still wasn't telling.

'I thought we were friends.'

'We are.'

'No point coming round here if you don't want to talk.'

He sighed, sipped some coffee, leaving a milky residue along his top lip. 'You know Big Ger Cafferty?' he said. The question was entirely rhetorical. 'Word is, if you burrow deep enough, it's his name you'll find.'

Siobhan sat forward. 'Cafferty?'

'He's not exactly advertising the fact, and he never goes near the place.'

'How do you know?'

Bain wriggled in his chair, not at all comfortable with this conversation. 'I've been doing some work for the SDEA.'

'You mean Claverhouse?'

Bain nodded. 'It's hush-hush. If he finds out I've been blabbing . . .'

'They're after Cafferty again?'

'Can we drop it, please? I only have to get through this one job, then I'm off to the Forensic Computer Branch. Did you know their workload's increasing twenty per cent every three months?'

Siobhan was on her feet, walking over to the window. The shutters were closed, but she stood there as though staring at some startling new vista. 'Whose workload? The SDEA?'

'The FCB – you're not listening . . .'

'Cafferty?' she said, almost to herself.

Cafferty owned the Paradiso . . . Edward Marber had frequented the place . . . And there was a story that Marber had been cheating his clients . . .

'I was supposed to interview him today,' she said quietly.

'Who?'

She turned her head towards Bain; it was as if she'd forgotten he was there. 'Cafferty,' she told him.

'What for?'

She didn't hear him. 'He was across in Glasgow . . . due back tonight.' She checked her watch.

'It'll wait till Monday,' Bain said.

She nodded agreement. Yes, it could wait. Maybe if she could gather a bit more ammo first.

'Okay,' Bain said. 'So sit down again and relax.'

She slapped a hand against her thigh. 'How can I relax?'

'It's easy. All you do is sit yourself down, take a few deep breaths and start telling me a story.'

She looked at him. 'What sort of story?'

'The story of why it is that you're suddenly so interested in Morris Gerald Cafferty . . .'

Siobhan backed away from the window, sat down again and took a few deep breaths. Then she reached down and picked her phone up off the floor. 'There's just one thing I have to do first . . .'

Bain rolled his eyes. But then Siobhan's call was answered and he broke into a smile.

She was ordering pizza.

6

On Monday morning, Rebus was back at Tulliallan in time for breakfast. He'd spent most of Saturday in the Oxford Bar, passing time first with one set of drinkers, then with another. Finally, he'd headed back to his flat and fallen asleep in the chair, waking at midnight with a raging thirst and a thumping head. He'd not been able to get back to sleep until dawn, meaning he didn't wake until midday on Sunday. A visit to the laundrette had filled in the afternoon, and he'd gone back to the Ox in the evening.

All in all, then, not a bad weekend.

At least he wasn't having the blackouts any more. He could remember the conversations he'd had in the Ox, the jokes he'd been told, the TV shows playing in the background. At the start of the Marber inquiry, he'd been at a low ebb, the past seeming to suffocate him just as surely as the present. Memories of his marriage and the day he had moved into the Arden Street flat with his young wife. That first night, he'd watched from the window as a middle-aged drunk across the street leaned for all his life against a lamp-post, struggling for balance, seemingly asleep though standing. Rebus had felt an affection for the man; he'd felt affection for most things back then, newly married and with a first-time mortgage, Rhona talking about kids . . .

And then, a week or two before the tea-throwing incident, Rebus himself had become that man: middle-aged and clutching at the self-same lamp-post, struggling to focus, the crossing of the street an impossible proposition. He'd been due at Jean's for dinner, but had got comfortable at the Ox, slipping outside to phone her with some lie. He'd probably walked back to Arden Street; couldn't recall his journey. Hanging on to that lamp-post and laughing at the memory of the man. When a neighbour had tried to help, Rebus had gripped the lamp-post all the harder, crying out that he was useless, only good for sitting at a desk, making phone calls.

He hadn't been able to look the neighbour in the face since . . .

After breakfast, he stepped outside for a cigarette, and found a commotion on the parade ground. A lot of the probationers were out there. The CID intake were halfway through their five-week induction. As part of the training, they had to raise money for charity, and one of them had promised a parachute jump into the parade ground at 0915. There was a big letter X marking the spot. It was made from two lengths of shiny red material, weighted down with stones. A few of the probationers were squinting skywards, hands shading their eyes.

'Maybe got RAF Leuchars to help out,' one of them was suggesting.

Rebus stood with his hands in his pockets. He'd signed a sponsorship form, putting himself down for a five-quid donation should the jump succeed. A rumour was going around that a Land Rover with armed forces plates was parked in the driveway. Two men in light-grey uniforms could be seen at one of the windows in the building which fronted the parade ground.

'Sir,' one of the probationers said, making to pass Rebus. They usually did that; part of the training. You could get half a dozen of them in the corridors, all going 'Sir'. He tried to ignore it. A door was opening, all eyes turning towards it. A young man emerged, wearing a one-piece flight-suit, what looked like a parachute harness clamped around his chest. He was carrying a metal-framed chair. He nodded and beamed smiles at the crowd, who watched in silence as he made his way towards the X, planting the chair down firmly in its centre. Rebus blew out air through his mouth, shaking his head slowly at the knowledge of what was to come. The CID recruit climbed on to the chair, crouched and placed his hands together, as if readying to dive into a pool. And then he jumped. Dust kicked up as he hit the ground. He stood up straight, opened his arms wide as if to accept the acclaim of his audience. There was some muttering, confused looks. The recruit picked up the chair. Behind their window, the RAF officers were smiling.

'What was that?' someone asked in disbelief.

'That, son, was a parachute jump,' Rebus said, his admiration tempered only by the knowledge that he'd just lost a fiver. He recalled that when he'd been going through his CID training, he'd raised money by taking part in an all-day relay attempt on the assault course. These days, he'd be lucky if he could walk it once through . . .

Back in the syndicate room, he announced that the jump had been successful. There were frowns and shrugs. Jazz McCullough, who had been made senior investigating officer, was talking to Francis Gray. Tam Barclay and Allan Ward were busy compiling the filing system. Stu Sutherland was explaining the structure of the investigation to a twitchy-looking DCI Tennant. Rebus sat down and pulled a sheaf of papers towards him. He worked for a solid half-hour, glancing up every now and then to see if Gray had any message for him. When a break was announced, Rebus slipped a sheet of paper from his pocket and added it to the pile. With a beaker of tea in his hand, he asked McCullough if he fancied swapping jobs.

'Fresh perspective and all that,' he explained. McCullough agreed with a nod, went and sat down in front of the papers. Gray had just finished a short conversation with Tennant.

'He looks antsy,' Rebus commented.

'The brass are in the house,' Gray explained.

'What sort of brass?'

'Chief constables. Half a dozen of them, here for some meeting or other. I doubt they'll be bothering us, but Archie isn't so sure.'

'He doesn't want them meeting the remedial class?'

'Something like that,' Gray offered with a wink.

Just then, McCullough called out Rebus's name. Rebus walked over to the table. McCullough was holding the sheet of paper. Rebus made a show of reading it.

'Christ, that had clean escaped me,' he said, hoping he sounded surprised. Gray was at his shoulder.

'What is it?'

Rebus turned his head, fixing Gray's eyes with his own. 'Jazz has just dug this up. Two officers from Glasgow visited Edinburgh, looking for one of Rico's associates, a guy called Dickie Diamond.'

'So?' This from Tennant, who had joined the group.

'I was their liaison, that's all.'

Tennant read the sheet quickly. 'They don't seem too enamoured.'

'Covering their arses,' Rebus stated. 'Now that I remember, they spent the whole time in the boozer.'

Tennant was looking at him. 'This is you just remembering?'

Rebus nodded. Tennant kept staring, but Rebus wasn't offering anything more.

'Who is this Dickie Diamond?' McCullough asked.

'He was a local small-timer,' Rebus said. 'I barely knew him.'

'Past tense?'

'He could still be on the scene for all I know.'

'Was he a suspect?' McCullough asked.

Gray turned to the room. 'Anyone turned up a Richard Diamond?' There were shrugs, shakes of the head.

Tennant nodded towards the paperwork in front of McCullough. 'Nothing in there about him?'

'Not that I've found.'

'Well, there must be something in the files somewhere.' Tennant was talking to the room now. 'And if it had been correctly indexed in the first place, it would be right next to this report. As it is, we'd better flag the name up and keep looking.'

There were murmurs of 'Yes, sir.' Francis Gray added the name to the marker-board.

'Any chance your mates in Lothian and Borders could fill us in on this character?' Allan Ward asked, looking for a short cut.

'No harm in asking,' Rebus told him. 'Why don't you get on the phone?'

Ward frowned. 'It's your patch,' he informed Rebus.

'It's also Stu's patch,' Rebus reminded him. Ward glanced towards Stu Sutherland. 'But one of the skills we need to learn in an inquiry is trans-regional co-operation.' It was one of Tennant's own phrases, which was probably why the DCI made noises of agreement.

Ward looked frustrated by this turn of events. 'Fine,' he grunted. 'Give me the number.'

Rebus looked to Stu Sutherland. 'Do the honours, will you, Stu?'

'Be my pleasure.'

There was a knock at the door, causing Tennant to freeze. But when it opened a couple of inches, Andrea Thomson, rather than the feared posse of chief constables, was standing there. Tennant waved for her to enter.

'It's just that I'm supposed to be seeing DI Rebus this afternoon, but something else has come up.'

Result! Rebus was thinking.

'So I wondered if you could maybe spare him this morning instead . . .'

She was uncharacteristically tight-lipped on the walk

down the corridor, and Rebus gave up trying. But when they got to her door, she hesitated.

'You go in,' she told him. 'I'll just be a minute.'

Rebus looked at her, but she wouldn't meet his eyes. When he reached out to the door-handle, she turned and started walking away. Watching her, Rebus opened the door. He sensed movement from the corner of his eye. Seated in Andrea Thomson's chair was someone he'd been wanting to see. He entered the room, quickly closing the door.

'Clever,' he admitted. 'How much does she know?'

'Andrea will keep her mouth shut,' the man said. Then he reached out a hand for Rebus to shake. 'How have you been, John?'

Rebus took the hand, returned its grip, then sat down. 'Fine, sir,' he said. He was seated opposite his own chief constable, Sir David Strathern.

'Now then,' the Chief Constable said, getting comfortable again, 'what seems to be the problem, John . . . ?'

A little over two weeks had passed since their first meeting. Rebus had been working in St Leonard's when a call had come through from the Big House – could Rebus nip across the road to the Blonde restaurant?

'What for?' he'd asked.

'You'll find out.'

But as Rebus had made to cross the road, gripping his jacket shut against the fierce breeze, a car horn had sounded. The car was parked on the corner of Rankeillor Street, and a hand was waving from its window. He recognised the figure in the driver's seat, even without the customary uniform: Sir David Strathern. The pair had met in the past at official functions only, and infrequently at that. Rebus wasn't one for the sportsmen's dinners, the boxing bouts with cigars. And he'd never found himself on a platform being given some award for gallantry or good conduct. It didn't matter. Sir David seemed to know *him*.

It wasn't an official car: black, gleaming Rover – almost certainly the Chief Constable's own. There was a chamois cloth on the passenger-side floor, magazines and a carrier-bag on the back seat. As Rebus closed the door, the car pulled away.

'Sorry about the subterfuge,' Strathern said with a smile. The action creased the lines around his eyes. He was in his late fifties, not that much older than Rebus. But he was the boss, the chief, the big stick. And Rebus was still wondering what the hell he was doing here. Strathern was dressed in grey casual trousers and a dark crew-neck jumper. Mufti it might be, but he wore it like a uniform. His hair was silver, neatly clipped above his ears, the large bald spot only prominent when he turned his head to check for traffic at the next junction.

'You're not offering me lunch then?' Rebus guessed.

The smile widened. 'Too close to St Leonard's. Didn't want anyone seeing us together.'

'Am I not good enough for you, sir?'

Strathern glanced in Rebus's direction. 'It's a good act,' he commented, 'but then you've spent years perfecting it, haven't you?'

'What act is that, sir?'

'The wisecracks; that hint of insubordination. Your way of coping with a situation until you've had a chance to digest it.'

'Is that right, sir?'

'Don't worry, John. For what I'm about to ask you to do, insubordination is a prerequisite.'

Which left Rebus more baffled than ever.

Strathern had driven them to a pub on the southern outskirts of the city. It was close to the crematorium and got a lot of business from funeral meals, which meant it wasn't quite so popular with anyone else. Their corner of the bar was quiet. Strathern ordered sandwiches and halves of IPA, then attempted some conversation, as if this was a regular outing for the two of them.

'Are you not drinking?' Strathern asked at one point, noting Rebus's still-full glass.

'I hardly touch the stuff,' Rebus told him.

Strathern looked at him. 'That's not exactly been your reputation.'

'Maybe you've been misinformed, sir.'

'I don't think so. My sources are usually impeccable.'

There was little Rebus could say to this, though he did wonder who the Chief had been talking to. Assistant Chief Constable Colin Carswell, perhaps, who disliked Rebus intensely; or Carswell's acolyte, DI Derek Linford. Neither would have painted Rebus in anything but the darkest shades.

'With respect, sir,' Rebus said, sitting back, food and drink untouched, 'we can skip the foreplay if you like.'

He then watched his Chief Constable struggle to contain the anger mounting within him.

'John,' Strathern said at last, 'I came to you today to ask a favour.'

'One which requires a certain level of insubordination.'

The Chief Constable nodded slowly. 'I want you to get yourself kicked off a case.'

'The Marber case?' Rebus's eyes narrowed.

'The case itself has nothing to do with it,' Strathern said, sensing Rebus's suspicion.

'But you want me off it all the same?'

'Yes.'

'Why?' Without thinking, Rebus had raised the flat half-pint of beer to his lips.

'Because I want you somewhere else. Tulliallan, to be precise. There's a rehab course about to start there.'

'And I'll need rehab because I've been kicked off a case?'

'I think DCS Templer will demand it.'

'She knows about this?'

'She'll agree to it when I tell her.'

'Who else knows?'

'Nobody. Why do you ask?'

'Because I think you're asking me to go undercover. I don't know why yet, and I don't know that I'll do it, but that's the feeling I get.'

'And?'

'And there are people at Fettes who don't like me. I wouldn't like to think that they'd . . .'

Strathern was already shaking his head. 'Nobody would know except you and me.'

'And DCS Templer.'

'She'll be told only as much as I need her to know.'

'Which leads to the big question, sir . . .'

'Namely?'

'Namely,' Rebus said, rising to his feet, empty glass in hand, 'what's this all about?' He lifted the glass. 'I'd offer to get you another, sir, but you're driving.'

'And you said you hardly touch the stuff.'

'I was lying,' Rebus said, with the ghost of a smile. 'That's what you need, isn't it? A convincing liar . . .'

The way Strathern told it was: there was a drug-dealer on the west coast, a man called Bernard Johns.

'Bernie Johns, as he's more colloquially known. Or was until his untimely death.' The Chief Constable nursed his near-empty glass as he spoke. 'He died in prison.'

'Still protesting his innocence, no doubt?'

'No, not exactly. But he was adamant he'd been ripped off. Not that he ever said as much to us. It would hardly have helped his case, would it? "You're putting me away for eight kilos, but I had a lot more than that stashed away." '

'I can see it would have been awkward.'

'But word got around about a large amount of missing stuff. Either drugs or cash, depending who you talked to.'

'And?'

'And . . . the operation against Johns was big: you probably remember it. Ran from the winter of 'ninety-four to spring 'ninety-five. Three forces, dozens of officers, a logistical nightmare . . .'

Rebus nodded. 'But Lothian and Borders wasn't involved.'

'That's true, we weren't.' He paused. 'Not back then, at any rate.'

'So what's happened?'

'What's happened, John, is that three names keep coming up.' The Chief Constable leaned over the table, lowering his voice still further. 'You might know some of them.'

'Try me.'

'Francis Gray. He's a DI based in Govan. Knows the place like the back of his hand; invaluable for that reason. But he's dirty, and everybody knows it.'

Rebus nodded. He'd heard of Gray, knew the man's rep: not so dissimilar from his own. He wondered how much of it was bluff. 'Who else?' he asked.

'A young DC called Allan Ward, works out of Dumfries. He's learning fast.'

'Never heard of him.'

'The last one is James McCullough, a DI from Dundee. Basically clean, so far as anyone knows, but blows a fuse from time to time. They worked the case, John. Got to know each other.'

'And you think they took Bernie Johns's swag?'

'We think it's likely.'

'Who's we?'

'My colleagues.' By which Strathern meant the other chief constables in Scotland. 'It looks bad, something like that. Even if it is just a rumour. But it tarnishes everyone at the highest level.'

'And what's your role in all of this, sir?' Rebus was halfway down the pint he'd bought himself. The beer seemed to be weighing down his gut, as if what was liquid had suddenly become solid. He was thinking of the Marber case, the grind of all those cold-calls. His hands gripping a cold lamp-post.

'The three regions involved ... we couldn't ask a detective from any one of them to act on our behalf.'

Rebus nodded slowly: because it might get back to the three men involved. So instead they'd asked Strathern if he could think of anyone.

And apparently he'd thought of Rebus.

'So these three,' Rebus said, 'they're going to be at Tulliallan?'

'By accident, yes, all three will be on the same course.' The way he said it, Rebus knew it was anything but an accident.

'And you want me in there with them?' Rebus watched Strathern nodding. 'To do what exactly?'

'To find out what you can ... gain their confidence.'

'You think they'll suddenly open up to a complete stranger?'

'You won't be a stranger to them, John. Your reputation precedes you.'

'Meaning I'm a bent cop, same as them?'

'Meaning your reputation precedes you,' Strathern repeated.

Rebus was thoughtful for a moment. 'You and your ... "colleagues" ... do you have any evidence at all?'

Strathern shook his head. 'The little investigating we've been able to do, we can't find any trace of drugs or money.'

'You're not asking much of me, are you, sir?'

'I appreciate it's a tall order, John.'

'Tall? We're talking Jack and the beanstalk.' Rebus chewed his bottom lip. 'Give me one good reason why I should do this.'

'I think you like a challenge. Plus, I'm hoping you dislike dirty cops as much as the rest of us.'

Rebus looked at him. 'Sir, there are plenty of people out

there who think *I'm* a dirty cop.' He was thinking of Francis Gray, curious to meet the man.

'But we know they're wrong, don't we, John?' the Chief Constable said, rising to fetch Rebus another pint.

Tulliallan: no more Marber inquiry . . . a short break from the blackouts . . . and a chance to catch up with the man he'd once heard called 'the Glasgow Rebus'. The Chief Constable was studying him from the bar. Rebus knew Strathern didn't have long to go, retirement looming. Maybe the man was still hungry; unfinished business and all that . . .

Maybe Rebus would do it after all.

Now, in Andrea Thomson's room, Strathern sat with his hands clasped. 'So what's so urgent?' he asked.

'I haven't made much headway, if that's what you're wondering. Gray, McCullough and Ward act like they barely know each other.'

'They *do* barely know each other. There was just that one case they worked together.'

'They don't act like they've got riches salted away.'

'How do you expect them to act? Drive around in Bentleys?'

'Have their bank accounts been checked?'

The Chief Constable was shaking his head. 'There's nothing tucked away in their bank accounts.'

'Maybe in a wife's name . . . ?'

'Nothing,' Strathern stated.

'How long have they been under investigation?'

Strathern looked at him. 'Is that any concern of yours?'

Rebus shrugged. 'I just wondered if I was the straw you were clutching at.'

'We're close to losing them,' Strathern admitted at last. 'Gray's up for retirement in less than a year; McCullough probably won't be far behind him. And Allan Ward's disciplinary record . . .'

'You think he's looking for the early bath?'

94

'Maybe.' The Chief Constable was checking his watch, sliding the metal casing up and down his wrist. 'I should be getting back.'

'There's just one thing, sir . . .'

'About time.' Strathern took a deep breath. 'Go on then.'

'They've got us working an old case.'

'Trying you out as a syndicate, eh? I dare say Archie Tennant's in charge.'

'He is, yes. Thing is . . .' Rebus paused, considering just how much to tell his boss. 'Well, both Gray and me tie to the case.'

Strathern looked interested.

'Gray worked it from his end, and I was liaison when two of Glasgow's finest came through to Edinburgh on a recce. This was in 'ninety-five, same year as Bernie Johns . . .'

Strathern looked thoughtful. 'It's coincidence,' he said. 'Pure and simple.'

'Tennant doesn't know about . . . ?'

Strathern shook his head.

'And this case wasn't foisted on him?'

Another shake of the head. 'Is that why you wanted to see me?'

'Gray might think it's more than just coincidence.'

'I agree, it's awkward. On the other hand, if you play it right, it could get you closer to him. The pair of you already have something in common. D'you see what I mean?'

'Yes, sir. Do you think maybe somebody could ask?'

'Ask?'

'Ask DCI Tennant why he happened to choose that particular case.'

Strathern looked thoughtful again, pursing his lips. 'I'll see what I can do. That good enough for you?'

'That's fine, sir,' Rebus said, but he wasn't sure he believed his own words.

Strathern looked satisfied, and got up from the chair. The two men met by the door. 'You first,' the Chief Constable said. Then he raised a hand and patted Rebus's shoulder. 'Templer's mad at you, you know.'

'Because without my insights, the Marber case is doomed?'

Strathern accepted the joke. 'Because of how hard you threw that mug. She's taking it personally.'

'All part of the act, sir,' Rebus said, pulling open the door.

As he walked back along the corridor, he thought better of it and wandered downstairs instead to the break-out area. He needed a cigarette, but there were none in his pockets. Looking outside, he noted a distinct shortage of fellow addicts. There was a packet in his room, if he could be bothered walking there. Or he could linger in the hope that some Good Samaritan would come by.

The meeting had failed to put his mind at rest. He wanted to be sure that the Rico Lomax case *was* just a coincidence. And he couldn't shrug off the niggling suspicion that perhaps there was less to this than met the eye.

No cabal of worried chief constables.

No drug money.

No conspiracy between Gray, McCullough and Ward.

Just the Rico Lomax case . . . and his own involvement in it. Because John Rebus knew more about Rico Lomax than he was telling.

A hell of a lot more.

Did Strathern know? Was Gray working for Strathern . . . ?

Rebus took the stairs back up to CID two at a time, breathing hard as he made his way back down the corridor. He pushed open the door without knocking, but the Chief Constable wasn't there. Andrea Thomson's office was empty.

Strathern had to be headed to the original building, the castle itself. Rebus knew the way. Moved quickly, ignoring the young uniforms with their clipped 'Sir's. Strathern had paused for a moment to study one of the display cases which lined the main corridor, the corridor facing the now-empty parade ground. No chair or parachute; no X-marks-the-spot.

'A moment of your time, sir,' Rebus said quietly.

Strathern's eyes widened. He pushed open the nearest door. It led to a conference room, empty save for rows of chairs with writing-trays attached.

'You want your cover blown?' Strathern spluttered.

'I need more background,' Rebus stated. 'On all three of them.'

'I thought we'd discussed all that. The more you know, the more likely they are to suspect—'

'When did they take the money? How did they know about it? How come the three of them ended up working together?'

'John, nothing like that has exactly gone on the record . . .'

'But there must be notes. There must be *something*.'

Strathern looked wildly about him, as though fearing eavesdroppers. One thing Rebus knew: if the whole Bernie Johns story was a front, there could be no background, no notes . . .

'All right,' Strathern said, almost in a whisper. 'I'll get you what I can.'

'By tonight,' Rebus added.

'John, that might not—'

'I need it tonight, sir.'

Strathern almost winced. 'Tomorrow at the latest.'

The two men locked eyes. Eventually, Rebus nodded. He wondered if he was giving Strathern enough time to concoct a fantasy case. He didn't think so.

By tomorrow, he could be sure.

'Tonight if possible,' he said, heading for the door. This time, he made straight for his room and those cigarettes.

7

'Where's your homophobic friend?' Dominic Mann asked.

Siobhan and Mann were seated opposite one another at a tiny window table in a west end café. He was stirring his skimmed decaf latte while she'd already sunk one shot of her double espresso. The inside of her mouth felt coated with a fine residue, and she reached into her bag for the bottle of water she kept there.

'You noticed,' she said.

'I noticed he didn't want to make eye contact with me.'

'Maybe he's just shy,' Siobhan offered. She took a mouthful of water, rinsed and swallowed. Mann was glancing at his watch, the face of which he kept on the inside of his wrist. She remembered that her father had done the same, and when she'd asked him why he'd said it was to stop the face getting scratched. Yet the glass itself had been almost opaque with abrasions.

'I have to open at ten,' the art dealer said.

'You didn't feel like going to the funeral?' By which she meant Edward Marber's funeral, which had started almost half an hour ago at Warriston Crematorium.

Mann shuddered. 'I can't stand them. I was actually relieved to have an excuse.'

'Glad to be of help.'

'So what is it I can do for you?' The top two buttons of Mann's yellow shirt were undone, and he'd hooked a finger into the opening.

'I'm wondering about Edward Marber. If he'd been cheating . . . how would he have gone about it?'

'Depends *who* he was cheating: clients or artists?'

'Let's try both.'

Mann took a deep breath and raised one eyebrow. '*Five minutes, you said?*'

Siobhan smiled. 'Maybe it depends how fast you talk.'

Mann unhooked the finger from his shirt and went back to stirring his latte. It looked like he had no intention of actually drinking it. As he spoke, his eyes drifted to the window. Office staff were dragging their feet to work.

'Well, dealers can cheat potential buyers in all sorts of ways. You can exaggerate the importance of an artist, or the rarity and value of a piece by a deceased artist. You can offer fakes – those are the cases that usually make the headlines . . .'

'You don't think Mr Marber was dealing in fakes?'

Mann shook his head thoughtfully. 'Nor was he passing along stolen works. But then, if he was, it's unlikely anyone in Edinburgh would know.'

'How so?'

His eyes turned to her. 'Because such transactions tend to be sub rosa.' He saw her eyes narrow. 'Under the table,' he explained, watching her nod of understanding.

'And what about cheating the artists themselves?' she asked.

Mann shrugged. 'That could mean several things. One would be charging too high a commission – hardly cheating, but an artist might not see it that way.'

'Commissions tend to be what?'

'Anywhere between ten and twenty-five per cent. The better-known the artist, the lower the commission.'

'And someone like Malcolm Neilson . . . ?'

Mann pondered this. 'Malcolm's well enough known in the UK . . . and has his collectors in the States and the Far East . . .'

'He doesn't live like a rich man.'

'You mean his pied-à-terre? The Stockbridge Colonies?' Mann smiled. 'Don't be fooled. He uses that place as a studio. He has a much larger house in Inveresk and recently added a home in the Perigord to his property portfolio, if rumours are to be believed.'

'So just because he was left out of the Colourists doesn't mean he's hurting?'

'Not financially, at any rate.'

'Meaning?'

'Malcolm has an ego, same as any other artist. He doesn't like to feel excluded.'

'You think that's why he says Marber was cheating?'

Mann shrugged. He'd finally given up stirring the latte, and was now testing the temperature of the tall glass cup with the tips of his fingers. 'Malcolm doesn't just think himself a Colourist: he feels he should be leading the group.'

'They came to blows apparently.'

'So the story goes.'

'You don't believe it?'

He looked at her. 'Have you asked Malcolm?'

'Not yet.'

'Maybe you should. You might also ask him why he was at Edward's gallery that night.'

Siobhan suddenly had trouble swallowing the last of her espresso. It felt like sludge. She reached for the water bottle again. 'You were there?' she finally managed to ask.

Mann shook his head. 'I wasn't invited. But we dealers . . . we're always keen to know how the competition's doing. I just happened to be passing in a taxi. The place looked sadly busy.'

'And you saw Malcolm Neilson?'

Mann nodded slowly. 'He was standing on the pavement outside, like a child at the window of a toy-shop.'

'Why didn't you tell me this before?'

Mann grew thoughtful again, turning to face the outside world. 'Maybe it was the company you were keeping,' he said.

*

Back in her car, Siobhan checked her messages: three from Davie Hynds. She called him at St Leonard's.

'What's up?' she asked.

'Just wondered how the funeral went.'

'I didn't go.'

'That puts you in a distinct minority. Half St Leonard's seems to be there.'

Siobhan knew they'd be on the look-out for possible suspects, taking names and addresses from anyone attending the ceremony. 'Are you at the station?' she asked.

'Right now, I think I *am* the station. It was pretty much a skeleton crew over the weekend, too . . .'

'I didn't know you were working this weekend.'

'Thought I'd show willing. Have you heard the news?'

'No.'

'Marber's bank statements . . . seems he was renting a self-storage unit at a place down in Granton. Had been for the past month. I went there for a look-see, but it was empty. Owner says he doesn't think Marber had been near the place.'

'So what was he planning to do with it?'

'Maybe use it for storing paintings?'

'Maybe.' But Siobhan sounded sceptical.

'Neither his secretary nor Cynthia Bessant knew anything about it.'

'Did you happen to drop by Madame Cyn's again?' Siobhan asked archly.

'Had to put a few questions to her . . .'

'Over a glass or two of wine?'

'Don't worry, I took a chaperone.' Hynds paused. 'So if you gave the funeral a miss, whereabouts are you?'

'I'm in town. I was thinking of paying the artist another visit.'

'Malcolm Neilson? What for?'

'New information. Neilson went to the private viewing.'

'How come no one said?'

'I don't think he went in, just loitered on the pavement.'

'Says who?'

'Dominic Mann.'

There was another pause. 'You've been talking to him?'

'He called it in,' Siobhan lied. She didn't want Hynds to know she'd gone to Mann without him. They might yet turn out to be partners after all ... More than that, she was aware that she needed an ally at St Leonard's. It wasn't just the loss of Rebus or the appearance of Derek Linford. She knew she couldn't be everywhere at once, and would have to depend on others, forging alliances, not making enemies. The next step on the promotion ladder might be a way off, but that didn't mean she could afford to relax ...

'I didn't see anything about it,' Hynds was saying.

'He got me on my mobile.'

'Funny, it's been switched off whenever I've tried ...'

'Well, he did.'

There was a longer silence between them. She knew he was working it out.

'Want me with you when you talk to Neilson?' Hynds asked quietly. He *knew*.

'Yes,' she replied, too quickly. 'Want to meet me there?'

'All right. Half an hour?'

'Fine.' She thought of something. 'Have the victim's credit cards turned up yet?'

'Not a single transaction.'

Which was curious in itself: when you stole credit cards, you used them hard and fast before a stop could be put on them. Eric had been talking to her about Internet fraud: nowadays, shopping was twenty-four/seven. A credit-card thief could max out overnight, the purchases delivered to safe addresses. If you'd been on a night out and your cards were lifted, by the time you woke up and discovered they were gone, it was already too late. Why would an attacker take the cards and then not use them? Answer: to make the attack look like a simple robbery, when it was anything but ...

'I'll see you at Neilson's,' she said. She was about to cut the call when something struck her. 'Hang on, do you have Neilson's number?'

'Somewhere.'

'Better phone first. He has another place out at Inveresk.'

'If he knows we're coming, won't he try setting his lawyer on us again?'

'I'm sure you could dissuade him. If he's at Inveresk, call me back: I can pick you up on the way.'

But Malcolm Neilson wasn't at Inveresk. He was in his colonies terrace, wearing the same clothes as before. Siobhan doubted he'd washed or shaved in the intervening time. Hadn't tidied either.

'Just a couple more questions,' she said, keeping things brisk. She didn't bother sitting down, and neither did Hynds. The painter had slumped between the loudspeakers again. His fingers were stained and smeared, and she could smell paint fumes coming from the attic.

'Can I phone a friend?' he asked gruffly.

'You can even ask the audience if you think it'll help,' Hynds answered.

Neilson proffered a snort and the beginnings of a smile.

'Did you ever have a fight with Edward Marber?' Siobhan asked.

'Depends what you mean.'

'I mean a stand-up fight?'

'You never knew him, did you? He couldn't punch his way through a prawn cracker.'

Looking at the empty tin-foil cartons on the floor, Siobhan deduced that Neilson's last meal had been Chinese.

'Did you hit him?' Hynds asked.

'I just gave him a bit of a push, that's all. Eddie always liked to get up close, didn't seem to know the meaning of personal space.'

'Where was this?' Siobhan asked.

'In the chest.'

'I mean, was it here?'

'At his gallery.'

'After he'd turned you down for the exhibition?'

'Yes.'

'And that's all it was – a push?'

'He stumbled back, fell over some canvases.' Neilson shrugged.

'And you haven't been back to the gallery since?'

'Wouldn't wipe my arse on the place.'

'Really?' The question came from Hynds. Something about his tone of voice alerted the artist.

'Okay, I went there the night of the opening.'

'Did you go in?' Siobhan asked quietly.

'I'm assuming someone saw me, so you know damned fine I didn't.'

'What were you doing there, Mr Neilson?'

'The spectre at the feast.'

'You wanted to taunt Mr Marber?'

The artist ran a hand through his hair, further disturbing it. 'I don't know what I wanted exactly.'

'To make a scene?' Hynds suggested.

'If I'd wanted one of those, I'd have gone inside, wouldn't I?'

'How long were you there?'

'Not long. Five, ten minutes.'

'Did you see anything?'

'I saw fat people pouring champagne down their throats.'

'I meant anything suspicious.'

Neilson shook his head.

'Did you recognise any of the guests?' Siobhan asked, shifting her weight from one foot to the other.

'A couple of journalists . . . a photographer . . . a few of Eddie's buyers.'

'Such as?'

'Sharon Burns . . . It was galling to see her there. She's bought a few of my paintings in the past . . .'

'Anyone else?'

'Morris Cafferty . . .'

'Cafferty?'

'The businessman.'

Siobhan nodded. 'Does he own any of your own works?'

'I think he's got one, yes.'

Hynds cleared his throat. 'Did you happen to see any other artists?'

Neilson glowered at him, while Siobhan seethed that they'd gone off the subject of Cafferty. 'Joe Drummond was there,' the artist admitted. 'I didn't see Celine Blacker, but no way she'd pass up free booze and the chance to be fawned over.'

'What about Hastie?'

'Hastie doesn't do many parties.'

'Not even when he has paintings to sell?'

'He leaves that to the dealer.' Neilson's eyes narrowed. 'You like his stuff?'

'It has its moments,' Hynds offered.

Neilson shook his head slowly, as if in disbelief.

'Can I ask one more thing, Mr Neilson?' Siobhan interrupted. 'You've said that Edward Marber was a cheat. I'm not sure who he was cheating.'

'Bloody everyone. He'd sell a painting for full whack, then tell the artist he had to knock a bit off to secure the sale.'

'And how did that cheat the buyer?'

'Because they could probably have got it for the cheaper price. And take something like the New Colourists, that's just bloody marketing hype. Means he can bump up his prices again.'

'No one has to buy if they don't want to,' Hynds said.

'But they *do* buy, especially after Eddie's patter's done its trick.'

'You sell your own works direct, Mr Neilson?' Siobhan asked.

'Dealers have got the market sewn up,' Neilson spat. 'Blood-sucking bastards that they are . . .'

'So who represents you?'

'A London gallery: Terrance Whyte. Not that he seems to have what it takes . . .'

Outside, after another fifteen minutes of fairly unproductive grumbling from the artist, Siobhan and Hynds stepped on to the pavement. Siobhan's car was kerbside, Hynds double-parked alongside.

'He's still talking about Marber in the present tense,' Siobhan commented.

Hynds nodded. 'As if the murder hasn't really affected him.'

'Or maybe he's read the same psychology books we have, and knows it looks good for him.'

Hynds considered this. 'He saw Cafferty,' he said.

'Yes, I wanted to thank you for getting us away from that particular topic so promptly.'

Hynds paused to think back, then muttered an apology. 'Why are you so interested in Cafferty?'

She looked at him. 'What do you mean?'

'I've heard about Cafferty and DI Rebus.'

'What about them, Davie?'

'Just that they . . .' Hynds seemed finally to realise that he was digging himself into a hole. 'Nothing.'

'Nothing? You sure about that?'

He stared at her. 'Why didn't you take me with you to see Dominic Mann?'

She scratched at her ear, looking around before focusing on Hynds. 'Know what his first question to me was? "Where's your homophobic friend?" That's why I didn't take you. I thought I might get more out of him if you weren't there.' She paused. 'And I did.'

'Fair enough,' Hynds said, his shoulders dropping, hands seeking the shelter of his pockets.

'What are Neilson's paintings like, do you know?' Siobhan asked, keen to change the subject.

Hynds's right hand appeared from its pocket, clutching four postcards. They were works by Malcolm Neilson. They had titles like 'First Impressions Count Last' and 'Seeing How You Already Know'. The titles didn't go with the paintings: field and sky; a beach with cliff-face; moorland; a boat on a loch.

'What do you think?' Hynds asked.

'I don't know . . . I suppose I'd expected something a bit more . . .'

'Abstract and angry?'

She looked at him. 'Exactly.'

'Abstract and angry don't sell,' Hynds explained. 'Not to the people who decide which prints and postcards they'll foist on the public.'

'How do you mean?'

Hynds took the postcards and waved them at her. 'These are where the big money is. Greetings cards, framed prints, wrapping paper . . . Ask Jack Vettriano.'

'I would if I knew who he was.' She was thinking: hadn't Dominic Mann mentioned him . . . ?

'He's a painter. The couple dancing on the beach.'

'I've seen that one.'

'I'll bet you have. He probably makes more from card sales and the like than he does from his paintings.'

'You're joking.'

But Hynds shook his head, pocketing the postcards. 'Art's all about marketing. I was speaking to a journalist about it.'

'One of the ones from the viewing?'

Hynds nodded. 'She's art critic for the *Herald*.'

'And I wasn't invited?' He looked at her, and she took the point: *just like her and Dominic Mann.* 'Okay,' she said, 'I asked for that. Go on about marketing.'

'You need to get artists' names known. Plenty of ways to do that. The artist can cause a sensation of some kind.'

'Like whassername with her unmade bed?'

Hynds nodded. 'Or you stir up interest in some new school or trend.'

'The New Scottish Colourists?'

'The timing couldn't be better. There was a big retrospective last year of the original Colourists – Cadell, Peploe, Hunter and Fergusson.'

'You got all this from your art critic?'

He held up a single digit. 'One phone call.'

'Speaking of which . . .' Siobhan dug into her pocket for her mobile, punched in a number and waited till it was answered. Hynds had taken the postcards out again and was flicking through them.

'Is anyone speaking to the competition?' Siobhan asked him.

Hynds nodded. 'I think Silvers and Hawes did the interviews. They talked to Hastie, Celine Blacker and Joe Drummond.'

'Does this Hastie have a first name?'

'Not for professional purposes.'

There was no answer from the phone. Siobhan shut it off. 'And did anything come of the interviews?'

'They went by the book.'

She looked at him. 'Meaning?'

'Meaning they didn't know what questions to ask.'

'Unlike you, you mean?'

Hynds rested a hand against Siobhan's car. 'I've taken a crash course in Scottish art. You know it and I know it.'

'So speak to DCS Templer; maybe she'll let you do a fresh lot of interviews.' Siobhan noted some reddening on Hynds's neck. 'You already spoke to her?' she guessed.

'Saturday afternoon.'

'What did she say?'

'She said it looked like I thought I knew better than her.'

Siobhan muffled a smile. 'You'll get used to her,' she said.

'She's a ball-breaker.'

The smile disappeared. 'She's just doing her job.'

Hynds's lips formed an O. 'I forgot she's a friend of yours.'

'She's my boss, same as she is yours.'

'Way I heard it, she's grooming you.'

'I don't *need* grooming . . .' Siobhan paused, sucked in some air. 'Who've you been talking to? Derek Linford?'

Hynds just shrugged. Problem was, it could have been anyone really: Linford, Silvers, Grant Hood . . . Siobhan punched the number back into her phone.

'DCS Templer's got to be tough on you,' she said, controlling her voice. 'Don't you see? That's her job. Would you call her a ball-breaker if she was a bloke?'

'I'd probably call her something worse,' Hynds said.

Siobhan's call was picked up this time. 'It's Detective Sergeant Clarke here. I have an appointment with Mr Cafferty . . . just wanted to check we were still okay.' She listened, glanced at her watch. 'That's great, thank you. I'll be there.' She quit the call and slipped the phone back into her pocket.

'Morris Gerald Cafferty,' Hynds stated.

'Big Ger to those in the know.'

'Prominent local businessman.'

'With sidelines in drugs, protection and God knows what else.'

'You've had run-ins with him before?'

She nodded, but didn't say anything. The run-ins had been between Cafferty and Rebus; at best she'd been a spectator.

'So what time are we seeing him?' Hynds asked.

' "We"?'

'I assume you'll want me to cast an expert eye over his art collection.'

Which made sense, even though Siobhan was loath to admit it. Hynds's phone sounded now, and he answered it.

'Hello, Ms Bessant,' he said, winking at Siobhan. Then

109

he listened for a moment. 'Are you sure?' He was staring at Siobhan now. 'We're not far away, actually. Yes, five minutes . . . see you there.' He finished the call.

'What is it?' Siobhan asked.

'One of Marber's own paintings. Looks like someone's walked off with it. And guess what: it's a Vettriano . . .'

They drove to Marber's gallery, where Cynthia Bessant was waiting for them, still dressed in black from the funeral and with her eyes reddened from crying.

'I drove Jan back here . . .' She nodded towards the back office, where Marber's secretary was fussing with paperwork. 'She said she wanted to get straight back to work. That's when I noticed.'

'Noticed what?' Siobhan asked.

'Well, there was a painting Eddie liked. He'd kept it at home for a while, then decided to hang it in his office here. That's where I thought it was, which is why I didn't say anything when it wasn't with the rest of his collection at home. But Jan says he decided it might get stolen from the gallery, so he took it home again.'

'Could he have sold it?' Hynds asked.

'I don't think so, David,' Bessant said. 'But Jan is checking . . .'

Hynds's neck was reddening, knowing Siobhan's eyes were on him, amused by Bessant's use of his first name.

'What sort of painting was it?'

'Fairly early Vettriano . . . self-portrait with a nude behind him in the mirror.'

'How large?' Hynds had taken his notebook out.

'Maybe forty inches by thirty . . . Eddie bought it five or so years ago, just before Jack went stratospheric.'

'So what would it be worth now?'

She shrugged. 'Maybe thirty . . . forty thousand. You think whoever killed Eddie stole it?'

'What do you think?' Siobhan asked.

'Well, Eddie had Peploes and Bellanys, a minor Klee and

a couple of exquisite Picasso prints . . .' She seemed at a loss.

'So this painting wasn't the most valuable in the collection?'

Bessant shook her head.

'And you're sure it's missing?'

'It's not here, and it wasn't in the house . . .' She looked at them. 'I don't see where else it could be.'

'Didn't Mr Marber have a place in Tuscany?' Siobhan asked.

'He only spent a month a year out there,' Bessant argued.

Siobhan was thoughtful. 'We need to circulate this information. Would there be a photo of the painting anywhere?'

'In a catalogue probably . . .'

'And do you think you could go to Mr Marber's house again, Miss Bessant, just to make doubly sure?'

Cynthia Bessant nodded, then glanced in Hynds's direction. 'Would I need to go on my own?'

'I'm sure David would be happy to accompany you,' Siobhan told her, watching as the blood started creeping up Hynds's neck all over again.

8

When Rebus got back to the syndicate room, the team were gathered around Archie Tennant. Tennant was seated, the others standing behind him, peering over his shoulders at the sheaf of papers from which he was reading.

'What's that?' Rebus said, shrugging his arms out of his jacket.

Tennant broke off his recital. 'The file on Richard "Dickie" Diamond. Your amigos at Lothian and Borders just faxed it over.'

'That's strangely efficient of them.' Rebus watched from the window as a car drove down the access road. It could have been Strathern, heading home. Driver in front, passenger in the back.

'A bit of a lad, your Dickie,' Francis Gray said.

'He wasn't my Dickie,' Rebus responded.

'You knew him, though? Pulled him in a few times?'

Rebus nodded. No use denying it. He sat down at the opposite side of the table from the others.

'I thought you said you'd hardly heard of him, John?' Gray said, eyes twinkling. Tennant turned another sheet.

'I hadn't finished that,' Tam Barclay said.

'That's because you've the reading age of a muppet,' Gray complained, as Tennant handed the sheet to Barclay.

'I think I said I barely knew him,' Rebus stated, answering Gray's question.

'You arrested him twice.'

'I've arrested a lot of people, Francis. They don't all

become bosom buddies. He stabbed some guy in a nightclub, then poured petrol into someone else's letterbox. Except the latter never made it as far as court.'

'You're not telling us anything we don't know,' Jazz McCullough commented.

'Maybe that's because you're so fucking brainy, Jazz.'

McCullough looked up. They *all* looked up.

'What's wrong, John? Is it your time of the month or something?' This from Stu Sutherland.

'Maybe Andrea's not falling for John's charms after all,' Francis Gray offered.

Rebus looked at the eyes watching him, then released a pent-up breath, following it with a smile of contrition. 'Sorry, lads, sorry. I was out of order.'

'Which is why you're here in the first place,' Tennant reminded him. He prodded the file with a finger. 'This guy never turned up again?'

Rebus shrugged.

'And did a runner just before the Glasgow CID could come calling?'

Rebus shrugged again.

'Did a runner *or* got himself disappeared,' Allan Ward said.

'You still here, Allan?' Gray said. Rebus studied both men. There didn't seem to be much love lost. He wondered if Allan Ward was ripe to grass up his fellow conspirators. He doubted it. On the other hand, of the three supposed miscreants, he was definitely the wettest behind the ears . . .

'Allan's right,' Tam Barclay said. 'Diamond could have got himself killed. But whichever it was, it looks likely that he knew something . . . or was scared someone would think he did.'

Rebus had to concede, Barclay had taken his brainy pills this morning. Tennant was prodding the file again.

'This is just dead wood. It doesn't tell us anything about what's happened to Diamond in the years since.'

'We could circulate his description, see if he's turned up on another force's turf.' The suggestion came from Jazz McCullough.

'Good thinking,' Tennant conceded.

'The one thing this file *does* tell us, though,' Francis Gray said, 'is who Dickie Diamond hung around with. Someone like him goes walkies, there's always someone who knows. Back then, they may not have wanted to say anything, but time's passed . . .'

'You want to talk to his accomplices?' Tennant said.

'Can't do any harm. Years go by, stories start to get told . . .'

'We could ask Lothian and Borders to—'

Stu Sutherland's suggestion was cut short by Gray. 'I believe our friends in the east are a bit tied up.' He glanced towards Rebus. 'Isn't that right, John?'

Rebus nodded. 'The Marber inquiry's on the go.'

'Pretty high-profile, too,' Gray added. 'Which turned out not to be John's cup of tea.'

There were smiles at this. Gray had come around the table, so that he could lock eyes with Tennant.

'So what do you reckon, sir? Is it worth a day or two in Auld Reekie? It has to be your call in the end, not ours.' He opened his arms and gave a shrug.

'Maybe a couple of half-days,' Tennant agreed at last. 'Now what else have we got to go on . . . ?'

As it turned out, they did have something else by the end of that day's play. But first, there were classes to attend. The canteen was noisy at lunchtime, everyone relieved that the top brass had come and gone. Tennant seemed strangely subdued, and Rebus wondered if secretly he'd wanted them to come to watch his 'show'. It had crossed Rebus's mind that Tennant had to be in on it. Much easier to smooth Rebus's way into the course as a latecomer if the chief constables had someone on the inside. Then there was that niggling doubt about the 'coincidence' that their unsolved case just happened to be one Rebus had worked . . .

One Francis Gray had worked, too.

Gray as a mole, sent in by Strathern . . . ? Rebus couldn't get thoughts of the double-bluff out of his head. The lasagne on his plate had flattened itself out, a swirl of yellow and red, rimmed with orange grease. The more he stared at it, the more the colours seemed to blur.

'Lost your appetite?' Allan Ward asked.

'You want it?' Rebus replied. But Ward shook his head. 'Frankly, it looks like afterbirth.'

As the description took effect, Allan Ward smirked from behind a forkful of gammon.

Straight after lunch, some of the probationers took to one of the football pitches. Others took a stroll around the grounds. But up in Crime Management, the Wild Bunch were being taught how to put together a Manual of Murder Investigation, the MMI being, in the words of their tutor, 'the Bible of a good, tight inquiry'. It had to detail avenues taken and procedures followed. It showed that the investigating team had done their utmost.

To Rebus, it was paperwork.

And it was followed by Forensic Entomology, at the end of which they streamed out of the classroom.

'Gives me butterflies just thinking of it,' Tam Barclay said, referring to some of the slides they'd been shown. Then he winked and smiled. Down in the break-out area, they sprawled on the sofas, rubbing at their foreheads, eyes squeezed shut. Rebus and Ward headed down a further flight and outside for a ciggie.

'Does your head in, that stuff,' Ward said, nodding thanks as Rebus produced a lighter.

'Certainly makes you think,' Rebus agreed. They'd been shown close-ups of putrefying corpses and the bugs and insects found on them. They'd been told how maggots could help pinpoint time of death. They'd been shown floaters and bloaters and human forms reduced to something more akin to melted raspberry ripple.

Rebus thought of his uneaten lasagne and took another drag on his cigarette.

'Thing is, Allan, we let a lot of shite get in the way. We get cynical and maybe even a bit lazy. All we can see are brass breathing down our necks and another load of paperwork to be completed. We forget what the job's supposed to be about.' Rebus looked at the younger man. 'What do you think?'

'It's a job, John. I joined because no other profession would have me.'

'I'm sure that's not true.'

Ward thought about it, then flicked ash into the air. 'Ach, maybe not. It feels that way sometimes, though.'

Rebus nodded. 'You seem to have Francis on your back a lot of the time.'

When Ward looked up sharply, Rebus wondered if he'd introduced the subject too rapidly. But Ward just gave a wry smile.

'That stuff's like water off a duck's back.'

'You two know one another?'

'Not really.'

'It's just that I'm not sure Francis would try it with everyone . . .'

Ward wagged a finger. 'You're not so daft, are you? We did work one case. I mean, we weren't close or anything.'

'Understood. But you're not complete strangers, so he feels he can rag you a bit, right?'

'Right.'

Rebus took another draw on the cigarette, then exhaled. He was staring into the distance, as though maybe there was something of interest to him in the football match. 'What was the case?' he asked, finally.

'Some Glasgow drug-dealer . . . gangster sort of thing.'

'Glasgow?'

'This guy had tentacles everywhere.'

'Even as far south as your patch?'

'Oh, aye. Stranraer, you know – gateway to and from Ireland. Guns, drugs and cash bouncing backwards and forwards like a ping-pong ball.'

'What was the guy's name? Would I know him?'

'Not now you wouldn't. He's dead.' Rebus watched for some sign from Ward – a pause, or a hooding of the eyes. But there was nothing. 'Name was Bernie Johns.'

Rebus made a show of running the name through his memory. 'Died in jail?' he offered.

Ward nodded. 'Couldn't have happened to a more deserving bloke.'

'We've got one just like him in Edinburgh.'

'Cafferty?' Ward guessed. 'Yeah, I've heard of that bastard. Didn't you help put him away?'

'Problem was, they didn't keep him there.' Rebus squashed the remains of his cigarette underfoot. 'So you don't mind the ribbing Francis is giving you?'

'Don't you worry about me, John,' Ward said, patting him on the shoulder. 'Francis Gray will know when he's crossed the line . . . I'll make sure of that.' He made to turn away, but stopped. Rebus felt a tingling in his shoulder from where he'd been touched. 'You going to show us a good time in Edinburgh, John?'

'I'll see what I can do.'

Ward nodded. There was still some steel in his eyes. Rebus doubted it was ever completely absent. He knew it wouldn't do to underestimate Ward. But he still wondered if he could somehow turn him into an ally . . .

'You coming?'

'I'll catch you up,' Rebus said. He thought about another cigarette but dismissed the idea. There were roars from the football pitch, arms raised high on the sideline. One of the players seemed to be rolling around on the ground.

'They're coming to Edinburgh,' Rebus said quietly to himself. Then he shook his head slowly. *He* was supposed to be the one keeping tabs on the Wild Bunch, and now they'd be trespassing on *his* patch instead. They'd be sniffing around, asking questions about Dickie Diamond. Rebus blew the idea away with a wave of his hand, then got his mobile out and put in a call to Siobhan, who wasn't answering.

'Typical,' he muttered. So instead he called Jean. She was shopping at Napier's the Herbalist, which made him smile. Jean trusted to homoeopathy, and had a bathroom cabinet full of herbal medicines. She'd even made him use some when he'd felt flu coming on, and they'd seemed to work. But every time he looked in her cabinet, he felt he could use half the jars for cooking up a curry or a stew.

'Laugh all you like,' she'd told him more than once. 'Then tell me which of us is the healthier.'

Now Jean wanted to know when she'd see him. He told her he wasn't sure. He didn't mention that his work would be bringing him back into the city sooner than expected, didn't want that sense of expectation. If they made some arrangement, chances were he'd have to cancel at the last minute. Better for her not to know.

'I'm going round to Denise's tonight anyway,' she informed him.

'Good to see you're not pining.'

'You're the one who's done a runner, not me.'

'Part of the job, Jean.'

'Sure it is.' He heard her sigh. 'How was your weekend anyway?'

'Quiet. I tidied the flat, did some washing . . .'

'Drank yourself into a stupor?'

'That accusation wouldn't stand up in court.'

'How tough would it be to find witnesses?'

'No comment, Your Honour. How did the wedding go?'

'I wish you'd been there. Will I see you next time you're in town?'

'Of course.'

'And will that be any time soon?'

'Hard to say, Jean . . .'

'Well . . . take care of yourself.'

'Don't I always?' he said, ending the call with a 'bye' before she could answer the question.

Back inside, there was excitement in the break-out area. Archie Tennant stood with arms folded, chin tucked into his chest, as though deep in thought. Tam Barclay was waving his arms around as if trying to attract attention to the point he was making. Stu Sutherland and Jazz McCullough were wanting their own say. Allan Ward looked to have walked into the middle of it, and wanted an explanation, while Francis Gray was an oasis of calm, seated on one of the sofas, one leg crossed over the other, a black polished shoe moving from side to side like a baton controlling the performers.

Rebus didn't say anything. He just squeezed past Ward and took a seat next to Gray. A ray of low sunshine was coming in through the windows, throwing an exaggerated silhouette of the group on to the far wall. Rebus wasn't reminded of an orchestra any more, but of some puppet show.

With only one man pulling the strings.

Still Rebus said nothing. He noticed the mobile phone nestled in Gray's expansive crotch, took out his own phone again and decided that it was heavier and older. Probably obsolete. He'd taken an earlier model to a shop because of a fault, only to be told it would be cheaper to replace than fix.

Gray was studying Rebus's phone, too. 'I got a call,' he said.

Rebus looked up at the tumult. 'Must've been a good one.'

Gray nodded slowly. 'I had a few favours outstanding, so I put the word around Glasgow that we were looking at Rico Lomax.'

'And?'

'And I got a call . . .'

'Whoah, whoah,' Archie Tennant suddenly called out, unfolding his arms and raising them. 'Let's all slow down here, okay?'

The noise ceased. Tennant took in each man with his gaze, then lowered his arms. 'Okay, so we've got new information . . .' He broke off, fixing his stare on Gray. 'Your informant's one hundred per cent?'

Gray shrugged. 'He's reliable.'

'What new information?' Ward asked. Sutherland and Barclay started answering, until Tennant told them to shut up.

'Okay, so it turns out that Rico's pub, the one he'd been drinking in the night he died, was owned at the time by a certain Chib Kelly, who we know started winching Rico's widow soon after.'

'How soon after?'

'Does it matter?'

'Did the investigation know at the time . . . ?'

The questions were coming thick and fast, and once again Tennant had to appeal for quiet. He looked to Gray.

'Well, Francis, *did* the original inquiry team know about this?'

'Search me,' Gray said.

'Do any of you remember coming across this fact in any of the files?' Tennant looked around, received only shakes of the head. 'Big question then: is it material to the case?'

'Could be.'

'Got to be.'

'Crime of passion.'

'Absolutely.'

Tennant grew thoughtful again, letting the voices wash over him.

'Could be we need to talk to Chib himself, sir.' Tennant looked to the speaker: John Rebus.

'Yeah, sure,' Ward was saying. 'He's definitely going to incriminate himself.' The sneer reappeared.

'It's the proper course of action,' Rebus said, repeating a phrase they'd had drummed into them at the MMI talk.

'John's right,' Gray said, his eyes on Tennant. 'In a *real* investigation, we'd be out there asking questions, getting in people's faces, not sitting here like school-kids on detention.'

'I thought getting in people's faces was your precise problem, DI Gray,' Tennant said coolly.

'Could be. But it's been getting me results these past twenty-odd years.'

'Maybe not for much longer, though.' The threat lay in the air between the two men.

'Seems logical to at least talk to the man,' Rebus said. 'After all, this isn't just a test, it's a real, flesh-and-blood case.'

'You weren't half as keen to follow up the Edinburgh angle, John,' Jazz McCullough stated, slipping his hands into his pockets.

'Jazz has got a point,' Gray said, turning his head to face Rebus. 'Something you're not telling us, DI Rebus?'

Rebus wanted to grab Gray and hiss at him: *How much do you know?* Instead, he pocketed his mobile and rested his elbows on his knees. 'Maybe I just fancy a trip to the wild west,' he said.

'Who says *you're* going?' Allan Ward asked.

'I can't see us all in a room with Chib Kelly,' Stu Sutherland commented.

'What? Too much like hard work for you, Stu?' Ward taunted.

'This isn't getting us anywhere,' Tennant piped up. 'Since DI Rebus is suddenly all hot and bothered about "proper courses of action", the first thing we need to do is see whether this really is new ground. And that means ploughing back through the files, seeing if Chib Kelly's mentioned anywhere as landlord ... What was the pub called anyway?'

'The Claymore,' Gray offered. 'It's since become the Dog and Bone, gone a bit upmarket.'

'Still owned by Kelly?' Rebus asked.

Gray shook his head. 'Some English chain: all book-lined walls and clutter. More like walking into a junk shop than a pub.'

'The thing to do,' Tennant was saying, 'is get back into those files, see what we can come up with.'

'We could maybe manage an hour or two,' Gray offered, looking at his watch.

'Plans for tonight, Francis?' Tennant asked.

'John's shipping us through to Edinburgh for a night on the town.' Gray's hand landed heavily on Rebus's shoulder. 'Make a change from the lounge, eh, John?'

Rebus didn't say anything, didn't hear the rest of the group saying things like 'Nice one' and 'Good idea'. He was concentrating too hard on Francis Gray, wondering what the hell he was up to.

9

'What the hell are you up to?'

It was a snarling question, and it came from behind the closed door. There was a muffled reply. The secretary smiled up at Siobhan and Hynds. She had the telephone receiver to her ear. Siobhan could hear the phone buzzing somewhere behind the door. Then it appeared to be snatched up.

'What?'

The secretary actually flinched. 'Two police officers to see you, Mr Cafferty. They did make an appointment . . .' Sounding apologetic, a slight tremble in her voice. She listened to whatever her employer was telling her, then put the receiver down. 'He'll be with you in a moment, if you'll take a seat . . .'

'Must be a joy to work for.'

'Yes.' The secretary forced a smile. 'Yes, he is.'

'Plenty secretarial jobs going. Friday's *Scotsman*'s the place I'd start looking.'

Siobhan retreated to the line of three chairs, taking Hynds with her. There wasn't space in the outer office for a coffee table. Two desks: one currently occupied by the secretary, the other a shambles of paperwork. The place had probably been a shop until fairly recently. It was sandwiched between a baker's and a stationer's, its large window looking on to the nondescript street. They were west and south of the city centre, not far from Tollcross. The area held no fond memories for Siobhan, who had crashed her car once, years back, while confused by the range of options at the Tollcross road junction. Five routes criss-crossing at the lights, and her having not long passed her test, the car a gift from her parents . . .

'I couldn't work here,' Hynds was telling the secretary. He nodded in the direction of the street. 'That smell from the baker's.' Then he patted his stomach and smiled. The secretary smiled back, more from relief, Siobhan thought, than anything else – relief that Hynds wasn't meaning her employer . . .

The one-time shop was now MGC Lettings. Across the window was printed the legend 'The Answer to Your Property Needs'. When they'd arrived, Hynds had asked why a 'criminal genius' would need such a boring front. Siobhan couldn't answer that. She knew Cafferty had other interests in the city, predominantly a minicab firm out at Gorgie. The fresh paintwork and new carpet led her to believe that MGC Lettings was a recent venture.

'Hope that's not one of his tenants he's got in there,' Hynds said now. If the secretary heard him, she pretended otherwise. She'd slipped on a pair of headphones and looked to be typing out a letter from a dictation machine. Siobhan had picked up some of the sheets from the messy table. They were listings of properties to let. Most were tenement flats in the less salubrious parts of town. She handed one to Hynds.

'A lot of agencies, they'll say things like "No DSS". No mention of that here.'

'So?'

'Ever heard of landlords cramming their flats with people from Social Security, then ripping them off?' Hynds looked blank. 'The claimants have to hand over their benefit books. Landlord meantime gets the rent money from the DSS. He's quids in.'

'But this is a lettings agency. Anyone can walk in wanting a flat . . .'

'Doesn't mean everyone gets one.'

Hynds took time digesting this, then looked around the

walls. Two calendars and a week planner. No original works of art.

The door to the inner office opened and a ratty-looking man shuffled quickly towards the exit. Then a figure filled the doorway. He was wearing a white shirt, near-luminous in its newness, and a silk tie the colour of spilled blood. His sleeves were rolled up, the arms thick and hairy. The head was large and round, like a bowling ball, the wiry silver hair cropped short. The eyes sparkled darkly.

'Sorry to keep you waiting,' the mouth said. 'I'm Mr Cafferty. How can I help you?'

As Siobhan and Hynds stood up, Cafferty asked if they wanted tea or coffee. They shook their heads.

'Donna can fetch it from the baker's,' he assured them. 'No trouble.'

Still no takers, so he led them into his office. There wasn't much to it: a desk, with nothing but a telephone on it; a grey four-drawer filing-cabinet; a small window of frosted glass. The lights were on, but the place felt like a clean, well-lit cave. A dog had risen to its feet. It was a brown and white spaniel, and it made straight for Siobhan, sniffing her feet, wiping its wet nose against her hand when she held it out.

'Sit, Claret!' Cafferty snapped. The dog retreated to its corner.

'Nice dog,' Siobhan commented. 'Why Claret?'

'I'm a fiend for red wine,' Cafferty said with a smile.

Against one wall, still shrouded in bubble-wrap, were what looked like three or four framed pictures or paintings, reminding Siobhan of the ones in Marber's house. Hynds made straight for them, though Cafferty had directed him towards one of the chairs in front of the desk.

'Not got round to putting these up yet?' Hynds asked.

'Don't know that I ever will,' Cafferty replied.

Siobhan had seated herself, and, as intended, Cafferty

didn't know whether to focus his attention on her or Hynds. He couldn't keep an eye on both at once.

'DC Hynds is a bit of an aficionado,' Siobhan explained, as Hynds peered at each canvas in turn.

'Is he now?' Cafferty growled. His jacket was over the back of his chair, and he was sitting forward, as if fearful of crushing it in some way. His shoulders seemed massive. Siobhan thought he looked like a caged predator, not quite hiding its ability to pounce.

'Here's a Hastie,' Hynds said, lifting the painting so Siobhan could see. Covered in polythene as it was, she could just make out swatches of colour and a thick white frame. 'Did you buy this at the preview, Mr Cafferty?'

'No.'

Siobhan looked over to Hynds. 'None of the paintings have been moved from the exhibition,' she said, as if reminding him.

'Oh, yes,' he said, nodding, then he shook his head almost imperceptibly, letting her know the Vettriano wasn't there.

Siobhan turned her attention to Cafferty. 'Did you happen to buy anything on the night?'

'I didn't, as it happens.'

'Nothing there you fancied?'

Cafferty rested his forearms on the edge of the desk. 'You're Siobhan Clarke, aren't you?' He smiled. 'I'd forgotten, but now I remember.'

'And what exactly is it you remember, Mr Cafferty?'

'You work with Rebus. Only I hear he's been stuck back in training school.' He made a tutting sound. 'And Detective Constable Hynds here . . . his first name is David, correct?'

Hynds straightened up. 'That's right, sir.'

Cafferty was nodding.

'I'm impressed,' Siobhan said, keeping her voice level. 'You know who we are. So you should know why we're here.'

'Same reason you visited Madame Cyn: you want to ask me about Eddie Marber.' Cafferty watched as Hynds walked around to the front of the desk and sat down next to Siobhan. 'It was Cyn told me your name, DC Hynds,' he said with a wink.

'You were at the private view, the night Edward Marber was killed.'

'I was, yes.'

'You didn't sign the guest book,' Hynds stated.

'Didn't see any reason to.'

'How long did you stay at the party?'

'I arrived late, stayed till just about the end. A few people were heading on to dinner. They wanted Eddie to go with them, but he said he was tired. I . . . he called for a taxi.' Cafferty shifted his arms slightly. The hesitation interested Siobhan, and she knew Hynds had caught it as well. Neither of them filled the silence. Eventually, Cafferty continued. 'I think we all left the gallery around eight or quarter past. I went out for a few drinks.'

'Anywhere in particular?'

'That new hotel in the *Scotsman* building. I wanted to see what it was like. And after that, the Royal Oak, listened to a bit of folk music . . .'

'Who was playing?' Siobhan asked.

Cafferty shrugged. 'People just turn up and play.'

Hynds had his notebook out. 'Were you with anyone, Mr Cafferty?'

'A couple of business associates.'

'And their names?'

But Cafferty shook his head. 'That's a private matter. And before you go saying anything, I know you're going to try to set me up for this, but it won't work. I liked Eddie Marber, liked him a lot. I felt as miserable as anyone when I heard what happened.'

'You don't know of any enemies he might have had?' Siobhan asked.

'Not one,' Cafferty said.

'Not even the people he'd cheated?' Claret's ears suddenly pricked up, as though comprehending this last word.

Cafferty's eyes narrowed. 'Cheated?'

'We hear tell Mr Marber might have been cheating his artists and clients alike: charging over the odds, paying too little ... You haven't heard anything of those allegations?'

'News to me.'

'Feel any different about your old friend now?' Hynds asked.

Cafferty glared at him. Siobhan was on her feet. She saw Claret watching her, saw the dog's tail beginning to thump the floor. 'You realise,' she said, 'we're not going to be able to verify your alibi unless you can give us your friends' names?'

'I didn't say friends, I said "business associates".' Cafferty had risen to his feet too. Claret sat up.

'And I'm sure they're all upstanding citizens,' Hynds said.

'I'm a businessman these days.' Cafferty wagged a finger. 'A *respectable* businessman.'

'Who's unwilling to help himself with an alibi.'

'Maybe that's because I don't need one.'

'Let's hope that's the case, Mr Cafferty.' Siobhan shot out her hand. 'Thanks for taking the time to see us.' Cafferty stared at the hand, then shook it, a smile flitting across his face.

'Are you as hard as you seem, Siobhan?'

'It's Detective Sergeant Clarke to you, *Mr* Cafferty.'

Hynds felt obliged to offer his hand too, and Cafferty shook it. A little game between the three of them, pretending to be polite and objective, to be on the same side, cut from the same human cloth.

Out on the pavement, Hynds clicked his tongue against his teeth. 'So much for the infamous Big Ger Cafferty.'

'Don't let him fool you,' Siobhan said quietly. She knew

Hynds had been listening to the voice, seeing the shirt and tie ... But she'd been concentrating on Cafferty's eyes, and they'd seemed to belong to some alien species, predatory and cruel. What's more, he had confidence now – the confidence that no prison could ever hold him.

Siobhan was staring back in through the window, and was being watched in turn by Donna, until a bark from the inner office had the secretary leaping to her feet, running in and closing the door behind her. The bark had been human ...

'He only made that one slip,' Siobhan commented.

'About calling the taxi?'

Siobhan nodded. 'Know what I'm wondering? I'm wondering just who exactly it was called for the cab.'

'You think Cafferty did?'

She started nodding, turning to face Hynds. 'And which company do you think he would call?'

'His own?' Hynds guessed.

She kept on nodding, then noticed an old-style Jag parked across the road. She didn't know the driver, but the small figure in the back was the ratty-looking man who'd been getting an earful from Cafferty when they'd arrived. She thought he was called the Weasel ... something like that.

'Hang on here a second,' she told Hynds, then she walked to the edge of the pavement, checking right and left for traffic. But something had been said to the driver, and by the time she reached the middle of the carriage-way, the Jag was moving off, the Weasel's eyes staying on her through the rear window. It took the horn of an approaching moped to bring Siobhan back to life. She trotted back to where Hynds was waiting.

'Someone you know?' he asked.

'Cafferty's right-hand man.'

'Something you wanted to ask him?'

She thought about this, and had to suppress a smile.

There hadn't been anything she'd wanted to say to the Weasel . . . no reason for her to head off into the traffic.

Except that it was something Rebus would have done.

Back at the station, there was interest in the news of the missing painting. Marber's secretary had unearthed a colour photograph, which was now being copied, while DCI Bill Pryde itemised the expense. The reports from that morning's cremation were being collated. No one was claiming any great breakthrough. The Vettriano was as solid a piece of news as they had. Hynds was heading off to Marber's house, where he was due to meet Cynthia Bessant.

'Want to hook up for a drink later?' he asked Siobhan.

'Sure Madame Cyn will let you drag yourself away?' He smiled, but she was shaking her head. 'Quiet night for me,' she told him. She said much the same thing half an hour later when Derek Linford asked her out to dinner – 'nothing fancy . . . just somewhere local. A few of us are going . . .' When she gave him the brush-off, his face hardened. 'I'm trying to be nice here, Siobhan.'

'A few more lessons needed, Derek . . .'

Gill Templer wanted a report on the missing painting. Siobhan kept it succinct. Templer looked thoughtful. When her phone rang, she picked it up, broke the connection and left the receiver off the hook.

'Where do we go from here?' she asked.

'I don't know,' Siobhan admitted. 'It gives us something to look for. More than that, it gives us a question to work on. Namely: why *that* painting?'

'Spur of the moment?' Templer guessed. 'Grab the first thing that came to hand . . . ?'

'And remember to reset the alarm and lock up after you?'

Templer conceded that Siobhan had a point. 'You want to chase it up?' she asked.

'If there's anything to chase, I'll bring my running-shoes. For now, I think we file it under "Interesting".'

Siobhan watched Templer's face darken, and thought she knew the reason why: the Chief Super could hear John Rebus mouthing near-identical sentiments . . .

'Sorry,' Siobhan said, feeling colour rise to her cheeks. 'Bad habit.' She turned to leave.

'By the way,' Templer said, 'how was Big Ger Cafferty?'

'He's bought himself a dog.'

'Really? Think we could persuade it to be our eyes and ears?'

'This one was more nose and tail,' Siobhan said, finally making her exit.

10

'What's your poison, John?'

Each time he got a round in, Jazz McCullough asked the same question. They'd driven into Edinburgh in a two-car convoy. Rebus had agreed to be one of the designated drivers: that way, he'd be sure not to drink too much. Jazz had been the other driver, arguing that he didn't drink much in any case, so it was no skin off his nose.

They'd worked solidly until six on the case-notes, Archie Tennant sticking with them all the way. In the end, and with nothing to show, Ward had invited Tennant along for the evening. Maybe it was the looks from the other men, but Tennant had refused, albeit graciously.

'Not likely,' he'd said. 'You lot could drink me under the bloody table.'

Six of them in two cars: Rebus acting the chauffeur while Gray and Stu Sutherland sat in the back, Gray commenting that Rebus's Saab was 'a bit of a clunker'.

'And what is it you drive again, Francis? Bentley convertible?'

Gray had shaken his head. 'I keep the Bentley in the garage, use the Lexus as a runaround.'

It was true, he did drive a Lexus, a biggish model with leather interior. Rebus hadn't a clue how much one cost.

'How much does one of those rush you these days?' he'd asked.

'Bit more than in the old days,' was the answer.

Then Sutherland had started yakking about the cost of cars when he'd first learned to drive, Rebus taking occasional looks at Gray in the rear-view mirror. Really, he'd wanted Gray and Ward in the car together, see if he could force them still further apart. He'd almost have been as satisfied if Ward and Gray had pushed to go with McCullough: at least that would have shown them acting as a team. No luck either way.

They'd wanted to eat first, so he'd directed them to a curry house on Nicolson Street. And after that, into the Royal Oak. Four drinkers were sitting in a row at the bar. The ones either end were on their own; the two in the middle were together. All four were rolling cigarettes with the intensity of a championship contest. Seated in the corner, a guitarist faced a mandolin player, their eye contact passionate as lovers as they improvised a tune.

Rebus and his fellow drinkers filled what was left of the tiny bar.

'Bloody hell, John,' Tam Barclay said, 'where's the women?'

'Didn't realise you were after a lumber, Tam.'

They stayed at the Oak for just the one drink, then headed into the city centre. Café Royal, Abbotsford, Dome and Standing Order. Four pubs, four more drinks.

'A big night out in Edinburgh,' Barclay commented, staring at the quiet pockets of drinkers around them. 'I thought we were supposed to be the Wild Bunch?'

'Tam's started believing his own hype,' Jazz McCullough said.

'But it's why we've been kicked into rehab, isn't it?' Barclay persisted. 'We don't play by the fucking rules.' Saliva flopped from his mouth. He rubbed it away with the back of his hand.

'I like a man who speaks his mind,' Francis Gray said, laughing and slapping Barclay on the back.

'And I like one who can hold his drink,' McCullough muttered to Rebus.

'It would be different in Glasgow, wouldn't it, Francis?'

'What would, Tam?'

'A night out.'

'It can get pretty tangled, that's for sure.' Gray had his arm around Barclay's shoulders.

'I mean, this place for instance . . .' Barclay studied his surroundings. 'It's a palace, not a boozer!'

'Used to be a bank,' Rebus stated.

'It's not a *proper* pub, see what I'm saying?'

'I think,' Stu Sutherland said, 'you're saying you're pished.'

Barclay considered this, his face widening into a smile. 'Could be you're right, Stu. Could be you're bang on the money there.'

They all laughed, and decided to retrace their steps, maybe taking in some of the pubs they'd passed on the way. Rebus was of a mind to lead them down into the Cowgate, but even that, he decided, wouldn't be authentic enough for Barclay. The rowdier bars were the ones with teenage drinkers and thumping light-shows, places where the six of them would stick out like . . . well, like cops on a night out. Some of their ties might have been discarded, but they were still in suits, all except McCullough, who'd gone to his room to change into jeans and a polo shirt. They'd given him stick about that: old fart trying to look trendy . . .

When they reached the junction between South Bridge and the High Street, Francis Gray suddenly veered left into the High Street itself and started heading downhill, towards the Canongate. They followed, asking him where he was headed.

'Maybe he knows a good boozer,' Barclay commented.

Rebus's ears reddened slightly. It was true that he'd been sticking to the tourist route, keeping the group away from his more regular haunts. He wanted those pubs to remain *his*.

Gray had stopped in front of a kilt shop and was staring up at the building next to it.

'My mum brought me here when I was a kid,' he said.

'What is it?' Stu Sutherland asked.

'Right here, Stu.' Gray stamped his foot on the pavement. 'This is everything that makes us what we are!'

Sutherland looked around. 'I still don't get it.'

'It's John Knox's house,' Rebus said. 'It's where he lived.'

'Bloody right, it is,' Gray said, nodding. 'Anybody else's mum bring them here?'

'I came with a school trip,' Jazz McCullough admitted.

'Aye, me too,' Allan Ward said. 'Fucking boring it was, too.'

Gray wagged a finger. 'That's history you're insulting, young Allan. *Our* history.'

Rebus wanted to say something about how women and Catholics might not agree. He didn't know much about John Knox, but he seemed to recall the man hadn't been too keen on either group.

'Knoxland,' Gray said, stretching out his arms. 'That's what Edinburgh is, wouldn't you agree, John?'

Rebus felt he was being tested in some way. He offered a shrug. 'Which Knox, though?' he asked, causing Gray to frown. 'There was another: Doctor Robert Knox. He bought bodies from Burke and Hare. Maybe we're more like him . . .'

Gray thought about this, then smiled. 'Archie Tennant delivered us the body of Rico Lomax, and we're cutting it open.' He began to nod slowly. 'That's very good, John. Very good.'

Rebus wasn't sure it was exactly what he'd meant, but he accepted the compliment anyway.

The conversation had passed over Tam Barclay's head. 'I need a pee,' he said, turning towards the nearest close and disappearing down it.

Allan Ward was looking up and down the street. 'Dumfries is Times Square compared to this place,' he complained. Then his eye caught a couple of women, coming up the slope towards the group. 'At last, our luck changes!' He made a move forward. 'All right there, ladies? Listen, me and my pals are strangers in these parts ... maybe we could buy you a drink ... ?'

'No thanks,' one of the women said. Her eyes were on Rebus.

'Something to eat then?'

'We've just eaten,' the other woman said.

'Was it any good?' Ward asked. He had a conversation going, and wasn't about to lose it. The first woman was still looking at Rebus. Stu Sutherland was standing beside the window of the kiltmaker's, exclaiming at the prices.

'Come on, Denise,' the first woman said.

'Hey, Denise and me are talking here,' Ward snapped.

'Let them go, Allan,' Rebus said. 'Jean, I—'

But Jean was tugging at Denise's sleeve. She glowered at Rebus, then her eyes moved to his left as Tam Barclay appeared from the shadows, still zipping his fly.

Rebus started to say something, but her look stopped him. Ward was trying to prise Denise's phone number out of her.

'Christ's sake!' Barclay gasped. 'I go for a slash and it all happens! Where are you headed, ladies?'

But the ladies were already on their way. Rebus stood there, mute, watching them go.

'You dog, Allan,' Barclay was saying. 'Did you get her number?'

Ward just grinned and winked.

'She was old enough to be your mother,' Stu Sutherland commented.

'My auntie, maybe,' Ward conceded. 'Some you win, some you lose ...'

Rebus was suddenly aware of Gray standing by his side. 'Someone you know, John?'

Rebus nodded.

'She didn't look too happy with you. Jean, was that her name?'

Rebus nodded again.

Gray slid an arm around his shoulders. 'John's in the dog-house,' he announced. 'Looks like he's bumped into the one person he shouldn't have.'

'That's the trouble with this place,' Allan Ward stated. 'It's too bloody small! Capital city? Capital village, more like.'

'Cheer up, John,' Jazz McCullough said.

'Come on, let's have a drink,' Sutherland mooted, pointing to the nearest pub.

'Good idea, Stu.' Gray gave Rebus a squeeze. 'Maybe a drink would cheer you up, eh, John? Just the one . . .'

Rebus nodded slowly. 'Just the one,' he repeated.

'Good man,' Francis Gray said, walking towards the door with his arm still around Rebus. Rebus felt a tightness across his shoulders which had nothing to do with the physical contact. He imagined himself after seven or eight pints, suddenly breaking down and yelling into Francis Gray's ear the secret he'd kept all these years:

Rico Lomax's murder . . . it's all down to me . . .

And then asking Gray about Bernie Johns, a quid pro quo . . . and having Gray admit to nothing:

Smoke and mirrors, John, that's all it ever was. You're Strathern's unfinished business, don't you see?

Walking into the pub, Rebus was aware of Jazz and Ward directly behind him, as if to make sure he didn't back out . . .

The taxi-driver was loath to take six, but relented when a healthy tip was mentioned . . . that and the fact that they were cops. It was a tight squeeze but a short trip. They got out at Arden Street, and Rebus led them upstairs. He knew he had lager in the fridge, beer and whisky in the cupboard. Plus tea and coffee. The milk might not be too healthy, but they could always do without.

'Nice stairwell,' Jazz McCullough commented. He meant the patterned wall-tiles and mosaic floor, which Rebus hadn't really paid any attention to in years. They climbed

137

to the second floor and Rebus unlocked the door. There was some mail behind it, but not much.

'Living room's down there,' he announced. 'I'll fetch the drinks.' He went into the kitchen and filled the kettle, then opened the fridge. He could hear their voices, sounding strange to him. Almost no one visited the flat. Jean sometimes . . . a few others. But never so many people all at once . . . not since Rhona had moved out. He poured himself a glass of water from the tap and gulped it down. Caught his breath and then downed another. What had possessed him to bring them back here? It was Gray who'd put forward the proposition: *A wee nightcap at John's.* He tried to shake his head clear of the alcohol. Maybe . . . maybe having opened his home to them, *they'd* open up to him. It had been Gray's idea. Was Francis Gray hoping to glean something about Rebus from the visit?

'Just be careful in there, John,' he muttered to himself.

Suddenly he heard music, becoming clearer as the volume was turned up. Well, that might give the students next door something to think about. It was Led Zeppelin, 'Immigrant Song', Robert Plant's voice a wailing siren. By the time he arrived in the living room with the cans of beer and lager, Allan Ward was already asking for 'that pish' to be turned off.

'It's a classic,' Jazz McCullough informed him. McCullough, usually so poised in his movements, was down on all fours, arse to the group, as he scrutinised Rebus's record collection.

'Ah, cheers, John,' Sutherland said, taking a beer. Ward snatched a lager with a nod of thanks. Tam Barclay asked where the toilet was.

'Some great stuff here, John,' McCullough said. 'I've got a lot of it myself.' He'd pulled out *Exile on Main Street.* 'Best album ever made?'

'What is it?' Gray asked. When told the title, he grinned. 'Exiles on Arden Street, that's us, eh?'

'I'll drink to that,' Stu Sutherland said.

'Speaking of which . . . ?' Rebus held the cans towards Gray, who wrinkled his nose.

'A wee whisky maybe?' Gray said. Rebus nodded.

'I might join you.'

'Not driving us back then?'

'I've had five pints, Francis. Reckon I'll spend the night in my own bed.'

'Might as well . . . not much chance of spending it in Jean's, eh?' Gray saw the look on Rebus's face, and lifted a hand, palm out. 'That was out of order. Sorry, John.'

Rebus just shook his head, asked Jazz what he wanted. Coffee was the reply.

'If John's staying put, we can all squeeze into my car,' he announced.

Rebus had located the bottle of Bowmore and a couple of glasses. He poured and handed one to Gray. 'Any water with that?'

'Don't be daft,' Gray said, toasting him. 'Here's to the Mild Bunch.' He got a laugh from Tam Barclay, who was coming back into the room, zipping his fly.

'Mild Bunch,' he chuckled. 'Good one, Francis.'

'Jesus, Tam,' Ward complained, 'you ever think of zipping it shut before you leave the bathroom?'

Barclay ignored him, took one of the beers and opened it, then slumped on the sofa next to Sutherland. Rebus noticed that Gray was sitting in the chair he himself normally used. Gray looked at home in it, one leg slung over the side. Rebus's phone and ashtray were on the floor beside him.

'Jazz,' Gray said, 'you going to grace us with the pleasure of your backside's company all night?'

McCullough half turned and sat himself down on the floor. Rebus had brought over one of the dining chairs for himself.

'Haven't seen this one in years,' McCullough said, waving a copy of the first Montrose album.

'Jazz is like a pig in shit,' Gray announced. 'One whole

room of his house is full of records and tapes. Alphabetical order and everything.'

Rebus took a sip of whisky, fixed a smile to his face. 'You've been there then?' he asked.

'Where?'

'Jazz's.'

Gray looked at McCullough, who looked back at him. 'Cat's out the bag,' Gray said with a smile. Then, turning to Rebus: 'We go back a ways, me and Jazz. I mean, it falls a long way short of a *ménage à trois*, but I've been to the house a couple of times.'

'Managed to keep that quiet,' Sutherland said. Rebus was glad others were joining in.

'Aye, what's the score here?' Barclay asked.

'There's no "score",' McCullough said determinedly. Which caused Allan Ward to burst out laughing.

'Going to share it, Allan?' Rebus asked. He was wondering if Ward had laughed precisely because there *had* been a score ... At the same time, he wondered whether it really mattered one way or the other. A few grand ... even a few hundred grand ... pocketed with no comebacks, no harm done. What did it matter in the wider scheme? Maybe it mattered if it was drugs. Drugs meant misery. But Strathern had been vague about just what the 'rip-off' had entailed.

Shit! Rebus had told Strathern he wanted the details of the Bernie Johns inquiry – tonight if possible. And here he was thirty-odd miles from Tulliallan, finishing a glass of malt and readying for a refill ...

Ward was shaking his head. Gray was explaining that he'd been to McCullough's house years back, and not since. Rebus hoped Sutherland or Barclay would run with it, keep up the questions, but they didn't.

'Anything on the box?' Ward asked.

'We're listening to the music,' Jazz chided him. He'd swapped the Led Zeppelin for a Jackie Leven CD: the very album Rebus would have chosen.

'Call that music?' Ward snorted. 'Hey, John, got any videos? A bit of the old porn maybe?'

Rebus shook his head. 'Not allowed in Knoxland,' he said, gaining a weak smile from Gray.

'How long you been here, John?' Sutherland asked.

'Twenty years plus.'

'Nice flat. Must be worth a few bob.'

'Over a hundred grand, I'd guess,' Gray said. Ward had lit a cigarette for himself and was now offering to Barclay and Rebus.

'Probably,' Rebus told Gray.

'You were married, weren't you, John?' McCullough asked. He was studying the inner sleeve of Bad Company's first album.

'For a time,' Rebus admitted. Was Jazz merely curious, or was there some agenda here?

'While since this place had a woman's touch,' Gray added, looking around.

'Kids?' McCullough asked, putting the album back exactly where he'd found it, just in case Rebus had a system.

'I've got a daughter. She's down in England. You've two sons, right?'

McCullough nodded. 'Twenty and fourteen . . .' Thinking of them, his face broke into a smile.

I don't want to put this man away, Rebus thought. Ward was a prick, and Gray as sly as they came, but Jazz McCullough was different. Jazz McCullough he liked. It wasn't just the marriage and kids, or the taste in music: Jazz had an inner calm, a sense that he knew what his role was in the world. Rebus, who had spent much of his life confused and questioning, was envious.

'And are they wild like their dad?' Barclay was asking.

McCullough didn't bother answering. Stu Sutherland pulled himself forward on the sofa. 'You'll forgive me for saying so, Jazz, but you don't seem the type to get himself

141

in trouble with the High Hiedyins.' He looked around the room for confirmation.

'It's the quiet ones you have to watch, though,' Francis Gray said. 'Wouldn't you agree, John?'

'The thing is, Stu,' Jazz answered, 'someone gives me an order I don't agree with, I just nod and say, "Yes, sir," then go on with my own way of doing things. Most of the time, they don't even notice.'

Gray nodded. 'Like I say, that's the way to get away with it: keep smiling and kowtowing, but go your own way nevertheless. Kick up a big stink and they'll fillet you like the day's catch.' Gray's eyes were on Allan Ward as he spoke. Not that Ward noticed. He was stifling a belch and reaching for a second can. Rebus got up to refill Gray's glass.

'Sorry, Jazz,' he said, 'you never got that coffee.'

'Black, one sugar, please, John.'

Gray frowned. 'Since when did you stop taking milk?'

'Since the moment I realised there's probably no milk in the house.'

Gray laughed. 'We'll make a detective of you yet, McCullough, mark my words.'

Rebus went to fetch the coffee.

They finally left just after one, Rebus calling a cab to take them back to Jazz's car. He watched from the window as Barclay tripped over the kerb and nearly head-butted the taxi's passenger-side window. His living room smelled of beer and cigarettes: no mystery there. The last thing they'd listened to on the hi-fi was *Saint Dominic's Preview*. The TV was playing silently – a sop to Allan Ward. Rebus turned it off, but put the Van Morrison album back on, turning the volume down until it was just audible. He wondered if it was too late to phone Jean.

He *knew* it was too late, but wondered if he should do it anyway. He had the phone in his hand, stared at it for a while. When it started ringing, he nearly dropped it. It

would be one of those silly buggers, calling from Jazz's car.
Maybe they'd forgotten something . . . His eyes strayed to
the sofa as he held the phone to his ear.

'Hello?'

'Who's speaking?'

'You are,' Rebus said.

'What?'

'Never mind: it's an old Tommy Cooper line. What can I
do for you, Siobhan?'

'I just thought maybe someone had broken in.'

'Broken in where?'

'When I saw your lights on.'

Rebus went to the window and looked out. Her car was
double-parked, engine still running.

'Is this some new kind of Neighbourhood Watch?'

'I was just passing.'

'You want to come up?' Rebus took in the night's
detritus. Jazz had offered to help clear up . . .

'If you like.'

'On you come then.'

When he opened the door to her, she sniffed the air.
'Mmm, testosterone,' she said. 'Did you do that all by
yourself?'

'Not quite. Some of the lads from the college . . .'

She wafted her hand in front of her as she entered the
living room. 'Maybe if you opened a window . . . ?'

'Late-night tips on housekeeping . . .' Rebus muttered,
but he opened the window a couple of inches anyway.
'What the hell are you doing out at this hour?'

'Just driving around.'

'Arden Street's a bit off anyone's route.'

'I was on the Meadows . . . thought I'd take a look.'

'The lads wanted me to show them the sights.'

'And were they duly impressed?'

'I think the city fell a bit short.'

'That's Edinburgh for you.' She settled on the sofa.

'Ooh, still warm,' she said, wriggling her bottom. 'I feel like Goldilocks.'

'Sorry I can't offer any porridge.'

'I'll settle for coffee.'

'Black?'

'Something tells me I better say yes.'

When he came back through with the mugs, she'd swapped the Van Morrison for Mogwai.

'That's the album you gave me,' he said.

'I know. I was wondering what you thought.'

'I like the lyrics. How's the Marber case?'

'I had a very interesting talk this afternoon with your friend Cafferty.'

'People keep calling him my "friend".'

'And he's not?'

'Take away the r and you're getting close.'

'He was giving his lieutenant a bollocking when we arrived.'

Rebus, who'd just got comfortable in his chair, leaned forward. 'The Weasel?' She nodded. 'What for?'

'Couldn't tell. I get the feeling Cafferty's that way inclined with all his staff. His secretary was so jumpy, her nickname's probably Skippy.' Siobhan squirmed. 'This coffee's awful.'

'Did you learn anything from Cafferty?'

'He likes Hastie's paintings.' When Rebus looked blank, she kept going. 'According to gallery records, he hadn't bought anything from Edward Marber for a while. He was there that night, arrived late and stayed till the end. He may even have helped Marber get a taxi . . .'

'One of Cafferty's own?'

'I'm going to check in the morning.'

'That could be interesting.'

She nodded thoughtfully. 'What about you? How's Tulliallan treating you?'

'Like a prince. All mod cons and no stress.'

'So what have they got you doing?'

'Looking into an old case. An unsolved. We're supposed to be learning the old-fashioned virtues of teamwork.'

'And are you?'

He shrugged. 'We're probably going to be in Edinburgh the next day or two, looking for leads.'

'Anything I can help with?'

Rebus shook his head. 'Sounds to me like you've got your hands full as it is.'

'Where will you be working from?'

'I thought we might find a spare office at St Leonard's . . .'

Siobhan's eyes widened. 'You think Gill's going to go for that?'

'I hadn't really thought about it,' he lied. 'But I can't see a problem . . . can you?'

'Do the words "tea", "mug" and "lob" mean anything to you?'

'Tea mug lob? Is that a Cocteau Twins track?' He won a smile from her. 'So you really were just driving around?'

She nodded. 'It's something I do when I can't sleep. Why are you shaking your head?'

'It's just that I do the same thing. Or I used to. I'm that bit older and lazier these days.'

'Maybe there are dozens of us out there, only we don't know about each other.'

'Maybe,' he conceded.

'Or maybe it's just you and me.' She rested her head against the back of the sofa. 'So tell me about the others on this course.'

'What's to tell?'

'What are they like?'

'What would you expect them to be like?'

She shrugged. 'Mad, bad and dangerous to know?' she suggested.

'Bad for relationships, certainly,' he confessed.

She caught his meaning immediately. 'Uh-oh. What happened?'

So he told her.

11

When Siobhan arrived at work on Tuesday morning, clutching a bag of paperwork and a beaker of coffee, someone was seated at her desk, staring at her computer screen. The someone was Derek Linford. There was a new message scrolling across the screen itself: I SEE LOVER BOY'S BACK.

'I'm assuming this isn't your work?' Linford asked.

Siobhan put the bag down. 'No,' she said.

'Do you think they mean me?'

She prised the lid from her coffee and took a sip.

'Who's doing it, do you know?' Linford asked. She shook her head. 'You're not surprised, so I'm guessing this isn't the first time . . .'

'Correct. Now if you wouldn't mind getting out of my chair.'

Linford stood up. 'Sorry,' he said.

'That's all right.' She sat down and hit the mouse, so that the screen-saver disappeared.

'Did you switch the monitor off before you left last night?' Linford was standing too close to her for comfort.

'Saves energy,' she told him.

'So someone powered the system back up.'

'Looks like.'

'And knew your password.'

'Everyone knows everyone else's password,' she said. 'Not enough computers to go round; we have to share.'

'And by everyone, you mean . . . ?'

She looked at him. 'Let's just drop it, Derek.' The office was filling up. DCI Bill Pryde was making sure the 'bible' –

the MMI – was up to date. Phyllida Hawes was halfway down a list of phone calls. The previous afternoon she'd rolled her eyes at Siobhan, indicating that cold-calling wasn't the most thrilling part of an inquiry. Grant Hood had been called to DCS Templer's office, probably so they could talk media liaison – Hood's speciality.

Linford took half a step back. 'So what's your schedule for the day?'

Keeping you at arm's length, she wanted to say. 'Taxi-cabs,' were the actual words that came out. 'You?'

Linford rested his hands against the side of her desk. 'The deceased's financial affairs. A bloody minefield they are, too . . .' He was studying her face. 'You look tired.'

'Thanks.'

'Out carousing last night?'

'Party animal, that's me.'

'Really? I don't tend to go out much these days . . .' He waited for her to say something, but she was concentrating on blowing on her coffee, even though it was little more than lukewarm.

'Yes,' Linford ploughed on, 'Mr Marber's financial wheeler-dealings will take some unpicking. Half a dozen bank accounts . . . investment portfolio . . . VCTs . . .'

'Property?'

'Just the house in Edinburgh, and his villa in Tuscany.'

'All right for some.'

'Mmm, a week in Tuscany would just about do me right now . . .'

'I'd settle for a week at home on the sofa.'

'You set your standards too low, Siobhan.'

'Thanks for the vote of confidence.'

He didn't catch her tone. 'One slight anomaly in the bank statements . . .'

It was a tease, but she reacted anyway. 'Yes?' she prompted. Phyllida Hawes was putting down the receiver, ticking off another name, starting to scribble some notes to herself.

'Tucked away in one of his accounts,' Linford was saying. 'Quarterly payments to a lettings agency.'

'A lettings agency?' She watched Linford nod. 'Which one?'

Linford frowned. 'Does it matter?'

'It might. So happens I was at MGC Lettings yesterday, talking to the owner: Big Ger Cafferty.'

'Cafferty? Wasn't he one of Marber's clients?'

Siobhan nodded. 'Which is why I'm curious.'

'Yes, me too. I mean, why would someone with as much money as Marber need to rent a place anyway?'

'And the answer is . . . ?'

'I haven't quite got there yet. Give me a second . . .' He retreated to his desk – Rebus's old desk – and started shifting sheets of paper. Siobhan had some digging of her own to do, and DCI Pryde would have the answers.

'What can I do for you, Siobhan?' he asked as she approached him.

'The taxi that took the victim home, sir,' she said. 'Which company was it?'

Pryde didn't even need to look it up: that was what she liked about him. She wondered if he did his homework every night, memorising facts and figures. The man was a walking MMI.

'Driver's name is Sammy Wallace. He has a few priors: housebreaking, reset. Years back, mind. We've checked him out. He looks clean.'

'But which company does he work for?'

'MG Private Hire.'

'Owned by Big Ger Cafferty?'

Pryde stared at her, unblinking. He had a clipboard held to his chest, fingers drumming against it. 'I don't think so,' he said.

'All right if I check?'

'Go right ahead. You talked to Cafferty yesterday . . .'

She nodded. 'And now Linford's come up with a lettings

agency who were getting regular payments from Mr Marber.'

Pryde's mouth opened in an O. 'So go do your checking,' he said.

'Yes, sir.'

She trawled the office, noticing that Linford was still sifting through paperwork. Grant Hood came up to her, holding a photocopied page from Marber's guest book.

'What do you reckon that says?' he asked.

She examined the signature. 'Could be Marlowe.'

'Only there was no one called Marlowe on the guest list.' He exhaled noisily.

'Templer's got you trying to sort out who was there that night?' Siobhan guessed.

Hood nodded. 'Most of the work's been done, but there are some names we can't put faces to, and vice versa. Come and take a look . . .'

He led her to his computer and opened up a file. A floor-plan of the gallery appeared on the screen, with little crosses representing the guests. Another click of the mouse, and the perspective changed. The crosses had become figures, moving in spasms around the room.

'It's the latest software,' he told her.

'Very impressive, Grant. You worked over the weekend on this?'

He nodded, proud of his achievement, like a kid showing off something he'd made.

'And what exactly does it add to the sum of our knowledge?'

He looked up at her, realising she was mocking him. 'Sod off, Siobhan,' he said. She just smiled.

'Is one of these stick-men meant to be Cafferty?'

Another click and a list of witness descriptions appeared. 'That's Cafferty,' Hood said. Siobhan read down the column: stocky, silver-haired, black leather jacket more suited to a man half his age.

'That's him,' she agreed, patting Hood's shoulder and

moving off in search of a phone book. Davie Hynds had just come in, Pryde checking his watch and frowning. Hynds walked sheepishly into the room, catching Siobhan as she stood by George Silvers's desk, a tattered copy of *Yellow Pages* in her hands.

'I got stuck in traffic,' he explained. 'They're digging up George IV Bridge.'

'I must remember that one for tomorrow.'

He saw that the directory was open at taxi companies. 'Doing a bit of moonlighting?'

'MG Private Hire,' she said. 'The driver who took Marber home after the show.'

Hynds nodded, looked over her shoulder as her finger ran down the page.

'MG Cabs,' she said, tapping the name. 'Address in Lochend.'

'Owned by Cafferty?'

'I don't know,' she said. 'He's got that one cab firm out in Gorgie. Exclusive Cars or something . . .' Her finger ran back up the page. 'There they are.' Again her finger tapped the name. 'What do you think the MG stands for?'

'Maybe the cabs are actually sports cars.'

'Wake up, Davie. Remember his letting agency? MGC, it's called. Look at the letters of MG Cabs.'

'MGC again,' Hynds acknowledged.

'I'm not just a pretty face, you know.'

'It doesn't prove the firm's owned by Cafferty, of course.'

'Maybe the quickest way is to ask Mr Cafferty himself.' Siobhan walked back over to her desk and picked up the phone.

'Is that Donna?' she said when the call was answered. 'Donna, it's DS Clarke, we met yesterday. Any chance I could have a word with your boss?' She looked up at Hynds, who was eyeing her coffee greedily. 'Oh, is he? Could you maybe ask him to give me a call?' Siobhan gave the secretary her number. 'Meantime, I don't suppose you know if Mr Cafferty happens to own an outfit called MG Cabs?' Siobhan pushed her coffee towards Hynds, nodding when he looked at her. He smiled gratefully and took a couple of sips. 'Thanks anyway,' Siobhan was saying, putting down the receiver.

'Don't tell me he's fled the country?' Hynds asked.

'She's not sure where he is. She's already had to cancel his morning appointments.'

'Should we be interested?'

Siobhan shrugged. 'Let's give him the benefit of the doubt. If he doesn't call back, we'll go looking.'

Derek Linford was marching towards the desk, a sheet of paper in his hand.

'Morning, Derek,' Hynds said. Linford ignored him.

'Here it is,' he said, handing the sheet to Siobhan. The company was called Superlative Property Management. She showed Hynds the name.

'Can you do anything with those letters?'

He shook his head, and she turned her attention to Linford. 'So why was Mr Marber paying these people two thousand pounds a quarter?'

'I don't know that as yet,' Linford said. 'I'm speaking to them today.'

'I'll be interested to hear what they say.'

'Don't worry, you'll be the first to know.'

The way he said it, Siobhan felt the colour rising to her cheeks. She tried hiding behind her beaker of coffee.

'It would be useful to know who actually owns Superlative,' Hynds added.

Linford glared at him. 'Thanks for the advice, Detective *Constable* Hynds.'

Hynds shrugged, rose up on to his toes and then down again.

'We need to liaise on this,' Siobhan stated. 'It looks like Cafferty might own the cab company which took Marber home. He also owns a lettings agency ... Might be coincidence, but all the same ...'

Linford was nodding. 'We'll sit down together before the end of play today, see what we've got.'

Siobhan nodded back. It was enough for Linford, who turned away and strode back to his desk.

'I can't believe how *nice* he is,' Hynds said in an undertone. 'I really think he's fallen head over heels for me.'

Siobhan tried stifling a grin, but it happened anyway. She looked across towards Linford, hoping he wouldn't see it. He was staring straight at her. Seeing what looked like a radiant smile, he returned it.

Oh, Christ, Siobhan thought. *How the hell did I get into this?*

'Remember those flats we saw yesterday at MGC Lettings?' she asked Hynds. 'They averaged four hundred a month, twelve hundred a quarter.'

'Marber's let cost a lot more,' Hynds agreed. 'Wonder what the hell it is.'

'Not a storage unit, that's for certain.' She paused. 'I'm sure Derek will let us know.'

'He'll let *you* know,' Hynds said, failing to hide an edge of bitterness . . . maybe even jealousy.

Oh, Christ, Siobhan thought again.

'How many times do you need to hear this?'

The cab driver, Sammy Wallace, was in one of the interview rooms at St Leonard's. The sleeves of his check shirt were rolled up to show arms covered in tattoos, ranging from faded blue-ink jobs to professional renderings of eagles and thistles. His greasy black hair curled over his ears and hung down past his neck at the back. He was broad-shouldered and sported scar tissue on his face and the backs of his hands.

'How long since you did time, Mr Wallace?' Hynds asked.

Wallace stood up abruptly. 'Whoah! Just stop the horses fucking dead! I'm not having you lot dredge up shite on me just because you can't find any other bastard to stick in the frame.'

'Eloquently put,' Siobhan said calmly. 'Would you care to sit down again, Mr Wallace?'

Wallace did so, with a show of reluctance. Siobhan was skimming his file, not really reading it.

'How long have you worked at MG Cabs?'

'Three years.'

'So you got the job pretty soon after your release?'

'Well, there was a dearth of vacancies for brain surgeons that week.'

Siobhan squeezed out a smile thinner than a prison roll-up. 'Mr Cafferty's good that way, isn't he? Likes to help ex-offenders.'

'Who?'

'I mean, he's been in jail himself, so it's natural he would . . .' Siobhan broke off, as though she'd only just digested Wallace's question. 'Your employer,' she said. 'Mr Cafferty. He's the one gave you the job, right?'

Wallace looked from Siobhan to Hynds and back again. 'I don't know anyone called Cafferty.'

'Morris Gerald Cafferty,' Hynds said. 'MG Cabs has his initials.'

'And I've got Stevie Wonder's initials – doesn't make me a blind piano-player.'

Siobhan smiled again, with even less humour than before. 'With respect, Mr Wallace, you played it all wrong. Anyone who's served time will have heard of Big Ger Cafferty. Pretending not to recognise his name, *that's* where you got it wrong.'

'Big Ger? Of course I've heard of Big Ger . . . not someone called "Morris". Not even sure I ever knew his surname . . .'

'He never comes to the cab office?'

'Look, as far as I know, MG is run by my boss – Ellen Dempsey. She's the one gives me my jobs.'

'Your boss is a woman?' Hynds asked. Wallace just

looked at him, and Hynds cleared his throat, as if to acknowledge that it had been a stupid question.

Siobhan had her mobile out. 'What's the number?'

'Whose number?' Wallace asked.

'MG's.' Wallace gave it to her and she pushed the buttons. Her call was answered immediately.

'MG Cabs, how may we help?'

'Is that Ms Dempsey?' Siobhan asked.

There was a pause, and the voice became less welcoming. 'Who is this?'

'Ms Dempsey, my name is Detective Sergeant Clarke, St Leonard's CID. I'm currently interviewing one of your drivers, Samuel Wallace.'

'Christ, not again: how often do you need to hear the story?'

'Until we're satisfied that we have all the information we need.'

'So how can I help?'

'You could tell me how MG Cabs got its name.'

'What?'

'The letters MG: what do they stand for?'

'The sports car.'

'Any particular reason?'

'I like them. MG means you're going to get a cab *fast*.'

'And that's it?'

'I don't see what this has to—'

'Ever heard of a man called Morris Gerald Cafferty – Big Ger?'

'He's got a cab outfit in the west end: Exclusive Cars. Does a lot of top-end business.'

'Top-end?'

'Executives ... business people. They need Mercs to collect them at the airport.'

Siobhan looked at Sammy Wallace. She was trying to visualise him in a peaked cap and white gloves ...

'Well, thanks for your help.'

'I still don't see what this—'

'Any idea who made the call to MG Cabs?'

'Which call?'

'The one ordering a car for Mr Marber.'

'I assume he made it himself.'

'There's no record of it. We've checked his calls with the phone company.'

'What do you want me to do about it?'

'A man's dead, Ms Dempsey.'

'Plenty more clients out there, DS Clarke . . .'

'Well, thanks again for your help,' Siobhan said coldly. 'Goodbye.' She ended the call, placed the phone on the desk between her hands. Wallace had his own hands spread across it, palms down, fingers as wide apart as they would go.

'Well?' he said.

Siobhan picked up a pen and played with it. 'I think that's everything for now, Mr Wallace. DC Hynds, maybe you could show Mr Wallace out . . .'

When Hynds came back, he wanted to know what Ellen Dempsey had said, so Siobhan told him.

He snorted with laughter. 'And I thought I was making a joke . . .'

She shook her head slowly. 'MGs are fast and sporty, you see.'

'That's as may be,' Hynds said, 'but Mr Wallace's car is a K-reg Ford rustbucket. Added to which, when he got outside he was just getting a ticket.'

'Don't suppose that thrilled him.'

Hynds sat down. 'No, I don't suppose it did.' He watched Siobhan turning the pen over in her hands. 'So where do we go now?'

A uniform was standing in the open doorway. 'Wherever it is,' he said, 'you've got about five minutes to move.' He then started dragging a stack of four tubular metal chairs into the already cramped space.

'What's going on?' Hynds asked.

'I think we're about to be invaded,' Siobhan told him. Moreover, she suddenly remembered who and why . . .

12

Rebus had driven to Tulliallan that morning only to turn around and drive back again, this time taking Stu Sutherland and Tam Barclay with him. He'd watched the manoeuvrings concerning who should travel with whom. Gray had offered to take the Lexus, and Allan Ward had immediately volunteered to be one of the passengers.

'You better come along too, Jazz,' Gray had said. 'My sense of direction's hopeless.' Then he'd looked towards Rebus. 'You all right with Stu and Tam?'

'Fine,' Rebus had said, wishing there was some way to bug Gray's car.

On the drive and between hungover yawns, Barclay kept talking about the National Lottery.

'Wouldn't like to think how much I've wasted on it these past years.'

'All for good causes, though,' Sutherland told him, while trying to pick bits of breakfast bacon from between his teeth with a thumbnail.

'Thing is,' Barclay went on, 'once you've started, how can you stop? Week you don't put a line on is the week you'll win it.'

'You're trapped,' Sutherland agreed. Rebus was check-ing his rear-view mirror. The Lexus was right behind him. Nobody inside it seemed to be speaking. Gray and Jazz in the front, Ward slouched in the rear.

'Eight or nine million, that's all I want,' Barclay was saying. 'It's not like I'm greedy . . .'

'Guy I know won just over a million,' Sutherland

confided. 'He didn't even stop working, can you credit that?'

'Thing about the rich,' Barclay offered, 'they never seem to have any money. It's all tied up in shares and stuff. You've got a guy who owns a castle, but hasn't got the price of a packet of fags.'

Sutherland laughed from the back seat. 'True enough, Tam,' he said.

Rebus was wondering about that . . . about rich men who couldn't spend their money because it was tied up, or because as soon as they started to spend, they'd also look conspicuous . . .

'How much d'you think that Lexus costs?' Rebus asked, eyes again on the rear-view. 'Reckon Francis had a wee lottery win himself?'

Sutherland turned his neck to peer out of the back window. 'Maybe thirty grand,' he said. 'Be honest, it's not exactly outrageous on a DI's salary . . .'

'Then how come I'm driving a fourteen-year-old Saab?' Rebus said.

'Maybe you're not careful with your money,' Sutherland offered.

'Oh aye,' Rebus came back, 'you saw as much last night – every penny poured into the interior of my palatial bachelor pad.'

Sutherland snorted and went back to picking his teeth.

'Ever totted up what you spend on booze and ciggies?' Barclay asked. 'You could probably buy a new Lexus every year.'

Rebus didn't trust himself to do the calculation. 'I'll take your word for it,' he said instead. An A4-sized packet had been waiting for him at Tulliallan: Strathern's notes on Bernie Johns. He hadn't had time to open it yet, but was wondering if it would show any evidence at all that Jazz, Gray and Ward were high rollers. Maybe they had big houses or took expensive holidays . . . Or maybe they were

159

biding their time, the pay-out awaiting them on retirement.

Could that be why each man was having trouble with authority? Was it all a ruse to get them kicked off the force? Simpler surely just to tender your resignation . . . Rebus was aware of movement in his rear-view: the Lexus was indicating and pulling out to overtake, cruising past Rebus's Saab with a blare of its horn and Allan Ward's face smirking at the rear window.

'Look at that silly sod,' Barclay laughed. Jazz and Gray were smiling and offering little waves.

'Tennant's not behind us, is he?' Sutherland said, turning his head again.

'I don't know,' Rebus admitted. 'What car does he drive?'

'No idea,' Barclay said. DCI Tennant was due to follow them to Edinburgh. He wouldn't be able to monitor them throughout, but would be kept informed.

'It'll be good to get away from those bloody closed-circuit cameras,' Barclay said now. 'I hate the things, always think they're going to catch me scratching my balls or something . . .'

'Maybe they'll have cameras where we're going,' Sutherland said.

'At St Leonard's?' Rebus shook his head. 'We're still at the stage of cave paintings, Stu . . . *Jesus Christ!*'

The Lexus's brake lights had suddenly come on, causing Rebus to slam *his* foot on the brake. In the back, Sutherland was thrown forwards, his face connecting with Rebus's headrest. Barclay placed both hands on the dashboard, as if preparing for impact. Now the Lexus was speeding away, red lights still glowing.

'Bastard's got his fog-lights on,' was Barclay's explanation.

Rebus's heart was racing. The cars had come within three or four feet of one another. 'You okay, Stu?'

Sutherland was rubbing his chin. 'Just about,' he said.

Rebus shifted down into second and pressed the accelerator, his whole right leg trembling.

'We've got to get them for that,' Barclay was saying.

'Don't be stupid, Tam,' Sutherland replied. 'If John's brakes hadn't been in good nick, we'd have hit them.'

But Rebus knew what he had to do. He had to show willing. He pressed further on the accelerator, the Saab's engine urging him to go up a gear. Then, just as it looked like he would ram the pristine Lexus, he pulled out so that the two cars were side by side. The three men in the other car were smiling, watching his performance. Tam Barclay had gone very pale in the passenger seat, and Stu Sutherland was searching in vain for the rear seat-belt which, Rebus knew, was trapped somewhere beneath the upholstery.

'You're as bad as they are!' Sutherland called from the back, struggling to make himself heard above the whine from the engine.

That's the plan, Rebus felt like telling him. Instead, he pressed a little harder on the accelerator and, when his nose was ahead of the Lexus, turned the steering wheel hard, cutting across Gray's bows.

It was down to Gray: he could brake; he could go off the road; or he could allow Rebus's car to hit him.

He hit the brakes, and suddenly Rebus was in front again, the Lexus flashing its lights, horn sounding. Rebus gave a wave before acceding to the Saab's wishes and finally moving into third gear, then fourth.

The Lexus dropped its speed a little, and they were a convoy again. Rebus, eyes on the rear-view, knew that the three men were talking ... they were talking about *him*.

'We could have died back there, John,' Barclay complained, a tremor in his voice.

'Cheer up, Tam,' Rebus reassured him. 'If we had, your lottery numbers would have come up next week.'

Then he started laughing. It took a while for the laughter to cease.

They got practically the last two parking spots at St Leonard's. The car park was to the rear of the actual station. 'Not very prepossessing, is it?' Tam Barclay said, studying the building.

'It's not much, but I call it home,' Rebus told him.

'John Rebus!' Gray called, emerging from the Lexus. 'You are one mad, bad bastard!' He was still grinning. Rebus shrugged.

'Can't let some weegie go cutting me up, Francis.'

'It was a close one, though,' Jazz said.

Rebus shrugged. 'No adrenaline otherwise, is there?'

Gray slapped Rebus's back. 'Maybe we're not such a mild bunch after all.'

Rebus took a little bow. *Accept me*, he was thinking.

The high spirits evaporated the minute they saw their 'office'. It was one of the interview rooms, equipped with two tables and six chairs, leaving no space for anything else. High on one wall, a video camera was aimed at the main table. It was there to record the various interviews, rather than the Wild Bunch, but Barclay scowled at it anyway.

'No phones?' Jazz commented.

'We've always got our mobiles,' Gray said.

'Which *we* pay for,' Sutherland reminded him.

'Stop whingeing for two seconds and let's think about this.' Jazz folded his arms. 'John, is there any office space at all?'

'To be honest, I don't think so. We've a murder inquiry going on, remember. It's pretty much taken over the CID suite.'

'Look,' Gray was saying, 'we're only here for a day or two, right? We don't need computers or anything . . .'

'Maybe, but we could suffocate in here,' Barclay complained.

162

'We'll open a window,' Gray told him. There were two narrow windows high up on the outer wall. 'If all goes well, we'll be spending most of our time on the street anyway: talking to people, tracking them down.'

Jazz was still taking the measure of the room. 'Not much space for all the files.'

'We don't *need* the files.' Gray sounded ready to lose his temper. 'We need about half a dozen sheets of paper from the files – that's it.' His hand chopped the air.

Jazz sighed. 'I don't suppose we've much option.'

'It was us that asked to come to Edinburgh,' Ward admitted.

'This isn't the only cop shop in town,' Sutherland said. 'We could look around, see if someone else can offer better.'

'Let's just get on with it,' Jazz said, his eyes meeting Sutherland's, and somehow finally gaining a shrug of acceptance.

'Might as well,' Rebus said. 'It's not like we're going to find anything new on Dickie Diamond.'

'Great,' Jazz said caustically. 'Let's try and keep those positive vibes flowing, eh, lads?'

' "Positive vibes"?' Ward mimicked. 'I think you spent too long with John's record collection last night.'

'Aye, you'll be wearing beads and sandals next, Jazz,' Barclay added with a smile.

Jazz gave him two fingers. Then they arranged the chairs to their liking and got down to work. They had compiled a list of people they wanted to talk to. A couple of names had been crossed off because Rebus knew they were already dead. He'd considered not letting on . . . leading them down blind alleys . . . but couldn't really see the point. Cross-referencing and the computer at Tulliallan had thrown up the nugget that one name – Joe Daly – was an informant belonging to DI Bobby Hogan. Hogan was Leith CID; Rebus and he went back a ways. Hogan was to be their first stop. They'd only been in the interview room half an hour but already there was a bad smell about the place, even with door and windows open.

'Dickie Diamond used to hang out at the Zombie Bar,' Jazz said, reading from the notes. 'That's in Leith too, right, John?'

'I don't know if it's still open. They were always in trouble with their licence.'

'Isn't Leith where the working girls hang out?' Allan Ward asked.

'Don't you go getting ideas, young Allan,' Gray said, reaching over to ruffle his hair.

There were voices in the corridor, coming closer: '. . . best we could do, under the circs . . .'

'They won't mind roughing it . . .'

DCI Tennant stepped into the doorway, eyes widening at the scene within.

'Better stay where you are, sir,' Tam Barclay warned. 'One more in here and the oxygen runs out.'

Tennant turned to the figure beside him – Gill Templer.

'I did warn you it was small,' she said.

'You did,' he admitted. 'Settling in all right, men?'

'Could hardly be cosier,' Stu Sutherland said, folding his arms like a man not best pleased with his lot.

'We thought we'd put the coffee machine in the corner,' Allan Ward said, 'next to the mini-bar and jacuzzi.'

'Good idea,' Tennant told him, straight-faced.

'This'll do us fine, sir,' Francis Gray said. He slid his chair back and managed to squash one of Tam Barclay's toes under the leg. 'We won't be here long. You could almost look on our surroundings as an incentive.' He was on his feet now, beaming a smile at Gill Templer. 'I'm DI Gray, since no one's seen fit . . .'

'DCS Templer,' Gill said, taking the proffered hand. Gray introduced her to the other men, leaving Rebus till last. 'This one you'll already know.' Gill glared at Rebus, and Rebus looked away, hoping it was just part of the act.

'Well, if you'll excuse me, gentlemen, I've a murder inquiry to run . . .'

'Us too,' Ward said. Gill pretended not to hear, and headed down the corridor, calling back to Tennant that he might want to join her for coffee in her office. Tennant looked back into the room.

'Any problems, you've got my mobile number,' he reminded them. 'And remember: I'll be expecting progress. Anybody not pulling their weight, I'll find out.' He held a finger up in warning, then set off to follow Gill.

'Jammy bastard,' Ward muttered. 'And I bet her office is bigger than this.'

'Slightly smaller, actually,' Rebus said. 'But then there's only one of her.'

Gray was chuckling. 'Notice she didn't offer you a cup, John.'

'That's because John can't hold his beverages,' Sutherland said.

'Nice one, Stu.'

'Maybe,' Jazz broke in, 'we could think about doing a bit of work? And just to show willing, I'll use *my* mobile to phone DI Hogan.' He looked at Rebus. 'John, he's your mate . . . do you want to do the talking?'

Rebus nodded.

'You know his number?' Jazz asked. Again, Rebus nodded his head.

'Well then,' Jazz said, slipping his own phone back into his jacket, 'might as well use *your* mobile, eh?'

Francis Gray's face went pink with laughter, the colour reminding Rebus of a baby being lifted from its bathtub.

He didn't mind making the call actually. After all, he reckoned he'd had a pretty good morning so far. The only thing he was wondering was: when would he get a minute to himself to delve into Strathern's report?

13

Siobhan was splashing water on her face when one of the uniforms, WPC Toni Jackson, came into the women's toilets.

'Will we see you Friday night?' Jackson said.

'Not sure,' Siobhan told her.

'Yellow card if you miss three weeks on the trot,' Jackson warned her. She went to one of the cubicles, locked the door after her. 'There's no paper towels, by the way,' she called. Siobhan checked the dispenser: nothing inside but fresh air. There was an electric dryer on the other wall, but it had been broken for months. She went to the cubicle next to Jackson's, pulled at a clump of toilet roll and started dabbing at her face.

Jackson and some of the other uniforms went for a drink every Friday. Sometimes it went beyond a drink: a meal, then a club, dancing away all the frustrations of the week. They pulled the occasional bloke: never any shortage of takers. Siobhan had been invited along one time, honoured to have been asked. Hers was the only CID face. They seemed to accept her, found they could gossip freely in front of her. But Siobhan had started skipping weeks, and now she'd skipped two in a row. It was that old Groucho Marx thing about not wanting to be part of any club that would have her. She didn't know why exactly. Maybe because it felt like a routine, and with it the job became a routine, too . . . something to be endured for the sake of a salary cheque and the Friday-night dance with a stranger.

'What have they got you doing?' Siobhan called.

'Foot patrol.'

'Who with?'

'Perry Mason.'

Siobhan smiled. 'Perry' was actually John Mason, only recently out of Tulliallan. Everyone had started calling him Perry. George Silvers even had a name for Toni Jackson: he called her 'Tony Jacklin', or had done until a rumour had spread that Toni was sister to footballer Darren Jackson. Silvers had treated her with a bit of respect after that. Siobhan had asked Toni if it was true.

'Is it bollocks,' she'd said. 'But I'm not going to let that worry me.'

As far as Siobhan knew, Silvers still thought Toni was related to Darren Jackson, and he still treated her with respect . . .

The 'Toni' was short for Antonia: 'I never call myself that,' Toni had said one night, seated at the bar in the Hard Rock Café, looking around to see what 'talent' might be lurking. 'Sounds too posh, doesn't it?'

'You should try being called Siobhan . . .'

Siobhan had met almost no one who could spell her name. And if they saw it written down, they almost never connected it with her. 'See Oban?' they'd guess.

'Shi-vawn,' she would stress.

She had a Gaelic name but an English accent; Toni couldn't call herself Antonia because it was too posh . . .

Such a strange country, Siobhan thought to herself. From behind the cubicle door, she could hear Toni uttering a string of curses.

'What's up?' Siobhan called.

'Bloody loo roll's finished. Is there any next door?'

Siobhan looked: she'd used most of the paper drying her face. 'A few sheets,' she said.

'Chuck them over here then.'

Siobhan did as she was asked. 'Look, Toni, about Friday night . . .'

'Don't tell me you've got a date?'

Siobhan considered this. 'Actually, I have,' she lied. It was the one acceptable excuse she could think of for missing a Friday session.

'Who is he?'

'Not telling.'

'Why don't you bring him along?'

'I didn't know men were allowed. Besides, you lot would devour him.'

'Looker, is he?'

'He's not bad.'

'All right . . .' The toilet flushed. 'But I'll want a report afterwards.' The door clicked open and Toni emerged, adjusting her uniform and making for the sink.

'No towels, remember?' Siobhan told her, pulling open the door.

WPC Toni Jackson started cursing all over again.

Derek Linford was standing in the corridor directly outside. It was obvious to Siobhan that he'd been waiting for her.

'Can I have a word?' he said, sounding pleased with himself.

Siobhan led him down the corridor, wanting him out of the way before Toni emerged. She was afraid Toni would think Linford was her breakfast partner for Saturday. 'What is it?' she asked.

'I spoke to the lettings agency.'

'And?'

'No sign that it's owned by Cafferty . . . seems above board. The property they rented to Marber is a flat in Mayfield Terrace. Only, Edward Marber didn't live there.'

'Of course not. He had a bloody big house of his own . . .'

He looked at her. 'The woman's name is Laura Stafford.'

'What woman?'

Linford smiled. 'The woman who walked into the

168

lettings agency and asked about renting a flat. They showed her several, and she took one.'

'But the rent comes out of Marber's account?'

Linford was nodding. 'One of his more *obscure* accounts.'

'Meaning he wanted it kept hidden? You think this Laura woman was his mistress?'

'Except he wasn't married.'

'No, he wasn't.' Siobhan chewed at her bottom lip. The name Laura . . . there was something . . . Yes: the Sauna Paradiso. The two businessmen who'd had a drink. One of them had asked if Laura was on duty. Siobhan wondered . . .

'You going to talk to her?' she asked.

Linford nodded. He could see how interested she was. 'Want to tag along?'

'Thinking of it.'

He folded his arms. 'Listen, Siobhan, I was wondering . . .'

'What?'

'Well, I know things didn't work out between us . . .'

Her eyes widened. 'Tell me you're not about to ask me out?'

He shrugged. 'I just thought Friday, if you're not doing anything.'

'After last time? After you *spying* on me?'

'I just wanted to know you.'

'That's what worries me.'

He gave another shrug. 'Maybe you've got other plans for Friday?'

Something in his tone alerted her. 'You were listening at the door,' she stated.

'I was just waiting for you to come out. It's hardly my fault if you and your pal were yelling so loud half the station could hear.' He paused. 'Still want to go to Mayfield Terrace?'

She weighed up her options. 'Yes,' she stated.

'Sure?'

'Positive.'

'Ooh, look at the love-birds!' Toni Jackson said, pausing beside them. When Siobhan shot out an arm, Jackson actually ducked. But all Siobhan did was pick a remnant of toilet paper from her face.

Mayfield Terrace was only a five-minute drive from St Leonard's. It was a wide avenue between Dalkeith Road and Minto Street. Those two were busy routes in and out of the city, but Mayfield Terrace was a quiet oasis, with vast detached and semi-detached houses, most on three and four floors. Some of these had been split into flats, including the one where Laura Stafford lived.

'Didn't suppose she'd get a whole house around here for six-seventy a month,' Linford said. Siobhan remembered that property was something of an obsession with him. He would pore over the ESPC guide each week, comparing prices and areas.

'What do you reckon to buy one?' she asked.

He shrugged, but she could see he was doing the sums. 'You'd probably get a one-bedroom conversion for a hundred K.'

'And a whole house?'

'Detached or semi?'

'Detached.'

'Maybe seven, eight hundred K.' He paused. 'And rising.'

They'd climbed four steps to the front door. There were three names, three buzzers. None of the names was Stafford.

'What do you think?' Siobhan asked. Linford stood back, craned his neck. 'Ground, first and top,' he said. Then he looked down to either side of the steps. 'But there's a garden flat, too. Must have its own door.'

He went back down the steps, Siobhan following him around to the side of the house where they found the door, and a buzzer with no name. Linford pressed it and waited. When it opened, a woman was standing there. She was stooped and in her sixties. Behind her, they could hear the playful yelps of a child.

'Ms Stafford?' Linford asked.

'Laura's not in. She'll be back soon.'

'Are you her mother?'

The woman shook her head. 'I'm Alexander's granny.'

'Mrs. . . ?'

'Dow. Thelma Dow. You're from the police, aren't you?'

'Are we that obvious?' Siobhan asked with a smile.

'Donny . . . my son,' Mrs Dow explained. 'He used to be an awful one for getting in trouble.' She suddenly started. 'He's not . . . ?'

'It's nothing to do with your son, Mrs Dow. We're here to see Laura.'

'She's gone to the shops. Should be here any minute . . .'

'Do you mind if we wait?'

Mrs Dow didn't mind. She led them down a narrow set of stairs into the flat proper. There were two bedrooms, and a living room which opened into a bright conservatory. The door to the conservatory was open, showing a four-year-old boy playing in the back garden. The living room was cluttered with toys.

'I can't control him,' Mrs Dow said. 'I do my best, but laddies that age . . .'

'Or any age,' Siobhan said, raising a tired smile from the woman.

'They've split up, you know.'

'Who?' Linford asked, seemingly more interested in the room than his own question.

'Donny and Laura.' Mrs Dow was staring out at her grandson. 'Not that he minds me still coming here . . .'

'Doesn't Donny see much of Alexander?' Siobhan asked.

'Not much.'

'Is that his choice or Laura's?' Linford asked, still not

paying much attention. Mrs Dow decided not to answer, turning instead to Siobhan.

'It's tough enough being a single parent these days.'

Siobhan nodded. 'Or any days,' she added, noting that this struck a chord with the woman. Obviously, Thelma Dow had brought her son up by herself. 'Do you look after Alexander when Laura's at work?'

'Sometimes, yes ... There's a nursery he goes to, too ...'

'Does Laura work nights?' Siobhan asked.

Mrs Dow looked down at the floor. 'Sometimes, yes.'

'And you stay here with Alexander?' Siobhan watched the woman nod slowly. 'Thing is, you didn't ask why we're here, Mrs Dow. That would be the normal question. Makes me think Laura's had a few run-ins over the years, and you've become used to it.'

'I might not like what she does for a living, that doesn't mean I don't understand her reasons. Lord knows, I've been through plenty of hard times myself.' She paused. 'Years back, I mean. When Donny and his brother were young, and no money coming in ... Who knows now whether that thought ever crossed my mind back then?'

'You mean you thought of going on the game?' Linford asked coldly. Siobhan could have slapped him, but had to content herself with a glower.

'I apologise for my colleague, Mrs Dow,' she said. 'He has all the sensitivity of a goat.'

Linford looked at her, seeming shocked by this pronouncement. Just then a door opened and closed. Feet on the steps.

'Just me, Thelma,' a voice called. Moments later, Laura Stafford walked into the living room, carrying two bags marked 'Savacentre' – the name of the supermarket at the bottom of Dalkeith Road. Her eyes went from Siobhan to Linford and back again. Saying nothing, she walked into the kitchen and started emptying the shopping. It was a

172

small kitchen, not enough room for a table. Siobhan stood in the doorway.

'It's about Edward Marber,' she said.

'I wondered when you'd come.'

'Well, here we are. We can talk now, or make an appointment for later.'

Stafford looked up, sensing that Siobhan was doing her best to be discreet. 'Thelma?' she called. 'Think you could go play with Alexander for five minutes while I get this done with?'

Mrs Dow got up without a word and went into the garden. Siobhan could hear her talking to her grandson.

'We haven't said anything to her,' she said. Laura Stafford nodded.

'Thanks,' she said.

'Does she know about Marber?'

Stafford shook her head. She was five foot four, slim, late twenties. Short black hair in a neat cut with a side parting. She wore a little make-up on her face: eyeliner and maybe some foundation. No jewellery, and a white T-shirt tucked into faded blue denims. Open-toed pink sandals on her feet.

'I don't look like a whore, do I?' she said, making Siobhan aware that she'd been staring too hard.

'Not the stereotype, anyway,' Siobhan admitted. Linford was in the doorway, too, now.

'I'm DI Linford,' he said, 'this is DS Clarke. We're here to ask you a few questions about Edward Marber.'

'Of course you are, Officer.'

'He pays for this place?'

'Until the payments stop.'

'What happens then, Laura?' Siobhan asked.

'Maybe I'll keep the place on. I haven't decided.'

'You can afford it?' Linford asked, with what to Siobhan sounded almost like a hint of envy.

'I make enough,' Stafford said.

'You didn't mind being a kept woman?'

'His choice, not mine.' She leaned back against the kitchen worktop and folded her arms. 'Okay, here's the story . . .'

But Siobhan interrupted her. She didn't like Linford standing so close to her. 'Maybe if we sat down first?' she suggested.

They moved into the living room. When Linford settled into the sofa, Siobhan took the chair, meaning Laura Stafford had to sit next to Linford, a move which seemed to make him uncomfortable.

'You were saying . . . ?' he said.

'I was going to give you the story. It'll be short and to the point. Eddie was a client of mine, as you've already gathered.'

'At the Sauna Paradiso?' Siobhan interrupted. Laura nodded.

'That's where I met him. He came in every couple of weeks or so.'

'Did he always ask for you?' Linford asked.

'As far as I know. Maybe he came in sometimes when I wasn't on shift.'

Linford nodded. 'Go on, please.'

'Well, he was always wanting to know about me. Some of the punters are like that, but Eddie was different. He had that quiet, insistent sort of voice. In the end, I started talking. Me and Donny had split up. I had Alexander and we were in this poxy place in Granton . . .' She paused. 'Next thing I know, Eddie says he's fixed me up. I thought it was some kind of con. That's another thing the punters do: they're always offering you stuff that never comes to anything.' She had crossed one leg over the other. There was a thin gold chain around her right ankle. 'Eddie seemed to realise that. He gave me the address and number of this lettings agency, told me to head down there myself and pick out a flat for me and Alexander.' She looked around her. 'So here we are.'

'Nice place,' Siobhan said.

'And what did Mr Marber want in return?' Linford asked.

Stafford shook her head slowly. 'If there was a catch, he didn't stay around long enough for me to find out what it was.'

'No home visits?' Linford asked.

Stafford bristled. 'I don't do anything like that.' She paused. 'I'm still not sure why he did it.'

'Maybe he just fell for you, Laura,' Siobhan said, further softening her voice, prepared to play 'nice' to Linford's 'nasty'. 'I think there was a bit of the romantic in him . . .'

'Yeah, maybe.' Stafford's eyes were glinting with emotion, and Siobhan knew she'd said the right thing. 'Maybe that's what it was.'

'Did you ever go to his house?' Siobhan asked. Stafford shook her head. 'You knew what he did for a living?'

'He sold paintings, right?'

Siobhan nodded. 'Some of the paintings he owned, they were taken down from the walls – any idea why he'd do that?'

'Maybe to send to his place in Tuscany.'

'You know about it?'

'He told me about it. It's true then . . . ?'

Stafford had obviously heard a lot of stories and boasts in her time. 'He has a place in Italy, yes,' Siobhan confirmed. 'Laura, one of his paintings seems to be missing. He didn't give it to you, did he?' She held up the photo of the painting. Stafford looked at it, but wasn't really concentrating.

'He talked about Italy,' she said wistfully, 'how he'd take me there one day . . . I thought it was just . . .' She lowered her eyes.

'Eddie opened up to you then, Laura?' Siobhan asked quietly. 'He talked about himself?'

'Nothing too personal . . . a bit about his background, stuff like that.'

'Problems he was having?' Stafford shook her head. 'Nothing troubling him recently?'

'No, he seemed happy enough. Had some money coming to him, I think.'

'What makes you say that?' Linford asked brusquely.

'I think maybe he said something about it. When we were talking about this place, how he could afford it.'

'And he said he had money coming?'

'Yes.'

'Could he have meant the exhibition, Laura?' Siobhan asked.

'I suppose so . . .'

'You don't really think so?'

'I don't know.' She looked out through the conservatory. 'It's getting cold out there. Alexander needs to come in . . .'

'Just a couple more questions, Laura. I need to ask about the Paradiso.'

Stafford looked at her. 'What about it?'

'Who owns it?'

'Ricky Marshall.'

'You don't believe that,' Siobhan teased her. 'He might run the desk, but that's all, isn't it?'

'I've always dealt with Ricky.'

'Always?'

Stafford nodded. Siobhan let the silence lie between them for a minute.

'Have you ever come across a man called Cafferty? Big Ger Cafferty?'

Stafford shook her head. Again, Siobhan let the silence lie. Stafford shifted on the sofa, as if about to say something.

'And all the time,' Linford broke in, 'that Marber was paying for this place, he never asked you for any extras?'

Stafford's face became a mask, and Siobhan knew that they'd lost her.

'No,' she was saying, in reply to the question.

176

'You'll appreciate that we find that hard to believe,' Linford said.

'I don't,' Siobhan interrupted, her eyes on Stafford while Linford fixed her with a frown. 'I believe it,' Siobhan said. Then she got up and handed her card to Laura Stafford. 'Any time you want to talk . . .'

Stafford studied the card, nodded slowly.

'Well, thanks again for your time,' Linford said grudgingly.

They'd reached the door when they heard Stafford calling from the living room. 'I liked him, you know. That's more than I can say for most of them . . .'

Outside, they walked towards Linford's car in silence. After they'd got in and fastened their seat-belts, he turned the ignition, fixing his gaze on the road ahead.

'Well, thanks for your support back there,' he said.

'And thanks so very much for yours. Teamwork's what it's all about at the end of the day.'

'I don't remember saying *I* didn't believe *you*.'

'Let's just leave it, eh?'

He fumed for a good two minutes before speaking. 'The boyfriend . . . or whatever he is.'

'Donny Dow?'

Linford nodded. 'The mother of his kid is shacked up in a posh flat. He decides to thump the sugar daddy, but ends up thumping him too hard.'

'How did he know about Marber?'

'Maybe she told him.'

'Mrs Dow doesn't even know.'

'We've only the prossie's word for that.'

Siobhan screwed shut her eyes. 'Don't call her that.'

'Isn't that what she is?' When she didn't answer, his look said he'd won that particular argument. 'We need to talk to him anyway.'

Siobhan opened her eyes again. 'His mum said he used to get into trouble. He'll be on the files.'

Linford nodded. 'And so will his ex. Maybe there's more

to her than just soliciting, eh?' He risked a glance at Siobhan. 'You think Cafferty knew about the arrangement?'

'I don't even know for sure that he owns the Paradiso.'

'But it's likely?'

With a nod, Siobhan conceded that it was. She was thinking: *if* Cafferty had known about Marber's crush on Laura . . . well, then what? What could it mean? Was it even possible that *he* had put Laura up to it. Why would he do that? She could think of reasons. Maybe Marber had a painting or paintings Cafferty wanted . . . something Marber was unwilling to sell. She still didn't see how blackmail or anything like it would have helped. Marber was single. It was the married ones you blackmailed, the ones who needed to be whiter than white. Marber worked with artists, the wealthy, the cosmopolitan. Siobhan didn't think they'd be shocked to learn that their art dealer friend had been sleeping with prostitutes. If anything, it might have made him *more* popular.

Had some money coming to him, I think . . . Laura's words came back to her. How much money, and from what source? Enough money to get him killed? Enough to interest someone like Big Ger Cafferty?

'What do they do when they retire?' Linford was asking, signalling to pull into St Leonard's.

'Who?'

'Working girls. I mean, she looks okay just now, but that won't last. The work'll start to dry up . . . amongst other things.' He failed to stifle a grin.

'Jesus, Derek, you disgust me,' Siobhan said.

'So who is it you're seeing on Friday night?' he asked.

14

Leith police station was an elderly and distinguished building on the outside, but referred to by most of its occupants as 'the geriatric'. Pulling on his jacket as he led them back down its steps into the waiting afternoon, DI Bobby Hogan explained why.

'It's like somebody in a care home. They might look well enough dressed – presentable and all that – but inside, their body's started breaking down. The plumbing might leak, the heart's a bit dicky, and the brain's given up the ghost.' He winked at Allan Ward.

Three of them had made the trip from St Leonard's: Rebus was the obvious choice, of course, but Tam Barclay had made a song and dance about needing some fresh air, and Allan Ward had volunteered, even though Rebus suspected that what the young man wanted to see were signs of prostitution.

The day was bright but windy. Hogan's jacket flapped like a sail as he finally secured his arms into its sleeves. He was glad of the excuse to be out of the station. They'd only needed to mention the Zombie Bar and he'd sprung up from his desk, looking around him for his jacket.

'If we're in luck, Father Joe might be there,' he'd said, referring to his snitch, Joe Daly.

'It's not called the Zombie Bar any more,' he explained now, leading them along Tolbooth Wynd. 'That place lost its licence.'

'Too many brawls?' Allan Ward guessed.

'Too many drunken poets and writers,' Hogan corrected. 'The more they tart Leith up, the more people seem to come looking for the sleazy side.'

'And where's that to be found these days?' Ward asked. Hogan offered a smile, eyes turning to Rebus.

'We've got a live one here, John.'

Rebus nodded. Tam Barclay wasn't looking too lively: as the day had progressed, so had his hangover. 'Mixing the beer and whisky,' he said, rubbing at his temples. He wasn't looking forward to their trip to the pub . . .

'What's the Zombie called now?' Rebus asked Hogan.

'Bar Z,' came the answer. 'And here it is . . .'

Bar Z had windows which were all frosted glass except for a large letter Z in the centre of each. The interior was chrome and grey, the tables made from some light, trendy wood which captured and retained every beer-ring and cigarette burn. The music was probably called something like 'trance' or 'ambient', and a chalkboard menu offered 'Huevos Rancheros' – listed as 'a Tex-Mex all-day breakfast treat' – and 'Snack Attacks' such as blinis and baba ganoush.

However, something had gone badly wrong with the Bar Z. The only people drinking the afternoon away were the same mixture of desperate businessmen and down-at-heel drunks who had probably called the Zombie Bar home. The place carried an aroma of soured dreams. Hogan pointed to one of the many empty tables and asked the trio what they wanted.

'Our round, Bobby,' Rebus insisted. 'You're the one helping us out.' Ward decided on a bottle of Holsten, while Barclay only wanted cola – 'as much as you can fit in a glass'. Hogan, who said he was undecided, went up to the bar with Rebus.

'Is your man here?' Rebus asked in an undertone. Hogan shook his head.

'Doesn't mean he won't come in. Father Joe's the restless type: if he goes in a place and there's no one he knows, he moves on; never stays anywhere for more than two drinks.'

'Does he have a job?'

'He has a *vocation*.' Hogan saw the look on Rebus's face. 'Don't worry, he's not a real priest. It's just that he has the kind of face strangers tell their troubles to. That seems to fill Joe's days to the brim . . .' The barman came up, and Rebus put in their order, including a half of IPA for Hogan and the same for himself.

'A game of two halves, eh?' Hogan announced with a smile.

'Aye, it's a game all right, Bobby.'

Hogan picked up Rebus's meaning. 'So what's reopened this particular can of worms?'

'I wish I knew.'

'Dickie Diamond was an arsehole, whole world knew it.'

'Any of his other cronies still around?'

'There's one of them in here right now.'

Rebus looked around at the disconsolate, blank-eyed faces. 'Who?'

Hogan just winked, and waited till the drinks had been paid for. When the barman slouched back with Rebus's change, Hogan greeted him by name.

'Okay, Malky?'

The young man frowned. 'Do I know you?'

Hogan shrugged. 'Thing is, *I* know *you*.' He paused. 'Still on the smack?'

Rebus, too, had placed the young man as a drug user. It was something about the eyes, the facial muscles, something about the way the body held itself. In turn, the barman recognised pigs when he saw them.

'I'm off that stuff,' Malky said.

'Take your methadone religiously?' Hogan asked with a smile. 'DI Rebus here is wondering whatever happened to your uncle.'

'Which one?'

'The one we don't hear about so much these days . . . unless you know different.' Hogan turned to Rebus. 'Malky here is Dickie's sister's kid.'

'How long you been working here then, Malky?' Rebus asked.

'Nearly a year.' The barman's attitude had changed from indifference to surliness.

'Did you know the place when it was the Zombie?'

'I was too young, wasn't I?'

'Doesn't mean they wouldn't have served you.' Rebus lit a cigarette, offering one to Hogan.

'Has Uncle Dickie turned up?' Malky asked. Rebus shook his head. 'It's just that my mum . . . every now and then she gets all weepy, says Uncle Dickie must be dead and buried somewhere.'

'What does she think happened to him?'

'How should I know?'

'You could try asking her.' Rebus had one of his cards out. It had his pager number as well as the police switchboard. 'I'd be interested to know her answer.'

Malky stuck the card in the top pocket of his shirt.

'Dying of thirst over here!' Barclay called from the table. Hogan picked up two of the drinks. Rebus was staring at Malky.

'I mean it,' he said. 'You ever hear anything, I'd really like to know what happened to him.'

Malky nodded, then turned away to answer the phone. But Rebus had gripped his arm. 'Where do you live, Malky?'

'Sighthill. What's it to you?' Malky wrestled his arm free, picked up the phone.

Sighthill was perfect. Rebus knew someone in Sighthill . . .

'So what happened to this place?' Ward was asking Hogan when Rebus reached the table.

'They got their market research wrong, thought there'd be enough yuppies in Leith by now to make them a fortune.'

'Maybe if they hang on a few more years,' Barclay said, pausing halfway down his cola.

Hogan nodded. 'It's coming,' he agreed. 'Just a shame we didn't get the parliament.'

Rebus snorted. 'You'd've been welcome to it.'

'We wanted it.'

'So what was the problem?' Ward asked.

'The MSPs didn't want to be in Leith. Too out of the way.'

'Maybe they were scared off by the temptations of the flesh,' Ward proposed. 'Not that I'm seeing any around here . . .'

The door opened and another solitary drinker entered. He was all twitches and movement, as if someone had just wound up his mechanism. He saw Hogan and gave a nod of acknowledgement, but then started heading for the bar. Hogan, however, waved him over.

'Is this him?' Ward asked, already hardening his face, turning it into a mask.

'This is him,' Hogan said. Then, to the new arrival: 'Father Joe . . . I was wondering if your pastoral wanderings would bring you in here.'

Joe Daly smiled at the joke, and nodded as if it were part of some ritual between Hogan and himself. Hogan meantime was making introductions. 'Now talk to the good men,' he said in closing, 'while I fetch you a small libation. Jameson's and water, no ice, yes?'

'That would serve the purpose,' Daly said, his breath already sweetened by whiskey. He watched Hogan head for the bar. 'A good man in his way,' he commented.

'And was Dickie Diamond a good man too, Father Joe?' Rebus asked.

'Ah, the Diamond Dog . . .' Daly was thoughtful for a moment. 'Richard could be the best friend you'd ever had, but he could be a right bastard, too. He had no forgiveness in him.'

'You haven't seen him recently?'

'Not in five or six years.'

'Did you ever meet another friend of his called Eric Lomax?' Ward asked. 'Most people called him Rico.'

'Well, it was a long time ago, as I say . . .' Daly licked his lips expectantly.

'Of course, we'd pay the going rate,' Rebus informed him.

'Ah, well . . .' Daly's whiskey arrived and he toasted the company in Gaelic. Rebus reckoned it was a double or treble – hard to tell with the added water.

'Father Joe was just about to tell us about Rico,' Rebus explained to Hogan, who was sitting down now.

'Well,' Daly began, 'Rico was from the west coast, wasn't he? Gave a good party, so the story went. Of course, I was never invited.'

'But Dickie was?'

'Oh, assuredly.'

'This was over in Glasgow?' Barclay asked, his face more bloodless than ever.

'I suppose there *would* have been parties there,' Daly admitted.

'But that's not what you meant, is it?' Rebus asked.

'Well, no . . . I meant out at the caravans. There was a site in East Lothian, Rico stayed there sometimes.'

'Caravans plural?' Rebus checked.

'He owned more than one; rented them out to tourists and the like.'

And the like . . . They already knew Rico's reputation, bad men from Glasgow sheltering beside east coast beaches . . . Rebus noticed that Malky the barman was busying himself wiping down the already pristine tables in their vicinity.

'They were pretty close then, Rico and Dickie?' Ward asked.

'I don't know that I'd say that. Rico probably only came to Leith three or four times a year.'

'Did you think it strange,' Rebus asked, 'that Dickie did a bunk around the same time Rico was murdered?'

'Can't say I connected the two,' Daly said. He hoisted the glass to his mouth, drained the whiskey.

'I don't think that's quite true, Father Joe,' Rebus stated quietly.

The glass was placed back on the table. 'Well, maybe you're right. I suppose I *did* wonder about it, same as everyone else in Leith.'

'And?'

'And what?'

'And what conclusion did you draw?'

'None at all,' Daly said with a shrug. 'Except that Our Lord moves in mysterious ways.'

'Amen to that,' said Hogan. Allan Ward rose to his feet, said he'd get in another round.

'When you've finished polishing that ashtray . . .' he remarked to Malky. So he'd noted the barman's actions, too. Maybe he was sharper than Rebus had given him credit for . . .

Linford was not to be deflected from his pursuit of Donny Dow. He'd called up what records they had, and was poring over them. Alongside them on his desk was a slim file with Laura Stafford's name on it. Siobhan had taken a peek at the latter. The usual cautions and arrests: two sauna busts; one brothel bust. The brothel had been a flat above a video rental shop. The guy who owned the video shop, it was his girlfriend ran the operation upstairs. Laura had been one of the girls on duty the night the police, acting on a tip-off, had paid a visit. Bill Pryde had worked the case. His handwriting was in the margin of one page of the report: 'tip-off anonymous, probably the sauna down the road . . .'

'The deep-throat business can be cut-throat, too,' was Derek Linford's comment.

He was having more joy with Donny Dow, who had been fighting since the age of ten. Arrests for vandalism and drunkenness, then Dow had taken up a healthy physical activity: Thai kick-boxing. It had failed to keep him out of trouble: one charge of housebreaking – later dropped – several assaults, one drug bust.

'What sort of drugs?'

'Cannabis and speed.'

'A kick-boxing headcase on speed? The mind boggles.'

'He worked as a bouncer for a time.' Linford pointed to the relevant line of the typed report. 'His employer wrote a letter defending him.' He turned the page. The signature at the bottom of the letter was that of Morris G. Cafferty.

'Cafferty owned a security firm in the city,' Linford added. 'Parted company with it a few years back.' He looked at Siobhan. 'Still don't think he could have clouted our art dealer?'

'I'm beginning to wonder,' Siobhan admitted.

Back at her desk, Davie Hynds had pulled his chair up alongside and was drumming a pen against his teeth.

'At a loose end?' Siobhan asked.

'I feel like the spare prick at an orgy.' He paused. 'Sorry . . . that wasn't a good way of putting it.'

Siobhan thought for a moment. 'Wait here,' she said. She turned back towards Linford's desk, but another man had entered the room and was shaking Linford's hand. Linford nodded, as though the two knew each other, but not well. Frowning, Siobhan walked over.

'Hello,' she said. The man had picked up a sheet from Donny Dow's file and was reading it. 'I'm a DS here. Name's Siobhan Clarke.'

'Francis Gray,' the man said. 'Detective Inspector.' He shook her hand, almost swamping it in his own. He was tall and broad, with a thick neck and salt-and-pepper hair, cut short.

'You two know one another?' she asked.

'We met once . . . a while back, at Fettes, right?' Gray said.

'Right,' Linford confirmed. 'We've helped each other out by phone a couple of times.'

'I was just wondering how the inquiry was going,' Gray added.

'It's fine,' Siobhan said. 'You're part of the Tulliallan crew?'

'For my sins.' Gray put down the sheet of paper, picked up another. 'Looks like Derek here may be winding things up for you.'

'Oh, he's a great wind-up merchant,' Siobhan said, crossing her arms. Gray laughed, and Linford himself joined in.

'Siobhan's a bit of a Doubting Thomas,' he stated.

Gray's eyes widened. 'Means, motive, opportunity. Looks to me like you've got two out of three. Least you can do now is interview the suspect.'

'Thank you, DI Gray, maybe we'll take your advice.' The words came from behind Gray: Gill Templer had entered the room. Gray dropped the sheet. It wafted back to the desk. 'Might I ask what you're doing here?'

'Nothing, ma'am. Just out for a stroll. We have to take ten minutes every hour to stave off oxygen starvation.'

'I think you'll find the station has plenty of corridors. There's even a world outside, if you'd care to explore it. This, on the other hand, is the centre of a murder inquiry. Last thing we need are unnecessary interruptions.' She paused. 'Wouldn't you agree?'

'Absolutely, ma'am.' He glanced from Siobhan to Derek. 'My apologies for keeping you from your noble efforts.' And with a wink he was off. Templer watched him leave. Then, saying nothing, but with a twinkle in her eye, she headed back to her own office.

Siobhan felt like cheering. She'd been about to have a go at Gray herself, but doubted she could have scored so palpable a hit. DCS Gill Templer had just risen like a rocket in Siobhan's estimation.

'She can be a cold bitch, can't she?' Linford muttered. Siobhan didn't respond: she wanted a favour from Linford and upsetting him wasn't going to help.

'Derek,' she said, 'since you're hell for leather on Donny Dow, mind if Hynds takes a look at Marber's cash-flow? I know you've covered the ground already, but it'll give the poor sod something to do.'

She stood there, hands behind her back, hoping she didn't look and sound *too* drippy.

Linford gazed in Hynds's forlorn direction. 'Go ahead,' he said, reaching down to pull the relevant folder from the box on the floor beside him.

'Thanks,' Siobhan cooed, skipping back to her desk.

'Here you go,' she said to Hynds, her voice back to normal.

'What's this?' Hynds asked, staring at the folder but not touching it.

'Marber's finances. Laura Stafford seemed to think he had some big money coming to him. I want to know the why, when and how much.'

'And his records will tell me?'

Siobhan shook her head. 'But his accountant might. The name and phone number are in there.' She tapped the file. 'And don't say I'm not generous.'

'Who was that big bastard you were speaking to?' Hynds nodded in the direction of Linford's desk.

'Detective Inspector Francis Gray. He's part of the Tulliallan posse.'

'He's a big bloke.'

'The bigger they are, the harder they fall, Davie.'

'If that bugger ever looks like falling, here's hoping we're not in the vicinity.' He stared at the folder. 'Anything else I should be asking the accountant?'

'You could ask him if there's anything he's been hiding from us, or his client might have been hiding from *him*.'

'Rare paintings? Bundles of cash?'

'Those'll do for a start.' She paused. 'Think you can manage this one on your own, Davie?'

Hynds nodded. 'No problem, DS Clarke. And what will you be up to while I'm toiling at the workface?'

'I have to go see a friend.' She smiled. 'But don't worry: it's strictly business.'

Lothian and Borders Police HQ on Fettes Avenue was known to most of the local force as 'the Big House'. Either that or 'Rear Window', which didn't refer to the Hitchcock film but to an embarrassing episode when vital documents had been stolen from the building by someone who'd climbed in through an open window on the ground floor.

Fettes Avenue was a wide thoroughfare which ended at the gates to Fettes College – Tony Blair's old school. Fettes was where the toffs sent their kids, paying dearly for the privilege. Siobhan had yet to meet any police officers who'd been schooled there, though she knew a few from Edinburgh's other fee-paying schools. Eric Bain, for example, had spent two years at Stewart's Melville – years he described simply as 'rough'.

'Why rough?' she asked now as they walked down the first-floor corridor.

'I was overweight, wore specs and liked jazz.'

'Enough said.'

Siobhan made to turn into a doorway, but Bain stopped her. She'd just been priding herself on her remembrance of the building's geography, having served in the Scottish Crime Squad for a time.

'They've moved,' Bain told her.

'Since when?'

'Since the SCS became the SDEA.'

He led her two doors further along and into a large office. 'This is what the Drug Enforcement Agency get. Me, I'm in a cupboard next floor up.'

'So why are we here?'

Bain seated himself behind a desk. Siobhan found a chair and dragged it across.

'Because,' he answered, 'for so long as the SDEA need me, I get a window and a view.' He swivelled on his chair, peering out at the scenery. There was a laptop computer on the desk, a pile of paperwork beside it. On the floor were stacked little black and silver boxes – peripherals of some description. Most of them looked home-made, and Siobhan would bet that Bain had constructed them himself, maybe even designed them, too. In a parallel universe somewhere, a billionaire Eric Bain was sitting by the pool of his Californian mansion . . . and the Edinburgh police were struggling with cyber-crimes of all descriptions.

'So what can I do for you?' he asked.

'I'm wondering about Cafferty. I need some confirmation that he owns the Sauna Paradiso.'

Bain blinked a couple of times. 'Is that it? An e-mail or phone call would have sufficed.' He paused. 'Not that I'm not pleased to see you.'

She considered her response. 'Linford's back. Maybe I just wanted an excuse to get away.'

'Linford? Major Peeping Tom himself?' She'd told Bain all about Linford. It had come spilling out almost the first night he'd visited her. She'd told him why she was wary of visitors; why she closed her shutters most evenings . . .

'He's filling in for Rebus.'

'A tough job for anyone.' He watched her nodding. 'So how's he acting?'

'As slimy as I remember . . . I don't know, he seems to be trying . . . and then he lets the mask slip.'

'Ugh.'

She shifted in her seat. 'Look, I really didn't come here to talk about Derek Linford.'

'No, but I'm sure it helps.'

She smiled, acknowledging the truth of this. 'Cafferty?' she said.

'Cafferty's finances are Byzantine. We can't be sure if people are fronting for him, or if he might have money sunk into someone else's scheme, a sort of silent partner or shareholder.'

'With nothing put down in writing?'

'These aren't people who worry too much about Companies House.'

'So what have you got?'

Bain was already firing up his laptop. 'Not a whole lot,' he confessed. 'Claverhouse and Ormiston seemed interested for a while, but that appears to be passing. They've gotten all excited about something else ... something they're not exactly willing to share. Not long now till I'm dispatched to the broom cupboard ...'

'Why were they interested?'

'My guess is that they want Cafferty back behind bars.'

'So it was just a speculative trawl?'

'You have to speculate to accumulate, Siobhan.' Bain was reading what was written on the screen. Siobhan knew better than to manoeuvre around behind him to read it for herself. He would shut the screen down rather than let her see. It was a question of territory for him, despite their friendship. He could snoop around her flat, checking her cupboards and CDs, but there were things he felt he had to hide from her, keeping that slight but tangible distance. No one, it seemed, was allowed to get too close to Bain.

'Friend Cafferty,' he said now, 'has interests in at least two Edinburgh saunas, and may have spread his wings as far as Fife and Dundee. The thing about the Paradiso is, we don't really know who owns it. There's a paper trail, but it leads to semi-respectable business types who probably *are* a front for someone else.'

'And you're guessing that someone is Cafferty?'

Bain shrugged. 'Like you say, it's a guess ...'

Siobhan had a thought. 'What about taxi companies?'

Bain hit some more keys. 'Yep, private hire firms. Exclusive Cars in Edinburgh, and a few smaller outfits dotted around West Lothian and Midlothian.'

'Not MG Cabs?'

'Where are they based?'

'Lochend.'

Bain studied and screen and shook his head.

'You know Cafferty runs a lettings agency?' Siobhan asked.

'He started that particular venture two months ago.'

'Do you know *why*?' She waited while Bain considered her question. He shook his head, watching her. 'Care to make a guess?' she asked.

'I haven't a clue, Siobhan, sorry. Is it relevant?'

'Right now, Eric, I don't know *what's* relevant. I'm drowning in information, only none of it seems to add up to anything.'

'Maybe if you reduced it to binary . . .'

He was making fun of her, so she stuck out her tongue.

'And to what do we owe this honour?' a voice boomed. It was Claverhouse, sauntering into the office, followed so closely by Ormiston that the two might have been connected by ankle-chains.

'Just visiting,' Siobhan said, trying not to sound flustered. Bain had assured her the two SDEA men were out for the afternoon. Claverhouse slipped off his coat and hung it on a coat-stand. Ormiston, dressed for outdoors, kept his jacket on, hands in its pockets.

'And how's your boyfriend?' Claverhouse asked. Siobhan frowned. Did he mean Bain?

'Last seen at Tulliallan,' Ormiston added.

'I hear he's got someone his own age,' Claverhouse said, mock-casually. 'That must piss you off, Shiv.'

Siobhan stared at Bain, who was reddening, readying to leap to her defence. She managed to shake her head just enough for him to register the act. She had a sudden vision of Bain as a school-kid, bullied but fighting back, earning even more derision.

'And how's *your* love life, Claverhouse?' she countered. 'Ormie treating you okay?'

Claverhouse sneered, immune to such jibes.

'And don't call me Shiv,' she added. She could hear a

phone trilling distantly. It was hers, tucked deep down in her bag. She wrestled it out and held it to her ear.

'Clarke,' she said.

'You wanted me to call you,' the voice said. She placed it immediately: Cafferty. She took a second to compose herself.

'I was wondering about MG Cabs,' she said.

'MG? Ellen Dempsey's outfit?'

'One of their drivers took Edward Marber home.'

'So?'

'So it seemed like a strange coincidence, MG Cabs having the same initials as your lettings agency.' Siobhan had forgotten about the people around her. She was focusing on Cafferty's words, his phrasing and tone of voice.

'That's what it is, though: a coincidence. I noticed it myself a while back, even thought of stealing the name.'

'Why didn't you, Mr Cafferty?' Siobhan, with the phone tucked into her chin, couldn't see behind her, but Bain was suddenly staring over her shoulder. She glanced round and saw that Claverhouse was as rigid as a statue.

Because he knew now who was on the phone.

'Ellen's got friends, Siobhan,' Cafferty was saying.

'What sort of friends?'

'The sort it's not worth crossing.' She could almost see his cruel, cold smile.

'I doubt there's anyone you wouldn't cross, Mr Cafferty,' she offered. 'You're saying you have no dealings with MG Cabs?'

'None whatsoever.'

'Out of curiosity, who was it called a cab that night?'

'Not me.'

'I'm not saying it was.'

'Probably Marber himself.'

'You didn't see him do it?'

'You reckon MG Cabs had something to do with it?'

193

'I don't "reckon" anything, Mr Cafferty. I'm just going by the book.'

'I find that hard to believe.'

'What do you mean?'

'All that time with Rebus, didn't anything rub off on you?'

She chose not to answer. Something else had occurred to her. 'How did you get this number?'

'I called the station . . . one of your colleagues gave me it.'

'Which one?' She didn't like the idea of Cafferty having access to her mobile.

'The one I spoke to . . . I don't remember the name.' She knew he was lying. 'I'm not about to start stalking you, Siobhan.'

'Just as well for you.'

'You've got more balls than Tynecastle, did you know that?'

'Goodbye, Mr Cafferty.' She cut off the call, sat and watched the display for a moment, wondering if he'd call back.

'*Mr* Cafferty she calls him!' Claverhouse exploded. 'What was all that about?'

'He was returning a call.'

'Did he happen to know where you were?'

'I don't think so.' She paused. 'Only Davie Hynds knew I was coming here.'

'And me,' Bain added.

'And you,' she conceded. 'But he got my mobile number from someone at St Leonard's. I don't think he knew I was here.'

Claverhouse was pacing the room, while Ormiston rested his bulk against the edge of one of the desks, hands still in his pockets. It took more than a call from Cafferty to fire him up.

'Cafferty!' Claverhouse exclaimed. 'Right here in this room!'

'You should have said hello,' Ormiston suggested, his voice a quiet growl.

'It's like he's infected this fucking place,' Claverhouse spat, but his pace was slowing. 'What's *your* interest in him?' he finally got round to asking.

'He was one of Edward Marber's clients,' Siobhan explained. 'He was at the gallery the night Marber was killed.'

'That's your man then,' Claverhouse decreed. 'Look no further.'

'It would be nice to have some proof, though,' Siobhan told him.

'Is that what Brains is helping you with?' Ormiston asked.

'I wanted to know about Cafferty's relationship with the Sauna Paradiso,' she admitted.

'Why?'

'Because the deceased may have been a client.' She was hedging her bets, not wanting to give away too much. It wasn't just the Rebus connection; even between cops on the same force, there was this mistrust, this unwillingness to dilute information by spreading it around.

'Blackmail then,' Claverhouse said. 'That's your motive.'

'I don't know,' Siobhan said. 'There's a rumour Marber might have been cheating clients.'

'Bing!' Claverhouse said, snapping his fingers. 'Every frame you put on the wall, Cafferty fits it perfectly.'

'An interesting image, under the circs,' Bain commented.

Siobhan was thoughtful. 'Who would Cafferty not want to tangle with?' she asked.

'You mean apart from us?' Ormiston said with the beginnings of a smile. For a while, he'd sported a bushy black moustache, but had shaved it off. Siobhan noticed that the difference made him seem younger.

'Apart from you, Ormie,' she said.

'Why?' Claverhouse asked. 'What did he say?' He'd stopped pacing, but couldn't get comfortable, standing legs apart in the middle of the room, arms folded.

'Some vague mention of people he didn't want to cross.'

'He was probably bullshitting,' Ormiston said.

Bain scratched his nose. 'Anybody out there we don't know about?'

Claverhouse shook his head. 'Cafferty's got Edinburgh sewn up tight.'

Siobhan was only half listening. She was wondering if Ellen Dempsey maybe had friends *outside* Edinburgh ... wondering if it would be worthwhile taking a look at the owner of MG Cabs. If Dempsey wasn't fronting for Cafferty, was it possible she was doing it for someone else, someone trying to break Cafferty's grip on the city?

A little warning bell went off in her head, because if this was true, then wouldn't Cafferty have every reason for framing Dempsey? *Ellen's got friends, Siobhan ... the sort it's not worth crossing.* His voice had been seductive, intimate, almost reduced to a murmur. He'd been trying to get her interested. She doubted he would do that without a reason, without some ulterior motive.

Was Cafferty trying to use her?

Only one way to find out: take a closer look at MG Cabs and Ellen Dempsey.

As she zoned back in on the conversation, Ormiston was saying something about how Claverhouse and he should try to get some shut-eye.

'Surveillance op?' Bain guessed.

Ormiston nodded, but when Bain pressed for details he just tapped his nose.

'Top secret,' Claverhouse stated, backing up his colleague. His eyes were on Siobhan as he spoke. It was as if he suspected – *knew* even – that she wasn't telling him the full story about herself and Cafferty. She thought back to the time she'd spent at Fettes as part of the Crime Squad team. Claverhouse had referred to her as 'Junior', but that

196

seemed like a lifetime ago. She returned his stare confidently. When Claverhouse blinked first, it almost seemed like a victory.

15

'And you haven't seen him since?'

The woman shook her head. She was seated in her fifth-floor flat in The Fort, a high-rise on the edge of Leith. There would have been great coastal views from the windows of the cramped living room, if they hadn't been so filthy. The room smelled of cat pee and leftovers, not that Rebus could see any physical evidence of cats. The woman's name was Jenny Bell and she had been Dickie Diamond's girlfriend at the time he'd disappeared.

When the door had been answered by Bell, Barclay had given Rebus a look which seemed to suggest that he could see why Diamond had done a midnight flit. Bell wore no make-up, and her clothes were shapeless and grey. The seams of her slippers had given way, and so had her teeth – leaving her mouth shrunken and lacking the dentures she probably wore when expecting company. This made her speech difficult to understand, especially for Allan Ward, who sat now on the arm of the sofa, a frown of concentration drawing his eyebrows together.

'Haven't clapped eyes on him,' Bell stated. 'He'd've gotten a good kicking if I had.'

'What did everyone think when he offskied?' Rebus asked.

'That he owed money, I suppose.'

'And did he?'

'Me for starters,' she said, jabbing a finger into her prodigious bosom. 'Nearly two hundred he had from me.'

'In one go?'

She shook her head. 'Bit here, bit there.'

'How long had you been an item?' Barclay asked.

'Four, five months.'

'Was he staying here?'

'Sometimes.'

There was a radio playing somewhere, either in another room or in the flat next door. Two dogs were involved in some noisy challenge outside. Jenny Bell had the electric fire on, and the room was stifling. Rebus didn't suppose it helped that he and Ward had been drinking, adding alcoholic fumes to the general miasma. Bobby Hogan had given them Bell's address, but made some excuse and headed back to the station. Rebus didn't blame him.

'Miss Bell,' he said now, 'did you ever go to the caravan with Dickie?'

'A few weekends,' she admitted, almost with a leer. Meaning: *dirty* weekends. Rebus could sense Ward give an involuntary shiver as the image filled his consciousness. Bell's eyes had narrowed. She was concentrating on Rebus. 'I've seen you before, haven't I?'

'Could be,' Rebus admitted. 'I do a bit of drinking down this way.'

She shook her head slowly. 'This was a long time back. In a bar . . .'

'Like I say—'

'Weren't you with Dickie?'

Rebus shook his head; Ward and Barclay were studying him. Hogan had hinted that Bell's memory was 'shot to hell'. Hogan had been mistaken . . .

'About the caravan,' Rebus pressed on, 'whereabouts was it exactly?'

'Somewhere Port Seton way.'

'You knew Rico Lomax, didn't you?'

'Oh aye, nice man, Rico.'

'Ever go with Dickie to one of his parties?'

She nodded vigorously. 'Wild times,' she grinned. 'And no neighbours to kick up a stink.'

'Unlike here, you mean?' Ward guessed. At which

point, someone through the wall started shouting at their offspring:

'I'm telling you to clean that up!'

Bell stared at the wall. 'Aye, not like here,' she replied. 'There's more space in a bloody caravan for a start.'

'What did you think when you heard Rico had been killed?' Barclay asked.

She shrugged. 'What was there to think? Rico was what he was.'

'And what was he?'

'You mean apart from a bloody good shag?' She started cackling, offering a view of pale pink gums.

'Did Dickie know?' Ward asked.

'Dickie was *there*,' she declared.

'He didn't object?' Ward asked. She just stared at him.

'I think,' Rebus explained for Ward's benefit, 'Miss Bell is saying that Dickie was a participant.'

Bell grinned at the look on Ward's face as he digested this. Then she started cackling again.

'Is there a shower at St Leonard's?' Ward asked on the drive back.

'Reckon you need one?'

'Half an hour's scrubbing should suffice.' He scratched his leg, which made Rebus start to feel itchy.

'That's an image that will be with me to the grave,' Barclay stated.

'Allan in the shower . . . ?' Rebus teased.

'You know damned well what I mean,' Barclay complained. Rebus nodded. They were quiet for the rest of the journey. Rebus lingered in the car park, saying he needed a cigarette. After Ward and Barclay had disappeared inside, he reached for his mobile, called Enquiries and got the number for Calder Pharmacy in Sighthill. He knew the pharmacist there, a guy called Charles Shanks, who lived in Dunfermline and taught kick-boxing in his spare time. When his call was answered, he asked for Shanks.

'Charles? John Rebus here. Look, do pharmacists have some kind of Hippocratic oath?'

'Why?' The voice sounded amused . . . and a little suspicious.

'I just wanted to know if you were doling out methadone to an addict called Malky Taylor.'

'John, I'm really not sure I can help.'

'All I want to know is whether he's doing okay, sticking with the programme . . . ?'

'He's doing fine,' Shanks said.

'Thanks, Charles.' Rebus ended the call, slipped the phone back into his pocket and headed indoors. Francis Gray and Stu Sutherland were in the interview room, talking with Barclay and Ward.

'Where's Jazz?' Rebus asked.

'He said he was going to the library,' Sutherland answered.

'What for?'

Sutherland just shrugged, leaving Gray to explain. 'Jazz thinks it would help to know what else was happening in the world around the time Rico got hit and Mr Diamond did his vanishing act. How did you get on in Leith?'

'Zombie Bar's gone downwardly upmarket,' Ward commented. 'And we talked to Dickie's old girlfriend.' He made a face to let Gray know what he thought of her.

'Her flat was minging,' Barclay added. 'I'm thinking of investing in some disinfectant.'

'Mind you,' Ward said mischievously, 'I think she might have serviced John here sometime in the dim and distant past.'

Gray's eyebrows rose. 'That right, John?'

'She thought she recognised me,' Rebus stressed. 'She was mistaken.'

'*She* didn't think so,' Ward persisted.

'John,' Gray pleaded, 'tell me you never shagged Dickie Diamond's bird?'

'I never shagged Dickie Diamond's bird,' Rebus

repeated. Just then, Jazz McCullough walked in through the door. He looked tired, rubbing his eyes with one hand and carrying a sheaf of paper in the other.

'Glad to hear it,' he said, having just caught the last few words.

'Find anything at the library?' Stu Sutherland asked, as if doubting that Jazz had been within a hundred yards of one.

Jazz dropped the sheets on to the desk. They were photocopies of newspaper stories.

'Look for yourself,' he said. As they passed the sheets between them, he explained his reasoning. 'We had the newspaper cuttings at Tulliallan, but they were focusing on Rico's murder, and that was a Glasgow case.'

Which meant the Glasgow paper – the *Herald* – had covered the story more comprehensively than its east coast rival. But now Jazz had gone to the *Scotsman*, finding a few scant references to the 'disappearance of a local man, Richard Diamond'. There was a grainy photograph: it looked like Diamond leaving a courtroom, buttoning his check jacket. His hair was longish, sticking out over the ears. His mouth hung open, teeth angular and prominent, and he had stubby little eyebrows. Skinny and tall with what looked like acne on his neck.

'A bonny-looking bugger, isn't he?' Barclay commented.

'Does this lot tell us anything new?' Gray asked.

'It tells us O. J. Simpson's going to catch his wife's killer,' Tam Barclay said. Rebus looked at the front page. There was a picture of the athlete after his acquittal. The paper was dated Wednesday 4 October 1995.

' "Hopes Rise for an End to Deadlock on Ulster",' Ward said, quoting another headline. He looked around the table. 'That's encouraging.'

Jazz picked up one sheet and held it in front of him: ' "Police Stymied in Hunt for Manse Rapist".'

'I remember that,' Tam Barclay said. 'They drafted officers in from Falkirk.'

'And Livingston,' Stu Sutherland added.

Jazz was holding the sheet for Rebus to see. 'You remember it, John?'

Rebus nodded. 'I was on the team.' He took the photocopied story from Jazz and started to read.

It was all about how the inquiry was running out of steam, no result in sight. Officers were being sent back to their postings. *A core of six officers will continue to sift information and seek out new leads.* Those six had eventually dwindled to three, Rebus not among them. There wasn't much in the story about the assault itself, which was as brutal as anything Rebus had seen in his years on the force. A church manse in Murrayfield – leafy Murrayfield, with its large, expensive homes and pristine avenues. It had started as a break-in, most probably. Silver and valuables had been taken in the raid. The minister himself had been out visiting parishioners, leaving his wife at home. Early evening, and no lights on. That was probably why the man – just the one attacker, according to the victim – had chosen the manse. It was next door to the church, hidden behind a tall stone wall and surrounded by trees, almost in a world of its own. No lights on meant no one home.

Being blind, however, the victim had needed no lights. She'd been in the bathroom upstairs. The clatter of breaking glass. She'd been running a bath, thought maybe she'd misheard. Or it was kids outside, a bottle thrown. The manse had a dog, but her husband had taken it with him to give it a walk.

She felt the breeze from the top of the stairs. There was a telephone in the hall next to the front door, and she put one foot on the first step down, heard the floorboard creak. Decided to use the phone in the bedroom instead. She almost had it in her hand when he struck, snatching her by the wrist and twisting her around so that she fell on to the bed. She thought she remembered the sound of him turning on the bedside lamp.

'I'm blind,' she'd pleaded. 'Please don't . . .'

But he had, giving a little laugh afterwards, a laugh that stayed with her during the months of the inquiry. Laughing because she couldn't identify him. It was only after the rape that he tore her clothes off, punching her hard in the face when she screamed. He left no finger-prints, just a few fibres and a single pubic hair. He'd swept the phone to the floor with his arm and then stamped on it. He'd taken cash, small heirlooms from the jewellery box on her dressing table. None of the missing items ever turned up.

He hadn't said anything. She could give little sense of his height or weight, no facial description.

From the start, officers had refused to voice their thoughts. They'd given it their best shot. The business community had put up a £5,000 reward for information. The pubic hair had given police a DNA fingerprint, but there hadn't been a database around back then. They'd have to catch the attacker first, *then* make the match.

'It was a bad one,' Rebus conceded.

'Did they ever catch the bastard?' Francis Gray asked.

Rebus nodded. 'Just a year or so back. He did another break-in, assaulted a woman in her flat. This was down in Brighton.'

'DNA match?' Jazz guessed. Rebus nodded again.

'Hope he rots in hell,' Gray muttered.

'He's already there,' Rebus conceded. 'His name was Michael Veitch. Stabbed to death his second week in prison.' He shrugged. 'It happens, doesn't it?'

'It certainly does,' Jazz said. 'I sometimes think there's more justice meted out in jails than in the courts.'

Rebus knew he had just been given an opening. *You're right . . . remember that gangster who got stabbed in the Bar-L? Bernie Johns, was that his name?* But it felt too obvious. If he said it aloud, it would alert them, put them on their guard. So he held back, wondering if he'd ever take the chance.

'Got what he deserved anyway,' Sutherland stated.

'Not that it did his victim much good,' Rebus added.

'Why's that, John?' Jazz asked. Rebus looked at him, then held up the sheet of paper.

'If you'd extended your search a few weeks, you'd have found she committed suicide. She'd become a recluse by then. Couldn't stand the thought of him still being out there . . .'

Weeks, Rebus had worked on the manse inquiry. Chasing leads provided by informants desperate for the cash reward. Chasing bloody shadows . . .

'Bastard,' Gray hissed under his breath.

'Plenty of victims out there,' Ward suggested. 'And we're stuck with a toe-rag like Rico Lomax . . .'

'Working hard, are we?' It was Tennant, standing in the doorway. 'Making lots of lovely progress for your SIO to report to me?'

'We've made a start, sir,' Jazz said, his voice full of confidence, but his eyes betraying the truth.

'Plenty of old news stories anyway,' Tennant commented, his eyes on the photocopies.

'I was looking for possible tie-ins, sir,' Jazz explained. 'See if anyone else had gone missing, or any unidentified bodies turned up.'

'And?'

'And nothing, sir. Though I think I've discovered why DI Rebus didn't seem overly helpful when Glasgow CID came calling.'

Rebus stared at him. Could he really know? Here Rebus was, supposedly infiltrating the trio, and every move they made seemed calculated to undermine him. First Rico Lomax, now the Murrayfield rape. Because there was a connection between the two . . . and that connection was Rebus himself. No, not just Rebus . . . Rebus and Cafferty

. . . and if the truth came out, Rebus's career would cease to be on the skids.

It would be a car-wreck.

'Go on,' Tennant pressed.

'He was involved in another inquiry, sir, one he was loath to take time out from.' Jazz handed the rape story to Tennant.

'I remember this,' Tennant said quietly. 'You worked it, John?'

Rebus nodded. 'They pulled me off it to look for Dickie Diamond.'

'Hence your reluctance?'

'Hence my *perceived* reluctance, sir. Like I said, I helped the Glasgow CID as much as I could.'

Tennant made a thoughtful sound. 'And does this get us anywhere nearer Mr Diamond, DI McCullough?'

'Probably not, sir,' Jazz conceded.

'Three of us went down to Leith, sir,' Allan Ward piped up. 'Interviewed two individuals who had known him. It seems Diamond may have shared his old lady with Rico Lomax on at least one occasion.'

Tennant just looked at him. Ward fidgeted a little.

'In a caravan,' he went on, eyes darting to Rebus and Barclay for support. 'John and Tam were there too, sir.'

Tennant's eyebrows shot up. 'In the caravan?'

Ward reddened as laughter filled the room. 'In Leith, sir.'

Tennant turned to Rebus. 'A useful trip, DI Rebus?'

'As fishing expeditions go, I've been on worse.'

Tennant was thoughtful again. 'The caravan angle: is there any mileage in that?'

'Could be, sir,' Tam Barclay said, feeling left out. 'It's something I feel we should follow up.'

'Don't let me stop you,' Tennant told him. Then he turned to Gray and Sutherland. 'And meantime you two were . . . ?'

'Making phone calls,' Gray announced calmly. 'Trying to locate more of Diamond's associates.'

'But still finding enough time to go walkabout, eh, Francis?'

Gray knew he'd been rumbled, decided silence was the best policy.

'DCS Templer tells me you were nosing around *her* inquiry.'

'Yes, sir.'

'She wasn't happy about it.'

'And she came crying to you, sir?' Ward said belligerently.

'No, DC Ward . . . she quite properly *mentioned* it to me, that's all.'

'There's *us* and there's *them*,' Ward went on, his eyes scanning the Wild Bunch. Rebus knew what he meant: it wasn't so much a team thing, more something approaching a siege mentality.

There's us . . . and there's them.

Except that Rebus didn't feel that way. Instead, he felt isolated inside his own head. Because he was a mole, brought here to con the group, and now working a case which, if solved, would be his ruin.

'Take this as a warning,' Tennant was telling Gray.

'You're saying we shouldn't fraternise?' Gray asked. 'We're a leper colony now, are we?'

'We're here through the good graces of DCS Templer. This is *her* station. And if you want to get through this course . . .' He paused to allow them to prepare for his next words. 'You'll do *exactly* what you're told, understood?'

There were mutters of grudging acquiescence.

'Now get back to work,' Tennant said, checking his watch. 'I'm headed back to base, and I'll expect to see all of you at Tulliallan tonight. Just because you're in the big city, don't think you're here on anything other than parole . . .'

After he'd gone, they sat staring into space and at each other, wondering where they went from here. Ward was first to speak.

'That guy should be in porn films.'

Barclay frowned. 'Why's that then, Allan?'

Ward looked at him. 'Tell me, Tam, when did you last see a bigger prick?'

The laughter eased some of the tension. Not that Rebus felt inclined to join in. He was imagining a blind woman, suddenly feeling a stranger's hand grab her wrist. He was thinking of the terror involved. There was a question he'd asked of a psychologist at the time: 'Blind or sighted, which would have been worse?'

The psychologist had just shaken his head, unable to provide an answer. Rebus had gone home and fashioned a blindfold for himself. He'd lasted all of twenty minutes, then had collapsed into his chair, his shins bruised, crying himself towards sleep.

He took a break now and went to the toilet, Gray warning him not to stray too close to 'the *real* detectives'. When he walked in, Derek Linford was shaking his hands free of water.

'No towels,' Linford said, explaining his actions. He was studying his appearance in the mirror above the sinks.

'I heard you were filling my shoes,' said Rebus, approaching the urinals.

'I don't think we've got anything to say to one another, do you?'

'Fair enough.' The silence lasted only half a minute.

'I'm about to do an interview,' Linford couldn't help revealing. He tucked a stray hair behind one ear.

'Don't let me keep you,' Rebus said. As he faced the urinal, he could almost feel Linford's eyes drilling into his back. Then the door swung open again. It was Jazz. He started to introduce himself to Linford, but was interrupted.

'Sorry, I've got a suspect waiting for me.' By the time Rebus had zipped himself up, Linford was gone.

'Was it something I said?' Jazz mused.

'The only people Linford gives the time of day to are ones he thinks he should be sucking up to.'

'Career opportunist,' Jazz said, nodding his understanding. He went to the sink and ran his hands under the cold tap. 'What was that Clash song again . . . ?'

' "Career Opportunities".'

'That's the one. I always felt I wasn't supposed to like The Clash: too old, not political enough.'

'I know what you mean.'

'A good band's a good band, though.'

Rebus watched Jazz looking around for a towel of some kind. 'Cutbacks,' Rebus explained. Jazz sighed and took out his handkerchief.

'That night we ran into your . . . your girlfriend, was it?' He waited till Rebus nodded. 'Everything sorted now between the pair of you?'

'Not exactly.'

'They never tell you when you join, do they? That being a cop will screw up your love life.'

'You're still married, though.'

Jazz nodded. 'It's never easy, though, is it?' He paused. 'That rape inquiry got to you, I could see it in your eyes. The moment you read that story, you were back in the middle of it.'

'A lot of cases have got to me over the years, Jazz.'

'Why let them?'

'I don't know.' Rebus paused. 'Maybe I used to be a good cop.'

'Good cops put up barriers, John.'

'Is that what you do?'

Jazz took his time before answering. 'End of the day, it's just a job. Not worth losing sleep over, never mind anything else.'

Rebus saw an opening. 'I started coming to that same

conclusion . . . Maybe too late, though: I'll be retiring soon.'

'Meaning?'

'Meaning all that's waiting for me out there is a lousy pension. This job's taken away my wife, my kid . . . most of the friends I ever had . . .'

'That's pretty tough.'

Rebus nodded. 'And what's it given me?'

'Apart from the drinking problem and lack of discipline?'

Rebus smiled. 'Apart from those, yes.'

'I can't answer that, John.'

Rebus let the silence rest between them, then asked the question he'd been preparing for.

'You ever crossed the line, Jazz? I don't mean the little things, the short cuts we take . . . I mean, something *big*, something you had to learn to live with?'

Jazz stared at him. 'Why? Have you?'

Rebus wagged a finger. 'I asked first.'

Jazz grew thoughtful. 'Maybe,' he said. 'Just the once.'

Rebus nodded. 'Ever wished you could go back and change it?'

'John . . .' Jazz paused. 'Are we talking about me or you here?'

'I thought we were talking about both of us.'

Jazz took half a step closer. 'You know something about Dickie Diamond, don't you? Maybe even about Rico's murder . . . ?'

'Maybe,' Rebus conceded. 'So what's *your* big secret, Jazz? Is it something we can work out between us?' Rebus's voice was almost a whisper, inviting confession.

'I hardly know you,' Jazz stated.

'I think we know one another well enough.'

'I . . .' Jazz swallowed. 'You're not ready yet,' he said with something akin to a sigh.

'*I'm* not ready? What about you, Jazz?'

'John . . . I don't know what it is you . . .'

'I've been getting an idea, something to make my pension that touch more secure. Thing is, I'd need help, people I could trust.'

'We're talking something illegal?'

Rebus nodded. 'You'd need to cross that line again.'

'How risky?'

'Not very.' Rebus considered. 'Maybe medium . . .'

Jazz was about to say something, but the door flew open and George Silvers sauntered in.

'Afternoon, gents,' he said.

Neither Rebus nor Jazz returned the greeting, being too busy staring one another out.

Then Jazz leaned towards Rebus. 'Talk to Francis,' he whispered. And then he was gone.

Silvers had gone into one of the cubicles, but re-emerged almost immediately. 'No bloody bog roll,' he complained. Then he stopped. 'What you grinning at?'

'Progress, George,' Rebus said.

'Then you're doing a sight better than our lot,' Silvers muttered, disappearing into the second cubicle and slamming shut the door.

16

Derek Linford wasn't best pleased. Rebus and his cronies had been installed in Interview Room 1, which was larger than IR2, where Linford now sat. Also, in IR2, the windows didn't open. The place was stifling, an airless box. The desk was narrow and screwed to the floor. This was where you brought the suspects with a record of violence. There was a dual cassette recorder bolted to the wall, and a video camera high up above the door. There was a panic button, disguised to look like an ordinary light-switch.

Linford was seated alongside George Silvers. Opposite them sat Donny Dow. Dow was short and skinny, but his squared-off shoulders told you there was muscle on him. He had straight blond hair – a dye job – and three days' growth of dark stubble. He wore gold studs and loops in both ears, another stud in his nose. A small golden sphere glinted from where his tongue had been pierced. He had his mouth open, licking the edges of his teeth.

'What you working at these days, Donny?' Linford asked. 'Still a doorman?'

'I'm answering nothing till you tell me what this is all about. Shouldn't I have a solicitor or something?'

'What do you want us to charge you with, son?' Silvers asked.

'I don't do drugs.'

'Good boy.'

Dow scowled and gave Silvers the middle finger.

'It's your ex we're interested in,' Linford revealed.

Dow didn't blink. 'Which one?'

'Alexander's mum.'

'Laura's a hooker,' Dow stated.

'And you left her for a prop forward?' Silvers asked with a smile. But Dow stared at him blankly: not a rugby man then.

'What's she done anyway?' Dow asked Linford.

'A man she was seeing, we're interested in him.'

'Seeing?'

Linford nodded. 'Rich guy, set her up in a nice little flat. Well, not so little, actually . . .'

Dow bared his teeth and thumped the desk with both fists. 'That wee slut! And *she's* the one got custody!'

'Did you fight her for it?'

'Fight . . . ?'

Fighting meant only one thing to someone like Dow. 'I mean,' Linford rephrased, 'did you want custody of Alexander?'

'He's my son.'

Linford nodded again, knowing the answer to his question was no.

'Who's this fucker anyway? This *rich* guy?'

'He's an art dealer, lives out in Duddingston Village.'

'And she's in his flat, her and Alex? *Shagging* this bastard there! With Alex . . .' Dow's face had gone puce with rage. In the momentary silence, Linford could hear voices – maybe a laugh – from IR1. Those sods were probably laughing at the idea of him demoted to IR2.

'So what's this got to do with me?' Dow was asking. 'You just trying to get me wound up or what?'

'You've got quite a record of violence, Mr Dow,' Silvers said. Dow's file was on the desk, and Silvers patted its brown cardboard cover.

'What? A couple of assaults? I've been hit more times than I can count. See when I was bouncing, wasn't a week went by when I didn't have some knob-head having a go at me. You won't find any of *that* in there.' He pointed towards the file. 'You lot only see what it suits you to see.'

'You might have a point there, Donny,' Silvers said, leaning back in his chair and folding his arms.

'What we see, Donny,' Linford said quietly, 'is a man with a record of violence who has just gone into a rage over his ex's relationship with another bloke.'

'Fuck her! See if I care!' Dow slid his chair back and stuffed his hands into his pockets, both legs going like pistons.

Linford made a show of flipping through the file. 'Mr Dow,' he began, 'did you happen to read about a murder in the city?'

'Only if it made the sports pages.'

'An art dealer, struck repeatedly on the head outside his home in Duddingston Village.'

Dow's legs stopped pumping. 'Hold on a fucking minute,' he said, raising both hands, palms out.

'What did you say you did for a living?' George Silvers asked.

'What? Wait a second . . .'

'Laura's gentleman friend is dead, Mr Dow,' Linford was saying.

'You worked as a bouncer for Big Ger Cafferty, didn't you?' Silvers asked. Dow couldn't keep up with this; he needed time to think; *couldn't* think, and knew if he said anything – *anything* – it might . . .

A tapping at the door and Siobhan Clarke's head appeared.

'Any chance I could sit in?' she asked. Then, seeing the thunderous looks on both her colleagues' faces, she started to retreat. But Dow had sprung to his feet and was on his way to the door. Silvers went for him, but Dow gave him a straight-fingered chop to the throat. Silvers started wheezing, hands going to his collar. Linford was effectively trapped between Silvers, the desk and the wall. Dow lifted a foot and hefted Silvers backwards into

Linford, whose fingers sought the panic button. Siobhan had been trying to close the door, with herself on the outside, but Dow couldn't have that. He yanked the door open, grabbed her by her hair and threw her into the room. An alarm was going off in the corridor, but he ran. There were men in the room next door: they watched him as he sped past. One more corner, a set of doors, and he would be gone.

Back in IR2, Silvers was hunched in his seat, still trying to catch a breath. Linford was squeezing past him. Siobhan was lifting herself from the floor. A whole clump of hair seemed to be missing from the top of her head.

'Shit, shit, shit!' she squealed. Linford ignored her and ran into the corridor. His left leg was aching from where Silvers had connected with it. But it was his pride that felt the most bruised. 'Where is he?' he yelled.

Tam Barclay and Allan Ward looked at one another, then both pointed towards the exit.

'He went that-a-way, Sheriff,' Ward said with a grin. Problem was, no one had actually seen him *leave* the station. There was video surveillance of the main entrance, and Linford asked the comms room to run the tape. Meantime, he went from office to office, checking under desks and inside the station's few walk-in cupboards. When he got back to the comms room, they were running the tape. Donny Dow sprinting in full-colour time-lapse, right out the front door.

'We need patrols to search the area!' Linford said. 'Cars *and* foot. Get his description out!' The uniformed officers looked at each other.

'What are you waiting for?' Linford snarled.

'I think they're probably waiting for me to give them the okay, Derek,' a voice said from behind him.

DCS Gill Templer.

'Ouch!' Siobhan said. She was seated back at her desk, while Phyllida Hawes checked the damage to her head.

'You've lost a little bit of skin,' Hawes said. 'I think the hair will grow back.'

'Probably feels worse than it looks,' Allan Ward offered. The incident in IR2 seemed to have broken down barriers: Gray, McCullough and Rebus were present too, while Gill Templer 'debriefed' Linford and Silvers in her office.

'Name's Allan, by the way,' Ward said, for Phyllida Hawes's benefit. When she told him her name, he remarked that it was unusual. He was listening to her explanation when Siobhan got up and moved away. She didn't think either of them had noticed.

Rebus was standing by the far wall, arms folded, studying the display relating to the Marber case.

'He's a fast worker,' Siobhan said. Rebus turned his head, watched the interplay between Ward and Hawes.

'You should warn her,' he said. 'I'm not sure Allan's house-broken.'

'Maybe that's the way she likes it.' Siobhan dabbed at the patch of naked skin. It was at the crown of her head, and it stung like buggery.

'You could get a sick line on the strength of that,' Rebus informed her. 'I've known cops go on disability for less. Factor in the shock and stress . . .'

'You don't get rid of me that easily,' she said. 'Shouldn't you all be out chasing Donny Dow?'

'This isn't our patch, remember?' Rebus scanned the room. Hawes listening to Ward's patter; Jazz McCullough in conversation with Bill Pryde and Davie Hynds; Francis Gray sitting on one of the desks, swinging one leg as he leafed through an evidence file. He saw Rebus watching him and gave a wink, sliding off the desk and coming forwards.

'This is the sort of case they should have given us, eh, John?'

Rebus nodded but said nothing. Gray seemed to take the hint, and after a few words of commiseration to

Siobhan he moved away again, changing desks, picking up another file.

'I need to speak to Gill,' Siobhan said quietly, her eyes on Templer's closed door.

'Going on the sick after all?'

Siobhan shook her head. 'I think I recognised Donny Dow. He was the Weasel's driver the day I went to interview Cafferty.'

Rebus stared at her. 'You sure?'

'Ninety per cent. I only saw him for a matter of seconds.'

'Then maybe we should talk to the Weasel.'

She nodded. '*After* I've okayed it with the boss.'

'If that's the way you want to play it.'

'You said it yourself: this isn't your patch.'

Rebus looked thoughtful. 'What about if you kept it to yourself for the moment?'

She stared at him, uncomprehending.

'What if I talk to the Weasel on the quiet?' Rebus went on.

'Then I'd be withholding information.'

'No, you'd just be withholding an inkling . . . Maybe it'll take you a day to convince yourself that it was Dow you saw driving the Weasel's car.'

'John . . .' Without saying as much, she was asking him for something. She wanted him to share, to confide . . . to trust in her.

'I have my reasons,' he said, voice just above a whisper. 'Something the Weasel might help me with.'

It took her a full thirty seconds to make up her mind. 'All right,' she said. He touched her arm.

'Thanks,' he said. 'I owe you. What about something to eat tonight? My treat?'

'Have you called Jean yet?'

His eyes darkened. 'I've been trying. She's either out or not answering.'

'*She's* the one you should be asking to dinner.'

'I should have phoned her that night . . .'

'You should have *followed* her that night, apologising all the way.'

'I'll keep trying,' he said.

'And send her some flowers.' She had to smile at the look on his face. 'Last time you sent anybody flowers, it was probably a wreath, am I right?'

'Probably,' he admitted. 'More wreaths than bouquets, that's for certain.'

'Well, don't confuse the two this time round. Plenty of florists in the phone book.'

He nodded. 'Straight after I talk to Weasel,' he said, heading for the corridor. There were some calls that had to be made on a mobile rather than one of the office phones. Rebus now had a list of two.

But the Weasel wasn't in his office, and the best anyone could do was offer a tepid promise to pass on a message.

'Thanks,' Rebus said. 'By the way, is Donny there at the moment?'

'Donny who?' the voice said, before cutting the connection. Rebus cursed, went to the comms room for a *Yellow Pages*, then headed out into the car park to phone a florist. He ordered a mixed bunch.

'What sort of flowers does the lady like?' he was asked.

'I don't know.'

'Well, what about colours?'

'Look, just a selection, okay? Twenty quid's worth or thereabouts.' He reeled off his credit-card number and the deal was done. Sliding his phone back into his pocket, switching it for cigarettes and lighter, he realised he had no idea what twenty notes would buy. Half a dozen withered carnations, or some ridiculously huge spray? Whatever it was, it would be delivered to Jean's home this evening at 6.30. He wondered what would happen if she was staying late at work: would the florist leave them on the doorstep, prey to any passing thief? Or take them back to the shop and try again the next day?

He took a long drag on the cigarette, filling his lungs. Things always seemed to be more complicated than you expected. But then when he thought about it, he was adding the complications himself, looking at what could go wrong with the arrangement rather than hoping for the best. He knew he'd been a pessimist from an early age, realising that it was a good way to prepare for life. As a pessimist, if things went wrong, you were ready, while if things went right, it came as a pleasant surprise.

'Too late to change now,' he muttered.

'Talking to yourself?' It was Allan Ward, busily loosing a fresh packet from its cellophane bonds.

'What's up? Has your patter failed to impress DC Hawes?'

Ward started to nod. 'She's so unimpressed,' he said, lighting up, 'she's agreed to have dinner with me tonight. Any tips?'

'Tips?'

'Short cuts into her knickers.'

Rebus flicked ash from his cigarette. 'She's a good officer, Allan. More than that, I like her. I'd take it personally if she got hurt.'

'Just a bit of harmless fun,' Ward said defensively. Then his face changed to a smirk. 'Just because you're not getting any . . .'

Rebus swung round, grabbing both of Ward's jacket lapels in one hand, pushing him back against the wall of the station. The cigarette dropped from Ward's mouth as he tried to push Rebus away. A patrol car was pulling in through the gateway, the uniforms staring out at the spectacle. Then hands were on both men, separating them. It was Derek Linford.

'Ladies, ladies,' he was telling them. 'No fisticuffs.'

Ward was rearranging his jacket. 'What're you doing

here? Checking under the cars for a missing prisoner?' Flecks of saliva flew from his mouth.

'No,' Linford said, but he shifted his gaze to the car park, just in case ... 'I was actually wondering if any smokers were down here.'

'You don't smoke,' Rebus reminded him. He was breathing hard.

'I thought maybe I should give it a go. Christ knows, this is as good a time as any.'

Ward laughed, seeming to forget all about Rebus. 'Welcome to the club,' he said, offering his packet to Linford. 'Templer gave you a hard time, did she?'

'It's the fucking embarrassment as much as anything,' Linford admitted with a sheepish grin, while Ward lit the cigarette for him.

'Forget about it. Everybody's saying Dow's into kick-boxing. You don't want to mess with that.'

Ward seemed to be cheering Linford up. Rebus was wondering about Linford. He'd come across them brawling, yet hadn't asked why, being busy with his own concerns. Rebus decided to leave them to it.

'Hey, John, no hard feelings, eh?' Ward suddenly announced. Rebus didn't say anything. He knew that once he'd gone, Linford – now reminded – would probably ask about the fight, and his new best buddy would explain about the night out and Jean.

And suddenly Linford would have ammunition. Rebus wondered how long it would take him to use it. He was even starting to worry about the fact that Linford had been chosen to replace him on the Marber case. Why Linford of all people? As Rebus walked back into the station, he could feel how the tension was making his every movement more sluggish. He tried rolling his shoulders, stretching his neck. He remembered an old piece of graffiti: *Just because you're paranoid, it doesn't mean they're not after you* ... Was he becoming paranoid, seeing enemies and traps everywhere? Blame Strathern, for picking him in the first place. I don't even trust the man I'm working for, Rebus thought, so how can I trust anyone else? Passing one of the officers from the Marber inquiry, he thought how nice it would be to be seated at a desk in the murder room, making routine telephone calls, knowing how little any of it mattered. Instead, he seemed to be digging himself an ever-deeper hole. He'd promised Jazz an 'idea', a plan to make some money. Now all he had to do was deliver . . .

That evening, Rebus went drinking alone. He'd told the syndicate he had something to do, but might catch up with them later. They were undecided about whether to stay in Edinburgh for a few drinks, or head straight back to Tulliallan. Jazz was thinking of Broughty Ferry, but his car was back at the college. Ward was thinking of treating Phyllida Hawes to a Mexican place near St Leonard's. They were still arguing over strategies and alternatives when Rebus slipped away. After three drinks in the Ox, only half listening to the latest batch of jokes, he started feeling hungry. Didn't know where to eat . . . last thing he wanted was to walk into a restaurant and bump into Ward and Hawes playing footsie under the table. He knew he could cook himself something at home; knew, too, that this wouldn't happen. All the same, maybe he should be at home. What if Jean rang? Had she got the flowers yet? His mobile was in his pocket, just waiting for her call. In the end, he ordered another drink and the last leftover Scotch egg.

'Been there since lunchtime, has it?' he asked Harry the barman.

'I wasn't on at lunchtime. You want it or not?'

Rebus nodded. 'And a packet of nuts.' There were times he wished the Ox did a bit more in the catering line. He remembered the previous owner, Willie Ross, dragging some hapless punter outside after the man had asked to see the menu, pointing up at the Oxford Bar sign and asking: 'Does that say "Bar" or "Restaurant"?' Rebus doubted the client had become a regular.

The Ox was quiet tonight. Murmurs of conversation from a couple of tables in the lounge, and only Rebus himself in the front bar. When the door creaked open, he didn't bother turning to look.

'Get you one?' the voice beside him asked. It was Gill Templer. Rebus straightened up.

'My shout,' he said. She was already easing herself on to a bar stool, letting her shoulder-bag slump to the floor. 'What'll it be?'

'I'm driving. Better make it a half of Deuchars.' She paused. 'On second thoughts, a gin and tonic.' The TV was playing quietly, and her eyes drifted towards it. One of the Discovery Channel programmes favoured by Harry.

'What're you watching?' Gill asked.

'Harry puts this stuff on to scare away the punters,' Rebus explained.

'That's right,' Harry agreed. 'Works with every bugger but this one.' He nodded in Rebus's direction. Gill offered a tired smile.

'Bad one?' Rebus guessed.

'It's not every day someone does a runner from the interview room.' She gave him a sly look. 'I suppose you're pleased enough?'

'How?'

'Anything that makes Linford look bad . . .'

'I hope I'm not *that* petty.'

'No?' She considered this. 'Looks like *he* might be, though. Word's going around that you and another of the Tulliallan crew had a punch-up in the car park.'

So Linford *had* been talking.

'Just thought I'd warn you,' she went on, 'I think it's already reached the ears of DCI Tennant.'

'You came looking for me to tell me?'

She shrugged.

'Thanks,' he said.

'I suppose I was also hoping to have a word . . .'

'Look, if it's about the mug of tea . . .'

'Well, you did give it some welly, John, be honest.'

'If I'd pushed it off the desk with my pinkie, you'd hardly have had reason to send me into purdah.' Rebus paid for her drink, raised his own pint glass to her in a toast.

'Cheers,' she said, taking a long swallow and exhaling noisily.

'Better?' he asked.

'Better,' she confirmed.

He smiled. 'And people wonder why we drink.'

'One'll be enough for me, though – how about you?'

'Would you settle for a ballpark figure?'

'I'd settle for knowing how things are going at Tulliallan.'

'I've not made much headway.'

'Is that likely to change?'

'It might.' He paused. 'If I take a few risks.'

She looked at him. 'You'll talk to Strathern first, won't you?'

He nodded, but could see she wasn't convinced.

'John . . .'

Same tone Siobhan had used earlier in the day. *Listen to me . . . trust me . . .*

He turned towards Gill. 'You could always take a cab,' he told her.

'Meaning what?'

'Meaning you could have another drink.'

She examined her glass. It was already mostly ice. 'I could probably manage one more,' she conceded. 'It's my round anyway. What are you having?'

After the third gin and tonic, she confided to him that she had been seeing someone. It had lasted about nine months, then fizzled out.

'You kept that pretty quiet,' he said.

'There's no way I was ever going to introduce him to you lot.' She was playing with her glass, watching the patterns it made on the bar. Harry had retreated to the other end of the small room. Another regular had arrived, and the two of them were talking football.

'How are things with Jean and you?' Gill asked.

'We had a bit of a misunderstanding,' Rebus admitted.

'Want to talk about it?'

'No.'

'Want me to act as peacemaker?'

He looked at her and shook his head. Jean was Gill's friend; Gill had introduced them to one another. He didn't want her feeling awkward about it. 'Thanks anyway,' he said. 'We'll sort it out.'

She glanced at her watch. 'I better get going.' Slid off the stool and collected her shoulder-bag. 'This place isn't so bad,' she decided, studying the bar's faded decor. 'I might grab something to eat. Have you had dinner?'

'Yes,' he lied, feeling that a meal with Gill would be a betrayal of sorts. 'I hope you're not going to drive in that condition,' he called as she made for the door.

'I'll see how I feel when I get outside.'

'Think how much worse tomorrow will be if you're charged with drunk driving!'

She waved a hand and was gone. Rebus stayed for one more. Her perfume lingered. He could smell it on the sleeve of his jacket. He wondered if he should have sent Jean perfume instead of flowers, then realised he didn't know what kind she liked. Scanning the gantry, he guessed that when pushed he could reel off the names of over two dozen malts, straight from memory.

Two dozen malts, and he'd no idea what perfume Jean Burchill used.

As he pushed open the main door to his tenement, he saw a shadow on the stairwell: someone descending. Maybe one of the neighbours, but Rebus didn't think so. He looked behind him, but there was no one on the street. Not an ambush then. The feet came into view first, then the legs and body.

'What are you doing here?' Rebus hissed.

'Heard you were looking for me,' the Weasel replied. He was at the bottom of the stairs now. 'I wanted a bit of a chat anyway.'

'Did you bring anyone with you?'

The Weasel shook his head. 'This isn't the sort of meeting the boss would approve of.'

Rebus looked around again. He didn't want the Weasel in his flat. A bar would be okay, but any more drink and his brain would start clouding. 'Come on then,' he said, passing the Weasel and making for the back door. He unlocked it and dragged it open. The tenement's shared garden wasn't much used. There was a drying-green, the grass almost a foot long, surrounded by narrow borders where only the hardiest plants survived. When Rebus and his wife had first moved in, Rhona had replaced the weeds with seedlings. Hard to tell now if any of them still thrived. Wrought-iron railings separated the garden from its neighbours, all the gardens enclosed by a rectangle of tall tenement buildings. There were lights on in most of the windows: kitchens and bedrooms; stair landings. The place was well enough lit for this meeting.

'What's up?' Rebus asked, fishing for a cigarette.

The Weasel had stooped to pick up an empty beer can, which he crushed and dropped into his coat pocket. 'Aly's doing okay.'

Rebus nodded. He had almost forgotten the Weasel's son. 'You took my advice?'

'They've not let him off the hook yet, but my solicitor says we're in with a shout.'

'Have they charged him?'

The Weasel nodded. 'But only with possession: the spliff he was smoking when they picked him up.'

Rebus nodded. Claverhouse was playing this one cautiously.

'Thing is,' the Weasel said, crouching by the nearest flower border, picking up empty crisp bags and sweet wrappers, 'I think my boss might have got wind of it.'

'Of Aly?'

'Not Aly exactly . . . the dope, I was meaning.'

Rebus lit his cigarette. He was thinking about Cafferty's network of eyes and ears. It only needed the boffin from the police lab to tell a colleague back at base, and that colleague to tell a friend . . . There was no way Claverhouse was going to keep the haul under wraps for ever. All the same . . .

'That could be in your favour,' Rebus told the Weasel. 'Puts pressure on Claverhouse to do something about it.'

'Like charge Aly, you mean?'

Rebus shrugged. 'Or hand it over to Customs, so they all end up taking credit . . .'

'And Aly still goes down?' The Weasel had risen to his feet, pockets filled and rustling.

'If he co-operates, he could get a light sentence.'

'Cafferty's still going to nail him.'

'So maybe you should get your retaliation in first. Give the Drug Squad what they want.'

The Weasel was thoughtful. 'Give them Cafferty?'

'Don't tell me you haven't been thinking about it.'

'Oh, I've thought about it. But Mr Cafferty's been very good to me.'

'He's not family, though, is he? He's not blood . . .'

'No,' the Weasel said, stretching the single syllable out.

'Can I ask you something?' Rebus flicked ash from the cigarette.

'What?'

'Do you have any idea where Donny Dow is?'

The Weasel shook his head. 'I heard he'd been taken in for questioning.'

'He's done a runner.'

'That was silly of him.'

'It's why I wanted to talk to you, because now we have to send out search parties, which means talking to all his friends and associates. I'm assuming you'll co-operate?'

'Naturally.'

Rebus nodded. 'Let's say Cafferty does know about the drugs . . . what do you think he'll do?'

'Number one, he'll want to know who brought them up here.' The Weasel paused.

'And number two?'

The Weasel looked at him. 'Who said there was a number two?'

'There usually is, when there's been a number one.'

'Okay . . . number two, he might decide he wanted them for himself.'

Rebus examined the tip of his cigarette. He could hear sounds of tenement life: music, TV voices, plates colliding on the drying-rack. Shapes passing a window . . . ordinary people living ordinary lives, all of them thinking they were different from the rest.

'Did Cafferty have anything to do with the Marber murder?' he asked.

'When did I become your snitch?' the Weasel asked.

'I don't want you for my snitch. I just thought maybe one question . . .'

The small man stooped down again, as though he'd spotted something in the grass, but there was nothing, and he rose again slowly.

'Other people's shit,' he muttered. It sounded like a mantra. Maybe he meant his son, or even Cafferty: the Weasel cleaning up after them. Then he locked eyes with Rebus. 'How am I supposed to know something like that?'

'I'm not saying Cafferty did this himself. It would be one of his men, someone he'd hired . . . probably through *you*, so as to distance himself from it. Cafferty's always been good at letting other people take the fall.'

The Weasel seemed to be considering this. 'Is that what

those two cops were doing there the other day? Asking questions about Marber?' He watched as Rebus nodded. 'The boss wouldn't say what it was about.'

'I thought he trusted you,' Rebus said.

The Weasel paused again. 'I know he knew Marber,' he said at last, his voice dropping to a level where the slightest gust of wind would erase it. 'I don't think he liked him much.'

'I hear he stopped buying paintings from Marber. Is that because he found out Marber had been cheating?'

'I don't know.'

'Do you think it's possible?'

'It's possible,' the Weasel conceded.

'Tell me . . .' Rebus's own voice dropped further still. 'Would Cafferty organise a hit without your knowledge?'

'You're asking me to incriminate myself.'

'This is just between the two of us.'

The Weasel folded his arms. The rubbish in his pockets crackled and clicked. 'We're not as close as we once were,' he confided, ruefully.

'A hit like this one, who would he have gone to?'

The Weasel shook his head. 'I'm not a rat.'

'Rats are clever creatures,' Rebus said. 'They know when to leave a sinking ship.'

'Cafferty isn't sinking,' the Weasel said with a sad smile.

'That's what they said about the *Titanic*,' Rebus replied.

There wasn't much more to be said. They went back into the stairwell, the Weasel heading for the front door and Rebus for the stairs. He wasn't inside his flat two minutes when there was a knock at the door. He was in the bathroom, running a bath. He did *not* want the Weasel in here. This was where he could try shutting it all out and pretend he was like everyone else. Another knock, and this time he walked to the door.

'Yes?' he called.

'DI Rebus? You're under arrest.'

Put his face to the peep-hole, then unlocked the door.

Claverhouse was standing there, sporting a smile as thin and sharp as a surgeon's blade. 'Going to invite me in?' he said.

'Wasn't thinking of it.'

'Not entertaining, are you?' Claverhouse craned his neck to look down the hallway.

'I'm just about to get in the bath.'

'Good idea. I'd do the same, under the circumstances.'

'What are you talking about?'

'I'm talking about the fact that you've just spent a good fifteen minutes being contaminated by Cafferty's right-hand man. Does he often make house calls? You're not busy counting out a pay-off in there, are you, John?'

Rebus took two steps forward, backing Claverhouse against the stair-rails. It was a two-storey drop to the ground.

'What do you want, Claverhouse?'

The feigned humour had vanished from Claverhouse's face. He wasn't scared of Rebus; he was just angry.

'We've been trying to nail Cafferty,' he spat, 'in case *you've* forgotten. Now word's starting to leak out about the shipment, and Weasel's got a nasty little lawyer chewing at my balls. So we're on surveillance, and what do we find? Weasel himself paying *you* a visit.' He stabbed a finger into Rebus's chest. 'And how's *that* going to look in my report, Detective Inspector?'

'Fuck you, Claverhouse.' But at least Rebus knew where Ormiston was now: he was tailing the Weasel.

'Fuck me?' Claverhouse was shaking his head. 'You've got it all wrong, Rebus. It's *you* the boys in Barlinnie will be telling to bend over. Because if I can tie you to Cafferty and his operation, so help me I'll send you so far down they'll need a JCB to find you.'

'Consider me warned,' Rebus said.

'It's all starting to unravel for friend Cafferty,' Claverhouse hissed. 'Make sure you know whose side you're on.'

Rebus thought of the Weasel's words: *Cafferty isn't*

sinking. And the smile that had accompanied his words . . . why had the Weasel looked *sad?* He took a step back, giving Claverhouse room. Claverhouse saw it as a weakening.

'John . . .' reverting to Rebus's first name, 'whatever it is you're hiding, you need to come clean.'

'Thanks for your concern.' Rebus saw Claverhouse for what he was: a chip-on-the-shoulder careerist who had ideas he couldn't follow through on. Nailing Cafferty – or at the very least inserting a mole into Cafferty's operation – would, in his own eyes, be the making of him, and he couldn't see past it. It was consuming him. Rebus was almost sympathetic: hadn't he been there himself?

Claverhouse was shaking his head at Rebus's stubbornness. 'I see the Weasel was driving himself tonight. That because Donny Dow did a runner?'

'You know about Dow?'

Claverhouse nodded. 'Maybe I know more than you think, John.'

'Maybe you do at that,' Rebus agreed, trying to loosen him up. 'Such as what, exactly . . . ?'

But Claverhouse wasn't falling for it. 'I was talking to DCS Templer this evening. She was very interested to find out about Donny Dow's chauffeuring duties.' He paused. 'But you knew all the time, didn't you?'

'Did I?'

'You didn't manage to sound very surprised when I told you. Thinking back, you didn't sound surprised at all . . . so how come *she* didn't know? Keeping stuff to yourself again, John . . . maybe you just wanted to protect your pal the Weasel.'

'He's not my pal.'

'His lawyer came asking all the right questions, almost as if he'd been primed.' It was Claverhouse who had advanced on Rebus this time, not that Rebus was budging an inch. He could hear the bath still filling. Not long now and it would start to overflow. 'What was he doing here, John?'

'You wanted me to talk to him . . .'

Claverhouse paused. A glimmer of hope seemed to rise in his eyes. 'And?'

'Nice talking to you, Claverhouse,' Rebus said. 'Say hello to Ormie for me when you catch up with him.' He stepped backwards into his hall, and started closing the door. Claverhouse stood unmoving, almost as if he planned to stay there till morning. Not saying anything, because nothing needed to be said between them. Rebus padded back to the bathroom and turned off the tap. The water was scalding, and there wasn't enough room to add cold. He sat down on the toilet and held his head in his hands. It struck him that he actually trusted the Weasel more than he did Claverhouse.

Make sure you know whose side you're on . . .

Rebus didn't like to think about it. He still couldn't be sure that he hadn't landed in a trap. Was Strathern out to nail him, using Gray and the others as bait? Even if there *was* some dirty deal to uncover, something involving Gray, Jazz and Ward, could Rebus succeed without implicating himself? He got up and went through to the living room, found the whisky bottle and a glass. Picked up the first CD he found and stuck it on. REM: *Out of Time*. The title had never meant more to him than right here, this minute. He stared at the contents of the bottle but knew he wasn't going to touch it, not tonight. He swapped it for the phone, called Jean at home. Answering machine, so he left another message. He thought about driving to the New Town, maybe dropping in on Siobhan. But it wasn't fair on her . . . and she was probably out driving anyway, her scalp burning, eyes not quite focused on the road ahead . . .

He walked softly back to the door and put his eye to the peep-hole. The landing was empty. He allowed himself a smile, remembering the way he'd left Claverhouse dangling. Back into the living room and over to the window. No sign of anyone outside. On the hi-fi, Michael Stipe alternated between rage and grieving.

John Rebus sat down in his chair, prepared to let the night-time take its toll. And then the phone rang, and it had to be Jean returning his call.

But it wasn't.

'All right, big man?' Francis Gray said, in that soft west coast growl of his.

'Been better, Francis.'

'Never fear, Uncle Francis has the cure for all ills.'

Rebus rested his head against the back of his chair. 'Where are you?'

'The delightful surroundings of the Tulliallan officers' bar.'

'And that's the cure for my ills?'

'Could I be that heartless? No, big man, I'm talking about the trip of a lifetime. Two people with a whole world of possibilities and delights opening before them.'

'Someone been spiking your drinks, DI Gray?'

'I'm talking about *Glasgow*, John. And you'll have me as your guide to what's best in the west.'

'It's a bit late for all this, isn't it?'

'Tomorrow morning . . . just you and me. So be here at sparrowfart or you'll miss all the fun!'

The phone went dead. Rebus stared at it, considered calling back . . . Gray and him in Glasgow: meaning what? Meaning Jazz had spoken to Gray, told him Rebus had something to offer? Why Glasgow? Why just the two of them? Was Jazz distancing himself from his old friend? Rebus's thoughts turned again to the Weasel and Cafferty. Old ties could loosen. Old alliances and allegiances could crumble. There were always points of vulnerability; cracks in the carefully constructed wall. Rebus had been thinking of Allan Ward as the weakest link . . . now he was turning to Jazz McCullough. He went back through to the bathroom, gritted his teeth and plunged his hand into the super-heated bathwater, letting the plug out. Then he turned on the cold tap to restore some balance. Back through to the kitchen for a mug of coffee and a couple of vitamin C tablets. Then into the living room. He'd hidden Strathern's report under one of the sofa cushions.

His bath-time reading . . .

17

Bernie Johns had been a brute of a man, controlling a
large chunk of the Scottish drugs trade by means of
contacts and ruthlessness, disposing of any and all
contenders for his crown along the way. People had
turned up tortured, maimed or dead – sometimes all three.
A lot of people had simply disappeared. There had been
talk that such a lengthy and successful reign of terror
could only be achieved with the help of the police. In
other words, Bernie Johns had been a protected species.
This had never been proven, though the 'report', such as
it was, made mention of some possible suspects, all based
in and around Glasgow, but none of them Francis Gray.

Johns had lived for a large part of his life in an
unassuming council house on one of the city's toughest
estates. He'd been 'a man of the people', gifting money to
local charities and benefiting everything from toddlers'
play-schemes to old people's shelters. But the giver was
also a tyrant, his munificence tempered by the knowledge
that he was paying for power and invulnerability. Anyone
came within a hundred yards of him on his home turf, he
got to know about it. Police surveillance activities were
scuppered within ten minutes of their outset. White vans
were rumbled: flats were located and attacked. Nobody
was going to get near Bernie Johns. There were plenty of
pictures of him in the folder. He was tall, broad at the
shoulders, but not physically massive. He wore fashion-
able suits, his wavy blond hair always carefully groomed.
Rebus could imagine him as a child, playing the Angel
Gabriel in his school's Christmas show. The eyes had

hardened in the interim, as had the jaw, but Johns had been a handsome man, his face sporting none of the nicks and slashes associated with longevity in a gangster.

And then Operation Clean-Cut had come along, involving several forces in a long-term surveillance and intelligence operation which had ended with a haul of several thousand tabs of ecstasy and amphetamine, four kilos of heroin, and about the same weight of cannabis. The operation had been branded a success, and Bernie Johns had been put on trial. It wasn't the first time he'd appeared in a dock. Three previous charges, all dropped due to admin cock-ups or by dint of witnesses changing their minds.

The case against him wasn't watertight this time either – the Procurator Fiscal's office had admitted as much in a letter Rebus found in the folder. It could go either way, but they would give it their best shot. Any police officer even rumoured to have had links to Johns and his gang was sidelined throughout the investigation and trial. The team kept working even through the duration of the trial, ensuring evidence wasn't changed or witnesses lost. It was only after Johns's conviction that he started complaining that he'd been shaken down and ripped off. He wasn't naming any names, but the story seemed to be that he'd been told that certain pieces of evidence could be 'contaminated'. There was a price to pay, of course, and he'd been willing to pay it. One of his men had been dispatched to fetch the money from a secret stash. (Police had found little at Johns's actual home: around five thousand in cash and a couple of unlicensed pistols.) The underling didn't come back, and when he was tracked down, he told a story that he had been followed to the site and attacked by three men – almost certainly the same people who had done the deal in the first place. They had then cleaned Johns out. Precisely how much was involved was left to the rumour mill. The best estimate of Johns's accumulated wealth was around the three million mark.

Three million pounds . . .

'Give us some names and we might start to believe you,' Johns had been told by an investigating officer. But Johns had refused. That wasn't the way he worked; never had been, never would be. The underling, meantime, was found stabbed to death near his home after a night out: the price he'd had to pay for failure. Johns was adamant that this man could not by himself have tricked him, stolen from him. The man had done a runner only because he'd been terrified of the ramifications of the theft. Three million was not the sort of figure Bernie Johns was likely to shrug off as human error.

The stabbing was proof of that.

No doubt he'd had similar fates in mind for the cops – it was assumed they were cops – who'd double-crossed him, but he never got time to put any plan into effect. He'd been stabbed in the neck with a home-made shiv – the painstakingly sharpened end of a soup spoon – by one of the inmates while queueing for breakfast. This inmate, Alfie Frazer, known to all and sundry as 'Soft Alfie', had been one of Francis Gray's snitches – which gave the investigators their first inkling of who might have been involved in ripping off Bernie Johns.

Gray had been questioned, but had denied everything. It was never made clear precisely why Soft Alfie – known to be academically challenged and never the world's most perfect physical specimen – would commit a murder. All the investigators knew was that Gray had fought hard to keep Alfie out of prison, and that it was believed Alfie owed him as a result. But Alfie had been in on a three-year stretch: was it possible he would have committed himself to a far lengthier term by murdering Johns at Gray's behest?

The only other valuable piece of the jigsaw had come when it was discovered that on the day Johns's hapless henchman had been sent to fetch the cash, three officers – Gray, McCullough and Ward – had headed out in Gray's car. Their excuse when asked about it later: they'd gone out to celebrate the end of the investigation. They named pubs they'd been in, a restaurant where they'd eaten.

This was as much as the High Hiedyins had on the three men. They hadn't proved profligate spenders, and didn't appear to have money salted away in hidden bank accounts. The last page of the report detailed Francis Gray's disciplinary record. The sheet was handwritten and unsigned. Rebus got the feeling it came from Gray's own chief constable. Reading between the lines, the personal bitterness was all too evident: 'this man has been a disgrace . . .'; 'verbal abuse of senior officers . . .'; 'drunken antics at a social occasion . . .'. It was Gray they really wanted. Whatever Rebus's own reputation, Gray had raised the crossbar. It struck Rebus that they could have turfed Gray out at any time, so why hadn't they? His reasoning: they were hanging on to Gray, waiting for an opportunity to nail him for Bernie Johns. But with retirement in the offing, they were growing desperate. In their eyes, it was time for payback . . . at any price.

Rebus dried himself off and padded through to the living room. The Blue Nile on the hi-fi, and him on his chair. Stone-cold sober and thinking hard. The file was all conjecture, rumour, stories told by old lags. All the High Heidyins had to go on was the coincidence of the trio's day-trip taking place on the same day as the supposed money pick-up; that and the death of Johns at the hands of one of Gray's snitches. All the same . . . three million . . . he could see why they wouldn't want Gray and Co. getting away with it. A cool million apiece. Rebus had to admit, they didn't look like millionaires, didn't act like them either. Why not just resign and head off to spend the loot?

Because it would have been proof of a sort, and might have helped launch a full-scale inquiry. Soft Alfie had been questioned half a dozen times in the intervening years, but hadn't said anything worthwhile. Maybe he wasn't so soft after all . . .

Again, Rebus wondered if the whole thing was part of some elaborate set-up, meant to distract him, maybe leading him to incriminate himself in the Rico Lomax case. He concentrated on the music, but The Blue Nile weren't about to help him. They were too busy singing beautiful songs about Glasgow.

Glasgow: tomorrow's destination.

He tapped his fingers in time to the music, tapped them on the cover of the folder Strathern had given him . . .

When he woke up, the CD had finished and his neck felt stiff. He'd been dreaming that he was in a restaurant with Jean. Some posh hotel somewhere, but he was wearing clothes he'd been given by Rhona during their marriage. And he had no money on him to pay for the expensive meal. He'd felt so guilty . . . guilty of betraying Rhona and Jean . . . guilty about *everything*. Someone else had been in the dream, someone who had money enough to pay for it all, and Rebus had ended up following him through the maze of the hotel, everywhere from its penthouse to the cellars. Had he been going to ask for a loan? Was the figure someone he knew? Had he been going to take the money by force or duplicity from a total stranger? Rebus didn't know. He pulled himself to his feet and stretched tiredly. Couldn't have been asleep more than twenty minutes. Then he remembered that he had to be in Tulliallan by morning.

'No time like the present,' he told himself, snatching up his car keys.

Pony-tailed Ricky was back on the door of the Sauna Paradiso.

'Christ, not you again,' he muttered, as Siobhan walked in.

She looked around. The place was dead. One of the girls

238

was lying along a sofa, reading a magazine. There was baseball on the TV monitor, the sound turned off.

'You like baseball?' Siobhan asked. Ricky didn't look in the mood for conversation. 'I watch it sometimes,' she went on, 'if I'm awake through the night. Couldn't tell you the rules or half of what the commentators are talking about, but I watch it anyway.' She looked around. 'Laura in tonight?'

He thought about lying, but knew she'd spot it. 'She's with someone,' he said.

'Mind if I wait?'

'Take your coat off, make yourself at home.' He waved his arm in an exaggerated greeting. 'If a punter comes in and wants to take you downstairs, don't go blaming me.'

'I won't,' Siobhan said, but she kept her coat on, and was glad she was wearing trousers and boots. The woman on the sofa, now that Siobhan studied her, was ten years older than she'd originally thought. Make-up, hair and clothes: they could put years on you, or take them off. She remembered when she'd been thirteen, knowing she could pass for sixteen or older. Another of the women had appeared from the curtained doorway. She gave Siobhan a look of curiosity as she moved behind Ricky's desk. There was an alcove there with a kettle. She made herself a mug of coffee and reappeared, stopping in front of Siobhan.

'Ricky says you're looking for some action.' She was in her mid-twenties with a pretty, rounded face and long brown hair. Her legs were bare, with black bra and panties visible beneath a knee-length negligee.

'Ricky's having you on,' Siobhan informed her. The woman looked in the direction of the desk and stuck her tongue out, displaying a silver stud. Then she dropped into the chair next to Siobhan's.

'Careful, Suzy, you might catch something.' This from the woman on the sofa, who was still flicking through her magazine.

Suzy looked at Siobhan. 'She means I'm a cop,' Siobhan said.

'And is she right? Am I going to catch something?'

Siobhan shrugged. 'I've been told I've got an infectious laugh.'

Suzy smiled. Siobhan noticed that she had a bruise on one shoulder which the negligee was failing to conceal. 'Quiet tonight,' Siobhan commented.

'There's always a bit of a rush after the pubs close, then it calms down again. You here to see one of the girls?'

'Laura.'

'She's got a punter with her.'

Siobhan nodded. 'How come you're talking to me?' she asked.

'Way I see it, you've got your job to do, same as I have.' Suzy held the chipped mug to her lips. 'No sense getting worked up about it. You here to arrest Laura?'

'No.'

'Asking her questions then?'

'Something like that.'

'Your accent's not Scottish . . .'

'I was brought up in England.'

Suzy was studying her. 'I had a friend sounded a bit like you.'

'Past tense?'

'This was at college. I did a year at Napier. I can't remember where she was from . . . somewhere in the Midlands.'

'That could be about right.'

'That where you're from?' Suzy was wearing frayed moccasin-style slippers. She had crossed one leg over the other and was letting one moccasin dangle from her painted toes.

'Around there,' Siobhan said. 'Do you know Laura?'

'We've worked some of the same shifts.'

'She been here long?'

Suzy stared at Siobhan, but didn't answer.

'All right then,' Siobhan said, 'what about you?'

'Nearly a year. That's me just about ready to quit. Said I'd do it for a year and no longer. I've got enough saved now to go back to college.'

The woman on the sofa snorted.

Suzy ignored her. 'You make good money in the police?'

'Not bad.'

'What . . . fifteen, twenty thousand?'

'A bit more actually.'

Suzy shook her head. 'That's nothing to what you can make in a place like this.'

'I don't think I could do it, though.'

'That's what I thought. But when college fell through . . .' She got a faraway look. The woman on the sofa was rolling her eyes. Siobhan didn't know how much of it to believe. Suzy had had nearly a year to fashion her story. Maybe it was her way of coping with the Sauna Paradiso . . .

A man suddenly came out from behind the curtain. He looked around the room, surprised to find no other men there except Ricky. Siobhan recognised him: the less drunk businessman from her previous visit, the one who'd mentioned Laura by name. With head down, he walked briskly to the front door and made his exit.

'Has he got a tab or something?' Siobhan asked.

Suzy shook her head. 'They pay us, then we settle with Ricky later.'

Siobhan looked across the desk, where Ricky was standing watching her. 'Going to let Mr Cafferty know I'm here?' she called.

'You still on about him?' Ricky grinned. 'I keep telling you, *I* own this place.'

'Sure you do,' Siobhan said, winking at Suzy.

'Another month tops, that's me out of here,' Suzy was saying, to herself more than anyone, as Siobhan got up and made for the curtained doorway.

Only one cabin had its door closed. She knocked and

opened it. She could hear a shower running. It was behind a frosted glass door. The room had a wide bench topped with a mattress, a spa bath in one corner, and not much else. Siobhan was trying not to breathe in the foetid air.

'Laura?' she called.

'Who's that?'

'It's Siobhan Clarke. All right if I wait for you outside?'

'Give me two minutes, will you?'

'No problem.'

Siobhan climbed back up the stairs. The place was still dead. 'Tell Laura I'm right outside,' she ordered Ricky. Her car was actually across the road. She sat in it, the radio playing softly, window rolled down. A few cars and taxis rumbled past. Not too far away, she knew the street-walkers were plying their trade: a trade less safe than that enacted in places like the Paradiso. Men would pay for sex: it was a fact of life. And as long as the demand was there, there'd be no shortage of suppliers. It struck Siobhan that what troubled her most about the business was that it was run *by* men *for* men, with the women themselves reduced to merchandise. Okay, so they'd maybe made the choice themselves, but for what reasons? Because there was nothing else, at least in their eyes? From desperation, or coercion? Her stomach felt tight, as though some cramp was coming on. It was a feeling she was getting more frequently these days, as though she might be about to seize up completely. She saw herself frozen like a statue, while Cafferty, Ricky and all the others got on about their business.

The door of the sauna opened and Laura stepped out. She was dressed in a tight black mini-skirt and matching sleeveless top, with knee-length black leather boots. No coat or jacket, so she was intending going back to work afterwards.

'Laura!' Siobhan called. Laura crossed the road and got into the passenger side, rubbing her arms.

'Not warm tonight,' she commented.

'Have you heard from Donny?' Siobhan asked without preamble.

Laura looked at her and shook her head.

'We took him in for questioning earlier today.' Siobhan made sure she had eye contact. 'He did a runner.'

Laura's eyes went vacant.

'He knows about your . . . arrangement,' Siobhan said quietly.

'What arrangement?'

'You and Edward Marber.'

'Oh . . .'

'Will he come after you?'

'I don't know.'

'What about Alexander?'

Laura's eyes widened. 'He wouldn't hurt Alexander!'

'But might he try to snatch him?'

'Not if he knows what's good for him!'

'Maybe we could have some officers watch your home . . .'

Laura was shaking her head. 'I don't want that. Donny won't hurt me or Alexander . . .'

'You could always ask Mr Cafferty for help,' Siobhan stated nonchalantly.

'Cafferty? I already told you . . .'

'Donny worked for Cafferty, did you know that? Maybe you could ask Cafferty to keep Donny away from you.'

'I don't know anyone called Cafferty!'

Siobhan stayed silent.

'I *don't*,' Laura persisted.

'Well then, you've nothing to worry about, have you? Maybe I wasted my time coming out here this time of night to warn you . . .'

Laura looked at her. 'I'm sorry,' she said. Then: 'And thank you.' She reached over and laid her hand on Siobhan's. 'I appreciate it.'

Siobhan nodded slowly. 'Did Suzy ever go to college?' she asked.

Laura seemed taken aback by the question. 'Suzy? I think she thought about going . . . maybe six or seven years ago.'

'Is that how long she's worked in saunas?'

'At a rough guess.'

They heard the door to the Paradiso opening. A man, his back to them, face in shadow as he disappeared inside.

'I better get going,' Laura said. 'Could be one of mine.'

'You have a lot of regulars, don't you?'

'A fair few.'

'Means you must be good.'

'Or they must be desperate.'

'Was Edward Marber desperate?'

Laura looked slighted. 'I wouldn't have said so.'

'What about the punter who was leaving as I came in? He's a regular, too, isn't he?'

'Maybe.' Becoming defensive now, opening the car door and stepping out. 'Thanks again.'

She started to cross the road. The sauna's door was opening, throwing light on to the street. The same man emerging, only now with his front to them rather than his back.

Donny Dow.

'Laura!' Siobhan called. 'Get back in the car!' At the same time she was struggling to find the door-handle, which seemed to have moved a few inches from where she normally found it. Pushed open the door and started to get out.

'Laura!' Siobhan calling out her name almost at the same time he did, their voices clashing in the air above their heads.

'Come here, you whore!'

Donny Dow rushing at Laura. Laura screaming. And in the background, a sound Siobhan would hear for the rest of the night – the sound of the lock clicking shut on the inside of the door to the Sauna Paradiso.

Dow had Laura, grabbing her shoulders, shoving her

backwards against the car. Then his arm went up and Siobhan knew, though she couldn't see it, that there was a weapon there, a blade of some sort. She launched herself across the bonnet, one hand propelling her across it so that she flew feet first, catching him low down on one side. It wasn't enough to deflect him. The knife sliced into Laura's flesh, making a soft sound almost like a mild reproach. *Tsssk!* Siobhan grabbed for the knife arm, trying to lock it behind him, while listening to an elongated gasp from Laura, the air escaping from her as blood leaked from the puncture. Dow flung his head sideways, catching Siobhan on the bridge of her nose. Tears welled in her eyes, and she momentarily lost strength.

Tsssk!

The knife again finding its target. Siobhan let go his arm and aimed her knee into his groin, connecting with all the force she could muster. Dow staggered backwards, his voice a rising complaint of pain. Siobhan watched Laura sag visibly. She was hanging on to the car's door-handle, knees buckling. There were rivulets of blood.

Got to end this now!

Siobhan aimed another kick at Dow, but he dodged it, turning full circle. The knife – it was one of those builder's blades, the kind you bought in a DIY store – was still gripped in his right hand. Siobhan filled her lungs and let out a scream, making sure he took the full force of it.

'Help, somebody! Help us here! She's dying! Donny Dow's murdered her!'

At the sound of his name, he paused. Or maybe it was the word *murdered*. He stared unblinking at Laura. Siobhan made a move towards him, but he backed away. Three, four, five steps.

'You bastard!' she shouted at him. Then she gave another scream, searing the inside of her throat. Lights were coming on in the tenement windows above the sauna. 'Nine-nine-nine . . . ambulance and police!' Faces at the windows, curtains pushed aside. Dow was still walking backwards. She had to follow him. But what about Laura? Siobhan glanced back, and as she broke eye contact Dow took his chance, jogging and swaying his way back into darkness.

Siobhan crouched beside Laura, whose lips looked almost black in the street-light, maybe because her face was so white. Going into shock. Siobhan sought the wounds. There'd be two . . . had to get pressure on them. The sauna's door stayed resolutely closed.

'Bastard,' Siobhan hissed. She couldn't see Dow any more. There was warm blood oozing from between her fingers. 'Hang on, Laura, ambulance is coming.' Her mobile was in her pocket, but she didn't have any free hands.

Shit, shit, shit!

Then one of the neighbours was standing beside her. He seemed to be asking if everything was all right.

'Put some pressure here,' she said, showing him where. Then she fumbled for her phone, as it slid away from her bloodied grasp. The man was looking horror-struck. He was in his late fifties, thin hair flapping down over his forehead. She couldn't push the numbers; her hands were shaking too much. She ran across to the sauna, gave the door a kick, then rammed it with her shoulder. Ricky opened up. He was shaking too.

'Christ . . . is she . . . ?'

'Did you call nine-nine-nine?' Siobhan asked.

He nodded. 'Ambulance and . . .' He swallowed. 'Just ambulance,' he corrected.

She thought she could hear a siren in the distance, hoped it was coming this way. 'Did you tell him she was out here?' Siobhan spat.

Ricky shook his head. 'Guy looked in a rage . . . I said she wasn't on shift . . .' He swallowed again. 'I thought he was going to do me.'

'Well, aren't you the lucky one?' Siobhan ran past the woman from the sofa, who was now standing, arms folded protectively in front of her, and found the pile of towels and robes. She could hear sobbing from the actual sauna; didn't have time to look, but knew it was Suzy, probably cowering in fear for herself. Siobhan dashed outside again, pushing towels hard against the wounds. 'Lots of pressure,' she told the man. He was sweating, looked scared, but he nodded anyway and she patted his shoulder. Laura was sitting on the ground, legs folded beneath her. Her fingers clung resolutely to the door-handle. Maybe she was remembering Siobhan's instruction: *Get back in the car!* Mere centimetres from safety . . .

'Don't die on me,' Siobhan commanded, running a hand through Laura's hair. Laura's eyelids were open a fraction, but the eyes themselves were glassy, like the marbles boys used to play with. She was breathing through her mouth, little gasps of pain. The siren was a lot closer now, and then it was rounding the corner from Commercial Street, sending sweeps of blue light across the buildings.

'They're here, Laura,' Siobhan cooed. 'You're going to be fine.'

'Just hang in there,' the man said, looking to Siobhan for reassurance that he'd said the right thing. Too many episodes of *Casualty* and *Holby City*, Siobhan thought.

You're going to be fine . . . The lie that brings no peace. The lie that only exists because the speaker needs to hear it.

Just hang in there . . .

Four in the morning.

She wished Rebus was there. He would make some joke about the song of the same name. He'd done it before when they'd been on hospital vigils, villain stakeouts. He'd sing half a misremembered verse of some country and western song. She couldn't remember the name of the original singer, but Rebus would know it. Farnon? Farley? Somebody Farnon . . .

247

These games Rebus played to take their minds off the situation. She'd thought of phoning him, but had reconsidered. This was something she had to get through on her own. She was crossing a line . . . could feel it. She wasn't at the hospital; they hadn't wanted her there. A quick shower and change of clothes at home, the patrol car waiting to take her back to St Leonard's. The Leith police would take the investigation: it was their patch. But they wanted her at St Leonard's for debriefing.

'At least you got him a good kick in the charlies,' her uniformed driver had said. 'Should slow him down a bit . . .'

She stood in her shower and wished it had a bit more pressure. The water dripped on to her. She wanted sharp needles, a pummelling, a torrent. She held her hands over her face, eyes screwed shut. She leaned against the tiled wall, then slid down it until she was crouching again, the way she'd crouched over Laura Stafford.

Who's going to tell Alexander? Mummy's dead . . . Daddy did it. It would be Grandma's job, in between the tears . . .

Who would break the news to Grandma? Someone would already be on their way out there. The body needed to be ID'd.

Her machine was flashing to let her know she had phone messages. They could wait. There were dishes in the sink needed washing. She was drying her hair with a towel as she moved through the flat. Her nose was red, and she kept needing to blow it. Her eyes were bloodshot, pink-rimmed and puffy.

The towel she dried her hair with was dark blue. *No more white towels for me . . .*

DCS Templer was waiting for her at the station. The first question was an easy one: 'Are you all right?'

Siobhan made all the right noises, but then Templer said: 'Donny Dow's an animal, works for Big Ger Cafferty.'

Siobhan wondered who'd been talking. Rebus? But then Templer explained all: 'Claverhouse told me. You know Claverhouse?' To which Siobhan nodded. 'SDEA have had their eye on Cafferty for a while,' Templer went on. 'Not getting very far, if their track record's anything to go by.'

All of which was just by way of filler, working up to the real story. 'You know she's dead?'

'Yes, ma'am.'

'Christ, Siobhan, no need for the formal stuff. It's Gill here, remember?'

'Yes . . . Gill.'

Templer nodded. 'You did what you could.'

'It wasn't enough.'

'What were you supposed to do? Set up a blood transfusion on the pavement?' Templer sighed. 'Sorry . . . that's the middle of the night talking, not me.' She ran her hands through her hair. 'Speaking of which, what were you doing down there?'

'I'd gone to warn her.'

'At that time of night?'

'Best time to find her at work, I thought.' Siobhan was answering the questions, but her mind was elsewhere. She was still on that street. The click of the lock on the sauna parlour door . . . the hand gripping her car for dear life.

Tsssk!

'Leith are handling it,' Templer said, unnecessarily. 'They'll want to talk to you.'

Siobhan nodded.

'Phyllida Hawes has gone to break the news.'

She nodded again. She was wondering if Donny Dow had bought the blade that same afternoon. There was a DIY store practically next door to St Leonard's . . .

'It was premeditated,' Siobhan stated. 'I'll say so in my report. No way that bastard's getting off with manslaughter . . .'

Templer's turn to nod. Siobhan knew what she was thinking: good lawyer behind him, Dow would push for manslaughter . . . a moment of madness . . . diminished responsibility. *My client, your honour, had only just learned that his ex-wife, the woman charged with the care of his son,*

249

*was not only a prostitute but that she was living in
accommodation provided for her and the child by one of her
clients. Faced with this revelation – a revelation made by police
officers, no less – Mr Dow fled from a police station and was
allowed to roam free, the balance of his mind affected . . .*

Dow would be lucky to serve six years.

'It was horrible,' she said, voice reduced to a whisper.

'Of course it was.' Templer reached out and took her
hand, reminding Siobhan of Laura . . . Laura so alive,
reaching out to touch her hand in the car . . .

A blunt knock at the door, and not even a wait to be
asked to enter. Siobhan could see Templer readying to tear
a strip off the intruder. It was Davie Hynds. He glanced at
Siobhan, then fixed his eyes on Templer.

'Got him,' was all he said.

Dow's story was that he had given himself up, but the
arresting officers were saying he'd resisted. Siobhan had
said she wanted to see him. He was in one of the cells
downstairs. They were waiting for him to be transferred to
Leith, where the cells were ancient and the approximate
temperature of a deep freeze all the year round. He'd been
found at Tollcross. Looked like he was heading for the
Morningside road: maybe planning to hike south out of
the city. But then Siobhan remembered that Cafferty's
lettings agency was on that same stretch of road . . .

There was a knot of officers outside his cell door. They
were laughing. Derek Linford was one of them. Linford
was rubbing his knuckles as Siobhan approached. One of
the uniforms unlocked the cell. She stood in the doorway.
Dow sat on the concrete bed with head sunk into his
chest. When he lifted it, she saw the bruising. Both eyes
were almost closed.

'Looks like you did more than kick him in the nuts,
Shiv,' Linford said, provoking more laughter. She turned
to him.

'Don't pretend you did this for *me*,' she said. The

250

laughter ceased, the smiles evaporating. 'At best, I was the excuse . . .' Then she turned to face Dow. 'But I hope it hurts. I hope it keeps on hurting. I hope you get cancer, you repellent little shit.'

The smiles were back in place, but she just walked past them . . .

18

They'd taken the Lexus. Gray knew Glasgow. Rebus could have driven them to Barlinnie: the famous Bar-L jail was on the Edinburgh side of town, just off the motorway. But Chib Kelly wasn't in Barlinnie; he was under guard at a city-centre hospital. He'd had a stroke, hence the urgency of their visit. If they wanted Chib Kelly cogent, the sooner they talked to him the better.

'He could be faking it,' Rebus said.

'He could,' Gray agreed.

Rebus was thinking of Cafferty and his miracle recovery from cancer. Cafferty's story was that he was still being treated, albeit privately. Rebus knew it was a lie.

He'd woken early with someone thumping on his door. The Donny Dow story had already reached Tulliallan. Rebus had got on the mobile, trying first Siobhan's home and then her own mobile. Recognising his number, she'd picked up.

'You all right?' he'd asked.

'Bit tired.'

'Not hurt?'

'No bruises to report.' It was a good answer; it didn't mean she wasn't hurting in other ways.

'The rough stuff is supposed to be my job,' he'd chided her, keeping his voice light.

'You're not here,' she'd reminded him, before saying goodbye.

Rebus looked out of his passenger-side window. Glasgow roads all looked the same to him. 'I always get lost, driving round here,' he confessed to Gray.

'I'm like that in Edinburgh: all those bloody narrow streets, jinking this way and that.'

'It's the one-way system here, gets me every time.'

'Easy once you know it.'

'You Glasgow-born, Francis?'

'The Lanarkshire coalfields, that's where I'm from.'

'Fife coalfields me,' Rebus said with a smile, forging this new bond between them.

Gray just nodded. He was concentrating on the world beyond his windscreen. 'Jazz said there was something you wanted to talk about,' he said.

'I'm not sure.' Rebus hesitated. 'Is that why you picked me for this trip?'

'Maybe.' Gray paused, seemed to be watching the scenery. 'Anything you want to say, better be quick. Five minutes, we'll be in the car park.'

'Maybe later,' Rebus said. *Bait the hook, John. Make sure the point drives home.*

Gray gave a half-shrug, as though he didn't care.

The hospital was a tall modern building on the north side of the city. It looked to be ailing, stonework tarnished, windows clouded with condensation. The car park was full, but Gray stopped on a double yellow, placing a card next to the windscreen stating he was a doctor on emergency call.

'Does that help?' Rebus asked.

'Sometimes.'

'Why not use a police sign?'

'Get real, John. People round here see a cop car, they're likely to christen it with a half-brick.'

The admissions desk was next door to A&E. While Gray queued to find out Chib Kelly's ward number, Rebus eyed the array of walking wounded. Cuts and bruises; down-and-outs nursing worlds made of carrier-bags; sad-faced civilians for whom this was an experience devoutly to be forgotten. Teenage boys swaggered by in packs. They seemed to know each other, patrolled the aisles as though they owned the place. Rebus checked his watch: ten a.m. on a weekday.

'Imagine it at midnight on Saturday,' Gray said, seeming to read Rebus's thoughts. 'Chib's on the third floor. Lifts are over here . . .'

The lifts opened on to a waiting area and the first person Rebus saw he recognised from the photos they had on file: Fenella, Rico Lomax's widow.

She knew them for cops straight off, and was on her feet. 'Tell them to let me see him!' she cried. 'I've got my rights!'

Gray put a finger to his lips. 'You have the right to remain silent,' he said. 'Now behave yourself and we'll see what we can do.'

'You've no business being here. My poor man's had a heart attack.'

'We heard it was a stroke.'

She started wailing again. 'How am I supposed to know what it is? They won't tell me anything!'

'*We'll* tell you something,' Gray cajoled. 'Just give us five minutes, eh?' He put his hands on her shoulders and she allowed him to push her slowly back down on to the seat.

A member of the nursing staff was watching through a narrow vertical window in the doors to the ward. As they walked towards her, she pushed the doors open.

'We're thinking of having her ejected,' she said.

'How about giving her a bit of news instead?'

The nurse glared at Gray. 'When we *have* news, we'll tell her.'

'How is he?' Rebus asked, trying to calm things down.

'He had a seizure of some kind. There's paralysis down one side.'

'Would he be able to answer some questions?' Gray asked.

'Able, yes. Willing? I'm not so sure.'

She led them past beds filled with old men and young

men. A few of the patients were on their feet, shuffling in carpet slippers along a polished linoleum floor the colour of ox blood. There was a faint smell of fried food, mingled with disinfectant. The long, narrow room was stifling. Rebus was already beginning to feel the sweat cloying on his back.

The very last bed had been closed off by curtains, behind which lay a pasty-faced man, hooked up to machines and with a drip going into one arm. He was in his early fifties, a good ten years older than the woman outside. His hair was grey, combed back from the forehead. His chin and cheeks had been shaved erratically, silver stubble flecking the skin. Seated on a chair was a prison warder. He was leafing through a tattered copy of *Scottish Field*. Rebus noticed that one of Chib Kelly's arms was hanging down the side of the bed. The wrist had been handcuffed to the iron frame.

'He's that dangerous, is he?' Gray commented, eyeing the cuffs.

'Orders,' the warder said.

Rebus and Gray showed their ID, and the warder introduced himself as Kenny Nolan.

'Nice day out for you, eh, Kenny?' Gray said conversationally.

'Thrilling,' Nolan said.

Rebus walked around the bed. Kelly had his eyes closed. There didn't seem to be any movement behind the lids, and the chest was rising and falling rhythmically.

'You asleep, Chib?' Gray said, leaning down over the bed.

'What's all this?' a voice said behind them. A doctor in a white coat was standing there, stethoscope folded into one pocket, clipboard in his hand.

'CID,' Gray explained. 'We've got a few questions for the patient.'

'Does he really need those handcuffs?' the doctor was asking Nolan.

'Orders,' Nolan repeated.

'Any particular reason?' Rebus asked the warder. He knew that Kelly could be a violent man, but he hardly looked an immediate threat to the public.

Nolan wasn't about to answer the question, so Gray stepped in. 'Barlinnie lost a couple of prisoners recently. They walked away from hospital wards just like this one.'

Rebus nodded his understanding, while Nolan reddened at his starched white shirt-collar.

'How long till he wakes up?' Gray was asking the doctor.

'Who knows?'

'Will he be in a fit state to talk to us?'

'I've really no idea.' The doctor started moving away, checking a message on his pager.

Gray looked across to Rebus. 'These doctors, eh, John? Consummate professionals.'

'The crème de la crème,' Rebus agreed.

'Mr Nolan,' Gray said, 'if I give you my number, any chance you could page me when the prisoner comes round?'

'I suppose so.'

'You sure?' Gray made eye contact. 'Want to check first to make sure it's not against orders?'

'Don't listen to him,' Rebus advised Nolan. 'He's a sarky bugger when the mood takes him.' Then, to Gray: 'Give the man your number, Francis. I'm melting in here . . .'

They told Fenella Lomax what little they could, leaving aside any mention of the handcuffs.

'He's sleeping peacefully,' Rebus tried to reassure her, regretting his choice of words immediately. They were what you said just before someone died . . . But Fenella nodded silently and allowed them to lead her down to the ground floor, in search of something to drink. There was no cafeteria as such, just an ill-stocked kiosk. Rebus, who'd skipped breakfast, bought a dry muffin and an over-ripe banana to go with his tea. The surface of the liquid was the same grey colour as all the patients they'd seen.

'You're hoping he'll die, aren't you?' Fenella Lomax said.

'Why do you say that?'

'Because you're cops. That's why you're here, isn't it?'

'On the contrary, Fenella,' Gray said. 'We want to see Chib up and about. There are a few questions we'd like to ask him.'

'What sort of questions?'

Rebus swallowed a mouthful of crumbs. 'We've re-opened the case on your late husband.'

She looked shocked. 'Eric? Why? I don't understand . . .'

'No case is ever closed until it's solved,' Rebus told her.

'DI Rebus is right,' Gray said. 'And we've been given the job of dusting off the files, see if we can add anything new.'

'What's Chib got to do with it?'

'Maybe nothing,' Rebus assured her. 'But something came to light a day or so back . . .'

'What?' Her eyes darted between the two detectives.

'Chib owned your husband's local, the one he'd been in the night he died.'

'So?'

'So we need to talk to him about it,' Rebus said.

'What for?'

'Just so the file's complete,' Gray explained. 'Maybe you could help by telling us a little yourself?'

'There's nothing to tell.'

'Well, Fenella, that's not strictly true,' Rebus told her. 'For a start, it didn't seem to come out at the time that Chib owned the bar.' Rebus waited, but she just shrugged. A woman on crutches was trying to get past their table, and Rebus moved his chair, taking him a little closer to Fenella. 'When did you and Chib become an item?'

'It was months after Eric died,' she stressed. She was a pro, knew where they were going with this.

'But you were friendly before?'

Her eyes burnt into his. 'How do you mean, "friendly"?'

Gray sat forward. 'I think he's wondering if you and Chib were maybe a bit more than friends, Fenella?' Then he leaned back again. 'It's not the sort of thing you can hide, is it? Tight-knit community like that . . . I'm guessing we'd just have to ask around and we'd find out the score.'

'Ask all you like,' she said, folding her arms. 'There's nothing to tell.'

'You must have known, though,' Gray persisted. 'Women always do, in my experience.'

'Known what?'

'Whether Chib fancied you. That's all we're talking about.'

'No it isn't,' she said coldly. 'You're talking about framing Chib for something he didn't do.'

'We just need to be sure of the relationships involved,' Rebus said quietly. 'That way, we don't go jumping to conclusions or heading off down the wrong road.' He tried to inject a bit of hurt into his voice. 'We thought you might like to help with that.'

'Eric's death is ancient history,' she stated, unfolding her arms, reaching for her cup.

'Maybe we've just got longer memories than some,' Gray said, his tone gaining more edge as his patience waned.

'What's that supposed to mean?' She lifted the cup, as if to drink from it.

'I'm sure DI Gray didn't mean to suggest . . .' But Rebus didn't get the chance to finish the sentence. She'd hurled the tea into Gray's face, and was on her feet now, walking purposefully away.

Gray was on his feet too. 'Fucking hell!' He held a handkerchief to his face, rubbing it dry. His white shirt was stained. He glanced in Fenella's direction. 'We could have her for that, couldn't we?'

Rebus was thinking back to his own tea incident . . . 'If you want to,' he said.

'Jesus, it's not like I . . .' Gray realised his pager was sounding. He checked it. 'Patient's awake,' he said.

The lifts were at the far end of the building. Both men left the table and started walking, Rebus glad to see the back of his muffin and banana.

'Let's hope she doesn't beat us to it,' he said.

Gray was nodding, shaking drips from his shoes.

In fact, there was no sign of Fenella Lomax on the ward. Someone had put some pillows behind Chib Kelly's head, and he was accepting sips of water from a nurse. Nolan stood up when Rebus and Gray approached.

'Thanks for letting us know,' Gray said. 'That's a favour I owe you.'

Nolan just nodded. He'd noticed the stained shirt, but didn't ask. Chib Kelly had finished drinking and was resting his head against the pillows, eyes closed.

'How are you feeling, Mr Kelly?' Rebus asked.

'You're CID,' the voice croaked. 'I can practically smell it off you.'

'That's because they make us all wear the same deodorant.' Rebus sat down, watching the nurse. She was saying something to Gray about letting the doctor know Kelly was awake. Gray just nodded, but as she moved away he touched Nolan's arm.

'Go keep her talking, Kenny. Give us a few extra minutes.' He winked. 'You might even get a date.'

Nolan seemed happy with the challenge. Kelly had opened one eye. Gray sat down in the warder's vacated seat.

'We need to get those cuffs off you, Chib. I'll have a word when he comes back.'

'What do you want?'

'We want to talk about a pub you used to own: the Claymore.'

'I sold it three years ago.'

259

'Wasn't it making you any money?' Rebus asked.

'It didn't fit my portfolio,' Kelly said, closing the eye again. Rebus had thought his voice hoarse from sleep, but it wasn't. Something had affected it, so that only one side of the mouth was operating a hundred per cent.

'They keep telling me a portfolio's a good thing to have,' Gray said, eyes on Rebus. 'Money we make, we may never get the chance to find out.' He winked. Rebus wondered if he was trying to tell him something . . .

'My heart's bleeding,' Kelly slurred.

'Well, you're in the right place.'

'Rico Lomax used to drink in the Claymore, didn't he?' Rebus asked the patient.

Kelly opened both eyes. He didn't look surprised, just curious. 'Rico?'

'We're doing some housework on his case,' Rebus explained. 'Just a few loose ends to tidy up . . .'

Kelly was quiet for a moment. Rebus could see Nolan at the far end of the ward, engaging the nurse in conversation.

'Rico drank in the Claymore,' Kelly acknowledged.

'And as the owner, you'd drink there too sometimes?'

'Sometimes.'

Rebus nodded, even though the patient's eyes were closing again.

'So you'd have met him?' Gray chipped in.

'I knew him.'

'And Fenella, too?' Rebus added.

Kelly opened his eyes again. 'Look, I don't know what it is you think you're trying to pull . . .'

'Like we said, it's housekeeping.'

'And what if I told you to take your feather dusters elsewhere?'

'Well, obviously we'd find that highly amusing,' Rebus said.

'About as amusing as a stroke,' Gray added. Kelly looked at him, eyes narrowing.

260

'I know you, don't I?'

'We've met once or twice.'

'You're based out at Govan.' Gray nodded. 'With all the other bent cops.' Kelly tried his best to smile with both sides of his face.

'I hope you're not suggesting that my colleague is less than honest,' Rebus said, angling for details.

'They all are,' Kelly said. Then he looked at Rebus and corrected himself. '*You* all are.'

'Were Fenella and you an item before Rico got whacked?' Gray hissed, suddenly tired of the game-playing. 'That's all we want to know.'

Kelly considered his answer. 'It wasn't till after. Not that Fenella didn't spread herself a bit thin back then, but that was because she was with the wrong man.'

'Something she didn't realise till after Rico was dead?' Rebus asked.

'Doesn't mean I killed him,' Kelly said confidently.

'Then who did?'

'What do you care? Rico's just another blip on your clear-up rate.'

Rebus ignored this. 'You say Fenella had other men: care to give us some names?'

A doctor was approaching – different one from before. 'Excuse me, gentlemen,' he was saying.

'Give us something to work with, Chib,' Rebus demanded.

Kelly had his eyes closed. The doctor was bedside now. 'If you'll just leave us for a few minutes,' he was saying.

'You're welcome to him,' Gray said. 'But take my advice, Doc: don't strain yourself . . .'

They took the lift back down, stepped outside. Rebus lit a cigarette. Gray stared at it greedily.

'Thanks for putting temptation my way.'

'Funny thing about hospitals,' Rebus said. 'I always need to smoke afterwards.'

'Give me one,' Gray held out a hand.

'You've stopped.'

'Don't be a bastard all your life.' Gray flicked his hand towards himself, and Rebus relented, offering both a cigarette and the lighter. Gray inhaled, held the smoke in his lungs, then exhaled noisily. His eyes were screwed shut in ecstasy.

'Christ, that's good,' he said. Then he examined the tip of the cigarette, let it fall from his fingers and crushed it underfoot.

'You might have nipped it and given it back,' Rebus complained.

Gray was studying his watch. 'Suppose we could head back,' he said, meaning back to Edinburgh.

'Or . . . ?'

'Or we could take that tour I was promising you. Bugger is, I can't drink if I'm driving.'

'Then we'll stick to Irn-Bru,' Rebus said.

'I suppose we could visit the Claymore, see if anyone remembers any names for us.'

Rebus nodded, but didn't say anything.

'Waste of time?' Gray asked.

'Could be.'

Gray smiled. 'Why is it I get the feeling you know more about this case than you're letting on?' Rebus concentrated on finishing his cigarette. 'That's why you were so keen at Tulliallan, wasn't it? Getting to the files before anyone else?'

Rebus nodded slowly. 'You were right about that. I didn't want my name coming up.'

'Yet you still let it happen? In fact, you *made* it happen. You could have kept that page of the report hidden . . . destroyed it even.'

'I didn't want to be in your debt,' Rebus confided.

'So what is it you know about Rico Lomax?'

'That's between me and my conscience.'

Gray snorted. 'Don't tell me you've still got one of those?'

'Dwindling to the size of my pension.' Rebus flipped his cigarette stub down a grating.

'Dickie Diamond's old girlfriend really did recognise you, didn't she?'

'I knew Dickie a bit back then.'

'I know what Jazz is thinking.'

'What?'

'He's wondering if there could be any connection with that attack at the manse.'

Rebus shrugged. 'Jazz has an active imagination.' *Don't give too much away, John,* his brain was telling him. He had to convince Gray he was dirty without giving the man too much ammo. If he incriminated himself at any turn, it was something they – the trio and the High Hiedyins both – could use against him. But Gray's mind was working away: Rebus could see it in the very way he was standing, head angled, hands in pockets.

'If you *did* have anything to do with the Rico case . . .'

'I'm not saying I did,' Rebus qualified. 'I'm saying I knew Dickie Diamond.'

Gray accepted the point. 'All the same, doesn't it strike you as quite a coincidence that we've ended up working that exact same case?'

'Except that we haven't: it's Rico Lomax we're investigating, not Dickie Diamond.'

'And there's no connection between the two?'

'I don't remember going quite that far,' Rebus said.

Gray looked at him and laughed, shaking his head slowly. 'You think the brass have got an inkling and are out to get you?'

'What do *you* think?'

Rebus was pleased and disturbed that Gray's mind was taking him down this road. Pleased because it deflected Gray's thoughts from another coincidence: namely, that of him, Jazz and Ward being thrown together into

Tulliallan, with Rebus a late and sudden recruit. Disturbed because Rebus himself was wondering about the Lomax case, too, and whether Strathern had some agenda that he was keeping to himself.

'I was talking to a couple of guys who've been on our course before,' Gray said. 'Know what they told me?'

'What?'

'Tennant always uses the same case. Not an unsolved: a murder that happened in Rosyth a few years back. They got the guy. That's the case he always uses for his syndicates.'

'But not for us,' Rebus stated.

Gray nodded. 'Makes you think, eh? A case both you and I worked . . . what're the chances?'

'Think we should ask him?'

'I doubt he'd tell us. But it does make you wonder, doesn't it?' He came up close to Rebus. 'How far do you trust me, John?'

'Hard to tell.'

'Should I trust you?'

'Probably not. Everyone will tell you what an arse I can be.'

Gray smiled for effect, but his eyes remained bright, calculating orbs. 'Are you going to tell me what it was you couldn't tell Jazz?'

'There's a price attached.'

'And what's that?'

'I want the tour first.'

Gray seemed to think he was joking, but then he started nodding slowly. 'Okay,' he said. 'You've got a deal.'

They walked back to the car, where someone had attached a parking ticket to Gray's windscreen. He tore it off.

'Merciless bastards!' he growled, looking around for the culprit. There was no one in view. The DOCTOR ON CALL badge was still visible on the dashboard. 'That's Glasgow for you, eh?' Gray said, unlocking the car and getting in.

'A city full of Prods and Tims, each and every one of them a callous, godless bastard.'

It wasn't what you'd call the city's tourist route. Govan, Cardonald, Pollok and Nitshill . . . Dalmarnock, Bridgeton, Dennistoun . . . Possilpark and Milton . . . There was an almost hypnotic sameness to a lot of the streets. Rebus let his eyes drift out of focus. Tenement walls, play-parks, corner shops. Kids watchful but bored. Now and then Gray would relate some story or incident – no doubt with embellishments collected over the years of telling. He provided thumbnail sketches of villains and heroes, hard men and their women. In Bridgeton, they passed the ground of Celtic FC: Parkhead to civilians like Rebus; Paradise to the club's supporters.

'This'll be the Catholic end of town then,' Rebus commented. He knew that the Rangers stadium – Ibrox – was practically next door to Govan, where Gray was stationed. So he added: 'And you'll be a blue-nose?'

'I support Rangers,' Gray agreed. 'Have done all my life. Are you a Hearts man?'

'I'm not really anything.'

Gray looked at him. 'You must be something.'

'I don't go to games.'

'What about when you watch on TV?' Rebus just shrugged. 'I mean, there's only two teams playing at any one time . . . you must take *sides*?'

'Not really.'

'Say it was Rangers against Celtic . . .' Gray was growing annoyed. 'You're a Protestant, right?'

'What's that got to do with it?'

'Well, Christ's sake, man, you'd be on Rangers' side, wouldn't you?'

'I don't know, they've never asked me to play.'

Gray let out a snort of frustration.

'See,' Rebus went on, 'I didn't realise it was meant to be religious warfare . . .'

'Fuck off, John.' Gray concentrated on his driving.

Rebus laughed. 'At least I know now how to wind you up.'

'Just don't wind the mechanism too tight,' Gray cautioned. He saw a sign for the M8. 'Time to head back yet, or do you want to stop somewhere?'

'Let's go back into town and find a pub.'

'Finding a pub should present no major difficulties,' Gray said, indicating right.

They ended up in the Horseshoe Bar. It was central and crowded with people who took their drinking seriously, the kind of place where no one looked askance at a tea-stained shirt, so long as the wearer had about him the price of his drink. Rebus knew immediately that it would be a place of rules and rituals, a place where regulars would know from the moment they walked through the door that their drink of preference was already being poured for them. It had gone twelve, and the fixed-price lunch of soup, pie and beans, and ice-cream was doing a roaring trade. Rebus noticed that a drink was included in the price.

They each opted for pie and beans – no starters or dessert. There was a corner table just emptying, so they claimed it. Two pints of IPA: as Gray had argued, they could manage one pint apiece, surely.

'Cheers,' Rebus said. 'And thanks for the tour.'

'Were you impressed?'

'I saw places I'd never been before. Glasgow's a maze.'

'Jungle would be a better description.'

'You like working here, though.'

'I can't imagine living anywhere else.'

'Not even when you retire?'

'Not really.' Gray took a mouthful of beer.

'You'll be on full pension, I suppose.'

'Not long now.'

'I've thought about retiring,' Rebus confessed, 'but I'm not sure what I'd do with myself.'

'They'll turf you out one day.'

Rebus nodded. 'I suppose they will.' He paused. 'That's why I've been thinking of supplementing my pension.'

Gray knew they were at long last coming to the point. 'And how will you do that?'

'Not on my own.' Rebus looked around, as though someone in the noisy bar might be listening in. 'Could be I'll need some help.'

'Help to do what?'

'Knock off a couple of hundred grand's worth of drugs.' There, it was out. The single, mad bloody scheme he could think of . . . something to snare the trio and maybe even manoeuvre them away from Rico Lomax . . .

Gray stared at him, then burst out laughing. Rebus's face didn't change. 'Jesus, you're serious,' Gray eventually said.

'I think it can be done.'

'You must have put your arse on backwards this morning, John: you're supposed to be one of the good guys.'

'I'm one of the Wild Bunch, too.'

The smile had left Gray's face by degrees. He stayed quiet, sipped at his drink. Their food arrived, and Rebus squirted brown sauce on to his pie-crust.

'Christ, John,' Gray said. Rebus didn't answer. He wanted to give Gray time. After he'd demolished half the pie, he put down his fork.

'You remember I got called out of class?' Gray nodded, not about to interrupt. 'There were these two SDEA men downstairs. They took me back into Edinburgh. There was something they wanted to show me: a drug bust. They've got it tucked away in a warehouse. Thing is, they're the only ones who know about it.'

Gray's eyes narrowed. 'How do you mean?'

'They haven't told Customs. Or anyone else for that matter.'

'That doesn't make sense.'

'They're trying to use it as leverage. There's someone they want to get to.'

'Big Ger Cafferty?'

It was Rebus's turn to nod. 'They're not going to get him, but they haven't quite realised it yet. And meantime, the dope is just sitting there.'

'But protected?'

'I assume so. I don't know what security's like.'

Gray grew thoughtful. 'They showed you this stuff?'

'A chemist was grading it at the time.'

'Why did they show it to you?'

'Because they wanted to do a trade. I was the intermediary.' Rebus paused. 'I don't really want to get into it . . .'

'But if someone lifts the consignment, it has to be you. Who else have they shown it to?'

'I don't know.' Rebus paused. 'But I don't think I'd be their number one suspect.'

'Why not?'

'Because word is, Cafferty knows about it too.'

'So he might make a bid to get to it first?'

'Which is why we'd have to act fast.'

Gray held up a hand, trying to stem Rebus's enthusiasm. 'Don't go saying "we".'

Rebus bowed his head in a show of repentance. 'The beauty of it is, they'll lift Cafferty for it. Especially if he finds himself with a kilo or so planted on him . . .'

Gray's eyes widened. 'You've got it all figured out.'

'Not all of it. But enough to be going on with. Are you in?'

Gray ran a finger down the condensation on his glass. 'What makes you think I'd help? Or Jazz, come to that?'

Rebus shrugged, tried to look disappointed. 'I just thought . . . I don't know. It's a lot of money.'

'Maybe it is, if you can shift the drugs. Something like that, John . . . you'd have to range far and wide, selling a bit at a time. Very dangerous.'

'I could sit on them a while.'

'And watch them go stale? Drugs are like pies: at their best when fresh.'

'I bow to your superior knowledge.'

Gray grew thoughtful again. 'Have you ever tried anything like this before?'

Rebus shook his head, eyes fixing on Gray's. 'Have you?'

Gray didn't answer. 'And you just thought this up?'

'Not straight away . . . I've been looking for something for a while, some way of making sure I could kiss the job goodbye in style.' Rebus noticed their glasses were empty. 'Same again?'

'Better get me a softie if I'm driving.'

Rebus approached the bar. He had to work hard not to turn around and study Gray. He was trying to look nonchalant but excited. He was a cop who'd just stepped over the line. Gray had to *believe* him . . . had to believe in the *scheme*.

It was the only one Rebus had.

He bought a whisky for himself, something with which to toast his new-found bravado. Gray had wanted an orange and lemonade. Rebus placed it before him.

'There you go,' he said, sitting down.

'You'll appreciate,' Gray said, 'that this dream of yours is pure mental?'

Rebus shrugged, placed his glass to his nose and pretended to savour the aroma, even though his mind was so stretched he couldn't smell anything.

'What if I say no?' Gray asked.

Rebus shrugged again. 'Maybe I don't need any help after all.'

Gray smiled sadly and shook his head. 'I'm going to tell you something,' he began, lowering his voice a little. 'I pulled off something a while back. Maybe not as grand as this . . . but I got away with it.'

Rebus felt his heart lift. 'What was it?' he asked. But

Gray shook his head, not about to answer. 'Were you alone, or did you have help?' Gray's head continued its slow arc: not telling.

Was it Bernie Johns and his millions? Rebus ached to ask the question. Stop this stupid game and just *ask*! He was holding the glass, trying to appear relaxed, and all the time he felt it might splinter in his grasp. He stared down at the table, willing himself to place the glass there, nice and slow. But his hand didn't move. Half his brain was warning him: you'll smash it, you'll drop it, your hand will shake the contents out of it . . . *Maybe not as grand as this* . . . What did that mean? Was Johns's stash disappointing, or did he just not want Rebus to know?

'You got away with it, that's the main thing,' he said, his throat just loose enough to form recognisable words. He tried a cough. It felt like invisible fingers were busy squeezing, just beneath the skin.

I'm losing this, he thought.

'You all right?' Gray asked.

Rebus nodded, finally putting down his glass. 'It just feels . . . I'm a bit edgy. You're the only person I've told – what if I can't trust you?'

'Should've thought of that first.'

'I *did* think of it first. It's just that I'm having second thoughts.'

'Bit late for that, John. It's not your idea any longer. It's out in the public domain.'

'Unless I take you outside . . .'

He left it for Gray to finish the thought: 'And kill me with a baseball bat? Like what happened to Rico?' Gray broke off, gnawed his bottom lip. 'What *did* happen to him, John?'

'I don't know.'

Gray stared at him. 'Come on . . .'

'I really don't know, Francis. On my kid's life.' Rebus held his hand to his heart.

'I thought you knew.' Gray seemed disappointed.

You bastard . . . did Strathern plant you? Are you feeding me a line about Bernie Johns so that I'll spill the beans about Rico . . . ?

'Sorry,' was all John Rebus said, sitting on his hands to stop them shaking.

Gray took a mouthful of the fizzy drink, stifled a belch. 'Why me?'

'How do you mean?'

'Why tell me? Do I *look* that corruptible?'

'As it happens, yes.'

'And what if I run back to Archie Tennant, tell him what you've just said?'

'There's nothing he can do,' Rebus guessed. 'No law against having a dream, is there?'

'But this isn't just a dream, is it, John?'

'That depends.'

Gray was nodding. Something in his face had changed. He'd come to some decision. 'Tell you what,' he said. 'I like listening to this dream of yours. What about if you fill in some of the spaces on the drive back to base?'

'Which spaces exactly?'

'Where this warehouse is . . . who might be guarding it . . . what sorts of drugs we're talking about.' Gray paused. 'Those'll do for starters.'

'Fair enough,' Rebus said.

19

Siobhan had slept in, phoning to apologise as she waited for the water in the shower to run hot. No one at the station seemed too worried by her absence. She told them she was coming in, no matter what. She'd forgotten about her scalp until the water hit it, after which her bathroom was filled with the sound of cursing.

Donny Dow had been transferred to Leith, and she made that her first stop. DI Bobby Hogan went over the statement she'd made last night. It didn't need any changes.

'Do you want to see him?' he asked afterwards.

She shook her head.

'Two of your guys – Pryde and Silvers – will be sitting in on our interviews.' Hogan was pretending to busy himself writing a note. 'They're going to tie him to Marber.'

'Good for them.'

'You don't agree?' He'd stopped writing, his eyes lifting to meet hers.

'If Donny Dow killed Marber, it was because he knew about Marber's relationship with Laura. So why did Dow explode when told about it by Linford?'

Hogan shrugged. 'If I put my mind to it, I could come up with a dozen explanations.' He paused. 'You can't deny, it would be nice and neat.'

'And how often does a case end like that?' she said sceptically, rising to her feet.

At St Leonard's, the talk was all about Dow . . . except for Phyllida Hawes. Siobhan bumped into her in the corridor, and Hawes signalled towards the women's toilets.

When the door had closed behind them, Hawes confessed that she had gone out with Allan Ward the previous evening.

'How did it go?' Siobhan asked quietly, lowering her voice and hoping Hawes would follow suit. She was remembering Derek Linford, listening outside the door.

'I had a really good time. He's pretty hunky, isn't he?' Hawes had ceased to be a CID detective: they were supposed to be two women now, gossiping about men.

'Can't say I've noticed,' Siobhan stated. Her words had no effect on Hawes, who was studying her own face in the mirror.

'We went to that Mexican place, then a couple of bars.'

'And did he see you home like a gentleman?'

'Actually, he did . . .' She turned to Siobhan and grinned. 'The swine. I was just about to invite him up for coffee, and his mobile rang. He said he had to hotfoot it back to Tulliallan.'

'Did he say why?'

Hawes shook her head. 'I think he was pretty close to not going. But all I got was a peck on the cheek.'

Known, Siobhan couldn't help thinking, as the kiss-off. 'You seeing him again?'

'Hard not to when we're both in the same station.'

'You know what I mean.'

Hawes giggled. Siobhan had never know her so . . . was coquettish the right word? She seemed suddenly ten years younger, and distinctly prettier. 'We're going to arrange something,' she admitted.

'So what did the pair of you find to talk about?' Siobhan was curious to know.

'The job mostly. The thing is, Allan's a really good listener.'

'So mostly you were talking about you?'

'Just the way I like it.' Hawes was leaning back against

the sink, arms folded, legs crossed at the ankles, looking pleased with herself. 'I told him about Gayfield, and how I'd been seconded to St Leonard's. He wanted to know all about the case . . .'

'The Marber case?'

Hawes nodded. 'What part I was playing . . . how it was all going . . . We drank margheritas – you could buy them by the jug.'

'How many jugs did you get through?'

'Just the one. Didn't want him taking advantage, did I?'

'Phyllida, I'd say you *definitely* wanted him taking advantage.'

Both women were smiling. 'Yeah, definitely,' Hawes agreed, giggling again. Then she gave a long sigh, before a look of shock came over her face and she slapped a hand to her mouth.

'Oh God, Siobhan, I haven't asked about *you*!'

'I'm okay,' Siobhan said. It was the reason she thought Hawes had brought her in here: Laura's murder.

'But it must have been horrible . . .'

'I don't really want to think about it.'

'Have they offered you counselling?'

'Christ, Phyl, why would I need that?'

'To stop you bottling things up.'

'But I'm *not* bottling things up.'

'You just said you didn't want to think about it.'

Siobhan was becoming irritated. The reason she didn't want to think about Laura's death was that she had something else niggling away at her now: Allan Ward's interest in the Marber case.

'Why do you think Allan was so interested in your work?' she asked.

'He wanted to know all about me.'

'But specifically the Marber case?'

Hawes looked at her. 'What are you getting at?'

Siobhan shook her head. 'Nothing, Phyl.' But Hawes was looking curious, and a little worried. Would she go straight to Ward and start blabbing? 'Maybe you're right,' Siobhan pretended to concede. 'I'm getting worked up about stuff . . . I think it's because of what happened.'

'Of course it is.' Hawes took her arm. 'I'm here if you need someone to talk to, you know that.'

'Thanks,' Siobhan said, offering what she hoped was a convincing smile.

As they walked back to the office together, her mind turned again to the scene outside the Paradiso. The lock clicking: she hadn't said anything to Ricky Ponytail about it . . . but she would. She'd replayed the event so many times in the past few hours, wondering how she could have helped. Maybe leaning over to the passenger-side door, pushing it open for Laura, so that she could simply fall backwards into the car before Dow got to her . . . being faster out of the driving seat herself, faster across the bonnet . . . tackling Dow more effectively. She should have disabled him straight away . . . Shouldn't have let Laura lose so much blood . . .

Got to push it all aside, she thought.

Think about Marber . . . Edward Marber. Another victim seeking her attention. Another ghost in need of justice. Rebus had confessed to her once, after too many late-night drinks in the Oxford Bar, that he saw ghosts. Or didn't see them, so much as sense them. All the cases, the innocent – and not so innocent – victims . . . all those lives turned into CID files . . . They were always more than that to him. He'd seemed to see it as a failing, but Siobhan hadn't agreed.

We wouldn't be human if they didn't get to us, she'd told him. His look had stilled her with its cynicism, as if he was saying that 'human' was the one thing they weren't supposed to be.

She looked around the inquiry room. The team was hard at work: Hood, Linford, Davie Hynds . . . When they saw her, they asked how she was. She fended off their concern, noting that Phyllida Hawes was blushing:

ashamed not to have had the same reaction. Siobhan wanted to tell her it was okay. But Hynds was hovering by her desk, needing a word. Siobhan sat down, slipping her jacket over the back of the chair.

'What is it?' she asked.

'It's the money you asked me to look for.'

She stared at him. *Money? What money?*

'Laura Stafford thought Marber was in line for some big pay-out,' Hynds explained, seeing her confusion.

'Oh, right.' She was noting that someone had been using her desk in her absence: coffee rings, a few loose paper-clips. Her in-tray was full, but looked as though it had been disturbed. She remembered Gray, flicking through case-notes . . . and others from Rebus's team, wandering through the room . . . And Allan Ward, asking Phyllida about the inquiry . . .

Her computer monitor was switched off. When she switched it on, little fish swam across the screen. A new screen-saver – not the scrolling message. It looked as if her anonymous gremlin had taken pity on her.

She only realised that Hynds had been saying something when he stopped. The silence drew her attention back to him.

'Sorry, Davie, I didn't catch that.'

'I can come back,' he said. 'Can't be easy for you, coming in today like this . . .'

'Just tell me what it was you were saying.'

'You sure?'

'Bloody hell, Davie . . .' She picked up a pencil. 'Have I got to stab you with this?' He stared at her, and she stared back, suddenly aware of what she'd said. She watched the way her hand was holding the pencil . . . holding it like a knife. 'Christ,' she gasped, 'I'm sorry . . .'

'Don't be.'

She dropped the pencil, picked up the receiver instead. She signalled for Hynds to wait while she made the call to Bobby Hogan.

'It's Siobhan Clarke,' she said into the mouthpiece. 'Something I forgot: the blade Dow used . . . there's a DIY shop next door to here. Maybe that's where he bought it. They'll have security cameras . . . could be staff will recognise him.' She listened to Hogan's response. 'Thank you,' she said, putting the receiver down again.

'Have you had any breakfast?' Hynds asked.

'I was just about to ask the same thing.' It was Derek Linford. The look of concern on his face was so exaggerated, Siobhan had to suppress a shiver.

'I'm not hungry,' she told both men. Her phone buzzed and she picked it up. The switchboard wanted to transfer a call. It was from someone called Andrea Thomson.

'I've been asked to call you,' Thomson said. 'I'm a . . . well, I hesitate to use the word counsellor.'

'You're supposed to be a career analyst,' Siobhan said, stopping Thomson in her tracks.

'Someone's been talking,' she said after a long silence. 'You work with DI Rebus, don't you?'

Siobhan had to admit, Thomson was sharp. 'He told me you'd denied being a counsellor.'

'Some officers don't like the idea.'

'Count me among them.' Siobhan glanced at Hynds, who was gesturing encouragement. Linford was still trying for the sympathetic look, not quite getting it right. Lack of practice, Siobhan guessed.

'You might find that it helps to talk through the issues,' Thomson was saying.

'There aren't any issues,' Siobhan replied coldly. 'Look, Ms Thomson, I've got a murder case to be getting on with . . .'

'Let me give you my number, just in case.'

Siobhan sighed. 'Okay then, if it'll make you feel better.'

Thomson started reeling off two numbers: office and mobile. Siobhan just sat there, making no effort to record them. Thomson's voice died away.

'You're not writing them down, are you?'

'Oh, I've got them, don't you worry.'

Hynds was shaking his head, knowing damned well what was going on. He lifted the pencil and held it out to her.

'Give them to me again,' Siobhan told the receiver. Call finished, she held up the scrap of paper for Hynds to see.

'Happy?'

'I'll be happier if you eat something.'

'Me too,' Derek Linford said.

Siobhan looked at Andrea Thomson's phone numbers. 'Derek,' she said, 'Davie and I have got to have a meeting. Can you take any messages for me?' She started shrugging her arms back into her jacket.

'Where will you be?' Linford asked, trying not to sound peeved. 'In case we need you . . .'

'You've got my mobile number,' she told him. 'That's where I'll be.'

They went around the corner of the station and into the Engine Shed. Hynds admitted he hadn't known it was there.

'It really was an engine shed,' she told him, 'Steam engines, I suppose. They pulled goods trains . . . coal or something. There are still bits of the railway line, they run down to Duddingston.'

In the café, they bought tea and cakes. Siobhan took one bite and realised she was starving.

'So what is it you've found?' she asked.

Hynds was primed to tell the story. She could see he'd been keeping it to himself, not wanting to dilute its effect before she heard it.

'I was talking to Marber's various financial people: bank manager, accountant, book-keeper . . .'

'And?'

'And no hint of any large amount about to accrue.' Hynds paused, as though uncertain whether 'accrue' was the right word.

'And?'

'And I started looking at debits instead. These are listed in his bank statements by cheque number. No clue as to who each cheque was paid to.' Siobhan nodded her understanding. 'Which is probably why one debit slipped by without us noticing.' He paused again, his meaning clear: for *us* read *Linford* . . . 'Five thousand pounds. The book-keeper found the cheque stub but the only thing written there was the amount.'

'Business cheque or personal?'

'The money was drawn from one of Marber's personal accounts.'

'And you know who it was to?' She decided to take a guess. 'Laura Stafford?'

Hynds shook his head. 'Remember our artist friend . . . ?'

She looked at him. 'Malcolm Neilson?' Hynds was nodding. 'Marber gave Neilson five grand? When was this?'

'Only a month or so back.'

'It could have been payment for a work.'

Hynds had already thought of this. 'Marber doesn't represent Neilson, remember? Besides, anything like that would have gone through the business. No need to tuck it away where no one would see it.'

Siobhan was thinking hard. 'Neilson was outside the gallery that night.'

'Looking for more money?' Hynds guessed.

'You think he was blackmailing Marber?'

'Either that or selling him something. I mean, how often do you have a blazing row with someone, then pay them a four-figure sum for the privilege?'

'And what exactly was he selling him?' Siobhan had forgotten all about her hunger. Hynds nodded towards the cake, willing her to finish it.

'Maybe that's the question we should be asking him,' he said. 'Just as soon as you've cleared your plate . . .'

*

Neilson appeared at St Leonard's with his solicitor, as requested by Siobhan. Both interview rooms were empty: Rebus's crew were said to be touring caravan sites. Siobhan sat down in IR2, taking the same seat Linford had been in yesterday when Donny Dow had made his escape.

Neilson and William Allison sat opposite her, Davie Hynds to her side. They'd decided to tape the meeting. It could put pressure on the subject; sometimes they got nervous around microphones ... knew that whatever they said could come back to haunt them.

'It's for your benefit as much as ours,' Siobhan had explained, this being the standard line. Allison made sure that there'd be two copies, one for CID and one for his client.

Then they got down to business. Siobhan switched the tape machines on and identified herself, asking the others present to do the same. She studied Malcolm Neilson as he spoke. The artist sat with eyebrows raised, as though surprised to find himself suddenly transported to such surroundings. His hair was its usual wild self, and he was wearing a thick, loose cotton shirt over a grey T-shirt. Whether by accident or design, he had buttoned the shirt wrongly, so one side was lower than the other at the neck.

'You've already told us, Mr Neilson,' Siobhan kicked off, 'that you were outside the gallery the night Edward Marber died.'

'Yes.'

'Remind us why you were there.'

'I was curious about the show.'

'No other reason?'

'Such as?'

'You only have to answer the questions, Malcolm,' Allison interrupted. 'You don't need to add your own.'

'Well, since Mr Neilson *has* asked the question,' Siobhan said, 'perhaps I can let my colleague answer.'

Hynds opened the slim manilla folder in front of him

and slid a photocopy of the cheque across the desk. 'Would you care to enlighten us?' was all he said.

'DC Hynds,' Siobhan said, providing commentary for the tapes, 'is showing Messrs Neilson and Allison a copy of a cheque, made out in the sum of five thousand pounds to Mr Neilson and dated one calendar month ago. The cheque is signed by Edward Marber and comes from his personal bank account.'

There was silence in the room when she finished.

'Might I consult with my client?' Allison asked.

'Interview paused at eleven forty hours,' Siobhan said curtly, stopping the machine.

It was times like this she wished she smoked. She stood with Hynds outside IR2, tapping her foot against the floor and a pen against her teeth. Bill Pryde and George Silvers arrived back from Leith and were able to report on their first full interview with Donny Dow.

'He knows he's going down for his wife,' Silvers said. 'But he swears he didn't kill Marber.'

'Do you believe him?' Siobhan asked.

'He's a bad bastard . . . I never believe anything those kind tell me.'

'He's in a bit of a state about his wife,' Pryde commented.

'That really tugs my heart-strings,' Siobhan said coldly.

'Are we going to charge him with Marber?' Hynds asked. 'Only, we've got another suspect in there . . .'

'In which case,' a new voice added, 'what are you doing out here?' It was Gill Templer. They'd told her they wanted to bring in Neilson, and she'd agreed. Now she stood with hands on hips, legs apart, a woman who wanted results.

'He's consulting with his lawyer,' Siobhan explained.

'Has he said anything yet?'

'We've only just shown him the cheque.'

Templer shifted her focus to Pryde. 'Any joy down in Leith?'

'Not exactly.'

She exhaled noisily. 'We need to start making some progress.' She was keeping her voice low, so the lawyer and painter wouldn't hear, but there was no missing the sense of urgency and frustration.

'Yes, ma'am,' Davie Hynds said, turning his head as the door to IR2 swung open. William Allison was standing there.

'We're ready now,' he said. Siobhan and Hynds retreated back inside.

With door closed and tapes running, they sat across the desk once more. Neilson was pushing his hands through his hair, making it stick up at ever more ungainly angles. They waited for him to speak.

'When you're ready, Malcolm,' the lawyer prodded.

Neilson leaned back in his chair, eyes staring ceiling-wards. 'Edward Marber gave me five thousand pounds to stop being a nuisance to him. He wanted me to shut up and go away.'

'Why was that?'

'Because people were starting to listen to me when I spoke about him being a cheat.'

'Did you ask him for the money?'

Neilson shook his head.

'We need it out loud for the tape,' Siobhan prompted.

'I didn't ask him for anything,' Neilson said. 'It was him that came to me. He only offered a thousand at first, but eventually it went up to five.'

'And you were at the gallery that night because you wanted more?' Hynds asked.

'No.'

'You wanted to see how well the show was doing,' Siobhan stated. 'That might suggest that you were wondering whether there was any more money to be made out of your nuisance value. After all, you'd accepted the money, and there you were still hassling Marber.'

'If I'd wanted to hassle him, I'd have gone in, wouldn't I?'

'Then maybe all you wanted was a quiet word . . . ?'

Neilson was shaking his head vigorously. 'I didn't go near the man.'

'But you did.'

'I mean I didn't *speak* to him.'

'You were happy with the five?' Hynds asked.

'I won't say happy . . . but it was a kind of vindication. I took it because it represented five thousand of crooked money that *he* wouldn't be spending.' The artist's hands went to the sides of his face, making a rasping sound against a day's growth of beard.

'How did you feel when you heard he was dead?' The question came from Siobhan. Neilson locked eyes with her.

'I got a bit of a kick out of it, if I'm being honest. I know that's hardly the humane response, but all the same . . .'

'Did you wonder if we'd start looking into your relationship with Mr Marber?' Siobhan asked.

Neilson nodded.

'Did you wonder if we'd find out about this payment?'

Another nod.

'So why didn't you just tell us?'

'I knew how it would look.' Sounding sheepish now.

'And how do you think it looks?'

'It looks as though I had motive, means and whatever.' His eyes never left hers. 'Isn't that right?'

'If you didn't do anything, there's no reason to worry,' she said.

He angled his head. 'You've got an interesting face, Detective Sergeant Clarke. Do you think I might paint you, when this is finished?'

'Let's concentrate on the present, Mr Neilson. Tell us about the cheque. How was the eventual sum reached? Was it posted to you or did you meet?'

*

Afterwards, Hynds and Siobhan bought themselves a late lunch at a baker's. Filled rolls, cans of drink from the fridge. The day was warm, overcast. Siobhan felt like taking another shower, but really it was the inside of her head she wanted to sluice, ridding it of all the confusion. They decided to walk back to St Leonard's the long way round, eating as they went.

'Take your pick,' Hynds said. 'Donny Dow or Neilson.'

'Why not both of them?' Siobhan mused. 'Neilson watching Edward Marber, alerting Dow when Marber's taxi arrived.'

'The two of them in cahoots?'

'And while we're stirring the pot, let's add Big Ger Cafferty, not a man you want to be found ripping off.'

'I can't see Marber conning Cafferty. Like you say, it's too fraught.'

'Anyone else with a grudge?'

'What about Laura Stafford? Maybe she got sick of their arrangement . . . maybe Marber wanted to take things a bit further.' Hynds paused. 'What about Donny Dow as Laura's pimp?'

Siobhan's face fell. 'That's enough,' she snapped.

Hynds realised he'd said the wrong thing. He watched as she tossed the rest of her roll into a bin, brushed crumbs and flour from her front.

'You should talk to someone,' he said quietly.

'Counselling, you mean? Do me a favour . . .'

'I'm trying to. Seems like you don't want to listen.'

'I've seen people killed before, Davie. How about you?' She had stopped to face him.

'We're supposed to be partners,' he said, sounding aggrieved.

'We're supposed to be senior and junior officer . . . sometimes I think you get muddled over who's who.'

'Christ, Shiv, I was only—'

'And don't call me Shiv!'

He made to say something further, but seemed to think

better of it, took a swig of his drink instead. After a dozen paces, he took a deep breath.

'Sorry.'

She looked at him. 'Sorry for what?'

'For making jokes about Laura.'

Siobhan nodded slowly; a little of the tension left her face. 'You're learning, Davie.'

'I'm trying.' He paused. 'Truce?' he suggested.

'Truce,' she agreed. After which, they resumed their walk in a silence that could almost have been called companionable.

When Rebus and Gray got back to the station, IR1 was full. The rest of the team had split into two pairs, spent the day hitting the east coast's caravan parks, talking to the site owners, long-term users and residents. Now they were back . . . and weary.

'Didn't know there were static parks,' Allan Ward said. 'People living in these four-berth jobs like they were proper houses, little flowerbeds outside and a kennel for the Alsatian.'

'Way house prices are going,' Stu Sutherland added, 'could be the wave of the future.'

'Must be freezing in winter, though,' Tam Barclay said.

DCI Tennant was listening to all this with arms folded, as he leaned against the wall. He turned slowly towards Rebus and Gray. 'I hope to Christ you two have got something more for me than property speculation and gardening tips.'

Gray ignored him. 'You didn't get anything?' he asked Jazz McCullough.

'Bits and pieces,' Jazz answered. 'It *was* six years ago. People move on . . .'

'We spoke to the owner of one site,' Ward said. 'He hadn't been there when Rico was around, but he'd heard stories: all-night parties, boozed-up arguments. Rico used two caravans on that site ... supposedly with another two or three elsewhere.'

'Are the caravans still there?' Gray asked.

'One of them is; other went on fire.'

'Went on fire or was *set* on fire?'

Ward shrugged a response.

'You see why I'm impressed?' Tennant announced. 'So bring me glad tidings from dear old Glasgow town.'

It only took Gray and Rebus five minutes to summarise their trip, leaving out everything except the hospital visit. At the end of it, Tennant looked less than cheered.

'If I didn't know better,' he told them, 'I'd say you lot were pissing into the wind.'

'We've hardly started,' Sutherland complained.

'My point exactly.' Tennant wagged a finger at him. 'Too busy enjoying the good life, not busy *enough* doing the work you're supposed to be here for.' He paused. 'Maybe it's not your fault; maybe there's nothing here for us to find.'

'Back to Tulliallan?' Tam Barclay guessed.

Tennant was nodding. 'Unless you can think of a reason to stay put.'

'Dickie Diamond, sir,' Sutherland said. 'There are friends of his we still need to talk to. We've got feelers out with a local snitch . . .'

'Meaning all you're doing here is waiting?'

'There's one other avenue, sir,' Jazz McCullough said. 'At the time Diamond went AWOL, there was that rape case at the manse.' Rebus concentrated hard on the room's mud-coloured carpet-tiles.

'And?' Tennant prodded.

'And nothing, sir. It's just a coincidence that might be worth following up.'

'You mean in case Diamond had anything to do with it?'

'I know it sounds thin, sir . . .'

'Thin? You could use it as a pizza topping.'

'Maybe just another day or two, sir,' Gray advised. 'There are some loose ends we could do with tying up, and since we're already here,' he glanced towards Rebus, 'with an expert to guide us . . .'

'Expert?' Tennant's eyes narrowed.

Gray had slapped a hand on to Rebus's shoulder. 'When it comes to Edinburgh, sir, John knows where the bodies are buried. Isn't that right, John?'

Tennant considered this, while Rebus said nothing. Then Tennant unfolded his arms, stuck his hands in the pockets of his suit jacket. 'I'll think about it,' he said.

'Thank you, sir.'

After Tennant had left the room, Rebus turned to Gray. 'I know where the bodies are buried?'

Gray shrugged, gave a little laugh. 'Isn't that what you told me? Metaphorically speaking, of course.'

'Of course.'

'Unless you know different . . . ?'

Later that afternoon, Rebus stood by the drinks machine, considering his options. He had a handful of change, but his mind was on other things. He was wondering who to tell about the heist scheme. The Chief Constable, for instance. Strathern wouldn't know about the warehouse stash, he was sure of that. Claverhouse had gone to Carswell, the Assistant Chief. The two of them were mates, and Carswell would have given his blessing to the project, without feeling the need to bother the Big Chief. If Rebus told Strathern about it, the Chief would most likely blow his top, not liking the notion of having been side-lined on such an important bust. Rebus wasn't sure what the result would be, but he couldn't see it doing his heist scheme any good.

What he needed at the moment was for the knowledge of the bust's existence to remain as secret as possible. It wasn't as if he was actually going to carry out any heist. It was a smokescreen, a way to infiltrate the trio and hopefully glean some information on Bernie Johns's missing millions. He wasn't sure that Gray and Co. would go for it . . . in fact, it worried him that Gray had proved so attentive. Why would Gray consider such a scheme when he already had much more salted away than any raid on the warehouse would bring him? All Rebus had wanted the story to do was prove to the trio that he too could be tempted, that he, like them, could fall.

Now he had to consider a further possibility: that the trio would want to take it further, make the plan a reality.

And why would they do that if they were so stinking rich on their ill-gotten gains? The only answer Rebus could think of was that there *were* no gains. In which case he was back to square one. Or, even worse, he *was* square one: instigator of a plot to steal several hundred grand's worth of dope from under the noses of his own force.

Then again . . . if Gray and Co. *had* gotten away with it . . . maybe all they'd learned was that they could do it again. Could greed stop them thinking straight? The worry was, Rebus knew they probably *could* do it. The security around the warehouse wasn't over-zealous: last thing Claverhouse wanted was for the site to start looking heavily guarded. All that would do was attract attention. A gate, a couple of guards, maybe a padlocked warehouse . . . So what if there was an alarm? Alarms could be dealt with. Guards could be dealt with. A decent-sized estate car would accommodate the haul . . .

What are you contemplating, John?

The game was changing. He still didn't know much about the three men, but now Gray knew that Rebus knew something about Dickie Diamond. *John knows where the bodies are buried.* The slap Gray had given him on the shoulder had been a warning, letting him know who was in charge.

Suddenly Linford was behind him. 'You using that machine or just counting your savings?'

Rebus couldn't think of a comeback, so simply stepped aside.

'Any chance of another ringside seat?' Linford said, slotting his coins home.

'What?'

'You and Allan Ward – have you made your peace?' Linford pressed the button for tea, then cursed himself. 'Should have made that coffee. Tea has a way of flying around here.'

'Just crawl back into your fucking hole,' Rebus said.

'CID's a lot quieter without you: any chance of making it permanent?'

'Not much hope of that,' Rebus told him. 'I promised I'd retire when you lost your cherry.'

'*I'll* have retired before that happens,' Siobhan said, walking towards the two men. She was smiling, but with little amusement.

'And who was it deflowered *you*, DS Clarke?' Linford smiled right back at her, before shifting his gaze to Rebus. 'Or is that something we don't want to get into?'

He started walking away. Rebus moved a step closer to Siobhan. 'That's what the women say about Derek's bed, you know,' he said, loud enough for Linford to hear.

'What?' Siobhan asked, playing along.

'That it's something they don't want to get into . . .'

After Linford had disappeared, Siobhan got herself a drink. 'Not having anything?' she asked.

'Gone off the idea,' Rebus stated, dropping the coins back into his pocket. 'How are you?'

'I'm fine.'

'Really?'

'Well, mostly,' she confided. 'And no, I don't want to talk about it.'

'I wasn't going to offer.'

She straightened up, manoeuvring the hot plastic cup. 'That's what I like about you,' she said. Then: 'Got a minute? I need to pick your brains . . .'

They went down to the car park, Rebus lighting a cigarette. Siobhan made sure there were no other smokers around, no one to eavesdrop.

'All very mysterious,' Rebus said.

'Not really. It's just something that's niggling me about your friends in IR1.'

'What about them?'

'Allan Ward took Phyllida out last night.'

'And?'

'And she'd nothing to report. Ward was quite the gentleman . . . took her home but wouldn't go upstairs when she offered.' She paused. 'He's not married or anything?' Rebus shook his head. 'Not going steady?'

'If he is, it doesn't show.'

'I mean, Phyl's a bonny enough girl, wouldn't you say?' Rebus nodded his agreement. 'And he'd been paying her plenty of attention all night . . .'

The way she said this made Rebus focus on her. 'What sort of attention?'

'Asking her how the Marber case was coming along.'

'It's a natural enough question. Aren't women's magazines always saying men should do more listening?'

'I wouldn't know, I never read them.' She looked at him archly. 'Didn't realise you were such an expert.'

'You know what I mean, though.'

She nodded. 'The thing is, it made me think about the way DI Gray has been mooching around the inquiry room . . . and that other one . . . McCullen?'

'McCullough,' Rebus corrected her. Jazz, Ward and Gray, spending time in the inquiry room . . .

'Probably doesn't mean anything,' Siobhan said.

'What could it mean?' he asked.

She shrugged. 'Something they wanted . . . someone they were interested in . . . ?' She thought of something else. 'The case you're working on, did anything happen last night?'

He nodded. 'Someone we wanted to speak to, he was

rushed into hospital.' Part of him wanted to tell her more . . . tell her everything. He knew she was one person he *could* trust. But he held back, because there was no way of knowing whether telling her would put her in danger, somewhere down the line.

'The reason Ward didn't go upstairs with Phyl,' she was saying, 'was because he got a call on his mobile and had to head back to the college.'

'That could have been him hearing about it.'

Rebus remembered that when he'd arrived at Tulliallan himself, pretty late on, Gray, Jazz and Ward had still been awake, sitting in the lounge bar with the dregs of their drinks in front of them. The bar itself had stopped serving, no one else about, and with most of the lights extinguished.

But the three of them, still awake and seated around the table . . .

Rebus wondered if they'd summoned Ward back so they could discuss what to do about Rebus, the chat he'd had with Jazz . . . Gray coming up with the idea to take Rebus as his partner to Glasgow, maybe quiz him further. When Rebus had walked in, Gray had told him about Chib Kelly and repeated that he wanted Rebus with him. Rebus hadn't really questioned the decision . . . He remembered asking Ward how his date with Phyllida Hawes had gone. Ward had shrugged, saying little. It hadn't sounded like there was going to be a repeat performance . . .

Siobhan was nodding thoughtfully. 'There's something I'm not getting, isn't there?'

'Such as?'

'I'll only know that when you tell me.'

'There's nothing to tell.'

She stared at him. 'Yes there is. Something else you need to know about women, John: we can read you lot like a book.'

He was about to say something, but his mobile was

trilling. He checked the number, held a finger up to let Siobhan know he needed this to be private.

'Hello,' he said, moving across the car park. 'I was hoping I'd hear from you.'

'The mood I was in, believe me, you *didn't* want to hear from me.'

'I'm glad you're calling now.'

'Are you busy?'

'I'm always busy, Jean. That night on the High Street . . . I was roped into that. Group of guys from the college.'

'Let's not talk about it,' Jean Burchill said. 'I'm phoning to thank you for the flowers.'

'You got them?'

'I did . . . along with two phone calls, one from Gill, one from Siobhan Clarke.'

Rebus stopped and looked back, but Siobhan had already retreated indoors.

'They both said the same thing,' Jean was telling him.

'And what was it?'

'That you're a pig-headed lout, but you've got a good heart.'

'I've been trying to call you, Jean . . .'

'I know.'

'And I want to make it up to you. How about dinner tonight?'

'Where?'

'You choose.'

'How about Number One? *If* you can get us a table . . .'

'I'll get us a table.' He paused. 'I'm assuming it's expensive?'

'John, you muck me about, it's always going to cost. Lucky for you, this time it's only money.'

'Seven-thirty?'

'And don't be late.'

'I won't be.'

They finished the call and he headed back inside, stopping at the comms room to find a phone number for the restaurant. He was in luck: they'd just had a cancellation. The restaurant was part of the Balmoral Hotel on Princes Street. Rebus didn't bother to ask how much it was likely to cost. Number One was a special-occasion place; people *saved* to dine there. Atonement wasn't going to come cheap. Nevertheless, he was in good spirits as he walked back to the interview room.

'Someone looks frisky,' Tam Barclay commented.

'And wasn't that the fragrant DS Clarke we saw coming back from the car park?' Allan Ward added.

They started whistling and laughing. Rebus didn't bother to say anything. One man in the room wasn't smiling: Francis Gray. He was seated at the table with a pen clenched between his teeth, playing out a rhythm on it with his fingernails. He wasn't so much watching Rebus as *studying* him.

When it comes to Edinburgh, John knows where the bodies are buried.

Said metaphorically? Rebus didn't think so . . .

20

By six that evening, the inquiry room had emptied. Siobhan was glad to see them go. Derek Linford had been giving her foul looks ever since the drinks machine. Davie Hynds had spent the afternoon writing up the report on Malcolm Neilson's pay-off. The only break he'd taken had been to interview – with Silvers as his partner – a good-looking woman, who turned out to be Sharon Burns, the art collector. Siobhan had asked Silvers afterwards who she'd been. He'd explained, then grinned.

'Davie said you'd be jealous . . .'

Phyllida Hawes had been sitting moon-faced and anxious ever since lunch, checking her watch and the doorway, wanting Allan Ward to pay another visit. But no one from IR1 had come near. Eventually Hawes had asked Siobhan if she fancied a drink after work.

'Sorry, Phyl,' Siobhan had lied, 'I've got a prior engagement.' Last thing she wanted was Hawes crying on *her* shoulder because Ward was giving her the cold one. But Silvers and Grant Hood were up for a pint, and Hawes had joined them. Hynds had waited to be asked, and eventually he was.

'I could probably manage one,' he'd said, trying not to sound too desperate.

'Might join you,' Linford had said, 'if that's all right.'

'More the merrier,' Hawes had told him. 'Sure you can't come, Siobhan?'

'Thanks anyway,' Siobhan had replied.

Leaving her alone in the office at six o'clock, the sudden silence relieved only by the hum of the strip-lighting.

Templer had left much earlier to attend some meeting at the Big House. The brass would want to know what progress was being made on the Marber case. As her eyes drifted over the Wall of Death, Siobhan could have told them: precious little.

They'd be keen for a result. Which was precisely when mistakes could be made, short cuts taken. They'd be wanting Donny Dow or Malcolm Neilson to fit the frame, even if it meant reshaping them . . .

One of her teachers at college had told her years back: it wasn't the result that mattered, it was how you got there. He'd meant that you had to play fair, stay open-minded; make sure the case lacked any slow punctures, so the Procurator Fiscal wouldn't kick it straight back at you. It was up to the courts to decide guilt and innocence, the job of CID was merely to stitch the pieces together into a ball . . .

She looked down at her desk. Her notepad was a mass of doodles and squiggles, some in blue ink, some in black, not all of them hers. She knew she drew little tornadoes when she was on the phone. And cubes sometimes. And rectangles that looked like Union Jacks. One of the designs belonged to 'Hi-Ho' Silvers: arrows and cacti were his specialities. Some people never doodled. She couldn't remember Rebus ever doing it, or Derek Linford. It was as if they might give too much away. She wondered what her own graffiti would reveal to an expert. The tornado could be her way of giving some shape to the chaos of an investigation. The cubes and flags? Same thing, more or less. Arrows and cacti she wasn't so sure about . . .

One name on her pad had been ringed and then half obliterated by a phone number.

Ellen Dempsey.

What was it Cafferty had said . . . ? Ellen Dempsey had 'friends'. What sort of friends? The kind Cafferty didn't want to tangle with.

'Is this what promotion does to you?' Rebus said. He was leaning against the door-frame.

'How long have you been there?'

'Don't worry, I'm not spying.' He walked into the room. 'They've all buggered off then?'

'Full marks for spotting that.'

'The old powers of deduction haven't quite left the building yet.' Rebus tapped his head. His chair was behind what was now Linford's desk. He wheeled it out and placed it in front of Siobhan's.

'Don't let that ba'-heid sit in my seat,' he complained.

'Your seat? I thought you stole it from the Farmer's old office?'

'Gill didn't want it,' Rebus said, defending himself as he sat down and got comfortable. 'So what's on the menu for tonight?'

'Beans on toast probably. How about you?'

He made a show of thinking it over, resting his feet on the desktop. 'Boeuf en croûte, maybe, washed down with a good bottle of wine.'

Siobhan wasn't slow. 'Jean called?'

He nodded. 'I wanted to thank you for interceding on my behalf.'

'So where are you taking her?'

'Number One.'

Siobhan whistled. 'Any chance of a doggie bag?'

'There might be a bone or two left. What are you writing?'

She noticed what she was doing. 'Ellen Dempsey's name was down here, only it's been written over. I just wanted to write it again, to remind myself . . .'

'Of what?'

'I think she's worth looking at.'

'On what grounds?'

'On the grounds that Cafferty said she has friends.'

'You don't think it was Donny Dow who killed Marber?'

She shook her head. 'I could be wrong, of course.'

'What about this artist guy? I hear you had him in for questioning, too . . .'

'We did. He took a pay-off from Marber, promised to stop bad-mouthing him.'

'Didn't exactly work.'

'No . . .'

'But you don't see him for the killer either?'

She gave an exaggerated shrug. 'Maybe nobody did it.'

'Maybe a big boy did it and ran away.'

She smiled. 'Has anyone in the whole history of the world ever really used that as an alibi?'

'I'm sure I tried it, when I was a kid. Didn't you?'

'I don't suppose my mum and dad would have believed me.'

'I don't suppose *any* parent's been duped by it. Doesn't mean a kid wouldn't try it . . .'

She nodded thoughtfully. 'Neither Dow nor Neilson has an alibi for the night Marber was killed. Even Cafferty's story's a bit shaky . . .'

'You think Cafferty was involved?'

'I'm beginning to lean that way. He probably owns the Paradiso . . . he could have known about Laura and Marber . . . His driver happened to be Laura's ex, *and* Cafferty's a collector, someone Marber could have cheated.'

'Then bring him in.'

She looked at him. 'He's hardly likely to burst into tears and confess.'

'Bring him in anyway, just for the hell of it.'

She stared down at Ellen Dempsey's name. 'Why do I get the feeling that would be for *your* benefit, rather than mine?'

'Because you've a suspicious nature, DS Clarke.' Rebus checked his watch, rose to his feet.

'Got to go make yourself look pretty?' Siobhan guessed.

'Well, a change of shirt anyway.'

'Better find time for a shave, too, if you want Jean to get up close and personal.'

Rebus ran a hand over his chin. 'A shave it is,' he said.

Siobhan watched him go, thinking: men and women, when did it all get so complicated? And why?

She opened her notepad at a fresh sheet and lifted her pen. A few moments later, Ellen Dempsey's name was written there, at the still centre of an ink tornado.

Rebus had washed his hair, shaved, brushed his teeth. He had dusted off his good suit and found a brand-new shirt. Having removed its packaging and all the pins, he'd tried it on. It needed ironing, but he didn't know where the iron was . . . or whether he owned such an object, come to that. If he kept his jacket on, no one would see the creases. Pink tie . . . no. Dark blue . . . yes. No stains on it that he could see.

He gave his shoes a quick wipe with the dishcloth, dried them on the tea-towel.

Looked at himself in the mirror. His hair had dried a bit spiky, and he tried flattening it. His face was flushed. He realised he was nervous.

He decided to get there early. A chance to check out the prices, so he wouldn't look shocked in front of Jean. Besides, once he'd recce'd the place, he would feel more comfortable in general. Maybe time for a quick whisky just to steady him. The bottle peered at him from floor level. Not here, he thought: I'll have one when I get there. He decided to take the car. Jean didn't drive, and on the off-chance that they might end up at her place in Portobello, a car would be handy. It also gave him an excuse not to order too much wine; let her drink for both of them.

And if he *did* drink, he could leave the car in town, fetch it later.

Keys . . . credit cards . . . what else? Maybe a change of clothes. He could always leave them in the car. That way, if he stayed the night at her place ... no, no ... if he suddenly announced that he had spare clothes in the boot, she'd *know* he'd expected the night to end like that.

'No premeditation, John,' he warned himself. Last question: aftershave, yes or no? No. Same reasoning.

So ... out of the flat, realising halfway down the stairs that he hadn't checked his phone messages. So what? He had his mobile and pager with him. The car was in a sweet parking space, almost directly outside. Shame to lose it ... two minutes after he drove away, it would be taken. Still ... Might not need a space tonight.

Stop thinking like that!

What if the menu was all in French? She'd have to order for both of them. Maybe that would be a good ruse; ask her straight off to order for him. Putting himself in her hands, et cetera. He was trying to think what else could go wrong. Credit card bouncing on him? Doubtful. Using the wrong spoon? Very possible. There seemed already to be patches of sweat beneath his arms.

Jesus, John ...

Nothing was going to go wrong. He unlocked the car, slid into the driver's seat. Turned the key in the ignition.

The engine was behaving itself. Into reverse and out of the space. He shifted into first and started down the road. Arden Street had been reduced to a narrow lane by cars parked either side. Suddenly, one of them reversed out of a space right in front of him. Rebus hit the brakes.

Bloody stupid ...

He sounded the horn, but the driver just sat there. Rebus could see the shape of a head. No passengers.

'Come on!' he called, gesticulating. It was a twelve-year-old Ford with the exhaust practically hanging off. Rebus decided to memorise the licence plate and make sure the bastard got some grief.

Still the car wasn't budging.

Rebus undid his seat-belt and got out, slammed shut his own door. Started walking towards the light-blue Ford. He was ninety per cent of the way there when he suddenly thought: *Trap!* He looked around, but no one was coming up behind him. All the same, he stopped in his tracks, four feet from the driver's door. The man was still sitting there, hands on the steering-wheel. That was good. It meant he wasn't carrying a weapon.

'Hey!' Rebus called. 'Either move the car or let's talk about it!'

The hands slid from the wheel. The door opened with a dry, grating clunk, the sound of unoiled hinges.

The man placed one foot on the road, eased himself halfway out of the car. 'I want us to talk,' he said.

Rebus's eyes widened. Whatever he'd been expecting, it wasn't this.

This face . . . that voice . . .

This ghost.

'I can't,' he managed to say. 'I have to be somewhere in twenty minutes.'

'This'll take ten,' the voice said. Rebus's eyes were drawn to the mouth. There was new dental work there. Blackened teeth had been removed or polished.

The Diamond Dog was looking pretty good for a dead man.

'We can talk later,' Rebus pleaded.

Diamond shook his head, slid back into his car. He was reversing completely out of the parking spot. Rebus had to move aside so he wouldn't be crushed between the Ford and his own Saab. A hand appeared from the window, motioning for him to follow.

Rebus glanced at his watch. *Fuck!*

Looked up and saw the Ford trundling forwards, moving away from him.

Ten minutes. He could afford ten minutes. He'd still be at the restaurant ahead of time . . .

Fuck!

Rebus got back behind the wheel of his own car and started following Dickie Diamond.

*

They only drove the distance of two or three streets. Diamond parked on a single yellow – safe enough this time of the evening. Rebus stopped directly behind him. Diamond was already out of the Ford. They were next to Bruntsfield Links, a wide grassy slope where golfers occasionally practised their pitch 'n' putt skills. Recently, students had taken to holding barbecues on the links, using cheap disposable kits. The tin trays left charred rectangular marks on the grass. Diamond was testing one of these rectangles with his foot. He was dressed well. Nothing expensive or showy, but not bargain basement either.

'Who's the lady?' he asked, his eyes running the length of Rebus's suit.

'What the hell are you doing here?'

Diamond met Rebus's less-than-happy gaze. Then he gave a rueful smile and started walking down the slope. Rebus hesitated, then followed.

'What sort of game are you playing?' he asked.

'That's the question *I* should be asking!'

'I thought I told you never to set foot here.'

'That was before I got wind of what's been happening.' In the six years since they'd last met, Diamond's face had grown even thinner, as had his hair. What remained of the latter was an unnatural depth of black. There were dark half-moons beneath the eyes, but no sign of excess weight or any lessening of the faculties.

'And what exactly *has* been happening?' Rebus asked.

'You've got people looking for me.'

'That doesn't mean they're going to find you . . . unless, of course, you come charging back into town.' Rebus paused. 'Who told you? Was it Jenny Bell?'

Diamond shook his head. 'She doesn't even know I'm alive.'

'It was Malky then?' Rebus was guessing, but it hit home. Diamond revealed as much by saying nothing. Malky in the Bar Z, hovering near the table . . . 'My advice,' Rebus continued, 'is that you get back in your car and high-tail it out of town. I meant it when I told you to stay away.'

'And I've been good as my word until now.' Diamond had started rolling himself a cigarette. 'So why the sudden interest?'

'Coincidence, that's all. I'm on a training course and they happened to pick out Rico Lomax as an exercise.'

'An exercise in what?' Diamond licked the edge of the paper. Rebus watched as he pulled a few stray strands of tobacco from the finished roll-up and put them back in the tin.

'They wanted us working a case, see how they could turn us back into team players.'

'A team player? *You?*' Diamond chuckled and lit his cigarette. Rebus checked his watch.

'Look,' he said, 'I've really—'

'I hope you're leading them up the crow road, Rebus.' His voice had assumed an edge of menace.

'And what if I don't?' Rebus said stubbornly.

'I've been away a long time. I miss the place. It'd be nice to come back . . .'

'I told you at the time . . .'

'I know, I know. But I was maybe too scared of you back then. I'm not so scared now.'

Rebus pointed a finger. 'You were part of it. You come back here, *somebody*'ll get you.'

'I'm not so sure. More I think about it, more I get the feeling it's your arse I've been protecting all these years.'

'You want to walk into a police station, be my guest.'

Diamond examined the tip of his cigarette. 'That'll be for me to decide, not you.'

Rebus bared his teeth. 'You little turd, I could have had you buried . . . remember that.'

'It's Rico I remember. I think of him often. How about you?'

'*I* didn't kill Rico.'

302

'Then who did?' Diamond chuckled again. 'We both know the score, Rebus.'

'And what about you, Dickie? Did you know Rico was giving your girlfriend one? Way she tells it, you were there at the time. Is that right? Maybe *you're* the one who had the grudge, the one who wanted revenge.' Rebus nodded slowly. 'That could be the way I'll tell it in court. You whacked your old pal and did a runner.'

Diamond was shaking his head, chuckling once more. He looked around, slid the tobacco tin back into his jacket pocket.

Pulled out a snub-nosed revolver and aimed it at Rebus's gut.

'I'm in the frame of mind to shoot you right now. Is that what you want?'

Rebus looked around them. No one within a hundred yards; dozens of tenement windows ... 'This is great, Dickie. Blending in with your surroundings and all that. Nobody notices people brandishing firearms in the middle of Edinburgh.'

'Maybe I don't care any more.'

'Maybe you don't.' Rebus had his hands by his sides, bunched into fists. He was three feet or so from Diamond, but would he be quick enough ...?

'How long would I serve if I shot you? Twelve to fifteen, out in a bit less than that?'

'You wouldn't serve ten minutes, Dickie. You'd be on a death sentence as soon as the prison gates shut behind you.'

'Maybe, maybe not.'

'People I know have long memories.'

'I want to come home, Rebus.' He looked around again. 'I *am* home.'

'Fine ... but put the gun away. You've proved your point.'

Diamond glanced down at the revolver. 'Not even loaded,' he said.

Hearing which, Rebus swung at him, connecting with the hollow just beneath his breast-bone. He grabbed Diamond's gun-hand and prised the revolver away. Sure enough, its chambers were empty. Diamond was down on his hands and knees, groaning. Rebus wiped his own prints off the gun with his handkerchief and dropped it on to the grass.

'You try that again,' Rebus was hissing, 'and I'll break every one of your fingers.'

'You've dislocated my thumb,' Diamond bawled. 'Look.' He held his right hand up for Rebus's inspection, then launched himself at him, smashing him backwards on to the grass. The wind was knocked out of Rebus. Diamond was crawling over him, pinning him down. Rebus struggled, and as Diamond's grinning face came level with his own he head-butted him, then half rolled so that Diamond was forced off. Rebus clambered to his feet and swung a foot at Diamond, who wrapped his arms around it, trying to throw him off balance. Instead, Rebus dropped to both knees, his whole weight landing on Diamond's chest.

The man groaned and spluttered.

'Let go!' Rebus spat.

Diamond let go. Rebus got to his feet once more, this time stepping back out of range.

'I heard a rib snap,' Diamond complained as he writhed.

'The hospital's the other side of the Meadows,' Rebus told him. 'Good luck.' He looked at himself. Grass stains and mud on his trousers, shirt hanging out. His tie was over to one side, hair rumpled.

And he was going to be late.

'I want you to get in your car,' he told the prone figure, 'and keep driving. It's like the Sparks song said: this town ain't big enough for the both of us. I see you here again after tonight, you're dead meat. Understood?'

The body said something, but Rebus couldn't make it

304

out. He guessed Diamond wasn't complimenting him on the welcome home . . .

He parked directly outside the restaurant and ran down the steps. Jean was in the cocktail bar, pretending to study the menu. Her face was icy as he approached. Then, despite the understated lighting, she finally saw that something had happened.

'What did you do?' As he bent down to kiss her cheek, she touched her fingers to his forehead. It stung, and he realised he'd grazed it.

'A bit of a disagreement,' he said. 'Am I presentable enough for a place like this?' The maître d' was hovering.

'Can you bring John a large whisky?' Jean asked.

'A nice malt perhaps, sir?'

Rebus nodded. 'Laphroaig if you've got it.'

'And some ice,' Jean added. 'In a glass by itself.' She smiled at Rebus, but with concern in her eyes. 'I can't believe I'm going to have dinner with a man who'll be holding an ice-pack to his face.'

Rebus studied his surroundings. 'Place like this, they probably have someone to do that for you.'

She smiled more openly. 'You're sure you're all right.'

'I'm fine, Jean, honest.' He lifted her hand, kissed the inside of her wrist. 'Nice perfume,' he said.

'Opium,' she told him. Rebus nodded, filing the information away for future use.

The meal was long and wonderful, Rebus relaxing a little more with each course. Jean asked just once about the 'disagreement', Rebus muttering a few words of concocted explanation before she held up a hand and stopped him.

'I'd rather you told me to mind my own business, John . . . just don't start making up a story. It's ever-so-slightly insulting.'

'Sorry.'

'One day, maybe you'll feel like opening up to me.'

'Maybe,' he agreed, but inside he knew the day would never come. It hadn't happened with Rhona during all the years of his marriage, no reason to think things would be any different now . . .

He'd drunk just the one large malt, followed by two glasses of wine, and as a result felt fine to drive. As one of the waiters helped Jean into her coat, Rebus asked if he could give her a lift. She nodded.

They drove to Portobello, well fed and friends again, an old Fairport Convention tape providing background music. As they turned into her street, she spoke his name, drawing it out. He knew what she was about to say and pre-empted it.

'You don't want me coming in?'

'Not tonight.' Turning towards him. 'Is that all right?'

'Of course it is, Jean. No problem.' There weren't any parking spaces, so he just stopped in the middle of the road outside her house.

'It was a lovely meal,' she said.

'We'll have to do it again.'

'Maybe not quite so extravagantly.'

'I didn't mind.'

'You took your punishment very nobly,' she said, leaning over to kiss him. Her fingers touched his face. He placed both hands on her shoulders, feeling awkward, much the way he'd felt as a teenager. First dates . . . not wanting to screw things up . . .

'Good night, John.'

'Can I phone you tomorrow?'

'You better had,' she warned, opening her door. 'It's rare that I give someone a second chance.'

'Scout's honour,' he said, lifting two fingers to his right temple. She smiled again and was gone. She didn't look back, just climbed the steps to her front door, unlocked it and closed it after her. The hall light was already on – the lazy person's deterrent. He waited till the lights came on upstairs – hallway and bedroom – then put the car into gear and moved off.

There was no space for the Saab in Arden Street. He had a quick look to make sure Dickie Diamond wasn't lurking, but there was no sign. He parked a two-minute walk away, enjoying the fresh air. The night was crisp, almost autumnal. The dinner had gone well, he decided. No interruptions: he'd switched off his mobile, and his pager hadn't sounded. Trying his mobile now, he found that he had no new messages.

'Thank Christ for that,' he said, pushing open his tenement door. He was going to have one more whisky, albeit a large one. He was going to sit in his chair and listen to some music. He'd already pencilled in Led Zeppelin's *Physical Graffiti*. He wanted something that would blow everything else away. He might even fall asleep in the chair, and that wouldn't matter.

Things were back on track with Jean. He thought so . . . hoped so. He'd phone her first thing in the morning, maybe again after work.

He reached his landing, stared at his door.

'For Christ's sake . . .'

The door was wide open, the hall dark within. Someone had used an implement of some kind to bust the lock. There were shards of freshly splintered wood. He peered into the hall. No signs of life . . . no sounds. Not that he was going to risk it. The memory of Diamond's revolver was too recent. Diamond probably had the ammo hidden somewhere, maybe even in his car . . . Rebus called on his mobile, asked for back-up. Then he stood on the landing and waited. Still no signs of life from within. He tried the light-switch by the front door. Nothing happened.

Five minutes had passed when, downstairs, the main door opened and closed. He'd heard a car screeching to a halt. Feet on the staircase. He leaned over to watch Siobhan Clarke climbing towards him.

'You're the back-up?' he said.

'I was in the station.'

'This time of night?'

She paused, four steps down from him. 'I can always go home . . .' She half turned, as if to leave.

'Might as well stay,' he said, 'now you're here. Don't suppose you've got a torch on you?'

She opened her bag. There was a large black torch inside. She clicked it on.

'Fuse box is over there,' he said, pointing into the hall. Someone had turned the electricity off. Rebus flipped the switch and the lights came on. They moved through the rest of the flat as a team, quickly sensing that no one was there.

'Looks like a straightforward break-in,' she commented. He didn't respond. 'You don't agree?'

'I'd feel happier with the diagnosis if anything was actually missing.'

But nothing was, nothing he could see. The hi-fi, TV, his albums and CDs, his booze and books . . . all present and correct.

'To be honest, I'm not sure I'd bother nicking anything either,' Siobhan said, picking up the cover of a Nazareth LP. 'Do you want to call it in as a housebreaking?'

Rebus knew what that would mean: a fingerprint team leaving dust everywhere; giving a statement to a bored woolly-suit . . . And everyone at the station knowing he'd been turned over. He shook his head. Siobhan looked at him.

'You sure?'

'I'm sure.'

She seemed only now to spot that he was wearing a better suit than usual. 'How was the meal?'

He looked at himself, started removing his tie. 'Fine.' He popped the top button on his shirt and felt some of the pressure ease. 'Thanks again for calling her.'

'Anything to help.' She was studying the living room once more. 'You're sure nothing's been taken?'

'Pretty sure.'

'Then why would someone break in?'

'I don't know.'

'Care to try a few guesses?'

'No.' *Dickie Diamond . . . Gray . . . the Weasel . . .* Plenty of people seemed to know where he lived. But what would any of them be looking for? Maybe it was the students through the wall, desperate to play some decent music for a change . . .

Siobhan sighed, pinching the bridge of her nose between her fingers. 'Why is it that when you say "no", I know you've already got some names in mind?'

'Woman's intuition?'

'Not my finely honed detective's skills then?'

'Those, too, of course.'

'Have you got a joiner you can phone?' she meant the door: emergency repair needed.

'I'll wait till morning. They charge an arm and a leg otherwise.'

'And what if someone comes tiptoeing in here through the night?'

'I'll hide under the bed till they've gone.'

She came forwards till she was standing directly in front of him, slowly lifted her hand. Rebus didn't know what she was going to do. But he didn't shy away. Her forefinger touched his brow.

'How did that happen?'

'It's just a graze.'

'A fresh one, though. Wasn't Jean, was it?'

'I just fell into something.' They locked eyes. 'And I *wasn't* drunk, God's honest truth.' He paused. 'But speaking of drink . . .' He picked up the bottle. 'Care to join me, now you're here?'

'Can't have you drinking alone, can we?'

'I'll fetch a couple of glasses.'

'Any chance of a coffee to go with it?'

'I've no milk.'

She went into her bag again, producing a small carton. 'I was saving this for home,' she said, 'but in the circumstances . . .'

He retreated to the kitchen and Siobhan slipped off her coat. She was thinking that she would redecorate this room, given the chance. A lighter carpet, for definite, and junk the 1960s light-fittings.

Through in the kitchen, Rebus took two glasses from the cupboard, found a milk jug and poured some cold water into it, just in case Siobhan felt the need. Then he opened the freezer compartment of his fridge, lifted out a half-bottle of vodka, a packet of venerable fish fingers and a shrivelled morning roll. There was a polythene carrier bag beneath, and in it the Chief Constable's report on Bernie Johns. Rebus was fairly sure no one had tampered with it. He put it back, along with the fish fingers and the roll. Filled the kettle and switched it on.

'You can have vodka instead if you prefer,' he called.

'Whisky's fine.'

Rebus smiled and closed the freezer door.

'Did you ever listen to that Arab Strap tape I made you?' Siobhan asked as he returned to the living room.

'It was good,' he said. 'Drunk guy from Falkirk, right? Lyrics all about getting his end away?' He poured, handed her the glass. Offered water, but she shook her head.

They both sat down on the sofa, sipped their drinks. 'There's a saying, isn't there?' Rebus asked. 'Something about drinking and friendship?'

'Misery loves company?' Siobhan guessed mischievously.

'That's it,' Rebus said with a smile, raising his glass. 'Here's to misery!'

'To misery,' Siobhan echoed. 'Where would we be without it?'

He looked at her. 'You mean it's part and parcel of human life?'

'No,' she said. 'I mean you and me would be out of a job . . .'

21

As soon as he woke up, Rebus called Jean. He'd actually made it as far as his bed last night, but when he walked through to the living room the hi-fi was still playing. Wishbone Ash's *There's the Rub* – he must have pressed the 'repeat' button by mistake. The whisky glasses were on the dining table. Siobhan had left a good half-inch untouched. Rebus thought about finishing it, but dribbled it back into the bottle instead. Then he reached for the telephone.

Jean was still asleep. He imagined her: tousled hair, sun streaming in through her cream hessian curtains. Sometimes when she woke up there were fine white accumulations at the corners of her mouth.

'I said I'd call,' he told her.

'I was hoping it might be at a civilised hour.' But she was good-humoured about it. 'I take it you didn't manage to pick up any unsuitable women on your way home?'

'And what sort of woman do you think would be unsuitable for me?' he asked, smiling. He'd already decided that she needn't know about the break-in . . . or about Siobhan's little visit.

They chatted for five minutes, then Rebus placed another call – this time to a joiner he knew, a man who owed him a favour – after which he made himself coffee and a bowl of cereal. There wasn't quite enough milk for both, so he watered the carton down from the cold tap. By the time he'd eaten, showered and got dressed the joiner had arrived.

'Pull the door shut after you, Tony,' Rebus told him,

making his way out on to the landing. As he walked downstairs, he wondered again who might have been behind the break-in. Diamond was the obvious candidate. Maybe he'd wanted to wait for Rebus but had got fed up. As Rebus drove to St Leonard's, he replayed the scene on Bruntsfield Links. He was furious that Diamond had pulled a gun on him. Loaded or not, it didn't matter. He tried to recall how he'd felt. Not scared exactly . . . in fact, fairly calm. When someone aimed a gun at you, it was pointless to worry – you were either going to get shot or you weren't. He remembered that his whole body had tingled, almost vibrating with an electric energy. Dickie Diamond . . . the Diamond Dog . . . thinking he could get away with something like *that* . . .

He parked the car and decided to skip his usual cigarette. Instead he went to the comms room and gave the word that he wanted patrols to be on the lookout for a certain motor vehicle. He gave the description and number-plate.

'Nobody's to go near it: all I want is the whereabouts.'

The uniform had nodded, then started speaking into the mike. Rebus was hoping Diamond would have heeded his warning to clear out of town. All the same, he needed to be sure.

It was another half-hour before the rest of the Wild Bunch arrived. They'd come in the one car. Rebus could tell which three had been squeezed into the back seat – Ward, Sutherland and Barclay. They were doing stretching exercises as they walked into the room.

Gray and Jazz: driver and front-seat passenger. Once again, Rebus wondered about Allan Ward, about how he felt being so often the odd man out. He was yawning, his back clicking as he raised and lowered his shoulders.

'So what did you lot get up to last night?' Rebus asked, trying to make it sound like a casual enquiry.

'A few drinks,' Stu Sutherland said. 'And early to bed.'

Rebus looked around. 'What?' he asked in apparent disbelief. 'All of you?'

'Jazz nipped home to see his missus,' Tam Barclay admitted.

'See *to* her more like,' Sutherland added with a leering grin.

'We should hit a nightclub some evening,' Barclay said. 'Kirkcaldy maybe . . . see if we can get a lumber.'

'You make that sound so appetising,' Allan Ward muttered.

'So the rest of you were in the bar at Tulliallan?' Rebus persisted.

'Pretty much,' Barclay said. 'We weren't pining for you.'

'Why the interest, John?' Gray asked.

'If you're afraid of being left out,' Sutherland added, 'you should move back there with us.'

Rebus knew he daren't push it any further. He'd got back to his flat around midnight. If the intruder had come from Tulliallan, they'd have had to leave the college around half past ten, eleven o'clock at the latest. That would have given them time to drive into Edinburgh, search the flat and get out again before he arrived home. How had they known he would be out? Something else to think about . . . Dickie Diamond had known he was headed for a rendezvous, reinforcing his position as most likely culprit. Rebus half hoped one of the patrols would call in a sighting. If Diamond was still in Edinburgh, Rebus had a few things to put to him . . .

'So what's the schedule today?' Jazz McCullough asked, closing the newspaper he'd been reading.

'Leith, I suppose,' Gray informed him. 'See if we can track down any more of Diamond's pals.' He looked at Rebus. 'What do you think, John?'

Rebus nodded. 'Anyone mind if I stay here for a bit? I've a couple of jobs to do.'

'Fine with me,' Gray said. 'Anything we can help you with?'

Rebus shook his head. 'Shouldn't take too long, Francis. Thanks all the same.'

'Well, whatever happens,' Ward said, 'if we don't come up with something, Tennant's going to have us back at Tulliallan pronto.'

They nodded agreement. It would happen . . . today or tomorrow, it would happen, and the Rico case would become paperwork again, and brain-storming sessions, and making a card-index, and all the rest. No more side-trips, no chances for breaks at the pub or the odd meal out.

The Rico case would have died.

Gray was staring at Rebus, but Rebus kept his eyes on the wall. He knew what Gray was thinking: he was thinking that John Rebus would like that state of affairs just fine . . .

'I'm only doing this because you asked so nicely.'

'What's that, Mr Cafferty?' Siobhan asked.

'Letting you bring me here.' Cafferty looked around IR2. 'To be honest, I've had prison cells bigger than this.' He folded his arms. 'So how can I help you, Detective Sergeant Clarke?'

'It's the Edward Marber case. Your name seems to be cropping up at all sorts of tangents . . .'

'I think I've told you everything I can about Eddie.'

'Is that the same as telling us everything you *know*?'

Cafferty's eyes narrowed appraisingly. 'Now you're just playing games.'

'I don't think so.'

Cafferty had shifted his attention to Davie Hynds, who was standing with his back against the wall opposite the desk.

'You all right there, son?' He seemed pleased when

315

Hynds failed to respond. 'How do you like working under a woman, DC Hynds? Does she give you a rough ride?'

'You see, Mr Cafferty,' Siobhan went on, ignoring everything he'd said, 'we've charged Donny Dow – your driver – with the murder of Laura Stafford.'

'He's not *my* driver.'

'He's on *your* payroll,' Siobhan countered.

'Diminished responsibility anyway,' Cafferty stated with conviction. 'Poor bugger didn't know what he was doing.'

'Believe me, he knew *exactly* what he was doing.' When she saw Cafferty's smile, Siobhan cursed herself for letting him push her buttons. 'The woman Dow murdered worked in the Sauna Paradiso. I think if I dig deep enough, I'll find that you're its owner.'

'Better buy a big shovel then.'

'You see how already you connect to both the murderer and his victim?'

'He's not a murderer till he's convicted,' Cafferty reminded her.

'You speak with a wealth of experience in that area, don't you?'

Cafferty shrugged. He still had his arms folded, and looked relaxed, almost as if he was enjoying himself.

'Then there's Edward Marber,' Siobhan pressed on. 'You were at the private viewing the night he was killed. You were one of his clients. And ironically, *he* was one of yours. He met Laura Stafford at the Sauna Paradiso. He rented a flat for her and her son . . .'

'Your point being . . . ?'

'My point being that your name keeps cropping up.'

'Yes, you said. I think the phrase you used was "at all sorts of tangents". That's what we're talking about here, DS Clarke: tangents, coincidences. That's all we're ever going to be talking about, because I didn't kill Eddie Marber.'

'Did he cheat you, Mr Cafferty?'

'There's no proof he cheated anyone. Way I hear it, it was one man's word against his.'

'Marber paid that man five thousand pounds to shut up.'

Cafferty grew thoughtful. Siobhan realised she had to be careful how much she gave away to this man. She got the feeling Cafferty coveted information the way other people did jewellery or fast cars. She already had one small result, however: when she'd slipped a mention of the Paradiso into the conversation, Cafferty hadn't denied ownership.

A knock came at the door. It opened and a head appeared round it. Gill Templer.

'DS Clarke? Can I have a word?'

Siobhan rose from her chair. 'DC Hynds, look after Mr Cafferty, will you?'

Out in the corridor, Templer was waiting, looking around at the officers, who moved with more efficiency once they'd spotted her. 'My office,' she told Siobhan.

Siobhan was hitting the mental rewind button, trying to think what she'd done that might have merited a bollocking. But Templer seemed to relax once she was in her own room. She didn't ask Siobhan to sit, and stayed standing herself, hands behind her, gripping the edge of her desk.

'I think we might try charging Malcolm Neilson,' she announced. 'I've been talking it through with the Fiscal's office. You've done a thorough job, Siobhan.'

Meaning the dossier Siobhan had compiled on the painter. She could see it on the desk.

'Thank you, ma'am,' Siobhan said.

'You don't sound too enthusiastic.'

'Maybe I just think there are some loose ends . . .'

'Dozens, probably, but look at what we've got. He'd fallen out with Marber, a very public and bitter argument. He'd taken money – either that or extorted it. He was hanging around outside the gallery on the night in question – witnesses have placed him there.' Templer counted off on her fingers: 'Means, motive and opportunity.'

Siobhan remembered Neilson himself saying much the same thing.

'At the very least we can get a search warrant,' Templer was saying, 'see if it throws up any tidbits. I want you to organise it, Siobhan. That missing painting could be hanging in Neilson's bedroom for all we know.'

'I don't think it would be to his taste,' Siobhan commented, knowing it sounded lame.

Templer stared at her. 'Why is it that every time *I* try to do you a good turn, *you* try to pull the rug out from under me?'

'Sorry, ma'am.'

Templer studied her, then sighed. 'Any luck with Cafferty?'

'At least he didn't bring a lawyer with him.'

'Might just mean he doesn't rate the competition.'

Siobhan pursed her lips. 'If that's everything, ma'am . . . ?'

'Well, it isn't. I want to go through the warrant for Neilson's arrest. Shouldn't take us too long. Let Mr Cafferty sweat for a while . . .'

'I never could work with a woman boss,' Cafferty told Hynds. 'Always needed to be my own man, know what I mean?'

Hynds had taken Siobhan's seat. He was the one sitting with arms folded now, while Cafferty leaned over the desk, palms pressed downwards. Their faces were so close, Hynds could have taken a punt on which toothpaste the gangster used.

'Not a bad job, though, is it?' Cafferty ran on. 'Being a copper, I mean. Don't get as much respect as in the old days . . . maybe not as much fear either. Boil down to the same thing sometimes, don't they, fear and respect?'

'I thought respect was something you earned,' Hynds commented.

'Same with fear, though, isn't it?' Cafferty raised a finger to stress the point.

'You'd know better than me.'

'You're right there, son. I can't see you putting the frighteners on too many folk. I'm not saying that's a fault, mind. It's just by way of an observation. I should think DS Clarke's a scarier proposition than you when she's roused.'

Hynds thought back to the few times she'd snapped at him, the way she could suddenly change. He knew he was to blame; he had to think before he opened his trap . . .

'She's had a pop at you, has she?' Cafferty was asking, almost conspiratorially. He leaned further still across the desk, inviting some confidence or other.

'You don't half talk a lot for a man who's supposed to be under a death threat.'

Cafferty offered a rueful smile. 'The cancer, you mean? Well, let me ask you something, Davie: if you only had so long to live, wouldn't you want to make the most of every moment? In my case . . . maybe you're right . . . maybe I do talk too much.'

'I didn't mean . . .'

Hynds's apology was cut short when the door burst open. He stood up, thinking it would be Siobhan.

It wasn't.

'Well now,' John Rebus said, 'isn't this a surprise?' He looked at Hynds. 'Where's DS Clarke?'

Hynds frowned. 'Isn't she out there?' He thought for a moment. 'DCS Templer wanted her. Maybe they're in her office.'

Rebus put his face close to Hynds's. 'What're you looking so guilty about?' he asked.

'I'm not.'

Rebus nodded towards Cafferty. 'He's the serpent in the

319

tree, DC Hynds. Whatever he says, it isn't worth hearing. Got that?'

Hynds gave a vague nod.

'*Got that?*' Rebus repeated, baring his teeth. The nod this time was vigorous. Rebus patted Hynds's shoulder, then took the seat he'd just vacated. 'Morning, Cafferty.'

'Long time no see.'

'You just keep popping up, don't you?' Rebus said. 'Like a greasy spot on some adolescent's arse.'

'Would that make you the adolescent or the arse?' Cafferty asked. He was leaning back in his chair, spine straight, arms by his sides. Hynds noticed that the two men's postures were almost identical.

Rebus was shaking his head. 'It would make me the man with the Clearasil,' he said, causing Hynds to smile. He was the only man in the room who did. 'You're in this up to your neck, aren't you?' Rebus went on. 'Circumstantial evidence alone would see you in a courtroom.'

'And out again the same afternoon,' Cafferty countered. 'This is harassment, plain and simple.'

'DS Clarke isn't that way inclined.'

'No, but you are. I wonder who it was put her up to dragging me in here.' He raised his voice a little. 'Are you a betting man, DC Hynds?'

'Nobody in their right mind would bet with the devil,' Rebus stated, closing Hynds's mouth almost before he'd opened it. 'Tell me, Cafferty, what's the Weasel going to do without his chauffeur?'

'Get a new one, I expect.'

'Donny was a bouncer for you, too, wasn't he? Probably handy for selling stuff to all those young club-goers.'

'I don't know what you're talking about.'

'You didn't just lose a driver, did you? You didn't even just lose some muscle.' Rebus paused. 'You lost a dealer.'

Cafferty laughed drily. 'I'd love to spend twenty minutes in your head, Rebus. It's a regular fun house.'

'Funny you should mention that,' Rebus said. 'It's the

title of a Stooges album: *Fun House* . . .' Cafferty turned to stare at Hynds, as if offering him the chance to concur that Rebus was a couple of waltzers shy of a fairground.

'It's got a track on it that just about sums you up,' Rebus was saying.

'Oh aye?' Cafferty winked in Hynds's direction. 'What's that then?'

'Just a one-word title,' Rebus informed him. ' "Dirt".'

Cafferty turned his attention slowly towards the man seated opposite him. 'Do you know the only thing that's stopping me reaching across this desk and crushing your windpipe like an empty fucking chip-bag?'

'Do tell.'

'It's the feeling I get that you'd actually enjoy it. Would I be correct in that assumption?' He turned his head towards Hynds again. 'What do you reckon, Davie? Think DI Rebus here likes a bit of domination? Maybe that piece of his in Portobello does the leather and stilettos routine . . .'

The chair crashed as Rebus flew to his feet. Cafferty rose too. Rebus's arms had snaked across the space between them, grabbing the narrow lapels of Cafferty's black leather jacket. One of Cafferty's own hands had a grip on Rebus's shirt-front. Hynds took a step forwards, but knew it would be like a toddler refereeing a cock-fight. None of them noticed the door opening. Siobhan plunged in, taking hold of both men's arms.

'That's enough! Break it up or I hit the panic button!'

Cafferty's face seemed to have drained of blood, while Rebus's had filled, almost as if there'd been a transfusion of sorts between the two men. Siobhan couldn't tell who eased off first, but she managed to separate them.

'You better get out of here,' she told Cafferty.

'Just when I'm starting to enjoy myself ?' Cafferty looked confident enough, but his voice was shaky.

'Out,' Siobhan ordered. 'Davie, make sure Mr Cafferty doesn't hang around.'

'Unless it's by his neck,' Rebus spat. Siobhan slapped him on the chest, but didn't say anything until Cafferty and Hynds had left the room.

Then she exploded.

'What the hell are you playing at?'

'Okay, I lost the rag at him . . .'

'This was *my* interview! You had no right to interfere.'

'Jesus, Siobhan, listen to yourself, will you?' Rebus picked up his chair and slumped back down on to it. 'Every time Gill talks to you, you come out sounding like you've just left the college.'

'I'm *not* going to let you twist this around, John!'

'Then sit down and let's talk about it.' He had a thought. 'Maybe in the car park . . . I could do with a smoke.'

'No,' she said determinedly, 'we'll talk here.' She sat down in Cafferty's chair, pulled it in towards the desk. 'What did you say to him anyway?'

'It was what *he* said to *me*.'

'What?'

'He knows about Jean . . . knows where she lives.' Rebus saw the effect of his words on Siobhan. What he couldn't tell her was that Cafferty's utterance had been only part of the problem. There was also the small matter of a message from the comms room. The note was folded in Rebus's breast pocket. It told him that Dickie Diamond's car had been spotted parked in the New Town, already with a ticket on its windscreen and looking abandoned . . . So Diamond, wherever he was, hadn't obeyed orders.

The real catalyst, however, was Rebus's own sense of frustration. He'd wanted Cafferty in St Leonard's so he could probe how much the man knew about the SDEA's secret cache. But when it had come down to it, there'd been no way of asking, not without coming straight out with it.

The only person who might know . . . who might have access . . . was the Weasel. But the Weasel was no snitch

– he'd said it himself. And he'd also confided that Cafferty and him were not as close as had once been the case.

There was, quite simply, no way for Rebus to know . . .

And that sense of impotence had boiled up within him, finally gushing out when Cafferty had mentioned Jean.

The bastard had played his trump card, knowing the effect it would have. *The feeling I get that you'd actually enjoy it . . . a bit of domination . . .*

'Gill wants to bring in Malcolm Neilson,' Siobhan was saying.

Rebus raised an eyebrow. 'We're charging him?'

'Looks like.'

'In which case, Cafferty's off the hook?'

'Not until we cut the line. Problem is, if we do that we might lose a man overboard.'

Rebus smiled. 'Don't be so melodramatic.'

'I'm serious,' she said. 'Go read *Moby Dick* some time.'

'I don't really see myself as Captain Ahab. He was Gregory Peck in the film, wasn't he?'

Siobhan started shaking her head, eyes never leaving his. Rebus didn't think she was disagreeing with the casting . . .

There was a noise in the corridor, then a knock at the door. Not Gill Templer this time, but a grinning Tam Barclay.

'Hynds said we'd find you here,' he told Rebus. 'Want to come and take a look at what we found down in Leith?'

'I don't know,' Rebus said. 'Is it contagious?' But he allowed himself to be taken out of the room, past Ward and Sutherland, who were sharing a joke in the corridor, and into IR1, where Jazz McCullough and Francis Gray were standing, almost like zoologists studying some new and exotic creature in their midst.

The creature in question was supping tea from a polystyrene beaker. Its eyes never met Rebus's, though by no means unaware of his sudden presence in the cramped room.

'Can you believe it?' Gray said, slapping his hands together. 'First stop is the Bar Z, and who should we meet coming out as we're going in?'

Rebus already knew the answer to that. It was seated not four feet from him. He'd known the answer from the moment Barclay had put his head round the door.

Richard Diamond, aka the Diamond Dog . . .

'Just to finish the introductions,' Barclay told Diamond, 'this is DI Rebus. You might remember him as your arresting officer once upon a time.'

Diamond stared straight ahead. Rebus glanced in Gray's direction. All Gray did was wink, as if to say Rebus's secret was safe with him.

'We were just about to ask Mr Diamond a few questions,' Jazz McCullough said, taking the seat opposite his prey. 'Maybe we could start with the break-in and rape at a manse in Murrayfield . . .'

This got a reaction from Diamond. 'What's that got to do with anything?'

'It coincided with your disappearance, Mr Diamond.'

'Did it bollocks.'

'Then why *did* you disappear? Funny that you pop up again just when we've started looking for you . . .'

'Man's got a right to go where he wants,' Diamond said defiantly.

'Only if he has a good reason,' Jazz argued. 'We're curious as to what yours was.'

'What if I say it's none of your business?' Diamond folded his arms.

'Then you'd be mistaken. We're investigating the murder of your good friend Rico Lomax, over in Glasgow. CID came looking for you at the time, and suddenly nobody could find you. It wouldn't take a conspiracy theorist to see a connection.'

The rest of the team had squeezed into the room, leaving the door open. Diamond looked around him, eyes failing to meet Rebus's. 'This is all getting a bit cosy, isn't it?' he commented.

'Sooner you tell us, sooner you'll be on your way back to anonymity.'

'Tell you what exactly?'

'Everything,' Francis Gray growled. 'You and your good pal Rico ... the caravan sites ... the night he got whacked ... his wife and Chib Kelly ...' Gray opened his arms expansively. 'Start wherever you like.'

'I don't know who killed Rico.'

'Got to do better than that, Dickie,' Gray said. 'He got hit ... you ran.'

'I was scared.'

'Don't blame you. Whoever wanted Rico out of the way might have been after you next.' He paused. 'Am I right?'

Diamond nodded slowly.

'So who was it?'

'I've told you: I don't know.'

'But you were scared anyway? Scared enough to leave town all this time?'

Diamond unfolded his arms, clasped his hands over his head. 'Rico had made a few enemies down the years. Could have been any one of them.'

'What?' Jazz looked dismissive. 'Don't tell me they *all* had it in for you too?'

Diamond shrugged, said nothing. There was silence in the room, until Gray broke it.

'John, you got anything you want to ask Mr Diamond?'

Rebus nodded. 'Do you think Chib Kelly could have been behind the killing?'

Diamond looked like he was thinking this over. 'Could be,' he said at last.

'Any way of proving it?' Stu Sutherland broke in.

Diamond shook his head. 'That's your job, lads.'

'If Rico really *was* your friend,' Barclay said, 'you'd want to help us.'

'What's the point? It was a long time ago.'

'Point is,' Allan Ward answered, not wanting to be left out, 'the killer's still out there somewhere.'

'Maybe, maybe not,' Diamond replied. He brought his hands down from his head. 'Like I say, I don't think I can help you.'

'What about the caravans?' Jazz asked. 'Did you know one of them got torched?'

'If I did, I'd forgotten it.'

'You used to go out there, didn't you?' Jazz continued. 'You and your girlfriend Jenny. A bit of a *ménage à trois* going on there, way she tells it.'

'That what she told you?' Diamond seemed amused.

'You're saying she's lying? See, we were starting to wonder if there mightn't have been some jealousy there . . . you being jealous of Rico? Or maybe Rico's wife found out he was playing away from home . . . ?'

'I can see you've got an active fantasy life,' Diamond told Jazz. Francis Gray seemed to have heard enough.

'Do me a favour, will you, Stu – shut that door.'

Sutherland complied. Gray was standing behind Diamond's chair. He leaned down and brought one arm around until he was fixing Diamond to the chair by his chest. Then he tilted the chair back, so their faces weren't more than three inches apart. Diamond struggled, but he wasn't going anywhere. Allan Ward had taken hold of him by both wrists, pressing them against the table-top.

'Something we forgot to say,' Gray hissed at the prisoner. 'Reason they put us on this case is, we're the lowest of the low, the absolute fucking zero as far as the Scottish police force goes. We're here because we don't care. We don't care about *you*, we don't care about *them*. We could kick your teeth down your throat, and when they came to tell us off, we'd be laughing and slapping our thighs. Time was, buggers like you could end up inside one of the support pillars for the Kingston Bridge. See what I'm saying?' Diamond was still struggling.

Gray's arm had slid upwards, and was now around his throat, the crook of the elbow crushing his larynx.

'He's turning beetroot,' Tam Barclay said nervously.

'I don't care if he's turning fucking blue,' Gray retorted. 'If he gets an aneurysm, the drinks are on me. All I want to hear from this slimy, watery trail of shite is something approximating the truth. What about it, Mr Richard Diamond?'

Diamond made a gurgling sound. His eyes were protruding from their sockets. Gray kept the pressure up, while Allan Ward burst out laughing, as if this was the most enjoyment he'd had in weeks.

'Let the man answer you, Francis,' Rebus said.

Gray glanced towards Rebus, then released the pressure. Dickie Diamond started coughing, mucus dribbling from his nose.

'That's repulsive,' Ward said, letting go the hands. Diamond instinctively reached for his own throat, reassuring himself that it was still intact. Then his fingers went to his eyes, wiping away the water that had been squeezed from them.

'Bastards,' he coughed hoarsely. 'Stinking bunch of bastards . . .' He got a handkerchief from his pocket, blew his nose. The door had only been closed a couple of minutes, but the place was like a sauna. Stu Sutherland opened it again, letting some air in. Gray, still behind Diamond, had straightened up, and was standing with an arm on each of the seated man's shoulders.

'Easier all round if you just start talking,' Jazz said quietly: suddenly playing sympathetic cop to Gray's monster.

'All right, all right . . . somebody get me a can of juice or something.'

'*After* we've listened to your story,' Gray insisted.

'Look . . .' Diamond tried meeting their eyes, lingering longest on Rebus. 'All I know is what was being said at the time.'

'And what was that?' Jazz asked.

'Chib Kelly . . .' Diamond paused. 'You were right about him. He was after Fenella. She found out about Rico playing away from home and told Chib. Next thing, Rico's dead . . . simple as that.'

Gray and Jazz shared a glance, and Rebus knew what they were thinking. Dickie Diamond was telling them what he thought they wanted to hear, what he thought they'd *believe*. He'd taken the information they'd gifted him, and he was running with it. He'd even lifted Jazz's own phrasing: *playing away from home*.

Gray and Jazz weren't falling for it. The others in the room looked more excited.

'Knew it all along,' Stu Sutherland muttered. Tam Barclay was nodding, and Allan Ward seemed entranced.

Gray's eyes sought Rebus's, but Rebus wasn't playing. He stared down at his shoes while Diamond embroidered the story further.

'Chib knew about the caravan . . . that's where Rico would take all his women. It was Chib had it torched – he'd have done anything to win over Fenella . . .'

Rebus could see that Gray was beginning to apply pressure to Diamond's shoulders.

'Th-that's about all I can tell you. Nobody crossed Chib Kelly . . . why I had to do a runner . . .' Diamond's face was creasing with pain as Gray's fingers did their work.

'Is this a private party, or can anyone join in?' The voice belonged to Archie Tennant. Relief flooded Rebus's veins as Gray let go of Diamond. Barclay and Sutherland started talking at once, filling Tennant in.

'Whoah, whoah . . . one at a time,' Tennant ordered, holding up a hand. Then he listened to the story, the others chipping in when a bit was missed. All the time, Tennant was studying the seated figure, Diamond staring back, aware that he was in the presence of someone important, someone who could get him out of this place.

When the story was finished, Tennant leaned down

with clenched fists on the desk, his knuckles bearing his weight. 'Is that a fair summary, Mr Diamond?' he asked. Diamond nodded vigorously. 'And you'd be willing to make a statement to that effect?'

'With respect, sir,' Jazz McCullough interrupted, 'I'm not so sure we're not being led up the garden path here . . .'

Tennant stood up, turned his gaze on Jazz. 'And what makes you say that?'

'Just a feeling, sir. I don't think I'm the only one.'

'Really?' Tennant looked around the room. 'Anyone else find Mr Diamond's story less than tenable?'

'I have a few doubts myself, sir,' Francis Gray piped up. Tennant nodded, his eyes seeming to home in on Rebus.

'And yourself, DI Rebus?'

'I found the witness credible, sir,' he said, the words sounding as stiff to him as to anyone else in the room.

'With respect, sir . . .' Jazz repeating the gambit. 'Taking a statement from Mr Diamond is one thing, but letting him walk out afterwards probably means we're not going to see him again.'

Tennant turned to Diamond. 'DI McCullough isn't sure he trusts you, sir. What do you have to say to that?'

'You can't keep me here.'

Tennant nodded. 'He's got a point there, DI McCullough. I'm assuming Mr Diamond would be willing to give us his address in the city?' Diamond nodded with enthusiasm. 'And a permanent address also?' The nodding continued.

'Sir, he could make up any number of addresses,' Jazz continued to protest.

'Oh ye of little faith,' Tennant commented. 'Let's start with a statement anyway . . .' He paused. 'Always supposing that's okay with you, DI McCullough.'

Jazz said nothing – precisely what was expected of him.

'Here endeth the lesson,' Tennant intoned, pressing the palms of his hands together as if in prayer.

Barclay and Sutherland took Diamond's statement, the others vacating IR1, leaving them to get on with it. Tennant motioned to Jazz that he wanted a word with him in private, the two of them heading towards the station's reception area. Allan Ward said he was heading out back for a smoke. Rebus declined to join him, went to the drinks machine instead.

'He did a good job of protecting you,' Francis Gray said. He was already at the machine, awaiting delivery of his white coffee.

'I thought so,' Rebus admitted.

'I don't think anyone else noticed that the two of you knew one another better than you should.' Rebus didn't say anything. 'But you weren't exactly surprised to see him, were you? Did he warn you he was in town?'

'No comment.'

'We found him at the Bar Z. Probably means his nephew keeps in touch. Dickie knew we were after him, and came sneaking back ... Did he speak to you last night?'

'I didn't know I was working with Sherlock fucking Holmes.'

Gray chuckled, shoulders shaking as he leaned down to remove the cup from the machine. Rebus was reminded of the way the man had leaned down over Dickie Diamond, threatening to smother him completely.

Jazz was walking up the corridor. He made a show of rubbing his backside, as though the headmaster had just caned him.

'What did Half-Pint want?' Gray asked.

'Twittering on about how it's okay to argue your corner against a senior officer, but you have to know when to back off and not start taking it personally.'

Rebus was thinking: *Half-Pint*. Gray and Jazz had found their own private nickname for Tennant. They were close, these two ...

'I was just telling John,' Gray went on, 'about Dickie's wee acting lesson back there.'

Jazz nodded, eyes on Rebus. 'He didn't give you away,' he agreed.

So Gray had told Jazz all about Rebus's confession . . . Were there any secrets between the two men?

'Don't worry,' Gray assured him, 'you can trust Jazz.'

'He's going to have to,' Jazz himself added, 'if we're going to pull off this wee plan of his.'

The silence lay between them until Rebus could find his voice.

'You're up for it then?'

'Could be,' Gray said.

'Need to know a bit more first,' Jazz qualified. 'Lay-out, all that stuff. No point being unprofessional, is there?'

'Absolutely not,' Gray concurred.

'Right,' Rebus said, his mouth suddenly dry. *It was my calling-card, that's all. There is no 'wee plan' . . . is there?*

'You okay, John?' Jazz asked.

'Maybe getting cold feet,' Gray guessed.

'No, no, it's not that,' Rebus managed to say. 'It's just . . . you know, it's one thing to think about it . . .'

'But quite another to actually do it?' Jazz nodded his understanding.

If you bastards have got Bernie Johns's money . . . what do you want this for?

'Any chance you could give the premises a quick recce?' Gray was asking. 'We need a floor-plan, that sort of thing.'

'No problem,' Rebus said.

'Let's start with that then. You never know, John. It could still end up being pie in the sky.'

'I've been thinking,' Rebus said, recovering some composure. 'Maybe we need a fourth man. What do you think of Tam Barclay?'

'Tam's okay,' Jazz said, with little enthusiasm. 'But maybe young Allan is better.' He was sharing a look with Gray, who started nodding.

'Allan's our man,' Gray agreed.

'So who'll talk to him?' Rebus asked.

'Leave that side of things to us, John – just you concentrate on the warehouse . . .'

'Fine by me,' Rebus said, lifting his own cup from the machine. He stared at its surface, trying to remember if he'd pressed the button for tea, coffee or self-destruct. He had to tell Strathern. Tell him what exactly? No way the 'heist' was going to happen . . . no possible way. So what was there to tell?

22

At 4.10 p.m., Malcolm Neilson was arrested on suspicion of the murder of Edward Marber. DC Grant Hood, who'd been placed in charge of media liaison, was in his element. Two murders, two suspects in custody, both charged. The newspapers and TV wanted to know all about it, and he was the person they needed to charm. Hood knew what questions they would ask, and was scuttling around the inquiry room in search of answers. He'd nipped home and changed into a dark-grey suit which he'd had made for him at Ede and Ravenscroft. The sleeves had been shortened so as to expose a few inches of shirt-cuff, emphasising the gold cuff links.

Hood would tell you that it was all for the cameras. You had to look professional. Others had a different view.

'Is he a nancy-boy or something?' Allan Ward asked Rebus.

'Don't worry, Allan,' Rebus assured him. 'You're not his type.' They were in the car park: cigarette break. The team in IR1 was still brooding over Dickie Diamond's statement. Opinions ranged from 'not worth the paper it's printed on' to 'Chib Kelly's our man for sure'.

'What do you reckon?' Ward asked Rebus now.

'I'm with Tennant. Our job's to compile the evidence. It's down to someone else to decide if it's a pack of lies or not.'

'Not like you to side with Half-Pint,' Ward commented.

That nickname again: *Half-Pint*. Rebus wondered if any of the others knew about it.

'Tell me, Allan . . . have Jazz and Francis had a chance to speak to you yet?'

'What about?'

'That sort of answers my question.' Rebus took pity on Ward's look of befuddlement. 'A wee scheme we've got going. You might qualify for a share.'

'What sort of scheme?'

Rebus tapped his nose. 'Tell me . . . how welcome would a bit of cash be?'

Ward shrugged. 'Depends whose cash it is.'

Rebus nodded but kept quiet. Ward was about to press him when the door burst open and a bunch of uniforms streamed out towards their cars, followed by Hynds, Hawes and Siobhan. Hawes cast a glance in Ward's direction, causing him to concentrate on his cigarette. The smile she'd been preparing melted away. Ward just wasn't interested.

'Off on a jaunt?' Rebus asked Siobhan.

'Search warrant came through.'

'Got room for one more?'

She looked at him. 'You're not part of—'

'Come on, Siobhan. Don't give me that routine.'

'Why the interest?'

'Who said I'm interested? I just want a break from this place.' He turned towards Ward. 'Can you square it with the others?'

Ward nodded with little enthusiasm. He still had questions for Rebus, and now he was being left hanging.

'Go talk to Jazz and Francis,' Rebus advised him. Then he stubbed out his cigarette and made for Siobhan's car. She'd already said something to Phyllida Hawes, who was vacating the passenger seat and joining Hynds in the back instead.

'Cheers, Phyl,' Rebus said, taking her place. 'So where are we off to?'

'Inveresk. Malcolm Neilson has a house there.'

'I thought he lived in Stockbridge?'

Hynds leaned forward. 'He mostly uses that as a studio. Something to do with the quality of the light . . .'

Rebus ignored this. 'So Inveresk first, Stockbridge next?'

Siobhan was shaking her head. 'Linford and Silvers are in charge of another team. They're headed for Stockbridge.'

'Leaving Neilson to stew back in the cells?'

'He's got Gill Templer and Bill Pryde for company.'

'Those two haven't conducted a decent interview in years.'

'Haven't let a prisoner escape either,' Phyllida Hawes added. Rebus looked in the rear-view, returned her smile.

'What exactly is it we're hoping to find?' he asked Siobhan.

'God knows,' she said through gritted teeth.

'Maybe he kept some sort of diary,' Hynds offered.

'*Why I'm a Cold-Blooded Killer?*' Hawes suggested as a title.

'Inveresk's nice, though,' Rebus mused. 'Must be a few bob in this painting lark.'

'He has a place in France, too,' Hawes added. 'Though I notice we're not getting the chance to search *that*.'

Siobhan turned towards Rebus. 'Local *gendarmes* will do the job for us, just as soon as we can find someone who knows enough French to submit the request.'

'Could take a while then.' Rebus glanced into the rear-view. 'Maybe that's where your diary is.'

'*Pourquoi Je Suis un Tueur Avec le Sang Froid?*' Hynds offered. Everything went very still in the car. Siobhan was first to speak.

'Why didn't you say you spoke French?'

'Nobody asked. Besides, I didn't want to be left off the search.'

'Soon as we get back,' Siobhan said coldly, 'you're going to tell DCI Pryde.'

'I'm not sure I know enough to write something as specific as—'

'We'll buy you a dictionary,' Siobhan stated.

'I'll help if I can,' Rebus offered.

'And how much French do *you* have?'

'How about *nul points?*'

There was laughter from the back seat. Siobhan's face tightened, and she seemed to grip the steering-wheel harder than ever, as though right now it was the only thing in her life that was under her control.

They'd driven through the rougher outskirts of Edinburgh – Craigmillar and Niddrie – crossing the city boundary and making for Musselburgh, the self-proclaimed 'Honest Toun'. Hynds asked how it had come by the title, but no one in the car could answer. Inveresk was a wealthy enclave on the edge of the town. New housing was encroaching only slowly. Most of the homes here were old, large and detached, hidden behind high walls or at the ends of long, meandering driveways. It was a place where politicians and TV celebrities could tuck themselves away from the public gaze.

'This is new to me,' Hynds said, peering out his side of the car.

'Me too,' Hawes admitted.

There wasn't much to Inveresk, and they soon found Neilson's house. Two patrol cars stood at its entrance – the local station had been alerted to their arrival. The media were there too, wanting photos of whatever trove was produced. The house itself was not large. Siobhan would have called it a cottage, albeit an extremely pretty one. The small front garden was well tended, consisting mostly of rose-beds. Though the building was a single-storey construction, dormer windows protruded from the tiled roof. Siobhan had the keys, offered up by Neilson himself once he'd been told that without them, police would force an entry. She ordered Hynds to fetch the roll of bin-bags from the boot.

Just in case they *did* find anything.

Hawes was in charge of the box of smaller polythene

bags, plus the tags which would be attached to any useful find. Everyone was pulling on pairs of gloves, while across the road the camera shutters clicked, motors humming as the film progressed to the next frame.

Rebus held back. This was Siobhan's show, and she was making sure everyone knew it. She'd gathered her team in a semicircle and was outlining their duties. Rebus lit a cigarette. At the sound of his lighter, she turned towards him.

'Not in the house,' she reminded him. He nodded. Contamination: ash dropped on a carpet could be misinterpreted. Rebus decided he was safer outdoors. After all, he hadn't come here to help with the search. What he'd needed was some time away from Gray and the others . . . time to think. Siobhan was unlocking the house, throwing open its door. The officers headed in. From what Rebus could see, the hallway was much like any other. From the way she'd acted in the car, Rebus knew Siobhan thought they were wasting their time, which meant she was far from convinced that the painter was the killer. It wouldn't stop her being thorough. The suspect's house had to be searched. And you never knew what you might find . . .

With most of the police having disappeared inside, the cameras had little to do but focus on the single detective left smoking a cigarette. And wouldn't *that* picture appeal to Gill Templer if it found its way into the newspapers? Rebus turned his back and walked around the side of the house. There was a long, narrow garden at the rear, with a summerhouse and shed at the furthest corners. A strip of lawn, bordered with flagstones. Flowerbeds looking overgrown, but that could have been on purpose: a wild, rambling garden . . . counterpoint to the order provided by the rose-beds. Rebus didn't know enough about either gardening or Malcolm Neilson to be able to say. He walked down to the summerhouse. It looked fairly new. Varnished wooden slats, with wood-framed and glass-panelled doors. The doors were closed, but not locked. He pulled them open. Inside: deckchairs stacked against one wall, awaiting better weather; one fairly solid wooden chair, boasting wide arm-rests one of which had been hollowed out to accommodate a cup or glass. Nice touch, Rebus thought, settling into the chair. He had a view across the garden to the house itself, and could imagine the artist sitting here, maybe with the rain falling outside, snug and cosy with a drink for company.

'Lucky bugger,' he muttered.

Shapes moved behind the upstairs and downstairs windows. They'd be working two to a room, the way Siobhan had instructed. Looking for what exactly? Anything incriminating or out of place . . . anything that gave them an inkling. Rebus wished them well. What he needed, he realised, was a place like this. It felt like a haven. Somehow, he didn't think the placement of a summerhouse in the back garden of his tenement would have the same effect. He'd thought before of selling his flat, buying a little house just outside the city – commuting distance, but a place where he could find a bit of peace. Problem was, you could have too much of a good thing. In Edinburgh, he had twenty-four-hour shops, myriad pubs within a short walk, and the constant background hum of street life. In a place like Inveresk, he feared the silence would get to him eventually, drawing him deeper into himself – not a place he really wanted to be – and defeating the whole point of the exercise.

'No place like home,' he told himself, rising out of the chair. He wasn't going to find any answers here. His troubles were his own, and a change of scenery couldn't alter that. He wondered about Dickie Diamond, hopefully now in the process of scurrying out of Edinburgh. He'd given his Edinburgh address as his sister's house in Newhaven. His permanent address was a high-rise in Gateshead. They'd sent a message south, requesting a check by the local force. He'd claimed he wasn't currently in work, but neither had he registered as unemployed. No bank account . . . didn't have his driving licence with him. He hadn't mentioned his car, and neither had Rebus. If they knew about the car, they could get an address from his licence plate. Rebus knew that the Gateshead address would be fake or out-of-date. The car might well be another matter. He got on his mobile, called the comms room at St Leonard's and asked if the Ford's last known sighting – looking abandoned in the New Town – could be re-checked.

But the comms room already knew. 'Car was lifted this morning,' the officer said. Which meant it would be in the pound, a hefty levy payable before it could be released. Rebus doubted Diamond would bother – the Ford was probably worth less than the charges now attached to it.

'Doesn't take long for them to clear rubbish from the New Town, does it?' Rebus said into the phone.

'It was parked outside a judge's front door, blocking the space for his own car,' the officer explained.

'Got the Ford's registration address?'

The officer reeled it off: same one Diamond had given them in the interview room. Rebus ended the conversation, slipped the phone back into his pocket. Dickie Diamond would be leaving town by bus or train, always supposing he lacked the wherewithal to steal someone else's car.

Either that or he'd be staying put, necessitating another meeting between them and some strong words from Rebus. Strong words and maybe strong actions to accompany them.

Was the gun hidden inside the car? He wondered if it was worth finding out, but shook his head. Dickie Diamond wasn't the kind to shoot anyone. The gun had been a prop . . . the prop of a weak, scared man. A fine insight in retrospect.

He'd stopped to light another cigarette and was crossing the garden to the shed. This was a much older construction than the summerhouse, its wooden sides mildewed and spattered with bird-droppings. Again, there was no lock on it, so Rebus pulled it open. A coiled hose, which had been attached to a nail on the inside of the door, slid off and fell with a clatter. There were shelves of DIY bits and pieces – screws and brackets, rawl-plugs, hinges . . . An old-style push-pull mower took up most of the floor space. But there was something tucked down beside it, something smothered in bubble-wrap. Rebus looked back at the cottage. He wasn't wearing gloves, but decided to pick it up all the same. It was a painting, or at any rate a frame. Heavier than he'd been expecting, probably the weight of the glass. He lifted it on to the lawn. Heard the sound of a window opening, then Siobhan's voice: 'What the hell are you doing?'

'Come take a look,' he called back. He was unfolding the wrapping. The painting showed a man in a crisp white shirt, the sleeves rolled up. He had long dark wavy hair, and was standing by a mantelpiece, atop which sat a mirror, which itself was reflecting a woman with long, lustrous black hair, the angles of her lower jaw picked out as though from firelight. Around the two figures all was shadow. The woman wore a black mask covering her eyes and nose. She had her hands behind her. Maybe they were tied together at the back. The artist's surname was written in capitals at bottom left: Vettriano.

'This'll be the missing painting then,' Rebus said, as Siobhan stood over him.

She stared first at the canvas, then at the shed. 'And it was just lying there?'

'Tucked down the side of the lawnmower.'

'The door wasn't locked?'

Rebus shook his head. 'Looks like he panicked. Brought the thing home, then didn't want it in the house . . .'

'How heavy is it?' Siobhan was walking around the painting.

'It's not light. What's your point?'

'Neilson doesn't own a car. No point, since he's never learned to drive.'

'Then how did he get the painting back here?' Rebus knew the way her mind was working. He stood up, watching her nodding slowly. 'Right now,' he told her, 'what matters is that you've found the painting stolen from the victim's house.'

'And isn't *that* convenient?' she said, staring at him.

'Okay, I admit it ... I had it hidden under my jacket ...'

'I'm not saying *you* put it there.'

'But someone else did?'

'Plenty of people knew Malcolm Neilson was a suspect.'

'Maybe his prints will be all over the glass. Would that be enough to satisfy you, Siobhan? Or how about a blood-stained hammer? Could be there's one tucked away in the shed, too ... And by the way, I meant what I said.'

'About what?'

'It was *you* that found the painting. Me, I'm not even here, remember? You go telling Gill that it was John Rebus who found the crucial piece of evidence, she's going to have *both* of us on the carpet. Get one of the woolly-suits to give me a lift back into town ... *then* let Gill know what you've found.'

She nodded, knowing he was right, but cursing the fact that she'd let him come here.

'Oh, and Siobhan?' Rebus was patting her on the arm. 'Congratulations. Everyone's going to start thinking you walk on water ...'

Presented with the evidence of the stolen painting, Malcolm Neilson offered no explanation at first, then said it had been a gift from Marber, before changing his mind again and stating that he'd neither seen nor touched the painting. His fingerprints had already been taken, and the painting itself was sitting at Howdenhall police lab, being

341

dusted for prints before undergoing other, more arcane tests.

'I'm curious, Mr Neilson,' Bill Pryde asked. 'Why that particular painting, when there were others more valuable right there under your nose?'

'I didn't take it, I tell you!'

William Allison, Neilson's solicitor, was rapidly jotting notes by his client's side. 'You say it was found in Malcolm Neilson's garden shed, DCI Pryde? Can I ask whether there was a lock of any kind on the door?'

Elsewhere in the station, the success of the search at Inveresk was being trumpeted, the noise bringing the Wild Bunch out of their lair and up to the murder room.

'You got a result then?' Francis Gray asked Derek Linford, slapping him on the back.

'*I* didn't,' Linford snapped back. 'Too busy wading through three feet of shit in his studio the other side of town.'

'Still, a result's a result, eh?'

The look Linford gave him seemed to dispute this. Gray just chuckled and moved away.

News was filtering down that fingerprints *had* been found on the picture frame. Problem was, they belonged to Edward Marber himself.

'At least we know we've got the right painting,' one officer said with a shrug. Which was true enough, though still not enough to satisfy Siobhan. She was wondering about the picture's subject matter, wondering if in Marber's eyes the woman in the mask had represented Laura. Not that the two shared physical similarities, but all the same . . . Did Marber place himself in the man's role? The voyeur, or maybe even the possessor . . . thinking about the merchandise?

The painting had to mean something. There had to be a reason why it alone had been removed from Marber's house. She remembered the sales chit for it, which had turned up among Marber's effects. Five years back he had paid £8,500 for it. These days, according to Cynthia Bessant, it might fetch four or five times that, a more than decent return on the investment, but still some way short of other paintings in the dealer's collection.

It had meant something to someone ... something more than mere monetary value.

What could it have meant to Malcolm Neilson? Was he perhaps jealous of artists more successful than himself?

Another hand slapped Siobhan's shoulder. 'Good work ... well done.' She'd already deflected a phone call from the Assistant Chief Constable, Colin Carswell. She knew he would want to share in her glory, and had no intention of talking to him. Not that she wanted the glory all to herself; far from it.

She wanted nothing whatsoever to do with it.

Because to her mind it fell well short of glory ... yet might end up putting an innocent man away.

One of the Tulliallan crew – Jazz McCullough – was standing beside her now.

'What's up?' he asked. 'Not joining in the fun and games? Case must be cut and dried, I'd've thought.'

'Maybe that's why they sent you back to training school.' She saw a rapid change in his eyes. 'Christ, sorry ... I didn't mean to say that.'

'I've obviously caught you at a bad time. I just wanted to offer my congratulations.'

'Which I'll gladly accept ... *after* we get a conviction.' She turned and walked away, aware of McCullough's eyes following her all the way to the door.

Rebus saw her go, too. He was catching a word with Tam Barclay, asking if he had a nickname for DCI Tennant.

'I can think of a few choice ones,' Barclay was saying. Rebus nodded slowly. He'd already spoken to Stu Sutherland, and knew damned well that 'Half-Pint' was a name used only by Gray, Jazz and Allan Ward. Now Jazz was motioning to him. Rebus wrapped up his conversation with Barclay and made to follow. Jazz walked down the corridor and into the toilets. He was standing by the wash-basins, hands in pockets.

'What is it?' Rebus asked.

The door opened again and Gray came in. He nodded a greeting and checked that no one was lurking in the cubicles.

'When are you going to recce the merchandise?' Jazz asked quietly. 'Only, if there's a chance it may be moved, best get your arse in gear.' His voice was cold and calculating, and Rebus felt his liking for the man start to ebb.

'I don't know,' he said. 'Maybe tomorrow?'

'Why not today?' Gray said.

'There's not much of today left,' Rebus told him, making a show of consulting his watch.

'There's enough,' Jazz persisted. 'If you went there right now. We could cover for you.'

'It's not like we're unused to you bunking off,' Gray continued. 'Funny you shot back here just before they found that picture . . .'

'What's that supposed to mean?'

'Let's focus on something else,' Jazz warned both men. 'We'll call it the *big* picture, if you like.'

Gray grinned at this.

'We need some fast info, something we can work from,' Jazz went on.

'What about Allan?' Rebus asked. 'Is he in or out?'

'He's in,' Gray said. 'Though he didn't like the way you teased him.'

'Does he know what's involved?'

'Less Allan knows, better he likes it,' Gray explained.

'I'm not sure I understand.' Rebus was angling . . . hoping for a bit more.

'Allan does what he's told,' Jazz said.

'The three of you . . .' Rebus hoped he sounded naïve enough. 'You *have* done something like this before?'

'That's on a need-to-know basis,' Gray told him.

'I need to know,' Rebus stated.

'Why?' The question came from Jazz.

'A little knowledge can be a dangerous thing,' Gray said into the silence. 'How about your friends in the SDEA? Are you going to pay them a visit or not?'

'What option do I have?' Rebus tried to sound disgruntled. He could feel Jazz's eyes still on him.

'It's still *your* show, John,' Jazz reminded him quietly. 'All we're saying is that it can't be put off for ever.'

'I know that,' Rebus conceded. Then: 'Okay, I'll talk to them.' He grew thoughtful. 'We need to discuss the split.'

'The split?' Gray growled.

'It was my idea,' Rebus stressed, 'and so far I'm the only one doing anything about it . . .'

Jazz's air of absolute calm now seemed almost threatening. 'The split will be in your favour, John,' he said. 'Don't fret.'

Gray looked set to dispute this, but the words failed to come out. As Rebus turned towards the door, however, Jazz's hand landed softly on his arm.

'Just don't go getting greedy on us,' he said. 'Remember: you invited us in. We're here because you asked.'

Rebus nodded, made good his escape. Outside in the corridor, he could feel his heart pounding, the blood sizzling in his ears. They didn't trust him, yet they were ready to follow him.

Why? Were they *setting* him *up? And when was the time to tell Strathern?* His head told him 'now', but his gut said otherwise. Still, he decided to pay a little trip to the Big House.

It was past six, and he half expected that the SDEA offices would be empty, but Ormiston was hunched over a computer, the keys of the keyboard just too small for his oversized fingers to manage. As he cursed and pressed the delete key, Rebus walked into the room.

'Hiya, Ormie.' Trying to sound chatty, breezy. 'They've got you working late.'

The big man grunted, didn't raise his eyes from the screen.

'Is Claverhouse about?' Rebus went on, leaning his backside against a desk.

'Warehouse.'

'Oh, aye? Still got the stuff stashed there?' Rebus had picked up a stick of gum from the desk and unwrapped it, folding it into his mouth.

'What's it to you?'

Rebus shrugged. 'Just wondered if you wanted me to have another go at the Weasel.'

Ormiston glared at him, then turned back to his work.

'Fair enough,' Rebus said. Ormiston's look meant they'd given up on the Weasel. 'Bet Claverhouse would love to know why the Weasel visited me that night.'

'Maybe.'

Rebus had started pacing the room. 'Would *you* like to know, Ormie? I'd tell you before I'd tell your partner.'

'That gives me a warm glow all over.'

'Not that it was anything much . . .' Ormiston wasn't about to take the bait. Rebus decided to sweeten the hook. 'It was just something about Cafferty and the warehouse.'

Ormiston stopped typing, but kept his eyes on the screen.

'You see,' Rebus pressed on, 'the Weasel says Cafferty might be planning a hit on the warehouse.'

'We *know* he knows about it.'

'But that's just the word on the street.'

Ormiston turned his head, but it was no good. Rebus had stopped directly behind him. The big man had to swing around a hundred and eighty degrees in his chair.

'On the other hand,' Rebus continued, '*I* got it from the horse's mouth, so to speak.'

'You're sure it wasn't the horse's arse?'

Rebus just shrugged. 'That's for you and your *compadre* to decide.'

Ormiston folded his arms. 'And why in God's name would the Weasel grass his boss up to *you*?'

'That's what I want to talk to Claverhouse about.' Rebus paused. 'I want to apologise.'

Ormiston's eyebrows rose slowly. Then he unfolded his arms and reached for the phone.

'This I have to see,' he said.

'You're shipping it out?' Rebus guessed. He was in the warehouse. The carcass of the lorry had already been removed. Now the warehouse was more than half filled with new-looking wooden packing-cases. They were nailed closed and stacked two high across most of the floor. 'Does that mean you're splitting the glory with Customs and Excise?'

'Rules are rules,' Claverhouse said. Rebus ran his palm over the surface of one crate, then made a fist and rapped on it. Claverhouse smiled. 'Bet you can't guess which crate they're in.'

'Crate or crates?'

'That would be telling.'

There was the smell of fresh wood in the air. 'You're expecting someone to try taking them?' Rebus surmised.

'Not exactly, but we know the word is out. There's only so much you can do with security, but . . .'

'But this way at least it'll take them an hour or two to find the right boxes?' Rebus was nodding, actually quite impressed with Claverhouse's thinking. 'Why not just shift the drugs?'

'And they'd be safer where exactly . . . ?'

'I don't know . . . Fettes or somewhere.'

'The Big House? All open windows and no alarms?'

'Maybe not,' Rebus agreed.

'Anyway, you're right, they're going to be shifted. Just as soon as we've squared everything with Customs . . .'

Claverhouse thought of something. 'Ormie said you had some apology you wanted to make?'

Rebus nodded again. 'About Weasel. I think I was too soft on him. You told me it would be two fathers having a talk, and I let that happen . . . stopped thinking like a cop. So I wanted to apologise.'

'And that's why he came to your flat that night?'

'He came to warn me that Cafferty knew about the haul.'

'Information you decided to hold back from us?'

'You already knew, didn't you?'

'We knew word was out.'

'Well, anyway . . .' Rebus sniffed, gazed around him. 'You've got this place sewn up, right? Cafferty would have wanted to catch you unawares . . .'

'Security's round the clock,' Claverhouse confirmed. 'Padlocks on the gates, razor-wire fences . . . And my little puzzle to contend with at the end of it all.'

Rebus looked at Ormiston. 'Do you know which crates the stuff's in?'

Ormiston stared back, unblinking.

'Stupid question,' Rebus muttered aloud. Claverhouse smiled. 'I want you to know,' Rebus told him, 'that I really do feel bad about not snaring the Weasel for you. I gave him far too easy a ride. That sent the wrong message: he thought I was doing it on purpose, which meant he owed me.'

'And fed you the news on Cafferty to even things up?' Claverhouse was nodding.

'But now that I've opened a line of communication with him,' Rebus went on, 'maybe I can still bring him over to our side.'

'Too late for that now,' Claverhouse informed him. 'Looks like the Weasel has jumped ship. He hasn't been seen since the night he went to your flat.'

'What?'

'I think he panicked.'

'Which was what we wanted,' Ormiston admitted. The look he received from his partner shut him up.

'We put word out,' Claverhouse explained, 'that we were readying to charge Weasel's son with the whole shebang.'

'You thought if he got scared enough, he'd come in?' Claverhouse nodded.

'And he ran instead?' Rebus was trying to make sense of it. The Weasel had shown no sign at all that he was planning flight.

'Would he have flown, without taking Aly with him?'

Claverhouse seemed to contort his whole body into a shrug, letting Rebus know the subject was closed. 'Takes a big man to admit when he's wrong,' he said instead, addressing Rebus. 'I didn't think you had it in you.' Then he stuck out a hand, which Rebus, after only a moment's debate, accepted. He was still thinking of the Weasel, trying to assess whether the man could do any harm to Rebus and his plans. He came up blank. Whatever had happened to him, Rebus couldn't spare the time or space for conjecture. He had to focus, draw all his energy together.

Look after number one.

23

The six o'clock headlines were just ending when Siobhan switched off her engine. She was parked in the forecourt of MG Cabs. The large tarmac parking area boasted half a dozen assorted Vauxhalls, and a single brand-new, flame-red MG sports car. There was a white flagpole, from which drooped a St Andrew's Cross. The office was a pre-fab building, with a garage next to it, where a solitary mechanic in grey overalls was working on the engine of an Astra. Lochend wasn't far from Easter Road – home of Hibernian, Siobhan's chosen football team – but she didn't know the area at all. It seemed to be mostly low-rise and terraced housing with a smattering of neighbourhood shops. She hadn't really expected anyone to be here, but the cab business was round-the-clock, she now realised. All the same, she doubted Ellen Dempsey would still be on duty. That was fine: all she wanted was a feel for the place, maybe ask a couple of questions of the mechanic or anyone else she could find.

'Having trouble?' she asked, approaching the garage.

'That's it fixed,' he said, dropping the bonnet. 'Maintenance check.' He slid into the driver's seat, revved the engine a couple of times. 'Sweet as a nut. Office is in there.' He nodded towards the pre-fab. Siobhan was studying him. Through the oil and grease on the backs of his hands she could see old home-made tattoos. He was skinny, with a pale face and thinning hair which stuck out above the ears. Something about him made her think: ex-offender. She recalled that Sammy Wallace, the driver who'd taken Marber home, had boasted a police record.

'Thanks,' she told the mechanic. 'Who's manning the phone tonight?'

He looked at her, saw her for what she was. 'Mrs Dempsey's inside,' he said coldly. Then he shifted the Astra into reverse and started manoeuvring it out of the garage and into a parking space, the driver's-side door still open so that Siobhan had to take a step back or risk being hit by it. He glowered at her through the windscreen, and she knew she hadn't made a friend.

There were two steps up to the office. She tapped on the glass door. A woman was seated behind a desk. The woman looked up, sliding the spectacles from her nose, and gestured for her to enter. Siobhan closed the door after her.

'Mrs Dempsey? I'm sorry to trouble you . . .' She was opening her bag to find her warrant card.

'Don't bother with that,' Ellen Dempsey said, leaning back in her chair. 'I can see you're a cop.'

'Detective Sergeant Clarke,' Siobhan said by way of introduction. 'We spoke on the phone.'

'Indeed we did, DS Clarke. What can I do for you?' Dempsey motioned towards the chair on the other side of the desk, and Siobhan sat down. Ellen Dempsey was in her mid-forties. Full-figured but well preserved. The ringed creases of skin around her neck were a better indicator of her age than was her carefully made-up face. The dark-brown hair had probably been dyed, but it was hard to tell. No nail polish, no jewellery on her fingers, just a chunky ladies' Rolex on her left wrist.

'I just thought you'd like to know that Sammy Wallace is off the hook,' Siobhan said.

Dempsey was making a show of tidying some papers. In truth, the desk was about as neat as could be, the paperwork divided into four piles, with four labelled folders waiting to be filled.

'Was he ever on the hook?' Dempsey asked.

'He was the last person to see Mr Marber alive.'

'Apart from whoever murdered him,' Dempsey corrected. Now she looked up at Siobhan, narrowing her eyes slightly. Her glasses hung around her neck by a chain. 'If he was ever really a suspect, DS Clarke, it was because he already had a criminal record, and that's just laziness on your part.'

'I'm not saying we seriously considered—'

'What other reason was there?'

Siobhan paused, knowing this was an argument she couldn't win. Yes, they'd looked that bit more closely at Sammy Wallace precisely *because* of his criminal past. It had been as good a starting-point as any.

'Besides,' Dempsey said, reaching into the waste-basket and pulling out the latest edition of the *Evening News*, 'it was on the front page – all about this painter you've arrested. That's you, isn't it?' Dempsey had turned the paper round for Siobhan to see. There was a headline – MAN CHARGED IN ART DEALER MURDER – and a large colour photo of the search party as they made ready to enter the house at Inveresk. Obviously, the story had been printed just too early to use a photo of them coming out again, carrying their labelled bin-bags, in one of which was hidden the painting . . .

Dempsey was jabbing at one of the figures in the photograph. Yes, it was Siobhan, mouth open as she issued orders, finger pointing towards the house. But there was another figure at the very edge of the frame. Grainy, to be sure, but identifiable to those who knew him as Detective Inspector John Rebus. Chances of Gill Templer *not* seeing the photo? Astronomical. It took Siobhan a moment or two to recover.

'Mrs Dempsey,' she said, 'are all your employees ex-offenders?'

'Not all of them, no.' Dempsey folded the paper and put it back in the bin.

'Maybe it's some sort of principle . . . ?'

'It is, as it happens.' Dempsey's tone said this was another argument she was ready for.

'Men with convictions for violence, driving cabs around Edinburgh . . .'

'Men who have served their sentence. Men whose crimes are far in the past. I credit myself with an instinct for knowing which ones I can trust.'

'But your instinct could be wrong.'

'I don't think so.'

The silence in the room was broken by a phone ringing, not the phone on Dempsey's desk but another, on a long, waist-high shelf which ran the length of the window. Siobhan noticed that there was a two-way radio system tucked on a shelf beneath. The window itself could slide open, and she guessed that outside office hours, if anyone came to the site looking for a cab they had to stand at the window and offer details through the opening. It wasn't her drivers that Ellen Dempsey didn't trust, it was the public.

She watched Dempsey take the call, then get on the radio and offer the job to 'Car Four'. Two regulars needed picking up from a west end bar. Contract job, to be charged to one of the city's insurance firms.

'Sorry about that,' Dempsey apologised, coming back to the desk. Siobhan had been studying her clothes: matching blue jacket and skirt with a white blouse. Thickish ankles, low-heeled black shoes. Every inch the successful businesswoman.

'I can't help thinking this is an odd career choice,' Siobhan said with a smile.

'I like cars.'

'I'm guessing the MG outside is yours?'

Dempsey's eyes turned to the window. She'd parked the car so it would be visible from the desk. 'That's the eighth one I've owned. Two are still in the garage at home.'

'All the same . . . you don't see many women in charge of a cab company.'

'Maybe I'm breaking the mould.'

'You started from scratch?'

'If you're implying that the company was set up by some ex-husband or other, you're mistaken.'

'I was just wondering what you did beforehand.'

'Looking for some tips on changing your career?' Dempsey reached into a drawer and brought out cigarettes and lighter. She offered, but Siobhan shook her head. 'I always have one a day, around this time,' Dempsey explained. 'Somehow I can't bring myself to stop altogether . . .' She lit up, inhaled deeply, exhaled slowly. 'I started with a couple of taxis in Dundee – that's where I grew up. When I wanted to expand, I didn't think Dundee was ready for me. Edinburgh, on the other hand . . .'

'Your competitors can't have been too thrilled when you arrived.'

'We had some frank exchanges of views,' Dempsey admitted. She broke off to answer the phone again. Afterwards, Siobhan had a question for her.

'Including Big Ger Cafferty?'

Dempsey nodded. 'But I'm still here, aren't I?'

'In other words, he didn't scare you off?'

'Cafferty's not the only operator in town. Things can get a bit hairy . . . look at the trouble out at the airport.'

Siobhan knew she was referring to the constant battle between black taxis and licensed mini-cabs, vying for trade from the arriving planeloads.

'I've had slashed tyres, broken windscreens . . . a whole spate of fake bookings back in the early days. But they could see I was dug in. That's the type of person I am, DS Clarke.'

'I don't doubt it, Mrs Dempsey.'

'It's *Ms*.'

Siobhan nodded. 'I noticed you didn't wear a ring, but the mechanic outside called you "Mrs".'

Dempsey smiled. 'They all do. Gives me less grief if they think there might be a Mr Dempsey who could come down hard on them . . .' She glanced at her watch. 'Look, I don't want to rush you, but my night-shift telephonist will be coming in soon, and I want to get this paperwork finished . . .'

'Understood,' Siobhan said, rising to her feet.

'And thanks for dropping in.'

'No problem. Thanks for the career advice.'

'You don't need any advice, DS Clarke. Running a cab company is one thing, but being a female officer in the CID . . .' Dempsey shook her head slowly. 'Now there's one job I couldn't do for all the tea in China.'

'Luckily, I don't drink tea,' Siobhan said. 'Thanks again for your time.'

She drove as far as the end of the road, and squeezed into a kerbside parking space, turning off the ignition and letting her mind wander. What had she gleaned from the conversation? A few useful snippets. That Dempsey had recognised her for CID straight off was interesting. To employ ex-cons was one thing, but clocking a plainclothes cop took a certain skill, a skill that came with practice. Siobhan couldn't help wondering how Ellen Dempsey would have acquired such an ability . . .

Then there was Dundee to consider. The story of her time there almost rang true. Almost, but not quite. There had been enough pauses in her narrative to indicate that she was leaving things unsaid. Those were the things Siobhan wanted to know about. When her mobile sounded, she knew who it would be.

Gill Templer . . . and not in a mood to waste words.

'What in God's name was John Rebus doing out at Inveresk?'

'He tagged along,' Siobhan said, adopting a veneer of honesty as the best policy. A car was pulling into the forecourt of MG Cabs. The night shift, she guessed . . .

'Why?' Templer was asking.

'Wanted a break from St Leonard's.'

'And?'

'And nothing. I didn't let him near the house. As far as I know, he smoked a cigarette, then headed back.' Siobhan was thinking of all the officers who'd been present and could call her a liar. The ones who'd heard her bellowing out of the window at Rebus ... who'd seen her march down the garden towards where he crouched over the unwrapped object ...

'Why do I find that so hard to believe?' Templer was saying now, denting Siobhan's fragile confidence.

'I don't know ... maybe because you've known him longer than I have. But that's the way it happened. He said he needed a break ... I emphasised that he was no longer part of the Marber inquiry. He accepted that, made no effort to assist at the house, and left soon after.'

'He left before you found the painting?'

Siobhan took a deep breath. 'Before we found the painting,' she confirmed.

Templer was thoughtful for a few moments. Siobhan could see the red MG reversing out of the compound, turning in her direction.

'I hope for your sake John backs up your story,' Templer was saying as Siobhan turned the ignition.

'Understood.' There was a pause. Siobhan could sense that her boss had something else she was struggling to say.

'Well, if that's everything ...' she coaxed, and was rewarded when Templer broke in.

'Has John said anything to you about Tulliallan?'

'Just what you'd expect.' Siobhan frowned. 'Has something happened?'

'No, it's just ...' Templer sounded anxious.

'He *will* be coming back, won't he?' Siobhan asked.

'I hope so, Siobhan. I really do.'

Templer ended the call just as Ellen Dempsey's car roared past. Siobhan took her time easing out of the parking spot. This time of the evening, traffic would still be heavy, but a red sports car hard to miss. She thought back to Templer's closing words. Siobhan had been asking whether Rebus was for the chop, but the way Templer had answered made her wonder. It had all sounded much more ominous . . . She tried calling Rebus, but he wasn't answering. She wasn't sure why she was following Ellen Dempsey exactly, except that she wanted to know a little more about the woman. The way she drove could offer pointers, as could her home – the style of house, the part of the city . . . And at least when she was tailing Dempsey, she was keeping busy. She wasn't at the station, being fawned over . . . she wasn't at home, brooding over a ready meal . . .

She switched the car's CD player on: Mogwai, *Rock Action*. It had an edginess to it which she found soothing. Maybe she could relate to it. Edgy and samey but with sudden unpredictable shifts.

Just like an investigation.

And, maybe even, just like her . . .

What Siobhan hadn't been expecting was that Dempsey would head south out of the city until she hit the by-pass, then use it to start heading west and north at speed. Plainly, she didn't live in Edinburgh, and soon it became apparent that she didn't even live this side of the Firth of Forth. As they made for the Forth Road Bridge, Siobhan found herself checking her petrol gauge. If she had to pull into a service station, she would lose Dempsey. As it was, the bridge offered problems of its own. There were tailbacks of drivers waiting to pay their toll. Siobhan found herself in a separate queue from her prey, and one that seemed to be moving much more slowly. At this rate, Dempsey would be across the bridge and out of sight . . . But Dempsey seemed intent on sticking to the speed limit, which told Siobhan that she'd probably had a speeding fine in the recent past, either that or had clocked up enough points on her licence that any fresh violation might see her banned. Siobhan was in the outside lane, ignoring the regular roadside reminders that the limit on the bridge was fifty miles per hour. Over to her right, a train was crossing the rail bridge. The CD had finished, and she was trying to find the repeat button. Then, at the last minute, she saw Dempsey signalling to take the first turn-off after the bridge. The inside lane was clogged, and Siobhan couldn't see a gap that would let her in. She switched her indicator on and edged towards the dividing line. The car behind flashed at her angrily, but braked to let her in, the driver sounding his horn afterwards and flashing his lights again.

'I get the picture,' Siobhan snarled. There were three cars between her and Dempsey, and one of them also took the slip-road. They were heading for North Queensferry, a picturesque place on the banks of the Forth, with the rail bridge towering above the houses and shops. Dempsey was signalling to turn up a steep incline which was little more than the width of a single car. Siobhan drove past, then pulled over. When the traffic behind her had passed, she reversed to the bottom of the hill. Dempsey had reached the summit and was disappearing over the brow. Siobhan followed. A hundred yards further on, Dempsey had turned into a driveway. Siobhan waited a few moments, then drove past. She couldn't see much because of the tall hedge in front. In her favour, Dempsey couldn't see her either. The bungalow was pretty much at the eastern edge of the village, the steep climb giving it height, so that it looked down on the main street and surroundings. Siobhan would bet there were spectacular uninterrupted views from the back garden.

At the same time, it was a very private place, and North Queensferry was nicely anonymous. Another train was crossing the bridge: with her window open, Siobhan could hear it. Heading across Fife to Dundee and beyond. Fife was what separated Edinburgh from Dundee. She wondered if that was why Dempsey had chosen to make it her home: neither one place nor the other, but within reach of both. It felt right to her: Dempsey wasn't just visiting someone; she was home.

She also got the feeling Dempsey lived alone. No other cars outside the bungalow, and no garage ... Hadn't Dempsey said something about owning other MGs, about having them stored in her garage? Well, wherever that garage was, it wasn't here. Always supposing the cars existed at all. Why would she have lied? To impress her visitor ... to stress that the name of her company was down to her passion for the sports cars which bore that brand ... There could be multiple reasons. People lied to police officers all the time.

If they had something to hide ... If they were talking for the sheer sake of talking, because as long as *they* were talking, they weren't being asked any awkward questions. Dempsey had sounded confident enough, calm and collected, but that could have been all front.

What could she be hiding, this woman who hid herself away from the world? She drove a car that wanted you to look at it ... wanted you to admire the shiny surface, the promise of performance. But here was this other side to its owner: the woman who dressed immaculately only to spend her days alone in an office, enduring only a little physical contact with the outside world. Her employees called her 'Mrs' ... she didn't let them get too close, didn't want them to think she was single, available. And when she came home it was to this quiet haven, to a house hidden behind walls and a hedge.

There was a whole side to Ellen Dempsey which she kept away from the world. Siobhan wondered what it might consist of. Would she find any answers in Dundee? Dempsey had *friends*, people even Cafferty was wary of. Was she fronting for some Dundee villains? Where had the money come from to kick-start her business? A fleet of cars didn't exactly come cheap, and it was a bit of a step up from 'a couple of taxis in Dundee' to the operation she now ran at Lochend. A woman with a past . . . a woman who could spot CID and gave work to ex-cons . . .

Ellen Dempsey didn't just have a past, Siobhan realised. She had a police record of her own. It was the simplest explanation. What was it Eric Bain had told her? *Reduce it to binary*. His way of saying, keep it simple. Maybe she was trying to make everything too complex. Maybe the Marber case was simpler than it seemed.

'Reduce it to binary, Siobhan,' she told herself. Then she started the car and headed for the bridge.

By the time Rebus drove home, it was almost half past seven. His mobile had stored a couple of messages: Gill and Siobhan. Then it started ringing.

'Gill,' he said, 'I was just about to call you.' He was in a queue at traffic lights.

'Have you seen tonight's final edition?' He knew what she was going to say. 'You made the front page, John.'

Bingo . . .

'You mean they got a picture of me?' he pretended to guess. 'Hope it was my good side.'

'I wasn't aware that you *had* a good side.' A low blow, but he let her get away with it.

'Look,' he said, 'it was my own stupid fault. I wanted out of the station for an hour, and they were all heading for the cars. I insisted on going, so don't go blaming anyone else.'

'I've already spoken to Siobhan.'

'She told me to clear off, and that's pretty much what I did.'

'Which is almost exactly what she told me, except that in her version it was *you* who decided to leave voluntarily.'

'She's trying to make me look good, Gill. You know what Siobhan's like.'

'You're supposed to be off the Marber inquiry, John: remember that.'

'I'm also supposed to be the sort of cop who can't take a telling: do you want me to blow my cover at Tulliallan?'

She sighed. 'No luck so far then?'

'There's a ray of light in the tunnel,' he admitted. The lights had changed, and he drove across the junction into Melville Drive. 'Problem is, I'm not sure I want to go anywhere near it.'

'Dangerous?'

'I won't know that till I get there.'

'For Christ's sake, be careful.'

'It's nice to know you care.'

'John . . .'

'Speak to you later, Gill.'

He didn't bother responding to Siobhan, knew now what her message had been.

Gray, Jazz and Allan Ward would be waiting for him as arranged, but he'd already prepared his story. He didn't want them hitting the warehouse . . . not because it would or wouldn't work, but because it was *wrong*. He knew now that he could go to Strathern, tell him that he was able to lead the three men into a trap. He still doubted Strathern would go for it. It wasn't *clean*; it didn't answer the question. All the trio had to do was say they'd merely been following Rebus's lead.

He'd parked at the top end of Arden Street, but the trio had found a space right outside his tenement door. The headlamps flashed at him, letting him know they were there. One of the rear doors opened on his approach.

'Let's go for a drive, John,' Gray said from the front. Jazz was driving, leaving Allan Ward in the rear beside Rebus.

'Where are we going?' he asked.

'How did it go at the compound?'

Rebus looked into the rear-view, where he could connect with Jazz's eyes. 'It's a non-starter, lads,' he sighed.

'Tell us.'

'For a start, they've got twenty-four-hour security on

the gate. Plus there's an alarm system on the fence as well as some serious-looking razor-wire. Then there's the warehouse itself, which is locked tight and almost certainly alarmed, too. But Claverhouse has been cleverer than I'd have credited. He's filled the interior with packing-cases, dozens of them.'

'And the merchandise is in one of them?' Jazz guessed.

Rebus nodded, aware of the driver's eyes still on him. 'And he's not about to say which one.'

'So all it needs is a lorry,' Gray piped up. 'Take the whole damned lot of them.'

'Takes time to load a lorry, Francis,' Jazz told his friend.

'We don't need a lorry,' Ward pitched in, leaning forward. 'We just take whichever case feels the heaviest.'

'That's good thinking, Allan,' Jazz said.

'It still takes time,' Rebus argued. 'A hellish lot of time.'

'And meantime the forces of law and order are streaming towards the scene?' Jazz guessed.

Rebus knew he hadn't quite managed to dissuade them. His head was swimming. *They don't have Bernie Johns's money, always supposing there was any money to begin with. All they've got is this dream I've offered them, and they want to make it real. Which makes me the mastermind . . .* He started shaking his head without realising he was doing it. But Jazz noticed.

'You don't rate our chances, John?'

'There's one more problem,' Rebus said, thinking fast. 'They're moving the stuff over the weekend. Claverhouse is antsy that Cafferty will try something.'

'Tomorrow's Friday,' Ward said unnecessarily.

'Not much time to procure a lorry,' Gray grumbled. He pulled down on his seat-belt, making some slack so he could turn to face Rebus. 'You come to us with this big fucking plan of yours, and this is what it turns into?'

'It's not John's fault,' Jazz said.

'Then whose is it?' Ward asked.

'It was a nice idea, but it wasn't to be,' Jazz told him.

'It was a half-cocked idea that we should have kiboshed from the start,' Gray snarled, still giving Rebus the full force of his scowl. Rebus turned to peer out of the window.

'Where are we going?'

'Back to Tulliallan,' Ward explained. 'Tennant gave the word: that's the end of our wee holiday.'

'Hang on, I haven't got any of my stuff with me.'

'So?'

'So there are things I need . . .'

Jazz signalled, pulled over. They were approaching Haymarket. 'All right making your own way back from here, John?'

'If that's what's on offer,' Rebus said, opening his door. Gray's hand closed like a vice around his forearm.

'We're very disappointed in you, John.'

'I thought we were a team, Francis,' Rebus told him, twisting free of his grip. 'You want to walk into that warehouse, it's fine by me. But they'll catch you and they'll put you away.' He paused, 'Maybe another scheme will come along.'

'Aye, right,' Gray said. 'Don't call us and we won't call you . . .' He leaned back and pulled Rebus's door closed. The car took off again, leaving Rebus watching from the pavement.

That was it then. He'd blown it. He was never going to win them back, never going to find out the truth about Bernie Johns. And on top of all that, it might just turn out that they were on to him . . .

'Fuck it,' he said, wishing he'd never said yes to Strathern. He'd never meant for them to agree to his scheme. It was a way of getting them to open up about themselves. Instead of which, they were closing ranks, excluding him. The course had one more week to run. He could pull out now, or see it through to the end. It was something he'd have to consider. If he failed to see it through, whatever suspicions the trio harboured would appear confirmed. He turned and found that he was standing outside a pub. What better way to ponder the conundrum than over a pint and a double malt? With any luck, the place would do food too. They'd call him a cab afterwards to see him home. His problems would all have disappeared . . .

'I'll drink to that,' he told himself, pushing open the door.

24

It was two in the morning when the phone woke him. He was lying on the living room floor, next to the hi-fi, CD cases and album sleeves spread around him. He crawled on hands and knees to his chair and picked up the receiver.

'Yes?' he croaked.

'John? It's Bobby.'

Rebus took a moment to realise who Bobby was: Bobby Hogan, Leith CID. He tried focusing on his watch.

'How soon can you get down here?' Hogan was asking.

'Depends where "here" is.' Rebus was doing a stock-check: head cloudy but bearable; stomach queasy.

'Look, you can go back to bed if you like.' Hogan starting to sound aggrieved. 'I thought maybe I was doing you a favour . . .'

'I'll know that when you tell me what it is.'

'A floater. Pulled him out of the docks not fifteen minutes ago. And though I haven't seen him in a while, he looks awfully like our old pal the Diamond Dog . . .'

Rebus stared down at the album sleeves, not really seeing them.

'You still awake, John?'

'I'll be there in twenty minutes, Bobby.'

'He'll be on his way to the mortuary by then.'

'Even better. I'll meet you there.' Rebus paused. 'Any chance of this being an accident?'

'At this stage, we're supposed to be keeping an open mind.'

'You won't be too bothered if I don't do the same?'

'I'll see you at the Dead Centre, John . . .'

'Dead Centre' was what they called the mortuary. One of the workers there had come up with the phrase, telling everyone that he was proud to work 'at the dead centre of Edinburgh'. The building was tucked away on the Cowgate, one of the city's more secretive streets. Few pedestrians ever found themselves there, and the traffic was intent on being elsewhere. Things might change when the parliament opened its new building, less than a ten-minute walk away. More traffic, more tourists. At this time of night, Rebus knew the drive would take him five minutes. He wasn't sure his blood/alcohol level would pass muster, but after a quick shower he made for his car anyway.

He didn't know what he was thinking or how he was feeling about Dickie Diamond's death. Hard to say how many enemies had been harbouring their festering thoughts, just waiting for the night when they clapped eyes on Diamond again.

He cut across to Nicolson Street and headed for the city centre, turning right at Thin's Bookshop and taking the steep turn down to the Cowgate. A couple of taxis: a few drunks. *Dead centre*, he was thinking. He knew the easiest way into the mortuary this time of night was the staff entrance, so parked outside, making sure he wasn't blocking the loading-bay. For a long time, they'd had to carry out actual autopsies at one of the city's hospitals, due to the lack of a decent air-filtering system in the mortuary's autopsy suite, but that had been remedied now. Rebus walked into the building and saw Hogan in the corridor ahead of him.

'He's in here,' Hogan said. 'Don't worry, he wasn't long in the water.' Good news: the body underwent terrible changes after lengthy submersion. The short corridor led directly into the loading area, which itself led directly to the holding area – a wall of little doors, each one opening to reveal a trolley. One trolley was sitting out, a polythene-wrapped body lying on it. Dickie Diamond was still wearing the same clothes. His wet hair was slicked back from his face, and there was some kind of algae stuck to one cheek. His eyes were closed, mouth open. The attendants were readying to take him upstairs in the elevator.

'Who's doing the cutting?' Rebus asked.

'They're both on tonight,' Hogan told him. Meaning: Professor Gates and Dr Curt, the city's chief pathologists. 'It's been a busy one: drugs overdose in Muirhouse, fatal fire in Wester Hailes.'

'And four naturals,' an attendant reminded him. People dying of old age, or in hospital. Mostly they ended up here.

'Shall we go up?' Hogan asked.

'Why not?' Rebus said.

As they climbed the stairs, Hogan asked about Diamond. 'You lot were just interrogating him, weren't you?'

'Interviewing him, Bobby.'

'As a suspect or a witness?'

'The latter.'

'When did you let him go?'

'This afternoon. How long had he been dead when you fished him out?'

'I'd say about an hour. Question is: did he drown?'

Rebus shrugged. 'Do we know if he could swim?'

'No.'

They'd entered a glass-fronted viewing area. There were a couple of benches for them to sit on. On the other side of the glass, people moved around in surgical gowns and green wellingtons. There were two stainless-steel slabs, with drainage holes and old-fashioned wooden blocks for the head to rest on. Gates and Curt waved a greeting, Curt gesturing for the two detectives to come join the fun. They shook their heads, pointing to the benches to let him know they were fine where they were. The body-bag had been removed, and now Dickie Diamond's clothes were being discarded, placed in their own plastic bags.

'How did you ID him?' Rebus asked.

'Phone numbers in his pocket. One was for his sister. I recognised him anyway, but she did the formal ID downstairs just before you got here.'

'How was she?'

'She didn't seem too surprised, to be honest. Maybe she was just in shock.'

'Or maybe she'd been expecting it?'

Hogan looked at him. 'Something you want to tell me, John?'

Rebus shook his head. 'We reopened the case, went sniffing. Malky, the nephew, told Dickie what was happening. He came haring up here. We picked him up.' He shrugged. 'End of story.'

'Not as far as someone was concerned,' Hogan said, peering through the glass, as one of the attendants lifted something from the clothing. It was the revolver Diamond had pointed at Rebus. The attendant held it up for them to see.

'Managed to miss that in your search, Bobby,' Rebus said.

Hogan stood up, called out through the glass. 'Where was it?'

'Down the back of his underpants,' the attendant called back, voice muffled by the face-mask he was wearing.

'Can't have been too comfortable,' Professor Gates added. 'Maybe he'd a bad case of piles and was resorting to threats.'

When Hogan sat down again, Rebus noticed that he had reddened slightly at the neck.

'These things happen, Bobby,' Rebus sought to reassure him. He was wondering now if the gun had been tucked into Diamond's waistband when he'd been answering their questions in IR1 . . .

With the body stripped of its clothing, the autopsy

proper was beginning with the taking of body temperature. Rebus and Hogan knew what the pathologists would be looking for: alcohol levels; signs of injuries; head trauma . . . They would want to know whether Diamond had been alive or dead when he'd entered the water. Alive, and it could have been an accident – too much booze, maybe. Dead, and there was foul play involved. Everything from the state of the eyeballs to the contents of the lungs provided little clues. The body temperature would be used to calculate time of death, though immersion would make any exact calculations problematic.

After twenty minutes as spectator, Rebus said he needed a cigarette. Hogan decided to join him. They went to the staff room and helped themselves to mugs of tea, then walked outside. The night was clear and chilly. An undertaker's car had arrived to take charge of one of the 'naturals'. The driver bowed his head to them in sleepy acknowledgement. At this time of night, in this location, you had a bond of sorts. You were dealing with things most people – those with their heads warm against pillows, dreaming the time away until morning – shied away from.

'Undertaker,' Hogan mused. 'You ever thought it a bloody odd word to use in the circumstances? Funeral director, I can understand, but undertaker . . . ?'

'You getting philosophical on me, Bobby?'

'No, I'm just saying . . . ach, forget it.'

Rebus smiled. His own thoughts were of Dickie Diamond. Dickie had gifted them Chib Kelly's name. They could have accepted his gift, presented the case to Tennant and left it at that. But Gray and Jazz – Jazz in particular – hadn't been satisfied. Rebus was wondering if they'd decided to press Dickie further. They'd dumped Rebus at Haymarket, but that didn't mean they hadn't turned back. In fact, he was a damned good alibi. When last seen, the trio had been heading west out of town, while Dickie was found in the north-east corner of the city. The Wild Bunch had started life looking like an uneasy alliance of insubordinate officers who didn't like authority and were as likely to ignore an order as carry it out. But now Rebus was wondering if there were something more dangerous, more lethal at work. Gray, Jazz and Ward had been all too ready to help rip off the warehouse consignment. Force would have been necessary, but that hadn't seemed to bother them. Were they capable of killing Dickie Diamond? Then again, *why* would they have killed him? Rebus didn't have an answer for that, not yet.

He was leaning over the wall, watching the roadway, when he spotted the parked car. Movement within it. As the driver's door opened and the interior light came on, he recognised Malky. He looked for Malky's mother, but didn't see her. Malky was making to cross the road towards Rebus, but stopped at the centre-line and stretched his arm, pointing.

'You fucking killed him, ya bastard!'

Hogan was at the wall now, too. 'Calm down, Malky,' he called.

'Dickie told me he was going to have a word with you!' Malky shouted hoarsely. His finger moved towards the mortuary building. 'Is that what you call "a word"? Man comes to talk to you, you do him in!'

'What's he talking about, John?' Hogan said.

Rebus shook his head. 'Maybe Dickie *did* say he was coming to see me . . .'

'But never got round to it?' Hogan guessed.

'Or didn't get the chance.'

Hogan patted Rebus's arm. 'I'll go talk to him,' he said, making for the street, hands held up in front of him. 'Easy now, Malky, easy . . . It's a bad time for you, I know, but let's not go waking the neighbours, eh?'

For a moment, Rebus had thought he was going to say 'waking the dead' . . .

He headed back indoors, depositing his empty mug in the sink in the staff room. As he turned to leave, Dr Curt came in, no longer wearing his gown and boots.

'Any tea going?' Curt asked.

'Kettle's not long boiled.'

Curt busied himself with a fresh mug and tea-bag. 'He was dead when he went in the water,' he began. 'Happened around midnight, and the body went in the water not long after. Forensics might be able to tell us more from the clothing.'

'How did he die?'

'Windpipe was crushed.'

Rebus thought back to the interview room, the way Gray's forearm had slid around Diamond's throat . . .

'You got a spare cigarette?' Curt was asking now. Rebus opened his packet, and Curt picked one out, tucking it behind his ear. 'I'll have it with my tea. Simple pleasures, eh, John?'

'Where would we be without them?' Rebus said, his mind on the drive he was planning to take . . .

It was nearly dawn when he reached Tulliallan. He saw another detective in front of him, sneaking back in after a night in someone else's bed. Rebus recognised him, a young detective sergeant from the new City Centre force. He'd be here on one of the specialist programmes. Rebus drove around the car park, seeking Jazz's Volvo. There was dew on it, as with the cars either side, so it had been there a while. He touched the bonnet. It was cold; again, same temperature as the cars either side.

He did the same set of checks with Gray's Lexus, once he'd found it. Nothing to suggest it had been used in the recent past. Then he realised he didn't know what car Allan Ward drove. He supposed he could look for a dealer badge on the back windscreen, something indicating purchase in Dumfries . . . but that would take time, and he was pretty sure it would be a waste of effort. Instead, he headed indoors and along to the bedrooms, walking right past his own door and knocking loudly on Gray's, four along from him. When there was no answer, he knocked again.

'Who is it?' the voice coughed from within.

'It's Rebus.'

The door opened a crack, Gray squinting into the light. 'Hell's going on?' he asked. His hair was sticking up. He was dressed in a T-shirt and underpants. The room smelt stuffy.

'Been in bed long, Francis?' Rebus asked.

'What's it to you?'

'Dickie Diamond's just been found dead, windpipe crushed.'

Gray didn't say anything, just blinked a couple of times as if trying to wake from a dream.

'Afterwards, he was dumped in Leith docks, the killer trying to muddy the waters, as it were . . .' Rebus narrowed his eyes. 'Coming back to you now, is it, Francis? It was only four or five hours ago.'

'Four or five hours ago I was tucked up in bed,' Gray stated.

'Anyone see you come back?'

'I don't have to explain anything to you, Rebus.'

'That's where you're wrong.' Rebus pointed a finger. 'Round up your pals and meet me in the bar. You've got a serious amount of convincing to do if you want me off your case.'

Rebus went to the bar and waited. The place smelled of stale beer and cigarettes. There were a few glasses dotted around, left there by drinkers who'd stayed put after the place had closed. Most of the chairs had been stacked on tables. Rebus lifted one down and made himself comfortable. He was asking himself what the hell he was doing here. It wasn't that he was afraid of what Dickie Diamond might have told anyone. It was more that he just didn't care any more. Everything seemed to be falling apart, and the subtle undercover work hadn't accomplished anything, perhaps because subtlety had never been his strong point. Rather, he was going to shake things up, see how the trio reacted. What did he have to lose? That was a question he wasn't about to answer.

Five minutes later, the three men walked in. Gray had made some attempt to flatten his hair against his skull. Jazz looked wide awake, and had dressed with his usual care. Allan Ward, wearing only a baggy T-shirt and gym shorts, was yawning and rubbing his face. He'd slipped trainers on his feet, but no socks.

'Has Francis filled you in?' Rebus asked as they sat in a row across the table from him.

'Dickie Diamond's been found dead,' Jazz answered. 'And you seem to think Francis had a hand in it.'

'Maybe more of a forearm than a hand. Dickie's windpipe was crushed. Same sort of manoeuvre Francis pulled in IR1.'

'When did all this happen?' Jazz asked.

'Pathologist thinks around midnight.'

Jazz looked to Gray. 'We were back here by then, weren't we?'

Gray shrugged.

'You left me around eight,' Rebus said. 'Doesn't take four hours to drive from Haymarket to here.'

'We didn't come straight back.' Ward explained, still rubbing his face with both hands. 'We stopped for something to eat and a few drinks.'

'Where?' Rebus asked coldly.

'John,' Jazz said quietly, 'none of us went near Dickie Diamond.'

'Where?' Rebus repeated.

Jazz sighed. 'That road out of town . . . the one we were on after we left you. We stopped for a curry. After all, we had things to talk about, didn't we?' Now all three men looked at Rebus.

'We did,' Gray agreed.

'What was the restaurant called?' Rebus asked.

Jazz tried to laugh. 'Give me a break, John . . .'

'And afterwards? Where did you drink?'

'Couple of pubs on that same road,' Ward stated. 'Too good an opportunity, with Jazz driving . . .'

'Names?' Rebus said.

'Get stuffed,' Gray said. He leaned back and folded his arms. 'We don't need this paranoia of yours. Is it because you're in the huff? We'd given you the hump, left you standing there? So now you try pulling this . . . ?'

'Francis has a point, John,' Jazz said.

'If you went trawling Leith for Dickie Diamond, someone will have spotted you,' Rebus pressed on.

Jazz shrugged. 'Fine,' he said. 'But no one's going to come forward, because we were never there.'

'We'll see.'

'Yes,' Jazz said, nodding his head without his eyes ever leaving Rebus's, 'we will. But meantime, any chance we can go get some sleep now? Something tells me tomorrow's going to be a day and a half . . .'

Ward was already on his feet. 'Paranoia,' he said, echoing Gray. Rebus doubted he knew what the word meant.

Gray stood up without saying anything. His eyes burned into Rebus. Jazz was the last to leave.

'I know you did it,' Rebus told him.

Jazz seemed about to say something, but shook his head instead, as if to acknowledge that no words were going to change Rebus's mind.

'You need to admit it while there's still time,' Rebus went on.

'Time for what?' Jazz asked, genuinely curious.

'For resurrection,' Rebus answered quietly. But Jazz just winked at him before turning to go.

Rebus sat for a few more minutes before returning to his room, making sure the door was locked behind him. He was aware of the proximity of the three men, three men he'd just accused of murder and accessory to murder. He thought of placing his chair against the door. He thought of heading out to the car park and driving home. In truth, he wasn't sure they'd killed Dickie; he was only sure that they were capable of it. It all depended how much they knew and how much they suspected – about Rebus's involvement with Dickie, how it had led to Rico Lomax's murder and a burning caravan. But he'd wanted the trio shaken, and reckoned he'd succeeded – in spades. He considered who else might have wanted Dickie dead. There was one name, but thinking of it took him right back to the Rico Lomax case.

The name of Morris Gerald Cafferty . . .

25

Late down to breakfast, Rebus found the other five members of the Wild Bunch seated at one of the tables. He squeezed in between Stu Sutherland and Tam Barclay.

'What's this about Dickie Diamond?' Barclay said.

'Got himself throttled last night,' Rebus answered, concentrating on the plate in front of him.

Barclay whistled. 'Got to be our shout, hasn't it?'

'It's a Leith call,' Rebus told him. 'Body was fished out of the docks.'

'But it could tie in to the Lomax case,' Barclay argued. 'Which belongs to *us*.'

Sutherland was nodding. 'Bloody hell, we only talked to him yesterday.'

'Yes, funny coincidence,' Rebus said.

'John thinks one of us did it,' Allan Ward blurted out. Sutherland's jaw dropped, revealing chewed-up bacon and egg yolk. He turned to Rebus.

'He's right,' Rebus conceded. 'Diamond had the same neck-hold put on him that Francis used in the interview room.'

'I'd say you're leaping to conclusions,' Jazz said.

'Aye,' Barclay added, 'the kind of leap Superman used to make in the cartoons.'

'Just think for a minute, John,' Jazz pleaded. 'Try to rationalise it . . .'

Rebus sneaked a glance at Gray, who was working away at a crust of toast. 'What do you say, Francis?' he asked. Gray stared back at him as he answered.

'I say the pressure's got to you . . . you've stopped

thinking straight. Maybe a few extra sessions with wee Andrea are in order.' He reached for his coffee, preparing to wash down the mouthful of toast.

'Man's got a point, John,' Barclay argued. 'Why the hell would any of us want to do away with Dickie Diamond?'

'Because he was holding something back.'

'Such as?' Stu Sutherland asked.

Rebus shook his head slowly.

'If there's something you know,' Gray intoned, 'maybe now's the time to spit it out.'

Rebus thought of the little confession he'd made to Gray, the hint that he'd not only known Dickie better than he'd admitted, but that he also knew something about Rico Lomax's demise. Gray's threat was implicit: keep accusing me, I start talking. But Rebus had considered this, and didn't think anything Gray could say would do him much harm.

Unless he'd wrenched some confession out of the Diamond Dog . . .

'Morning, sir,' Jazz said suddenly, looking over Rebus's shoulder. Tennant was standing there. He tapped two fingers against Rebus's upper arm.

'I hear the situation has changed somewhat, gentlemen. DI Rebus, as you were present at the post-mortem examination, perhaps you could fill us in. From what I've been told, DI Hogan has yet to apprehend any suspects, and he's keen for whatever input we can provide.'

'With respect, sir,' Barclay spoke up, 'we should be in charge of this one, seeing how it might connect to Lomax.'

'But we're not an active unit, Barclay.'

'We've been doing a pretty good impersonation,' Jazz stated.

'That's as may be . . .'

'And you're not saying Leith wouldn't welcome a few extra pairs of hands?'

'Always supposing they were there to help,' Rebus muttered.

'What's that?' Tennant asked.

'No point in us being there if an ulterior motive's involved, sir. Hindering rather than helping.'

'I'm not sure I see what you're getting at.'

Rebus was aware of three pairs of eyes glowering at him. 'I mean, sir, that Dickie Diamond was strangled, and when we brought him in for questioning, DI Gray got a bit carried away and started throttling him.'

'Is this true, DI Gray?'

'DI Rebus is exaggerating, sir.'

'Did you touch the witness?'

'He was flannelling us, sir.'

'With respect, sir,' Stu Sutherland piped up, 'I think John's making a mountain out of a molehill.'

'A molehill can trip us as surely as any mountain,' Tennant told him. 'What do you have to say, DI Gray?'

'John's getting carried away, sir. He's got a bit of a rep for letting cases get beneath his skin. I was out last night with DI McCullough and DC Ward. They'll vouch for me.'

His two witnesses were already nodding.

'John,' Tennant said quietly, 'is your accusation against DI Gray based on anything other than what you say you saw in the interview room?'

Rebus thought of all the things he could say. But he shook his head instead.

'Are you willing to withdraw the accusation?'

Rebus nodded slowly, eyes still on his untouched plate of food.

'You sure? If Leith CID *do* ask us to help, I have to be sure we're heading there as a team.'

'Yes, sir,' Rebus said dully.

Tennant pointed to Gray. 'Meet me upstairs in five minutes. The rest of you, finish your breakfast and we'll convene in fifteen. I'll talk to DI Hogan and see what the state of play is.'

'Thank you, sir,' Jazz McCullough said. Tennant was already on his way.

Nobody said anything to Rebus during the rest of the meal. Gray was first to go, followed by Ward and Barclay. Jazz seemed to be waiting for Stu Sutherland to leave them alone, but Sutherland got himself a refill of coffee. As he rose to go, Jazz kept his eyes on Rebus, but Rebus focused on the remains of his egg-white. Sutherland settled back down with his replenished cup and took a loud slurp.

'Friday today,' he commented. 'POETS day.'

Rebus knew what he meant: Piss Off Early, Tomorrow's Saturday. The team were due a weekend's break, followed by the final four days of the course.

'Think I'll go to my room and start packing,' Sutherland said, getting up again. Rebus nodded, and Sutherland paused, as if preparing for some carefully considered speech.

'Cheers, Stu,' Rebus said, hoping to spare him the effort. It worked. Sutherland smiled as though Rebus was responding to something he'd said, some valuable contribution to Rebus's well-being.

Back in his room, Rebus was checking for messages on his mobile when it started to ring. He studied the number on the LCD display, and decided to take the call.

'Yes, sir?' he said.

'All right to talk?' Sir David Strathern asked.

'I've got a couple of minutes before I need to be somewhere else.'

'How's it going, John?'

'I think I've blown it big time, sir. No way I'm going to regain their trust.'

Strathern made a noise of irritation. 'What happened?'

'I'd rather not go into details, sir. But for the record, whatever they did with Bernie Johns's millions, I don't think they've got much of it left. Always supposing they had it in the first place.'

'You're not convinced?'

'I'm convinced they're not on the straight and narrow. I don't know if they've pulled any other scams, but if one presented itself, they'd be happy to take it on.'

'None of which gets us any further.'

'Not really, sir, no.'

'Not your fault, John. I'm sure you did what you could.'

'Maybe even a bit more than that, sir.'

'Don't worry, John, I won't forget your efforts.'

'Thank you, sir.'

'I suppose you'll want to be pulled out now? No use staying . . .'

'Actually, sir, I'd rather stick it out. Only a few more days to go, and they'd rumble me if I suddenly disappeared.'

'Good point. We'd be breaking your cover.'

'Yes, sir.'

'Very well then. If you're okay with that . . .'

'I'll just have to grin and bear it, sir.'

Rebus ended the call and thought about the lie he'd just told: he was staying put not because he feared being rumbled but because he still had work to do. He decided to phone Jean, let her know they'd have the weekend to themselves. Her response: 'Always supposing nothing comes up.'

He couldn't disagree . . .

The Wild Bunch reconvened in the Lomax inquiry room. It seemed like they'd been away from it a long time; longer still since they'd first met around its table. Tennant was seated at the head, hands clasped in front of him.

'Leith CID would like our help, gentlemen,' he began. 'Or more properly, *your* help. You won't be running the case – it's not your bailiwick, after all. But you will share any and all information with DI Hogan and his team. You will pass on to them your notes on the procedures you've followed, the progress you've made on the Lomax case. And especially anything pertaining to Mr Diamond and his circle. Clear enough?'

'Will we be based in Leith, sir?' Jazz McCullough asked.

'For today, yes. Make sure you take everything with you. There's a weekend coming up, and after that you'll be back here for four days of intensive final analysis. The plan was to retrain you and prepare you to work once more as effective team-players . . .' Rebus felt Tennant's eyes rest on him as he spoke these words. 'Your respective forces will need evidence that you have learned from this course.'

'How are we doing so far, boss?' Sutherland piped up.

'You really want to know, DS Sutherland?'

'Actually, now you mention it, I think I can wait.'

There were smiles at this, from everyone in the room but Rebus and Gray. Gray looked chastened after his little chat with Tennant, while Rebus was deep in thought, trying to gauge how safe he would be down in Leith. At least he'd be in Edinburgh – on home turf – and he'd have Bobby Hogan to watch his back.

Odds on him making it to the weekend in one piece? He'd give no better than even money.

The case against Malcolm Neilson was proceeding nicely. Colin Stewart from the Procurator Fiscal's office had arrived at St Leonard's that morning for a progress report. It would be Stewart and his team of lawyers who'd decide whether there was enough evidence to justify a trial. So far he seemed satisfied. Siobhan had been called into Gill Templer's office to answer a few of his procedural questions regarding the search of the house in Inveresk. Siobhan had countered with a few questions of her own.

'We've no actual physical evidence yet, have we?'

Stewart had removed his glasses, seeming to study the lenses for smears, while Gill Templer sat stony-faced beside him.

'We've the painting,' he commented.

'Yes, but it was found in an unlocked shed. Anyone

could have put it there. Aren't there more tests we could be doing to see whether anyone else handled it?'

Stewart glanced towards Templer. 'We appear to have a Doubting Thomas in our midst.'

'DS Clarke likes to play devil's advocate,' Templer explained. 'She knows as well as we do that further tests would take time and money – especially money – and probably wouldn't add anything to what we already know.'

It was something the officers on an inquiry were never allowed to forget: each case had to fall within a strict budget. Bill Pryde probably spent as much time adding up columns of figures as he did on actual detective work. It was another thing he was good at: bringing cases in under budget. The High Hiedyins at the Big House perceived this as a strength.

'I'm just saying that Neilson would be an easy target. He'd already had a very public falling-out with Marber. Then there was the hush money and . . .'

'The only people who know about the hush money, DS Clarke,' Stewart said, 'are the investigation team themselves.' He slipped his glasses back on. 'You're not implying that one of your own officers could have had some involvement . . . ?'

'Of course not.'

'Well then . . .'

And that had been that. Back at her desk, she called Bobby Hogan in Leith. It was something she'd been meaning to do. She wanted to know whether Alexander had been told about his mother's death, and how he was bearing up. She'd even considered paying the grandmother a visit, but knew there could be no easy conversation between them. Thelma Dow had to contend with the loss of Laura and the jailing of her own son. Siobhan hoped she would be able to cope, able to give Alexander what he needed. She'd even briefly considered contacting a pal in social work, someone who could check that both carer and grandson were going to manage. Staring at the office around her, she saw the case winding down. The telephones had stopped being busy. People were standing around, catching up on gossip. She'd seen Grant Hood on last night's TV news, acknowledging that a man had been charged, a house searched, and certain contents taken away for examination. It all had to be very coy now, so as not to jeopardise the legal case. The murder of Laura Stafford hadn't even made the front page of the tabloids. RED-LIGHT STAB HORROR was the headline Siobhan had seen, with a daytime photograph of the Paradiso's exterior and a much smaller photo of Laura, looking younger and with longer, bubble-permed hair.

Bobby Hogan was taking a while to come to the phone. Eventually, another officer answered for him.

'He's under the cosh right now, Siobhan. Is it anything I can help with?'

'Not really . . . They're keeping you busy down there then?'

'We had a murder last night. Rogue called Dickie Diamond.'

They chatted for a couple more minutes, then Siobhan hung up. She walked across to where George Silvers and Phyllida Hawes were sharing a joke.

'Hear what happened to Dickie Diamond?' she asked.

'Who's he when he's at home?' Silvers responded. But Hawes was nodding.

'That lot from Tulliallan had him in here only yesterday,' she said. 'Bobby Hogan was in first thing this morning, asking questions.'

'As long as he's not after poaching a few extra bodies,' Silvers commented, folding his arms. 'I think we all deserve a bit of a rest, don't you?'

'Oh, aye, George,' Siobhan told him, 'you've been breaking your neck on this one . . .'

His glare followed her back to her desk. WPC Toni Jackson entered the room, saw Siobhan and smiled.

'It's Friday,' she said, leaning against the side of the desk. Silvers had spotted her and was giving a sycophantic wave, still believing her to be related to someone famous. She waved back. 'Silly sod,' she muttered under her breath. Then, to Siobhan: 'You still got that date lined up?'

Siobhan nodded. 'Sorry, Toni.'

Jackson shrugged. 'It's your loss, not ours.' She gave a sly look. 'Still keeping lover boy's name under wraps?'

'Absolutely.'

'Well, that's your prerogative, I suppose.' Jackson eased herself off the desk. 'Oh, nearly forgot.' She handed over the sheet of paper she'd been carrying. 'Marked for your attention. Came through to our fax machine by mistake.' She wagged a finger. 'I want to hear *all* about it on Monday.'

'Right down to the forensic detail,' Siobhan promised, offering a smile as Jackson moved away. The smile melted as she studied the cover-sheet of the lengthy fax. It was from Dundee CID, responding to her request for gen on Ellen Dempsey. Just as she was starting to read, a voice interrupted her.

'No rest for the wicked, eh, Siobhan?'

It was Derek Linford. He seemed even better groomed than usual, with a pristine shirt, new-looking suit, and dapper tie.

'Going to a wedding, Derek?'

He looked down at himself. 'Nothing wrong with being presentable, is there?'

Siobhan shrugged. 'Wouldn't have anything to do with the rumour that we're in line for a visit from the Chief Constable?'

Linford raised an eyebrow. 'Are we?'

She gave a wry smile. 'You know damned well we are.

Bit of a fillip for the troops, telling us how hard we've all been working.'

Linford sniffed. 'Well, it happens to be true, doesn't it?'

'Speaking of which, some of us still have work to be getting on with.'

Linford angled his head, trying to read the fax. Siobhan turned it face down on her desk. 'Hiding something from your colleagues, Siobhan?' he teased. 'That's hardly being a team-player, is it?'

'So?'

'So maybe you've been learning all the wrong lessons from DI Rebus. Make sure you don't end up like him, kicked into rehab . . .'

He turned to go, but she called him back. 'When you're having your hand shaken by the Chief, just remember . . .' She pointed a finger at him. 'It was Davie Hynds who found the money Marber paid to Malcolm Neilson. You'd already been through Marber's bank statements and hadn't spotted it. Bear that in mind when you're taking all the credit for solving the case, Derek.'

He gave her a cold smile, said nothing. When he was gone, she tried getting back to her reading, but found it impossible to concentrate. Scooping up the fax, she decided she wanted to be elsewhere when the brass from the Big House came calling.

Settling for the Engine Shed, she bought herself some herbal tea and sat at a table by the window. A couple of mums were feeding jars of food to their infants. Otherwise, the place was quiet. Siobhan had turned off her mobile, pulled out a pen, and was preparing to mark any interesting snippets.

Having read the fax through once, she found that she'd underlined just about the whole damned thing. She realised that her hand was trembling slightly as she poured out more tea. Taking a deep breath, trying to clear her head, she started reading again.

The money to fund Ellen Dempsey's cab company hadn't come from shady businessmen; it had come from a few years' work as a prostitute. She'd been employed in at least two saunas, undergoing a single arrest in each when they were visited by police. The busts had been eighteen months apart. There was an additional note to the effect that Dempsey had also worked for an escort agency, and had been questioned after a foreign businessman 'mislaid' his cash and credit cards after a visit by Dempsey to his hotel room in the city. She was never charged. Siobhan looked for evidence that one or both of the saunas had been owned by Cafferty, but couldn't find any. Names were given, but they were the names of local entrepreneurs, one Greek in origin, one Italian. After the police raids, HM Inland Revenue and Customs and Excise had opened their own inquiries, looking into profits and VAT left undeclared. The owners had shut up shop and moved on.

By which time Ellen Dempsey was already running her small-time cab company. There were a couple of minor cases: a driver assaulted by a passenger who'd refused to pay the fare. The passenger – ready for an argument at the end of a long night's drinking – had found in the driver a willing sparring partner. The result had made it as far as an overnight stay in the cells, but had fallen short of a court appearance. The second case was similar, only Ellen Dempsey had been the driver, and she'd sprayed the client with mace. As mace was banned in Scotland, it was Ellen who'd ended up being charged, the passenger claiming that he'd only wanted a goodnight kiss, and that the two of them 'knew one another of old'.

Though this last phrase wasn't explored, Siobhan got an inkling of what had really happened. One of Ellen's old punters, probably not believing that she'd given up the sauna life, deciding that if he pressed, she'd be willing.

But she'd reached for the mace instead.

It might explain the move to Edinburgh. How could she

operate a legitimate business from Dundee without the threat of more ghosts appearing? Impossible to escape her old life, her old self ... So she'd set up in Edinburgh instead, and bought herself a house in Fife, somewhere she wouldn't be recognised, somewhere she could hide from the world.

Siobhan poured more tea, though it was tepid now and too strong. But it gave her something to do while she collected her thoughts. She flicked back four or five sheets, found the page she was looking for. There was a name not only underlined there, but circled, too. It cropped up a couple of times, once in connection with the raid on the sauna, once to do with the mace case.

A detective sergeant called James McCullough.

Or Jazz, as everyone seemed to call him.

Siobhan wondered if Jazz might be able to shed more light on Ellen Dempsey, always supposing there was light to shed. She thought back to Cafferty's words. There was no indication in the fax of any 'friends' Dempsey might have. She'd never been married, had no children. She seemed always to have supported herself ...

Pictures flickered across Siobhan's vision: Jazz McCullough, visiting the Marber inquiry, keeping up with developments ... Francis Gray, seated on one of the desks, reading transcripts ... Allan Ward buying Phyl dinner and pumping her for information.

Ellen Dempsey ... tangential to the case ... maybe worried, contacting her *friends*. Jazz McCullough and Ellen Dempsey ... ?

Coincidence or connection? Siobhan turned her mobile on, called Rebus on his. He picked up.

'I need to talk to you,' she said.

'Where are you?'

'St Leonard's. You?'

'Leith. Supposedly helping with the Diamond killing.'

'Are the others there with you?'

'Yes. Why?'

'I want to ask you about Jazz McCullough.'

'What about him?'

'It may be nothing . . .'

'You've got me curious. Want to meet?'

'Where?'

'Can you come down to Leith?'

'That would make sense. I can ask McCullough a few questions while I'm there . . .'

'Don't expect me to be much use in that department.'

She drew her eyebrows together. 'Why not?'

'I don't think Jazz is talking to me. Nor is anyone else, for that matter.'

'Hang in there,' Siobhan said. 'I'm on my way.'

Sutherland and Barclay had travelled to Leith in Rebus's car. A period of uncomfortable silence had been broken by some stilted conversation, before Barclay plucked up courage and asked Rebus if it was maybe worth reconsidering his accusations.

Rebus had just shaken his head slowly.

'No use arguing with the man,' Sutherland had muttered. 'Thank Christ for the weekend . . .'

At Leith police station, the atmosphere had been hardly less strained. They'd presented a report to Hogan and one of his colleagues, Rebus saying little as he concentrated on spotting anything the trio might be trying to leave out. Hogan had been aware of the tension in the room, his eyes requesting some sort of explanation from Rebus. None had been forthcoming.

'We don't mind sticking around,' Jazz had said at the end of the report. 'If you feel we've a contribution to make . . .' Then he'd shrugged. 'You'd be doing us a favour, keeping us away from Tulliallan.'

Hogan had smiled. 'All I can promise is office grind.'

'Better than classroom lessons,' Gray had opined, speaking, it seemed, for all of them.

Hogan had nodded. 'Fair enough then, maybe just for today.'

The inquiry room was old-fashioned and high-ceilinged, with peeling paint and chipped desks. The kettle seemed to be on constantly, with the most junior officers on a milk-buying rota. There wasn't much room for the Tulliallan contingent, which suited Rebus as it meant they had to split up, sharing desk-space with disgruntled locals. Rebus waited a good twenty minutes after Siobhan's call before she put her head around the door. He got up, joined her in the corridor, having signalled to Hogan with his palm spread, meaning he was taking five. He knew Hogan would relish the chance of a word, realising something was up and wanting to know what it was. But Hogan was in charge of the team, his time at a premium. So far, they hadn't managed a moment alone.

'Let's go walkies,' Rebus told Siobhan. When they got outside it was drizzling. Rebus pulled his jacket around him and took out his cigarettes. He gestured with his head, letting her know they were walking down towards the docks. He didn't know exactly where the Diamond Dog's body had been discovered, but it couldn't have been too far from here . . .

'I heard about Diamond,' Siobhan said. 'How come no one's talking to you?'

'Just a little falling-out.' He shrugged, concentrating on his cigarette. 'These things happen.'

'To you more than most.'

'Years of practice, Siobhan. So what's your interest in McCullough?'

'His name came up.'

'Where?'

'I was looking at Ellen Dempsey. She owns the cab that dropped Marber home that night. Dempsey moved her company here from Dundee. In a past life, she worked in a sauna.'

Rebus thought of Laura Stafford. 'Interesting coincidence,' he mused.

'And here's another one: Jazz McCullough arrested her a couple of times.'

Rebus seemed to concentrate harder than ever on his cigarette.

'And then I started remembering the way McCullough and Gray spent so much time flipping through the transcripts and notes in the inquiry room.'

Rebus nodded. He'd been there, seen them . . .

'And Allan Ward dating Phyl,' Siobhan was saying.

'Asking her questions,' Rebus added, still nodding. He'd stopped walking. Jazz, Gray and Ward . . . 'How to you think it plays?'

She shrugged. 'I just wondered if there was some connection between McCullough and Dempsey. Maybe they've kept in touch . . .'

'And he kept tabs on the Marber case at her behest?'

'Maybe.' Siobhan paused. 'Maybe because she didn't want her past to come up. I think she's tried hard to build a new life.'

'Could be,' Rebus said, not sounding entirely convinced. He'd started walking again. They were close to the docks now, heavy lorries passing them almost continuously, spewing out fumes, kicking up dust and grit. They walked with their faces turned to one side. Rebus could see Siobhan's unprotected neck. It was long and slender, a line of muscle running down it. He knew that when they reached the dockside the water would be oily and dotted with jetsam. No place for a body to end up. He touched her arm and took a detour, leading them down an alley. It would connect with one of the roads eventually, leading them back towards the station.

'What are you going to do about it?' he asked.

'I don't know. I thought I'd get McCullough's response.'

'I'm not sure about that, Siobhan. Maybe you'd be better off doing a bit more digging first.'

'Why?'

Rebus shrugged. What could he tell her? That to his mind Jazz McCullough, quiet and charming family man, was perhaps mixed up in murder and criminal conspiracy?

'I just think it might be safer.'

She stared at him. 'Care to elucidate?'

'It's nothing concrete . . . just a feeling.'

'A feeling that asking McCullough a few questions might not be *safe?*'

Rebus shrugged again. They'd come out of the alley. By turning right, they'd be heading towards the rear of the police station.

'I'm guessing this "feeling" of yours has something to do with the fact that nobody's talking to you?'

'Look, Siobhan . . .' He ran a hand down his face, as if trying to brush away a layer of skin. 'You know I wouldn't say anything if I didn't think it mattered.'

She considered this, then nodded her agreement. They were walking around the side of the station, a pavement drunk causing them to step on to the road. Rebus pulled Siobhan back to safety as a car hurtled past, horn blaring. Someone in a hurry.

'Thanks,' Siobhan said.

'I do what I can,' Rebus informed her. The drunk was making for the opposite pavement, stumbling blindly across the road. They both knew he'd make it. He was carrying a bottle: no way a motorist would want that flying through his windscreen.

'I've often thought pedestrians should be issued with hammers for just this situation,' Siobhan said, watching the car disappear into the distance. She said goodbye to Rebus on the steps of the police station, watched him disappear inside. She'd wanted to say something: *take care*, maybe, or *watch yourself*, but the words hadn't come out. He'd nodded anyway, reading her eyes with a smile. The problem wasn't that he thought himself indestructible –

quite the opposite. She worried that he relished the idea of his own fallibility. He was only human, and if proving it meant enduring pain and defeat, he would welcome both. Did that mean he had a martyr complex? Maybe she should give Andrea Thomson a call, see if the two of them could talk about it. But Thomson would want to talk about *her*, and Siobhan wasn't ready for that. She thought of Rebus and his ghosts. Would Laura Stafford now haunt *her* dreams? Might she be the first of many? Laura's face was already starting to fade, losing definition, leaving Siobhan with a hand locked to a car's door-handle.

She took a deep breath. 'Got to keep busy,' she told herself. Then she opened the door to the station and peered inside. No sign of Rebus. She walked in, showed her ID, climbed the stairs to the CID floor. It struck her that Donny Dow might still be in the cells, but by now he was probably on remand in Saughton jail. She could always ask, but wasn't sure that seeing him again would constitute any kind of exorcism.

'It's Siobhan, isn't it?' The voice startled her. The man had just appeared from out of an office. He was carrying a blue folder. She forced a smile.

'DI McCullough,' she said. 'That's funny,' the smile widening, 'I was just looking for you . . .'

'Oh yes?'

'I wanted a quick word.'

He looked up and down the corridor, then nodded to the room he'd just vacated. 'We'll have some privacy in here,' he said, leaning past her to open the door.

'After you,' she said, the smile frozen on her face. The office looked little used. Some old desks, chairs each missing a leg, stiff-drawered filing-cabinets. She left the door open, then remembered Rebus . . . didn't want him catching her here. So she closed the door behind her.

'All very mysterious,' McCullough said, placing the folder on a desk and folding his arms.

'Not really,' she said. 'It's just something that's cropped up in connection with the Marber case.'

He nodded. 'I hear you found the missing painting. That should give you a hike up.'

'I was promoted pretty recently.'

'Nevertheless . . . You go on breaking cases at this rate, sky's the limit.'

'I don't think the case is necessarily broken.'

He paused. 'Oh?' Sounding genuinely surprised.

'Which is why I have to ask a few questions about the owner of MG Cabs.'

'MG Cabs?'

'A woman called Ellen Dempsey. I think you know her.'

'Dempsey?' McCullough frowned, trying the name out a few times. Then he shook his head. 'Give me a clue?'

'You knew her in Dundee. Prostitute. She was working the night you raided a sauna. A while after that, she was off the game and running a couple of mini-cabs. Used mace against a customer, ended up in court . . .'

McCullough was nodding. 'Right,' he said, 'I've got her now. What did you say her name was? Ellen . . . ?'

'Dempsey.'

'That the name she was using back then?'

'Yes.'

He looked like he was still having trouble putting a face to the name. 'Well, what about her?'

'I just wondered if you'd kept in touch?'

His eyes widened. 'Why the hell would I do that?'

'I don't know.'

'DS Clarke . . .' Unfolding his arms, face turning angry. His hands had started to bunch themselves into fists. 'I should have you know I'm a happily married man – ask anyone . . . even your friend John Rebus! They'll tell you!'

'Look, I'm not suggesting anything improper here. It just seems a coincidence that the two of you—'

'Well, coincidence is all it *can* be!'

'Okay, okay.' McCullough's face had reddened, and she

393

didn't like those clenched fists . . . the door opened and a face peered round.

'You okay, Jazz?' Francis Gray asked.

'Far from it, Francis. This little bitch has just accused me of shagging some old pro I arrested once in Dundee!'

Francis Gray stepped into the room, closing the door softly behind him. 'Say that again,' he growled, eyes reduced to slits which were concentrated on Siobhan.

'All I'm trying to say is—'

'You better be careful *what* you say, dyke-features. Anybody starts bad-mouthing Jazz, they've got *me* to contend with, and I make Jazz here look like a pussy, though probably not the kind of pussy that interests *you*.'

Siobhan's face was suffusing with colour. 'Now hang on a minute,' she spat, trying to control the tremor in her voice. 'Before the pair of you go flying off the handle . . .'

'Did Rebus put you up to this?' McCullough was snarling, fingers of both hands pointed at her as though they were six-shooters. 'Because if he did . . .'

'DI Rebus doesn't even know I'm here!' Siobhan said, her voice rising. The two men seemed to glance at one another, and she couldn't tell what they were thinking. Gray stood between her and the door. She didn't think she was going to get past him in a hurry.

'Best thing you can do,' McCullough was warning her, 'is head back to your burrow and dig yourself in for the winter. You start telling tales, you could be headed for your Chief Constable's cooking-pot.'

'I think Jazz, as usual, is being too generous in his predictions,' Gray said, with quiet menace. He'd just taken half a step towards her and away from the door when it flew open, catching him in the back. Rebus had shouldered it, and was now standing there, surveying the scene.

'Sorry to gatecrash the party,' he said.

'What do you think you're trying to pull, Rebus?

Reckon you could drag your little girlfriend here into those paranoid fantasies of yours?'

Rebus looked at Jazz. He seemed upset, but Rebus couldn't tell how genuine it was, or what its cause might be. It was just as easy to be upset when maligned as when rumbled.

'You finished asking questions, Siobhan?' When she nodded, Rebus stuck out his thumb and jabbed it over his shoulder, letting her know it was time to leave. She hesitated, not liking the idea of him bossing her around. Then she gave McCullough and Gray the same withering stare, and squeezed past Rebus, striding down the corridor without looking back.

Gray offered Rebus a wicked grin. 'Want to shut that door again, John? Sort things out here and now?'

'Don't tempt me.'

'Why not? Just you and me. We'll leave Jazz out of it.'

Rebus's fingers were around the door-handle. He didn't know what was about to happen, but started pushing the door closed anyway, watching as Gray's grin widened, showing yellow, glinting teeth.

Then a fist rapped on the other side of the door, and Rebus let it swing open again.

'Getting all cosy in here?' Bobby Hogan said. 'I'll have no skiving on *my* shift.'

'Just conferencing,' Jazz McCullough said, face and voice suddenly back to normal. Gray had his own face lowered, pretending to adjust his neck-tie. Hogan looked at the three men, knowing something had been going on.

'Well,' he said, 'conference your arses out of here and back to what we in the human world call *work*.'

The human world . . . Rebus wondered if Hogan would ever know how close to the mark he'd been. In this room, for a matter of seconds, three men had been reconciled to acting like something less than human . . .

'Sure thing, DI Hogan,' Jazz McCullough said, picking up his folder and readying to leave the office. Gray's eyes caught Rebus's, and Rebus could see the man was having a hard time pulling himself back. It was like watching Edward Hyde decide he no longer needed Henry Jekyll. Rebus had told Jazz that there was still the chance for resurrection, but not in Francis Gray's case. Something had died behind his eyes, and Rebus didn't think he'd be seeing it again.

'After you, John,' McCullough was saying with a sweep of his arm. As he followed Hogan out of the room, Rebus could feel a tingling all down his spine, as though a blade was about to lodge itself there . . .

26

There was a tapping at Siobhan's window. It took her a moment to work out where she was: the St Leonard's car park. She must have driven there from Leith; couldn't remember anything about it. How long had she been sitting? It could have been half a minute or half an hour. More tapping. She got out of the car.

'What's up, Derek?'

'Shouldn't that be *my* question? You're sitting there like you've seen a ghost.'

'Not a ghost, no.'

'What then? Has something happened?'

She shook her head, as if trying to clear it of the memory of that office . . . Gray and McCullough . . .

Rebus had warned her, and she'd gone blundering in anyway with her sweeping accusations and half-formed questions. It was hardly what they taught you at Tulliallan. Even so, the reactions of McCullough and Gray had been startling: McCullough's sudden anger, Gray's snarling defence of his colleague. She'd expected a response, yes, but nothing quite so feral. It was as if the two men had been unravelling in front of her eyes.

'I'm fine,' she told Linford. 'Just in a dream, that's all.'

'Sure?'

'Look, Derek . . .' Her voice had hardened. She rubbed at a throbbing spot on her right temple.

'Siobhan . . . I *am* trying to mend the fences between us.'

'I know you are, Derek. But this isn't the time, okay?'

'Okay.' He held up both hands in surrender. 'But you

know I'm there for you if you need me.' She managed to nod her head. He shrugged, prefacing a change of subject. 'Friday night tonight. Shame you've got that date. I was going to suggest dinner at the Wichery . . .'

'Another time maybe.' She couldn't believe she was saying this. *I don't want to make any more enemies* . . . Linford was smiling.

'I'll hold you to that.'

She nodded again. 'I have to go to the office now . . .'

Linford checked his watch. 'I'm out of here. Might be back before the close of play. Otherwise, have a great weekend.' He seemed to think of something. 'Maybe we could do something together.'

'I need a bit more notice than that, Derek.' The throbbing was getting worse. Why wouldn't he just *go*? She turned and walked towards the station's rear door. He'd be standing there . . . watching her . . . waiting for her to turn so he could try out another sympathetic smile.

No chance.

Upstairs in the murder room, things were winding down. The team had been given the weekend off en masse. The Procurator Fiscal's office was happy enough with the case as it stood. They'd have more questions, more information they needed come Monday morning. But for now, everyone was relaxing. There was still paperwork to contend with, still loose ends to be gathered together and tied as tight as possible.

It could all wait till Monday.

Siobhan sat at her desk, staring at the cover-sheet of the Dundee fax. When she looked up, Hynds was moving in her direction. She could see by the look on his face that he was going to ask if anything was wrong. She held up a finger, warning him off. He stopped, shrugged and turned away. She started reading the text of the fax one more time, willing something – anything – to jump out at her. She supposed she could try talking to Ellen Dempsey, see if she'd let anything slip.

So what? she wondered. What difference did it make if McCullough did connect to Ellen Dempsey? It certainly seemed to make a difference to him. She knew almost nothing about McCullough, and didn't have any contacts in Dundee who could enlighten her. Then she turned back to the cover sheet.

To: DS Clarke, Lothian and Borders
From: DS Hetherington, Tayside

Hetherington ... a detective sergeant, just like her. Siobhan's request hadn't been addressed to any particular officer. She'd just got the fax number for Tayside Police HQ and sent it there. The cover-sheet was on headed paper, the telephone number just discernible. Then she noticed something typed below Hetherington's name: x242. Had to be an extension number. Siobhan picked up her phone and punched the digits.

'Police HQ, DC Watkins,' the male voice said.

'It's DS Clarke here, St Leonard's in Edinburgh. Any chance I could have a word with DS Hetherington?'

'She's not in the office right now.' *She* ... A smile cracked open Siobhan's face. 'Can I take a message?'

'Is she likely to be back?'

'Hang on a sec ...' There was the sound of the receiver being laid down on a desk-top. DS Hetherington was a woman. It gave them something in common, might make it easier for the pair of them to talk ... The receiver was picked up again. 'Her stuff's still here.' Meaning she'd be back to pick it up.

'Could I leave you a couple of numbers to pass on to her? I'd really like to talk to her before the weekend.'

'Shouldn't be a problem. We have to prise her out of the office usually.'

Better and better, thought Siobhan, giving Watkins her St Leonard's and mobile numbers. Afterwards, she stared at the telephone, willing it to ring. The room around her was emptying: early doors, as Rebus would have called it. She hoped he was all right. She didn't know why she hadn't called him . . . Actually, she had a vague memory of doing just that. Probably as soon as she'd got back to her car. But he hadn't been answering. She tried him again now. He picked up.

'I'm fine,' he told her without preamble. 'I'll talk to you later.' End of conversation.

She visualised Hetherington returning to her desk . . . maybe not noticing the message. Watkins hadn't sounded the type who had to be prised from anything but a bar-stool. What if he'd already made his escape before her return? What if she saw the message but was too tired to do anything about it? Maybe she'd had a long week . . . To Siobhan, it had lasted an eternity. She wasn't going to do anything this weekend but lie in bed and read, doze, then read some more. Maybe drag the duvet as far as the sofa and watch a black and white film. There were CDs she hadn't got round to playing: Hobotalk, Goldfrapp . . . She'd decided to give the football a miss. It was an away game at Motherwell.

The phone remained silent. Siobhan counted to ten, giving it a chance, then gathered her stuff and headed for the door.

She got in her car and put some driving music on: the latest REM. It was fifty-three minutes long, which meant it would see her most of the way to Dundee.

She hadn't allowed for the Friday-afternoon exodus from the city, ending with a long queue to pay the toll at the Forth Road Bridge. After that, she put her foot down. Her mobile was attached to its charger. Still no word from Hetherington. She picked it up every few minutes, just in case some new text message had escaped her attention. The further north she travelled, the better she felt. It wouldn't matter if there was nobody at the office when she arrived. It was good to be out of Edinburgh. It reminded her that there was another world out there. She didn't know Dundee professionally, but had visited the city plenty of times as a football fan. The two Dundee teams had stadiums practically next door to one another. There were a few pubs in the centre where Siobhan had enjoyed a drink before kick-off, her Hibs scarf hidden deep down in her shoulder-bag. There was a sign off the motorway to the Tay Bridge, but she'd made that mistake once before. It led to a long, winding trail through the villages of Fife. She stuck to the M90, bypassing Perth and heading into Dundee from the west. This approach turned into a seemingly endless series of roundabouts. She was steering the car around one of these when her phone sounded.

'I got your message,' the female voice said.

'Thanks for calling back. As it happens, I'm on the outskirts of town.'

'Christ, it must be serious.'

'Maybe I just fancied a Friday night in Dundee.'

'In which case, delete "serious" and add "desperate".'

Siobhan knew she was going to like DS Hetherington. 'My name's Siobhan, by the way,' she said.

'Mine's Liz.'

'Are you just about ready to shut up shop, Liz? Only, I know the pubs in this city better than I do your HQ.'

Hetherington laughed. 'I suppose I could be persuaded.'

'Great.' Siobhan named a pub, and Hetherington said she knew it.

'Ten minutes?'

'Ten minutes,' Hetherington agreed.

'How will we know one another?'

'I don't think that'll be a problem, Siobhan. Single women in that place tend to be an endangered species.'

She was right.

Siobhan only knew the place from Saturday afternoons, drinking in safety, a pack of Hibs fans around her. But as people clocked off, the weekend stretching ahead of them, the pub took on a very different character. There were office parties, loud laughter. The only people drinking alone were sour-faced men at the bar. Couples were meeting up after work, bringing their day's gossip with them. Supermarket carrier-bags held the evening meal. There was thumping dance music, and a TV sports channel playing silently. The interior was spacious, but Siobhan was having trouble finding somewhere to stand, somewhere she'd be conspicuous to anyone coming in. There were two doors into the place, which didn't help. Every time she thought she'd found a spot, drinkers would gather nearby, camouflaging her. And Hetherington was late. Siobhan's glass was empty. She went to the bar for a refill.

'Lime and soda?' the barman remembered. She nodded, quietly impressed. She turned to watch the door and saw that it had opened. A woman was standing there. Something Liz Hetherington had forgotten to mention: she had to be six feet tall or thereabouts. Unlike a lot of tall women, she made no attempt to make herself seem shorter, holding her back straight and wearing shoes with heels. Siobhan waved, and Hetherington joined her.

'Liz?' Siobhan said. Hetherington nodded. 'What're you having?'

'Just a dry ginger . . .' She paused. 'No, the hell with it. It's Friday, right?'

'Right.'

'So make it a Bloody Mary.'

There were no tables left, but they found a ledge by the far wall and placed their drinks there. Siobhan realised that she didn't want to stand next to Hetherington for too long: she might get a crick in her neck. She fetched two stools from the bar and they sat down.

'Cheers,' she said.

'Cheers.'

Liz Hetherington was in her mid-thirties. Thick shoulder-length black hair, which she kept trimmed without spending a fortune on new styles. Her slender frame thickened considerably at the hips, but her height helped her carry it. No rings on her left hand.

'How long have you been a DS?' Siobhan asked.

Hetherington puffed out her cheeks. 'Three years . . . Three and a half actually. You?'

'Nearer three weeks.'

'Congratulations. How's Lothian and Borders?'

'Much the same as up here, I'd expect. I've got a female DCS.'

Hetherington raised an eyebrow. 'Good for you.'

'She's okay,' Siobhan said thoughtfully. 'I mean, she's not the kind to give favours . . .'

'They never are,' Hetherington stated. 'Too much to prove.'

Siobhan nodded agreement. Hetherington was savouring a mouthful of her drink.

'Ages since I had one of these,' she explained, swirling the ice in her glass. 'So what brings you to the city of the three Js?'

Siobhan smiled. The three Js: jute, jam and journalism, of which, as far as she knew, only the third still provided much in the way of local jobs. 'I wanted to thank you for sending me that stuff I asked for.'

'A phone call would have sufficed.'

Siobhan nodded. 'There was a name mentioned . . . one of your colleagues. I may have to ask him a few questions.'

'And?'

Siobhan shrugged. 'And I was just wondering what he was like. His name's James McCullough. He's a DI. Maybe you know someone who can give me a bit of background?'

Hetherington studied Siobhan over her glass. Siobhan wasn't sure she was falling for the line she'd just spun. Maybe it wouldn't matter.

'You want to know about Jazz McCullough?'

Meaning Hetherington knew him. 'I just want to know how he'll react if I ask him some questions. Forewarned is forearmed and all that . . .'

'And knowledge is power?' She watched Siobhan shrug again, then gestured towards her drink. 'You need a refill.'

Siobhan knew Hetherington was giving herself time. 'Lime and soda,' she said.

'Want a gin or anything in that?'

'I'm driving.' Siobhan stared down at her near-empty glass. 'Go on then,' she said.

Hetherington smiled and headed for the bar.

When she came back, she'd made her decision. She'd also bought two packets of dry-roasted peanuts.

'Sustenance,' she said, placing them on the ledge. Then, as she sat down again: 'The hunters are out.'

Siobhan nodded. She'd seen them: men's eyes assessing her. Men from the office parties, but also men at the bar. They did, after all, appear to be two women at the start of a night out, making them possible prey . . .

'Good luck to them,' Siobhan said.

'Here's to professional women,' Hetherington said, chinking glasses. Then she paused. 'You don't realise how lucky you are.'

'Oh?'

'I mean, maybe it isn't luck. Could be it's instinct or kismet or something.' She paused to sip her drink. 'There are plenty of people in CID who know Jazz McCullough, and some of them might even be willing to talk to you. But not many would say very much.'

'He has a lot of friends?'

'He's *made* a lot of friends. Plenty of favours he's done for people down the years.'

'But you're not one of them?'

'I've worked with him a couple of times in the past. He acted like I was invisible, which, as you can imagine, is quite a feat.'

Siobhan could well imagine it: she reckoned Hetherington was probably a good half-inch taller than McCullough, maybe more.

'He didn't like you?'

Hetherington shook her head. 'I don't think it went that far. He just didn't think I was *necessary*.'

'Because you're a woman?'

Hetherington shrugged. 'Maybe.' She lifted her glass again. 'So don't expect him to welcome you with open arms.'

'I won't.' Siobhan thought back to the scene in Leith and had to suppress a shiver. The alcohol seemed to surge through her. She lifted a handful of nuts to her mouth.

'What is it you need to ask him anyway?'

'The notes you sent me . . .'

'I forget the woman's name.'

'Ellen Dempsey. McCullough arrested her a couple of times. Once for prostitution, then again for using mace against someone in a taxi. Dempsey may be part of a case I'm working.'

'What's it got to do with McCullough?'

'Probably nothing, but I need to ask anyway.'

Hetherington nodded her understanding. 'Well, I've told you what I know about Jazz . . .'

'You haven't mentioned that he's on a course at Tulliallan.'

'Oh, you know about that? Jazz isn't always very good at following orders.'

'A colleague of mine in Edinburgh's just the same. Happens to be at Tulliallan too.'

'Which is why you know Jazz is there? It's not that I was covering up for him, Siobhan. I just didn't see how it was relevant.'

'Everything's relevant, Liz,' Siobhan told her. 'My feeling – strictly between us . . .' she waited until Hetherington had nodded her agreement, 'is that McCullough may have kept in touch with this Ellen Dempsey character after she left Dundee.'

'Kept in touch in what way?'

'To the extent that he may want to protect her.'

Hetherington was thoughtful for a moment. 'I'm not sure I can help. I know he's married with kids, one of them grown up and studying at university.' She paused. 'There's some sort of separation going on . . .'

'Oh?'

Hetherington winced. 'This is going to sound like me having a go at him . . .'

'Not as far as I'm concerned, Liz.' Siobhan waited for her to speak.

Hetherington let out a sigh. 'He moved out a couple of months back, according to the rumour-mill. Still goes round there . . . I think he moved into a flat only a couple of streets away.'

'He lives in the city?'

Hetherington shook her head. 'Just outside, in Broughty Ferry.'

'On the coast?'

Hetherington nodded. 'Look, I really don't want to speak bad of the guy. If you talked to a dozen detectives, you'd hardly find anyone with a—'

'But he has a problem with authority?'

'He just happens to think he knows more than them. Who's to say he's wrong?'

'Reminds me of that colleague again,' Siobhan said with a smile.

'Hey, girls, looks like you could do with another drink.' Two men were approaching, pint-glasses in hands. They wore jackets, ties and wedding rings.

'Not tonight, fellahs,' Hetherington told them. The one who'd spoken gave a shrug.

'Only asking,' he said. Hetherington waved them goodbye.

'Maybe there's somewhere else you prefer?' Siobhan asked her.

'I really need to be getting home.' She tugged at her watch-strap. 'If you need to talk to Jazz, just dive in and do it. He won't bite.'

Siobhan didn't like to say that she wasn't sure about that.

They were heading in different directions, so shook hands outside the pub. The two men followed them out. 'Where you lassies off to then?'

'Never mind us, just get on home to your wives.'

The men glowered, then slouched off, muttering curses.

'Thanks for your help, Liz,' Siobhan said.

'I'm not sure I've done much.'

'You gave me an excuse to get out of Edinburgh.'

Hetherington nodded, as though she could understand. 'Come see us again some time, DS Clarke.'

'I'll do that, DS Hetherington.'

She watched the tall, confident figure striding away from her. Hetherington sensed it, threw a wave without bothering to look back.

Siobhan walked downhill to where she'd parked her car. The sky was losing light as she snaked her way back towards the motorway, replacing REM with Boards of Canada. When her mobile rang, she knew instinctively who it would be.

'How was the rest of your day?' she asked.

'I survived,' Rebus told her. 'Sorry I couldn't talk earlier.'

'You were in the same room as them?'

'And sticking as close to Bobby Hogan as I could. You managed to get under Jazz McCullough's skin – I'm impressed.'

'I should have taken your advice and steered clear.'

'I'm not so sure about that.'

'John . . . are you ready yet to tell me what the hell's going on?'

407

'Maybe.'

'I'm not doing anything else for the next hour.'

There was a long silence on the line. 'This has got to stay between us,' he told her.

'You know you can trust me.'

'Like I trusted you to stay away from McCullough?'

'That was more in the way of advice,' she said with a grin.

'Well, all right then. If you're sitting comfortably . . .'

'I'm ready.'

Another silence, and then Rebus's voice, sounding eerily disembodied. 'Once upon a time, in a land far away, there was a king called Strathern. And one day, he called one of his errant knights to him with news of a perilous quest . . .'

Rebus paced his living room as he told Siobhan the story, or as much of it as he felt she needed. He'd clocked off early and come straight home, but now the place felt like a trap. He kept peering from the window, wondering if someone was waiting for him below. The front door was locked, but that wouldn't keep anyone out. The joiner had replaced the door-jamb, but without adding any extra reinforcement. Another chisel or crowbar would open it as effortlessly as a key. The lights were off throughout the flat, but Rebus wasn't sure he felt any safer in the darkness.

Siobhan asked him a couple of questions when he was done. She didn't say anything about whether he'd been right or wrong to take on such a task. She didn't tell him he was mad for suggesting the drug heist to the trio. Rebus knew then that she was listening to him as a friend as well as a colleague.

'Where are you?' he thought to ask at last. From the sounds, she was still driving. He'd thought she was probably on her way home from St Leonard's, but that had been half an hour ago when he'd started his story.

'I've just passed Kinross,' she told him. 'I'm on my way back from Dundee.'

Rebus knew what Dundee meant. 'Digging dirt on Jazz McCullough?'

'Not that there was much to find . . . He's split from his wife, but that hardly makes him a monster.'

'Split from his wife?' Rebus was thinking back to their first days in Tulliallan. 'But he's always on the phone to her. Made a point of going home when he could.'

'They separated a few months back.'

The happy marriage had been smoke, Rebus realised. 'Then where was he going?' he asked.

'I wonder if Ellen Dempsey could tell us.'

'Me too . . .' Rebus grew thoughtful. 'What are you doing tonight?'

'Not much. Are you suggesting a stakeout?'

'Maybe a little one, just to see if we can confirm anything.'

'Dempsey lives in North Queensferry. I could be there in ten, fifteen minutes.'

'And McCullough has a house in Broughty Ferry . . .' Rebus went to his dining table, started sifting through the paperwork there. There was a sheet . . . they'd each been given one at the start of the course. Names and ranks of the participants, plus their work and home addresses. He lifted it out. 'Got it,' he said.

'Word is, he's rented a flat a couple of streets away,' Siobhan was saying. 'You sure you want to head up there? If his car's in North Queensferry, it's a wasted trip . . .'

'Anything's better than sitting here,' Rebus told her. He didn't add how much he felt like a target.

They agreed to keep in touch by mobile and he placed one last call to Jean, letting her know he would see her later on in the evening, how much later he couldn't say.

'If the lights are out, don't bother ringing the bell,' she told him. 'Call me in the morning instead.'

'Will do, Jean.'

He walked quickly from the tenement to his car, starting the engine and reversing out of the parking space. He didn't know what to expect: some ambush perhaps, or a car following him. But it was mid-evening quiet, and the Edinburgh streets were such that it was hard to tail someone if they were expecting you. It was all stop-start, traffic lights and junctions. Rebus didn't think he was being followed. The Wild Bunch had dispersed, supposedly on their way home to families, loved ones, drinking cronies. Allan Ward had complained of the long drive he faced: no fast, easy route to Dumfries. But that could have been just talk. Impossible to tell where any of the trio were. Rebus had imagined Jazz heading for the happy home he'd talked into existence. But there was no happy home. Hard to say what was real any more. Friday night, and the city was coming out to play: girls in short dresses; boys bouncing as they walked, filled with chemical bravado. Men in suits waving down taxis; music pounding from cruising cars. You worked hard all week, then prayed for oblivion. Having left Edinburgh behind, crossing the Forth Bridge, he looked down towards North Queensferry and gave Siobhan a call.

'No sign of life,' she told him. 'I've driven past a couple of times . . . no car in the driveway.'

'She might still be at work,' Rebus argued. 'Busy night and all that.'

'I called to book a cab. It wasn't her voice.'

Rebus smiled. 'Nice move.'

'Where are you?'

'If you wave, I might see you. I'm just crossing the bridge.'

'Let me know when you get there.'

Rebus ended the call, clearing his mind as he drove.

Broughty Ferry was on the coast just east of Dundee itself. It liked to think of itself as genteel and independent, like someone with enough money put aside for a comfortable retirement. He stopped to ask a local for directions, and soon found himself on Jazz McCullough's street, though mindful that McCullough himself could be in the vicinity. There were plenty of cars parked kerbside and in driveways, but no sign of McCullough's Volvo saloon. Rebus passed his house. It was detached but unostentatious. Maybe four bedrooms, leaded windows in the lounge. Light was pouring through them. There was a driveway but no garage. The car on view was a Honda Accord, probably the wife's. Rebus turned his Saab round at a neighbouring cul-de-sac and managed to park just close enough to the house to keep any comings and goings visible. He took a sheet of paper from his pocket and unfolded it: the list from Tulliallan. Jazz's phone number was printed next to his address. Rebus placed the call. A young male voice picked up: the fourteen-year-old son.

'Is your dad in?' Rebus asked cheerily.

'No . . .' The word stretched out longer than necessary as the boy tried to decide what else to tell the caller.

'I've got the right number for Jazz?'

'He's not here,' the boy said.

'I'm a friend of his from work,' Rebus explained.

The boy relaxed a little. 'I can give you another number if you've got a pen.'

'That'd be great.'

The number was recited from an address book or piece of notepaper. Rebus jotted it down. 'That's a great help, thanks.'

'No problem.' The boy put the phone down just as Rebus could hear the faint voice of a woman asking who was calling. He looked at the number he'd just been given. It was Jazz's mobile. No point trying that: it wouldn't help pinpoint a location. Rebus settled his neck against the head-rest, then called Siobhan.

'I'm here,' he told her. 'Any action your end?'

'Maybe they're down the pub.'

'I wish I was with them.'

'Me too. I had a gin a couple of hours ago and it's given me a thumping head.'

'For which the only cure is more alcohol,' Rebus agreed.

'What the hell are we doing, John?'

'I thought we were on surveillance.'

'But for whose benefit?'

'Our own.'

She sighed. 'I suppose you're right . . .'

'Don't feel duty-bound to stick around.' Rebus watched a sports car turn into the street. Its brake-lights glowed as it passed the house, but it kept going, signalling to turn into the road at the end. 'What car does Dempsey drive?' Rebus asked, starting his ignition.

'Latest-model red MG.'

'One just drove past me.' He made the same turn the MG just had, and saw it round another corner. Rebus kept up his commentary. 'Slowed down as if the driver wanted a quick recce of McCullough's family pile.'

'And now?'

Rebus made to turn into another street, but changed his mind when he saw the MG reverse into a tight parking spot. A man was standing on the pavement, looking to left and right.

Jazz McCullough.

With better lighting, he might have spotted Rebus, but Rebus had the feeling it was McCullough's wife he was watching for. A woman got out of the car, and he led her briskly indoors.

'Result,' Rebus told Siobhan. 'She's just gone into McCullough's flat.' He described the woman he'd seen.

'That's her all right,' Siobhan confirmed. 'What now?'

'I think we've got as much as we can expect. Jazz McCullough's playing away from home with Ellen Dempsey.'

'That's why he was so keen to keep tabs on the Marber case? He wanted to check we weren't hassling her?'

'I suppose so . . .'

'But why?' Siobhan persisted. 'What was it they thought we'd find?'

'I don't know,' Rebus admitted. He didn't see what else he could say.

'You're giving up?' Siobhan's voice asked.

'I just think it can wait till Monday,' he told her. 'It doesn't make me a bad person.'

'No, of course not . . .'

'Look, Siobhan, it's something you should take to Gill Templer. Whether she decides to act on it – or if there's anything for her to act *on* – is down to Gill herself.'

'She thinks the case is closed.'

'Maybe she's right.'

'What if she's wrong?'

'Jesus, Siobhan, what are you saying here? You take Dempsey and McCullough for some latter-day Bonnie and Clyde? You think they killed Edward Marber?'

'Of course not,' she answered, trying for the sound of a dismissive laugh.

'Well, then,' Rebus told her.

She went on to say he was right. She'd sleep on it, cogitate over the weekend, maybe put it into some kind of binary . . .

'Some kind of what?'

'Never mind.'

They ended the call, but Rebus didn't move the car, not quite yet. Dempsey and McCullough as Bonnie and Clyde . . . It had been said in jest, but now Rebus was starting to wonder, not about Bonnie and Clyde as such, but about the relationship between McCullough and Ellen Dempsey, and how it might tie in to something much bigger than even Siobhan could have imagined.

'Fuck it,' he said finally, unable to sort out the jumble of strands in his head. Then he turned the car around and headed south.

Jean's lights were still on.

When she opened the door he was standing there with a fish supper and a bottle of red wine.

'Enough for two,' he told her, as she stood back to let him in.

'I'm naturally flattered. First dinner at Number One, now this . . .'

He kissed her forehead. She didn't resist. 'Got any plans for the weekend?' he asked.

'Nothing I can't change if I feel like it.'

'I just thought we might spend some time together. There's a lot about you I need to get to know.'

'Such as?'

'Such as . . . for future reference, do you prefer perfume, bouquets or fish suppers with wine?'

'That's a tough one,' she admitted, closing the door behind them.

27

The weekend passed in a blur. Saturday morning, Rebus suggested they go for a drive. They headed over to the west coast, stopping for lunch at Loch Lomond, spending the afternoon as tourists, passing through Tarbet and Crianlarich. Rebus found them a hotel just outside Taynuilt and they checked in, laughing at their lack of baggage.

'How will you cope?' he asked her. 'There's not a Napier's the Herbalist within a hundred miles.' She just thumped his arm, then went out and found a chemist's shop, returning with toothbrushes and toothpaste. Replete after dinner, they managed a short stroll down to Airds Bay before retiring to their room. They left the curtains and the window open, so that the first thing they'd see on waking would be Loch Etive. Then they fell asleep in one another's arms.

Sunday, they didn't rise till nine, blaming the country air as they embraced and kissed. Neither felt the need for any breakfast, just orange juice and tea. Some of the other residents were reading newspapers in the lounge. Rebus and Jean said good morning and then walked outside. The grass was damp with dew underfoot, and there were thick grey clouds overhead. Yesterday's distant views across the loch had disappeared into the mist. They walked anyway. Jean was good at recognising birdsong. She knew plant names, too. Rebus took deep lungfuls of the air, reminded of childhood walks in the countryside around his home village in Fife, coal-mines coexisting with farmland. He wasn't used to walking, could feel his heart pumping, his breathing slightly laboured. Jean kept up a stream of conversation, but Rebus was eventually reduced to monosyllables. He'd smoked only eight cigarettes the whole weekend. Maybe lack of nicotine was slowing him down.

Back at the hotel, they checked out and settled into the car. 'Where now?' Jean asked.

'Home?' Rebus suggested, part of him itching to spend the afternoon in a smoky pub. Jean looked disappointed. 'The slow route,' he added, watching her face brighten.

They stopped in Callander and Stirling, after which Rebus took an unwilling detour because Jean wanted to see Tulliallan.

'I was expecting some sort of guard,' she said, as they stopped halfway up the driveway. 'Nice grounds, though.'

Rebus nodded, only half listening. Tomorrow, he would be back here. Four more days of the course to endure. Maybe Strathern was right; maybe he should bale out. Gray, McCullough and Ward might well feel cheated, feel there was unfinished business, but would they do anything about it?

Not if they didn't think he was a danger. He wondered if Siobhan might now look more of a threat to them . . .

'John?' Jean was saying.

'Hmm?'

'I think I lost you for a moment there. Thinking about next week?' He nodded. 'I shouldn't have brought you here,' she went on, squeezing his hand. 'I'm sorry.'

Rebus shrugged. 'Seen enough?' he asked. He was thinking of the three men's bedrooms, and whether there'd be anything there for him to find if he broke in. He doubted it, but all the same . . . And where were they anyway? Was Gray at home in Glasgow? Had he taken Ward there with him, the two of them plotting their next move? Would Jazz have joined them, or was he tucked up in bed with Ellen Dempsey? Risky, her visiting him at home. It meant his wife knew about them, or Jazz wanted her to find out.

Or Dempsey didn't want him in her own home . . . Which would mean what? That this was some sort of arrangement she went along with, without necessarily being too thrilled about it? That there was a large part of her life she didn't feel like sharing with him?

'John . . . ?'

He realised he'd completed two-thirds of a three-point turn, leaving the car stationary in the driveway.

'Sorry, Jean,' he said, moving the gear lever into first.

'It's okay,' she told him. 'I had you all to myself for a whole day. I'm rather proud I managed that.'

'You certainly took my mind off things,' he agreed with a smile.

'But now they're back?' she guessed.

'They're back,' he admitted.

'And they're not going away?'

'Not unless I do something about them,' he said, flooring the accelerator.

He dropped her home, said he wouldn't stay. They kissed and hugged. She held up her handbag.

'Want your new toothbrush?'

'Maybe we could keep it at your place,' he suggested.

She nodded slowly. 'All right,' she said.

He drove out of Portobello, trying to remember if the roads through Holyrood Park were closed on a Sunday. If they were, he should probably take the Duddingston road. His mind busy with calculations, he was slow to spot the blue light behind him. When he did see it, it was accompanied by flashing headlights.

'Hell is this?' he muttered, pulling over to the kerb. The patrol car stopped behind him, a uniform emerging from the passenger seat. Rebus was already out of his Saab.

'Planning to breathalyse me, Perry?' The passenger was PC 'Perry' Mason. Mason looked anxious.

'We've had cars out all day trying to track you down, sir.'

417

Rebus's face hardened. 'What's happened?' His mobile had been switched off since Friday night – and still was – while his pager was somewhere on the car's back seat . . . His first thought was: *Siobhan. Don't let anything have happened to Siobhan . . .*

The driver of the patrol car was on the two-way radio. 'We just had orders to be on the look-out for you.'

'Whose orders? What's going on?'

'We've to give him an escort!' the driver called out.

'I've really no idea what it's about, sir,' Mason told Rebus. 'I'm sure they'll explain everything when we get there.'

Rebus got back into his Saab and let the patrol car move ahead of him. It put its blue light and siren on and sped up, leaving Rebus to follow close behind. The driver was enjoying himself, breaking the speed limit, pulling out on to the wrong side of the road to pass strings of traffic, ignoring red lights at junctions. They crossed north Edinburgh in no time at all, Rebus tensing up not so much from the drive as from the sense of expectation. Something bad had happened. He didn't want to think what. He'd expected them to be making for the Big House, but they continued west. It wasn't until they hit Dalry Road that Rebus realised they were heading for the warehouse . . .

The gates were open, four cars parked in the compound. Ormiston was waiting for them. He pulled open Rebus's door.

'Fuck have you been?' he asked.

'What's happened?'

Ormiston ignored him, turning instead towards the officers who were just emerging from the patrol car. 'You lot can go,' he snapped. Mason and his driver looked disgruntled, but as far as Ormiston was concerned they'd already ceased to exist.

'Going to give me a clue, Ormie?' Rebus asked as he was led into the warehouse. Ormiston turned towards him.

'How's your alibi looking for last night?'

'I was in a hotel seventy-odd miles away.'

'Any company around midnight?'

'Asleep in the arms of a good woman.' Rebus grabbed Ormiston's arm. 'Jesus, Ormie, going to give me a break here?'

But they were inside the warehouse now, and it became crystal clear what had happened. Two or three of the crates nearest the front had been upended, wrenched open.

'Compound got turned over last night,' Ormiston explained. 'We were going to move the stuff today.'

Rebus's head reeled. 'What about the guard?'

'Guards plural: both of them nursing fractured skulls in the Western General.' Ormiston was leading him through the warehouse towards the back, where Claverhouse stood, peering into a single, open crate.

'They found the right one then?' Rebus guessed.

'All too easily,' Ormiston muttered, his eyes targeting Rebus, pupils as dark as the barrels of a shotgun.

'About time,' Claverhouse growled at Rebus.

'He was a long way away at the time,' Ormiston informed his colleague.

'That's what *he* says.'

'Whoah,' Rebus said. 'You saying *I* had something to do with this?'

'Half a dozen people knew about this place . . .'

'Did they bollocks. You said it yourself: news had leaked out all over town.'

Claverhouse was pointing a finger. 'But *you* knew about the packing-crates.'

'I didn't know which one the stuff was in, though.'

'He's got a point,' Ormiston said, folding his arms.

Rebus looked back at the opened boxes. 'They seemed to find it bloody quick.'

Claverhouse slapped the edge of the crate. A door in the warehouse's rear wall opened and three men stepped through. They'd been out back, carrying on what, from their faces, had been an angry conversation. Fingers were being pointed. The fingers belonged to two men Rebus hadn't seen before. They were being pointed at Assistant Chief Constable Colin Carswell.

'Customs?' Rebus guessed. Claverhouse didn't say anything, but Ormiston nodded. The two agents from Customs and Excise were turning to leave. Carswell looked furious as he came towards Rebus.

'Christ Almighty, what's *he* doing here?'

'DI Rebus knew about the packing-cases, sir,' Ormiston explained.

'But I didn't steal it,' Rebus added.

'Any idea who did?' Carswell asked.

'What did C&E say?' Claverhouse interrupted.

'They're absolutely fucking furious. Said it should have been their shout . . . lack of co-operation and all that shit. No way they're taking any portion of the blame.'

'Do the media have hold of it?' Rebus asked.

Carswell shook his head. 'Nor are they going to – I want that understood. We handle this internally.'

'That quantity of dope suddenly appears on the street, it won't stay quiet for long,' Rebus commented, rubbing in some salt.

Carswell's mobile rang. He looked at the display, ready to ignore it, then changed his mind. 'Yes, sir,' he said. 'Will do, sir . . . Right away.' He ended the call, started playing with the knot in his tie. 'Strathern's just arriving,' he said.

'Strathern knows?' Rebus asked Claverhouse.

'Course he bloody well knows!' Claverhouse spat back. 'No way he couldn't be told.' He kicked the side of the packing-case. 'Should have moved the stuff *yesterday*!'

'Bit late for that,' Carswell muttered, heading off to meet his fate. Rebus could hear one car leaving the compound – the Customs agents – and another, the Chief Constable's, arriving.

'Who knew the move was planned for today?' he asked.

'Necessary personnel,' Ormiston answered. 'We've been talking to them all morning.'

'No one saw anything? What about CCTV?'

'We've got it on tape,' Claverhouse admitted. 'Four men in balaclavas, two of them tooled-up.'

'Sawn-offs,' Ormiston added. 'They thumped the guards, put some cutters to the padlocks, drove in.'

'Stolen van, of course,' Claverhouse growled. He was pacing the room now. 'White Ford Transit. Picked it up this morning half a mile from here.'

'Two guards for that amount of stuff?' Rebus shook his head slowly. 'No prints?' he guessed.

Ormiston shook his head. 'Two vans, actually,' he said, correcting his colleague.

Four men, Rebus was thinking. He was wondering who the fourth might be . . . 'Can I take a look?' he asked.

'At what?'

'The video.'

Ormiston's eyes went to his partner's. Claverhouse shrugged.

'I'll show you,' Ormiston told Rebus, angling his head back towards the door. They left Claverhouse still staring into the empty crate. Exiting the warehouse, Rebus saw Carswell in the back of Strathern's car. The driver had got out for a smoke, leaving the two men alone. Carswell looked distinctly uncomfortable, which pleased Rebus more than it should.

He followed Ormiston to the gatehouse. There was a TV there, the screen quartered and showing exterior views.

'No interiors?' Rebus said.

Ormiston shook his head. He was slotting home a cassette.

'How come the gang didn't take the tape?'

'The recordings are made on another machine, hidden in a box behind the warehouse. Either they couldn't find it, or didn't think we were taping them.' He hit the play button. 'That's one little detail we seem to have managed to *keep* secret . . .' The action was stilted, the video working on what looked like a five-second delay. The Transit stopping at the gate . . . two men rushing the gatehouse, while another cut the padlock and a fourth drove the van into the compound. Rebus only had the men's builds to go by, and couldn't identify any of them. The van was backed up to the warehouse doors, which were pulled open, after which the van disappeared inside.

'This is the interesting bit,' Ormiston said. Then he speeded the film up.

'What's happening?' Rebus asked.

'Absolutely nothing, as far as we can tell. Then seven or eight minutes later . . . this.' The videotape now showed a second, smaller van arriving. It, too, reversed into the warehouse.

'Who's this?' Rebus asked.

'Dunno.'

One or two men in the van, the gang now totalling six. A matter of a few minutes later, both vans left the compound. Ormiston rewound the tape to the point where the second van arrived. 'Do you see?'

Rebus had to admit he didn't. Ormiston pointed to the front of the van, just below the radiator grille. 'The first van, you could just about make out the licence plate . . .'

Now Rebus saw. The second van's licence plate was obliterated. 'Looks like it's missing,' he said.

'Either that or taped up.' Ormiston stopped the video.

'What happens now?' Rebus asked.

Ormiston shrugged. 'You mean apart from the internal inquiry and me and Claverhouse getting the boot?' He spoke phlegmatically, and Rebus knew what he was thinking: Claverhouse was the team's senior partner. His idea, him for the boot. Ormie might just about hang in there. But Carswell knew, and Carswell hid the scheme from the Chief Constable. The sackings could go higher than just Claverhouse . . .

'Has the Weasel turned up?' Rebus asked.

Ormiston shook his head. 'You think maybe he . . . ?'

'Look, Ormie, word got out about what you were hiding in that compound. Isn't it feasible that there could have been another leak? Half the city could have known about Claverhouse's little ploy with the packing-cases.'

'But how did they know which one?'

Rebus shook his head. 'I can't answer that. Claverhouse apart, who knew which crate the stuff was in?'

'Just him,' Ormiston replied with a shake of the head. It sounded like this was already very old ground.

'And was there anything about the crate that made it different from the others?'

'Not apart from its weight.'

'There had to be some way of telling which one it was?'

'The corner furthest from the loading-bay. With another case on top of it.'

Rebus was thoughtful. 'Maybe the guards knew,' was all he could come up with.

'Well, they didn't.'

Rebus folded his arms. 'Sounds like it was your partner, then.'

Ormiston smiled without humour. 'He thinks you told your pal Cafferty.' He'd turned to watch from the cabin's window as Claverhouse marched across the compound towards them.

'The team were in and out of there in under ten minutes, Ormie,' Rebus explained patiently. 'They *knew* which box they were looking for.'

Claverhouse appeared at the cabin's open door. 'I was just explaining to Ormie here,' Rebus informed him, 'how it had to be you.'

Claverhouse stared at him, but Rebus wasn't blinking, so the SDEA man turned towards his partner.

'Don't go blaming *me*,' Ormiston said. 'We've been through this a dozen times . . .'

It looked like there might be a dozen more in the future, too. Rebus squeezed out of the booth.

'Well,' he said, 'I think I'll leave you gentlemen to grind and gnash your teeth. Some of us have got the last precious hours of the weekend to look forward to.'

'You're going nowhere,' Claverhouse told him. 'Not until you've made your report.'

Rebus stopped. 'What report?'

'Everything you know.'

'Everything? Even the little chat you wanted me to have with the Weasel?'

'Strathern already knows about it, John,' Ormiston told him.

'And he knows about the late-night visit the Weasel paid to you,' Claverhouse added, grim satisfaction bringing the ghost of a smile to his pale lips.

Just then, one of the doors to Strathern's car opened and Carswell stepped out, crossing briskly to the gate-house.

'Your turn,' he told Rebus.

The smile was lingering on Claverhouse's face.

'You didn't think it worth telling me any of this?' Strathern said. He held a notebook open on his lap, tapping it with a silver pen. They were seated in the back of his car. It smelt of leather and polished wood. Strathern looked annoyed, and his cheeks were tinged red. Rebus knew he was going to be a lot more annoyed by the end of their talk . . .

'Sorry for that, sir.'

'What's this about Cafferty's man?'

'DI Claverhouse asked me to speak with him.'

'Why you?'

Rebus shrugged. 'I suppose because I've had a few run-ins with him in the past.'

'Claverhouse thinks you're in Cafferty's pocket.'

'He's entitled to his opinion. It happens to be untrue.' Rebus watched as the SDEA men, accompanied by Carswell, disappeared inside the warehouse again.

'You didn't say anything to Cafferty's man?'

'Nothing DI Claverhouse didn't want me to say.'

'But he sought you out?'

'He came to my home, yes. We spoke for a few minutes.'

'About what?'

'He was still worried about his son.'

'And thought you could help?'

'I'm not really sure, sir.'

Strathern looked over some hand-written notes. 'You visited the warehouse twice?'

'Yes, sir.'

'And your second visit was . . . ?'

'Thursday, sir.'

'Why were you there? Claverhouse says you weren't invited.'

'That's not strictly true, sir. I went to HQ to speak to him. He was at the warehouse, and DS Ormiston was headed down here . . . DI Claverhouse knew I was coming. I think he was pleased at the prospect. It meant he could show off his little idea.'

'The crates? Bloody idiotic . . .' Strathern paused. 'He says you came to offer an apology. Doesn't sound like you, John.'

'It isn't,' Rebus said. His stomach tightened. Things were about to get uncomfortable. 'It was a pretext.'

'A pretext?'

'I'd come to the warehouse because Gray, McCullough and Ward asked me to.'

There was a long silence. The two men fixed eyes. Strathern twisted in his seat, trying to face Rebus as best he could in the cramped confines.

'Proceed,' he said.

So Rebus told him. The planned heist . . . his way into the gang . . . how it was never meant to come to anything . . . the way they'd dumped him once he'd gone cold on the idea.

'They knew about the crates?' Strathern asked, voice ominously quiet.

'Yes.'

'Because you told them?'

'I was trying to make them see how impossible the whole thing was . . .'

Strathern leaned forward, placed his head in his hands. 'Jesus Christ,' he whispered. Then he sat back up, took a deep breath.

'There were five of them,' Rebus said as Strathern struggled to regain his composure. 'Maybe even six.'

'What?'

'Four men in the van . . . the CCTV footage. Plus at least one other in the second van.'

'So?'

'So who were the others?'

'Maybe one of them was you, John. Maybe that's why I'm getting this story. You're setting up your co-conspirators.'

'I was at a hotel on the west coast.'

'Convenient alibi. Girlfriend with you?' Rebus nodded. 'Just the two of you, alone in the room all night? As I say, a convenient alibi.'

'Sir . . . supposing I *was* involved, why would I have told you any of it?'

'To set *them* up.'

'Fine,' Rebus said grimly. 'It was you and your cronies who wanted them . . . go get them. And arrest me while you're at it.' Rebus opened his door.

'We've not finished here, DI Rebus . . .'

But Rebus was already out of the car. He leaned back down into it. 'Better to get the air cleared, sir. Let's have all of it out in the open: the Bernie Johns case . . . bent cops . . . dope kept hidden from Customs . . . and a coven of chief constables who managed to fuck everything up!'

Rebus slammed the door closed after him and stalked towards his own car, then thought better of it. He needed a pee, so walked around the side of the warehouse. There, in the narrow, weed-filled conduit between security fence and corrugated-aluminium wall, he saw a distant figure. The man was at the far corner of the building, hands in pockets, head bowed forward as his whole body seemed to convulse.

It was Colin Carswell, the Assistant Chief Constable. Kicking the fence with all his might.

28

'You're not going to get away with it.'

Monday morning at Tulliallan. While parking his Saab, Rebus had seen McCullough getting out of his own car. McCullough had been reaching into the back seat for his holdall. He turned at the sound of Rebus's voice, but then decided to ignore him. There was a folder he wanted, further along the back seat. He stretched for it.

Rebus planted a knee in the small of his back, ducked down so he wouldn't hit his head on the top of the door. McCullough was stuck, writhing in the confined space.

'You're not going to get away with it,' Rebus repeated.

'Get off me!'

'Think you can pull a stunt like that?'

'I don't know what you're talking about!'

'The hit on the warehouse.'

McCullough stopped moving. 'Let me up and we'll talk.'

'You'll do more than that, McCullough: you'll hand the whole fucking lot back.'

Rebus heard a car screech to a stop behind him, a door opening with the motor still running. Gray's fist caught him in his right kidney, then grabbed him by the collar. Rebus stumbled backwards, off McCullough and out of the car, falling to his knees but rising quickly.

'Come on, you bastard!' Gray was shouting. He had both fists up, knees bent, feet shuffling. A bare-knuckle fighter who fancied his chances. Rebus was grimacing in pain. McCullough was extracting himself from the back seat, face red, hair dishevelled.

'He says we've turned over the warehouse,' he told his friend.

'What?' Gray's eyes darted from one man to the other. Abruptly, he stopped acting the boxer.

'I just want to know how you knew which crate to open,' Rebus hissed, one hand rubbing his side.

'You trying to stick us in the frame?' McCullough said accusingly. 'Was that the plan all along?' He pointed a finger. 'Anyone's got hold of the dope, it's you.'

'I was on the other side of the country.' Rebus's eyes were blazing. 'What about you, McCullough? Will Ellen Dempsey give you an alibi? That why you've been cosying up to her?'

McCullough didn't say anything, just shared a look with his partner. Rebus felt like wincing, because now he'd really blown it, letting them know he knew about Dempsey. But the look which passed between Gray and McCullough was curious. There was fear . . . fear mixed in there with everything else.

Fear of what?

What was it that was lurking there? Rebus got the feeling it had nothing to do with the warehouse.

Siobhan . . . ?

'So you know about Ellen,' Jazz was saying, trying to sound offhand. He shrugged. 'No big deal. I left my wife weeks back.'

'Yeah,' Gray added belligerently. Rebus looked at him.

'That the best you can do, Francis? Don't tell me I've got you at a loss for words.'

'I've always let actions do the talking for me.' Gray rubbed his fist with his palm.

'If you think I'm going to let you get away with this . . .'

'Get away with what?' Gray spat. 'It's your word against ours. Like Jazz says, *you're* the fucker who set it up in the first place. And that's precisely what we'll tell anyone who comes asking.'

Rebus had to admit, they didn't seem worried by his

accusations. Angered, yes; worried, no. His mention of Ellen Dempsey had touched a rawer nerve. He decided to save it . . . think it over. Turned away and walked back towards his car.

'See you inside,' Gray called to him, and Rebus couldn't know if he meant inside the college building or in one of Her Majesty's many fine Scottish prisons. He leaned against the Saab. Gray's punch still throbbed. He hoped there wouldn't be any damage. He watched a procession of other cars heading along the driveway towards him. Some might be fresh probationers, preparing for their first tentative steps on the career path. Others might be senior officers, coming to hone their skills, and learn new tricks.

I can't go back in there, Rebus told himself. He couldn't stay, not for another minute. The idea of sitting around Tennant's table, avoiding eye-contact with Gray and McCullough . . . keeping up with the sham . . . surrounded by hundreds of recruits for whom Tulliallan was teacher and nourisher, friend and mentor . . .

'Fuck it,' he said, sliding back behind the Saab's steering-wheel. He wouldn't even bother calling in sick. Let them ask questions, phone Gill Templer. He'd deal with it when he had to – *if* he had to.

If he felt like it.

Right now, he couldn't get that solitary moment out of his mind, Gray and McCullough sharing a look . . . a look as if they'd come one step closer to the edge. A step too close for either man.

Protecting Ellen Dempsey . . . or being protected *by* her? Rebus was starting to get an inkling, but he'd need help if he was to prove any of it. Help, and one hell of a lot of luck. As he started away down the drive, he saw Gray in his rear-view. The man was standing in the road, legs apart. He'd made a pistol of his right hand and was aiming it at the Saab, wrist recoiling as he fired the imaginary bullet, his mouth opening silently.

Bang.

'You don't think Neilson did it, do you?' Rebus whispered.

Siobhan locked eyes with him and shook her head. She was seated at her desk, Rebus leaning down over her. He could see that on her computer, she'd been writing a report on the connection between McCullough and Dempsey, without mentioning Friday night's non-approved surveillance.

'I need to take another look at the case.'

'You can't,' she whispered back. 'You're still *persona non grata* as far as Gill's concerned.'

He was about to tell her that this wasn't the case any more. One call to Strathern, and the boss would inform Gill that Rebus was back on board. But then he looked around the room. Eyes were staring at him, curious as to his sudden appearance there, and the way he was trying to talk in private with Siobhan. Hawes, Linford, Hood and Silvers . . . Rebus wasn't sure how far he could trust any of them. Hadn't Gray worked a case once with Linford? Could Hawes still fall under Allan Ward's spell?

'You're right,' he whispered. 'I *am* a non-person. And IR1 is probably still empty.' He nodded slowly, hoping she'd understand, then pushed himself back upright. 'See you,' he told her, reverting to his normal speaking voice.

'Bye,' she said, watching him leave.

Interview Room 1 had yet to be cleared of the desks and chairs used by the Wild Bunch, meaning that in the interim all interviews would be conducted next door in IR2.

There was a knock at the door and it opened. Siobhan sidled in, carrying a thick manilla folder. Rebus was seated at one of the desks, nursing a coffee from the machine.

'Anyone see you come in?' she asked him.

'Nope. Anyone notice you leaving the office with that lot?'

'Hard not to.' She shrugged. 'I don't think I was

followed, though.' She placed the folder on his desk. 'So what are we looking for?'

'Sure you can spare the time?'

She pulled out a chair. 'What are we looking for?'

'Ties that bind,' he answered.

'Dempsey and McCullough?'

He nodded. 'For starters. By the way, I blew it this morning, told McCullough I knew about the pair of them.'

'I don't suppose he was thrilled.'

'No. But it means they'll both be ready for us. We need to have some ammunition.'

'And you think it's hiding somewhere in here?' She patted the folder.

'I hope so.'

She blew air from her cheeks. 'No time like the present,' she said, opening the folder. 'Do we each take a chunk of the inquiry . . . ?'

Rebus was shaking his head, getting up and moving to the chair next to her. 'We work as partners, Siobhan. That means reading each and every page together, seeing what ideas we come up with.'

'I'm not the world's fastest reader.'

'All the better. Something tells me you know this case back to front anyhow. This way, I get the chance to read everything through twice to your once.'

He slid the first stapled set of sheets out of the folder and placed it on the desk between them. Then, like kids at primary school sharing a textbook, they started to read.

By lunchtime, Rebus's head was pounding. He'd covered six sides of lined A4 with comments and questions. No one had disturbed their session. Siobhan was standing up and stretching. 'Can we take a break?'

He nodded, checking his watch. 'Forty minutes for lunch. Can you fetch a bag from upstairs?'

She stopped in the middle of a neck-stretch. 'What for?'

Rebus had his hand on the folder. 'This goes with us,' he said. 'I'll meet you outside in five.'

He was smoking a cigarette when she came out. Something was weighing down her shoulder-bag, and he nodded his satisfaction.

'Tell me we're not working through lunch?'

'I just don't want anyone else to know what we're up to,' he explained.

'Well, since it's your idea ...' She handed him the shoulder-bag. 'You get to be in charge.'

They went to a sandwich bar near The Meadows, sat on high stools at the window, chewing their purchases. Neither spoke. Their heads were still cluttered, the passing world a good excuse to stare unblinking and unthinkingly. Both sipped from cans of Irn-Bru. Afterwards, on the way back to St Leonard's, Siobhan asked Rebus how his filled roll had been.

'It was fine,' he told her.

She nodded. 'What was the filling again?'

He thought for a moment. 'Can't honestly remember.' He looked at her. 'What was in yours?'

Watching her shrug, his face broke into a smile, which Siobhan returned.

There was no sign that anyone had been in IR1 in their absence. They'd brought extra cans of juice with them, and placed these on the desk, along with the folder and the lined pad of notes.

'Remind me,' Siobhan said, opening her drink, 'what are we looking for?'

'Whatever it is that was missed first time round.'

She nodded, and they got back to work. Half an hour later, they were in discussion about the missing painting.

'It means something,' Rebus was saying. 'Maybe not to us, but to someone ... When did Marber buy it again?' Rebus waited while Siobhan flipped through the sheets, finding the right one.

'Five and a half years back.'

Rebus tapped the desk with his pen. 'We've been talking

about Neilson trying to blackmail Marber ... What if it works both ways?'

'How do you mean?'

'Maybe Marber was putting the squeeze on someone else.'

'Neilson?'

Rebus shook his head. 'The big money he was expecting ...'

'We only had Laura's word for that. Marber could just have been trying to impress her.'

'Fair enough, but let's say he *did* have money coming ... or thought he did.'

'Blackmail money?'

Rebus was nodding. 'From someone he had no need to fear ...'

'Can't be too many people out there wimpier than Edward Marber.'

Rebus held up a finger. 'Exactly. But maybe Marber wasn't going to be around for much longer ...'

'Because he was going to be dead?' Siobhan was frowning, feeling she was failing to understand Rebus's train of thought.

He shook his head. 'He wasn't going to be *around*, Siobhan. The empty self-storage unit, the paintings all wrapped up as though ready to be shipped out ...'

'Going somewhere?'

Now Rebus nodded. 'This place of his in Tuscany. Maybe he was thinking of persuading Laura to go there with him.'

'She'd never have agreed.'

'I'm not saying she would. But if he was infatuated with her, maybe he couldn't see that. Think of the way he got her the flat in Mayfield Terrace: springing it on her. Could he have been planning the same sort of surprise with Italy?'

Siobhan was thinking it through. 'So he's going to put some of his stuff into storage, maybe take some of it with him ...?' She shrugged. 'And where does that get us exactly?'

Rebus was rubbing his chin. 'It brings us back to the Vettriano ...'

The door opened and a head popped round: Phyllida Hawes. 'Thought I heard voices,' she said.

'We're in conference here, Phyl,' Siobhan complained.

'That's as may be, but DCS Templer is looking for DI Rebus. Toot-sweet, as I believe they say in France ...'

Gill Templer looked to be rearranging the paperwork on her desk when Rebus walked in.

'You wanted to see me?' he said.

'Heard you'd been spotted on the premises.' She crumpled a sheaf of paper and added it to the contents of her overflowing bin.

'Marber case solved to your satisfaction, then?' he asked.

'Fiscal's office seem inclined to go to trial. Few loose ends they want us to tie up ...' She looked at him. 'I hear you're AWOL from Tulliallan?'

He shrugged. 'That's all finished with, Gill.'

'Really? Sir David hasn't said anything ...'

'Give him a bell.'

'Maybe I will.' She paused. 'Did you get a result?'

He shook his head. 'Anything else I can do for you, Gill? Only, there's some work I'm trying to catch up on ...'

'What sort of work?'

He was already halfway out of the door. 'Oh, you know ... loose ends.'

He walked into the murder room and stood next to Phyllida Hawes's desk. There were only a couple of officers around. Rebus crouched down so his head was the same level as hers.

'Where was it you found me?' he asked quietly.

She caught his meaning. 'Anywhere but IR1?' she guessed. He nodded slowly, stood back up.

'Anyone else know?'

She shook her head.

'Let's keep it that way,' he said.

Back downstairs, Siobhan had finished her drink. 'Vettriano?' she prompted him. 'I'm not seeing it.'

He sat down, picked up his pen. 'Why take that particular painting?'

'Like you said, it meant something to someone.'

'Exactly. Say Marber had blackmailed somebody, used some or maybe all the money to buy himself a painting. He wouldn't be the first person to get greedy later on, decide he could get himself a little extra . . .'

'Nor would he be the first to die for his efforts.' Siobhan pressed the tips of her fingers together. 'He was thinking of leaving the country anyway, so decided he might as well try an extra squeeze on whoever it was he'd blackmailed. They didn't like that, so they had him killed, taking the painting because they knew he'd bought it with money taken from them.'

'But the painting didn't mean anything to them other than that,' Rebus added. 'Stealing it was a gesture – and a pretty rash one. So when Neilson started to look good as a suspect, the killer decided it could be the final nail in his coffin.'

'Something the Procurator Fiscal said,' Siobhan mused. 'The money Marber had paid Neilson . . . no one knew about it but us.'

'Meaning?'

'Meaning the only people who knew how firmly Neilson was fitting the picture . . .'

'Were cops?' Rebus guessed, watching her nod.

'But we still don't know who it was Marber was blackmailing,' she said.

Rebus shrugged. 'I'm not so sure he'd blackmailed anyone . . . not the first time round.'

'Explain.' She narrowed her eyes. But Rebus shook his head.

'Not yet. Let's keep digging . . .'

When Siobhan took a break to fetch more coffees, she returned with news.

'Have you heard the rumour?'

'Is it about me?' Rebus guessed.

'For once, no.' She put their cups down. 'Moves afoot at the Big House.'

'Do tell.'

'Word is, Carswell's moving on.'

'Really?'

'And there's some shake-up at the SDEA.'

Rebus whistled, but his act was failing to convince her. 'You already knew,' she stated.

'Says who?'

'Come on, John . . .'

'Siobhan, cross my heart, I didn't know a thing about it.'

She stared at him. 'Linford's looking boot-faced. I think he'd gotten used to Carswell's protection.'

'It's a cold world at the Big House if no one's looking out for you,' Rebus agreed.

They pondered this for a moment, then broke into smiles.

'Couldn't happen to a more deserving bloke,' Rebus said. 'Now let's get back to the *real* work . . .'

They decided some foot-slogging was necessary, so left the station – bundling the folder and all their notes into the shoulder-bag again – and made for the self-storage facility, where the owner wasn't able to add much. Marber had arranged for a standing order to pay for the unit. He hadn't said why he might need it. Back at Marber's gallery, they found his secretary trying to clear out the office. She was on a retainer from the estate until the work was complete, and didn't seem in a hurry to hit the dole queue.

Her name was Jan Meikle. She was in her early forties, with tied-back hair and thick oval glasses, her frame seeming needle-thin amidst the haystack of boxes, papers and artefacts in the overheated room. The gallery itself was empty, the walls denuded of the pictures which had given it its personality. Rebus asked where they were.

'Gone to auction,' Jan Meikle replied. 'All monies to accrue to the estate.' It sounded like the line she'd been given by Marber's solicitor.

'Were Mr Marber's affairs in order at the time of his death?' Rebus asked. He was standing with Siobhan in the doorway, there being no floor-space worth mentioning inside the room itself, apart from two small patches which were currently being occupied by Miss Meikle's sandalled feet.

'As much as could have been expected,' she replied automatically. It wasn't the first time a police detective had asked the question.

'You didn't get the sense that the business was winding down in any way?' Rebus pressed.

She shook her head, but didn't look at him.

'Sure about that, Miss Meikle?'

She mumbled something neither of them caught.

'Sorry?' Siobhan said.

'Eddie was always getting ideas into his head,' the secretary repeated.

'He told you he was selling up, didn't he?' Rebus asked.

She shook her head again, defiantly this time. 'Not selling up, no.'

'Taking time off then?'

This time she nodded. 'His place in Tuscany . . .'

'Did he mention anyone he might have been taking with him?'

She looked up, working hard to keep the tears from flowing. 'Why must you *persist* in this?'

'It's our job,' Siobhan stated. 'You know Malcolm Neilson's in custody, charged with Mr Marber's murder?'

'Yes.'

'Do you think he did it?'

'I don't see why not.'

'You want it to be him because it brings all this to an end,' Siobhan said quietly. 'But wouldn't it be better to get the person who was really responsible?'

Meikle blinked at her. 'Not Malcolm Neilson?'

'We don't think so,' Rebus said. 'Did you know about Laura Stafford, Miss Meikle?'

'Yes.'

'And you knew she was a prostitute?'

The woman nodded, unwilling to speak.

'Did Eddie say he was going to go to Tuscany with Laura Stafford?'

Another nod.

'Do you know if he'd actually asked her?'

'As I say, Eddie was always getting ideas ... This wasn't the first time he'd spoken of it.' She paused. 'And *she* was by no means the first woman he'd spoken of taking with him on one of his jaunts.'

From her tone, Rebus guessed that maybe Miss Meikle had at one time thought herself one of those candidates.

'Could he have meant it this time?' he asked quietly. 'He was putting his paintings into mothballs. He'd rented a storage unit ...'

'He'd done that before, too,' she snapped.

Rebus thought for a moment. 'The Vettriano that went missing, would there be any records here about its purchase? The when and where?'

'The police took them.'

'Did they take any other records?' Rebus was looking towards two four-drawer filing-cabinets in a corner of the room. 'We're interested in sales and purchases, between six and five years ago.'

'All in there,' the secretary said, nodding not in the direction of the cabinets but towards two large boxes on the floor beside the desk. 'I've spent the last two days sorting them out. Lord knows why ... it'll all probably go to the dump.'

Rebus tiptoed gingerly into the room, removing the lid

from one of the boxes. There were bundles of invoices and receipts, wrapped in clear plastic envelopes and elastic bands, page-markers sticking out, showing relevant dates. He looked up at Miss Meikle.

'You've done a grand job,' he said.

An hour later, Rebus and Siobhan were seated on the floor of the gallery, the paperwork spread out and divided between them. A few curious passers-by had stopped to watch, perhaps thinking themselves spectators at some new style of art installation. Even when Siobhan had raised two fingers at a studenty couple, they'd just smiled, as if in appreciation that this, too, must be part of the performance. Rebus had his legs stretched out, ankles crossed, back resting against the wall. Siobhan sat with her legs folded beneath her, until pins and needles set her hopping across the whitewashed wooden floor. Silently, Rebus was blessing Miss Meikle. Without her organisational skills, their task might have taken days.

'Mr Montrose seems to have been a good customer,' Rebus said, watching Siobhan rubbing the circulation back into her foot.

'No shortage of those,' she said. 'I didn't realise people in Edinburgh had so much money to burn.'

'They're not burning it, Siobhan, they're investing it. Much nicer to hang your cash on the drawing room wall than have it moulder in a bank vault.'

'You've convinced me. I'm closing my savings account and buying an Elizabeth Blackadder.'

'I didn't know you had that much tucked away . . .'

She flopped down beside him so she could study Mr Montrose's purchases. 'Wasn't there a Montrose at the opening?'

'Was there?'

She reached over for her shoulder-bag and produced the Marber folder, busying herself flipping through its many sections. Rebus called through to Miss Meikle, who appeared in the doorway.

'I was thinking of heading home soon,' she warned him.

'All right if we take this lot with us?' Rebus indicated the sprawl of paperwork. The secretary looked disappointed at what had become of her careful filing. 'Don't worry,' Rebus assured her, 'we'll put it all back together again.' He paused. 'It's either that or leave it lying here till we can come back . . .'

This was the clincher. Miss Meikle nodded her agreement, and made to turn back into the office.

'Just one thing,' Rebus called out. 'Mr Montrose: how well do you know him?'

'Not at all.'

Rebus frowned. 'Wasn't he at the preview?'

'If he was, we weren't introduced.'

'Buys a lot of paintings, though . . . Or he did four, five years ago.'

'Yes, he was a good client. Eddie was sorry to lose him.'

'How did that happen?'

She shrugged, came towards him and dropped to a crouch. 'The numbers on these page-markers refer to other transactions.' She started sifting through the paperwork, plucking out this sheet and that.

'List of people at the party,' Siobhan said, brandishing a sheet of her own. 'We were dealing with signatures, remember, some more legible than others. One particularly nasty squiggle is down here as possibly Marlowe, Matthews or Montrose. I remember Grant Hood showing it to me.' She handed him a photocopy of the relevant page in the gallery's visitors' book. No first name, unless the squiggle *was* a first name. No address in the space left for one.

'Miss Meikle says Montrose stopped being a client of Mr Marber's.' He handed back the photocopy, which Siobhan now studied. 'Would he turn up at a preview?'

'He didn't get an invite,' the secretary stated. 'I never knew his address. Eddie always dealt with him direct.'

'Was that unusual?'

'A little. Some clients didn't want to be identified. Famous people, or the aristocracy, wanting a valuation and not wishing anyone to know they were needing to sell . . .' She drew out another sheet of paper, checked its page-marker, then started looking again.

'Makes sense,' Siobhan was saying. 'We had Montrose down as being Cafferty. I can't imagine him courting publicity.'

'You think it was Cafferty?' Rebus didn't sound so sure.

'Here we are,' Miss Meikle said, sounding proud that her system had already proved its usefulness.

Montrose – whoever he was – had purchased in bulk to start with. A quarter of a million pounds' worth of paintings in a matter of a few months. In the years that followed, there were a few sales, a few more purchases. The sales were always at a profit. Although Montrose's name appeared on the sales slips and buyers' notes, his address was given as c/o Marber Galleries.

'All these years, and you never met him?' Rebus asked. Meikle shook her head. 'You must have spoken to him on the phone?'

'Yes, but only to pass him over to Eddie.'

'How did he sound?'

'Curt, I'd say. A man of few words.'

'Scottish?'

'Yes.'

'Upper class?'

She thought about this. 'No,' she said, drawing out the single syllable. 'Not that I'm one to pre-judge people . . .' Her own cadences were Edinburgh private school. She spoke as though dictating each utterance to some slow-witted foreigner.

'When Montrose bought a painting, it must have gone to some delivery address,' Rebus guessed.

'I think they always came here. I could certainly check . . .'

Rebus shook his head. 'And after they arrived here, what then?'

'I really can't say.'

He looked at her. 'Can't or won't?'

'Can't,' she said, sounding peeved at his insinuation.

'Could Mr Marber have kept them?'

She shrugged.

'You're saying this Montrose character never actually kept any of his own paintings?' Siobhan sounded sceptical.

'Maybe, maybe not. Say he'd no interest in them, except as an investment.'

'He could still put them on his walls.'

'Not if people might suspect.'

'Suspect what?'

Rebus glanced towards Miss Meikle, letting Siobhan know this was a discussion they should carry on in private. The secretary was twisting her watch-band, anxious to close up for the night.

'One last question,' Rebus told her. 'What happened to Mr Montrose?'

She showed him the final sheet of transactions. 'He sold everything.'

Rebus looked down the list of paintings and prices fetched. Montrose had walked away with a third of a million, less commission.

'Did Mr Marber put everything through the books?' Siobhan asked.

Meikle suddenly looked furious. 'Of course!' she snapped.

'In which case, Inland Revenue will have been notified?'

Rebus saw her point. 'I don't suppose they've had any more luck tracking Mr Montrose down than we have. And if they haven't started looking by now, I think they're whistling "Dixie".'

'Because Montrose no longer exists?' Siobhan guessed.

Rebus nodded. 'Know the best way to make someone disappear, Siobhan?'

She thought for a moment, then shrugged.

'If they've never been there in the first place,' Rebus told her, beginning to gather up the papers.

They stopped for a Chinese takeaway and, already being on Siobhan's side of town, went to her flat.

'I'm warning you,' she said, 'it'll look like a bomb's hit it.'

And it did. Rebus could see how she'd spent her weekend: video rentals, a pizza box, crisp bags and chocolate wrappers, and a selection of CDs. As she went to fetch plates from the kitchen, he asked if he could put some music on.

'Be my guest.'

He perused the rack of titles, most of the names meaning nothing to him. 'Massive Attack,' he called to her, opening the lid. 'They any good?'

'Maybe not for our purposes. Try the Cocteau Twins.'

There were four to choose from. He opened one, dropped the CD on to the tray of the player, pressed the load button. He was opening more of the cases when she came back through carrying a tray.

'You put your CDs back the right way up,' he commented.

'You're not the first to notice. I should also tell you that I line up the tins in my cupboards with the labels facing out.'

'Profilers would have a field day with you.'

'Funny you should say that: Andrea Thomson offered me counselling after that attack on Laura.'

'You sound as though you liked her.'

'Thomson?' She was being obtuse.

'Laura,' Rebus corrected, accepting the plate and fork from her. They started prising open the cartons of food.

'I did like her,' Siobhan confessed, pouring soy sauce on

to her noodles. She sat down on the sofa. Rebus took the armchair. 'What do you think of it?'

'I haven't started yet,' Rebus said.

'I meant the music.'

'It's fine.'

'They're from Grangemouth, you know.'

'Must be all the chemicals in the water.' Rebus was thinking of the drive between Edinburgh and Tulliallan, passing the flare-towers of Grangemouth in the distance, looking like some low-budget *Blade Runner* set. 'You had a quiet weekend, then?'

'Mmm,' she said, mouth full of vegetables.

'Still seeing Brains?'

'His name's Eric. We're just friends. Did you see Jean at the weekend?'

'Yes, thanks.' He remembered the way it had turned out, with a patrol car leading him at speed through streets not far from here . . .

'Shall we call a truce on asking questions about one another's love life?'

Rebus nodded his agreement, and they ate in silence. Afterwards, they cleared the coffee table and placed all the paperwork there. Siobhan said she had some lagers in the fridge. Turned out they were Mexican. Rebus frowned at the bottle, but Siobhan paid no attention; she knew he'd drink it anyway.

Then they got back to work.

'Who exactly was at the party that night?' Rebus asked. 'Do we have a description of Montrose?'

'Always supposing he was there and the scribble didn't belong to a Marlowe or Matthews . . .' She found the relevant pages in the folder. They'd interviewed everyone they could, but there were still some uncertainties. Bound to be, with the place so crowded and not all of the guests acquainted. She remembered Hood's computer simulation. The gallery had sent out a hundred and ten invitations. Seventy-five had RSVP'd to accept, but not all of them had turned up on the night, and others, who hadn't got round to replying, *had* turned up.

'Like Cafferty,' Rebus said.

'Like Cafferty,' Siobhan agreed.

'So how many were actually there on the night?'

She shrugged. 'It's not a precise science. If they'd bothered to sign the guest book, we might have been in with a shout.'

'Montrose signed.'

'Or Matthews . . .'

He stuck out his tongue, then stretched his spine and groaned. 'So what exactly *did* you do with all the guests?'

'We asked them who else they could remember being there: the names of anyone they'd known or talked to, physical descriptions of anyone else they could think of.'

Rebus nodded. It was the kind of painstaking detail that was oftentimes useless to a case, but very occasionally threw up some nugget. 'And did you manage to put names to all the faces?'

'Not exactly,' she admitted. 'One guest described someone in a tartan jacket. Nobody else seemed to have spotted it.'

'Sounds like they'd had a bit to drink.'

'Or had been to too many parties that night. There are a lot of vague descriptions . . . we *did* try to match each and every one of them . . .'

'Not easy,' Rebus admitted. 'So what are we left with? Anyone put a name to Cafferty?'

'One or two, yes. He didn't seem keen on striking up conversations.'

'You still see him as Montrose?'

'We could always ask.'

'We could,' Rebus agreed. 'But maybe not yet.'

She pointed to a particular paragraph on one sheet. 'These are all the descriptions that seem to be indicating Cafferty.'

Rebus read down the list. 'Two of them have got him wearing a black leather jacket.'

'Which is what he usually wears.' Siobhan was nodding. 'He had it on when he came to the station.'

'But another two have got him in a brown sports jacket . . .'

'They got through four dozen bottles of champagne,' Siobhan reminded him.

'And one person's got him with darker hair . . . describes him as being "fairly tall". What's Cafferty – five-nine? Would you say that was tall?'

'Maybe if the person describing him was on the short side . . . What's your point?'

'My point is that we could be talking about two different people.'

'Cafferty and someone else?'

'Who happens to share some physical similarities.' Rebus was nodding. 'Taller than Cafferty, with hair not turned so grey.'

'And wearing a brown jacket. That narrows things down nicely.' She saw that her sarcasm was lost on Rebus. He was deep in thought. 'Our Mr Montrose?' she asked.

'Maybe we're just starting to see him, Siobhan. Only an outline, but definitely there . . .'

'So what now?' Siobhan looked suddenly tired. They'd been working flat out, and now she was home and feeling like a bath and an hour or two of mindless TV.

'Just to put your mind at rest, I thought we might pay Cafferty a visit.'

'Right now?'

'Could be we'll catch him at home. But I want to drop into Arden Street first, pick something up. Oh, and we'll need to talk to Miss Meikle. Look and see if she's in the phone book, will you?'

'Yes, boss,' Siobhan said, seeing bath and TV receding into the distance.

29

Rebus told her to wait for him in the car when they reached Arden Street. She peered up, saw the light come on in his living room. Less than five minutes later it went off again, and Rebus emerged from the building.

'Am I allowed to ask?' she said.

'Let's save the surprise,' he answered with a wink.

As he drove them out of Marchmont, she noticed that he seemed interested in the rear-view mirror.

'Someone behind us?' she guessed.

'I don't think so.'

'But you wouldn't be surprised if there was?'

'Lot of people seem to know my address,' he commented.

'Gray and McCullough?'

'To name but two.'

'And the others?'

'So far, one's turned up dead and the other's gone AWOL.'

She thought it through. 'Dickie Diamond and the Weasel?'

'We'll make a detective of you yet,' he told her.

She was silent for a few moments, until she thought of something. 'You know where Cafferty lives?' She waited till he'd nodded. 'Then you know more than I do.'

'That's why I'm the senior officer,' he said with a smile. When she stayed quiet, he decided she deserved more than this. 'I like to keep tabs on Mr Cafferty. It's by way of a hobby.'

'You know the rumours?'

He turned his head to her. 'That I'm in his pocket?'

'That the pair of you are too similar.'

'Oh, we're similar all right . . . like Cain and Abel were.'

Cafferty's home was a large detached house at the end of a cul-de-sac behind the Astley Ainslie Hospital, in the Grange area of the city. The street suffered from poor lighting – probably the only time it came into contact with an adjective like 'poor'.

'I think this is the one,' Rebus said.

Siobhan looked. There was no sign of Cafferty's red Jaguar. There was a garage at the side of the house, however, so maybe it had been put to bed for the night. Behind the downstairs curtains, the lights were on. Curtains weren't that usual in streets as des res as this one. The owners either used the original shutters, or else left them open, so that pedestrians could peer jealously through the windows. It was a solid-looking stone-built residence on at least three floors, matching bay windows to either side of the front door.

'Not bad for an ex-con,' Siobhan stated.

'Be a while before he has us as neighbours,' Rebus agreed.

'Unless he suddenly comes down in the world.'

There were three steps up to the front door, but when they tried the garden gate, it was locked. The gates to the driveway looked locked too. Movement-sensitive lights were suddenly bathing them in halogen. The curtains twitched, and a few seconds later the front door opened.

The man standing there was tall and wiry, with a tight black T-shirt showing off thick shoulder muscles and a flat stomach. His stance was classic club-doorman: legs apart, arms folded. *You're not coming in here*, it said.

'Can Big Ger come out to play?' Rebus asked. He could hear a dog barking inside. Next moment, it came flying from between the bodyguard's legs.

Siobhan snapped her fingers and made clicking noises with her tongue. 'Hello there, Claret.' At the sound of its name, the spaniel pricked its ears up and waggled its tail all the way to the gate, where Siobhan had dropped to a crouch so it could sniff her fingers. Moments later, it was off again, sniffing its way across the lawn.

The bodyguard had turned into the house to speak to someone, perhaps surprised that Siobhan had known the dog's name.

'Claret?' Rebus asked.

'I met her at Cafferty's office,' she explained. Rebus watched Claret pause to pee on the lawn, then turned his attention to the doorway. Cafferty was standing there in a thick blue bathrobe, rubbing his hair dry with a matching towel.

'Brought your cossies?' he cried out, nodding to the bodyguard before retreating back inside. The bodyguard pressed a button and the gate clicked open. Claret decided to follow them indoors.

The wide hallway boasted four marble pillars and two Chinese urns, each a similar height to Siobhan.

'Need bloody big flowers to fill those,' Rebus said to the guard, who was leading them towards the back of the house.

'Your name's Joe, isn't it?' Siobhan said suddenly. The guard stared at her. 'I recognise you from a club I sometimes visit with my mates.'

'I don't do that any more,' Joe said. Siobhan had turned to Rebus.

'Joe here was the doorman ... always a smile for the ladies.'

'Is that right, Joe?' Rebus said. 'What's your other name?'

'Buckley.'

'And how does Joe Buckley like working for the east coast's most notorious gangster?'

Buckley looked at him. 'I like it fine.'

'Plenty of chances to put the frighteners on people, eh? Is that in the job description, or just one of the perks?'

Rebus was smiling. 'Know what happened to the poor sod you've replaced, Joe? He's going down for murder. Just something for you to bear a mind. Club bouncer might have been the smarter career move.'

Through a door and down some steps they found themselves at another door, which led into a vast conservatory, most of the space taken up by an eight-metre swimming pool. Cafferty stood behind the poolside bar, dropping ice into three glasses.

'An evening ritual,' he explained. 'You still drink whisky, Strawman?'

Strawman: his nickname for Rebus. Because of a mix-up years back in court, the prosecutor thinking Rebus was another witness, a Mr Stroman.

'Depends what you've got.'

'Glenmorangie or Bowmore.'

'I'll take a Bowmore – without the ice.'

'No ice,' Cafferty acknowledged, emptying Rebus's glass. 'Siobhan, what about you?'

'DS Clarke,' she corrected him, noting that Buckley had left them.

'Still on duty, eh? I've got some bitter lemon – might suit that scowl on your face.'

They could hear Claret scratching at the door behind them. 'Basket, Claret! Basket!' Cafferty growled. 'This is the one part of the house that's out of bounds,' he told them. Then he lifted a bottle of bitter lemon from the fridge.

'Vodka and tonic,' Siobhan said.

'That's more like it.' Cafferty grinned as he poured. His hair was thin and spiky where he'd rubbed it with the towel. The robe, capacious as it was, barely stretched around him, so that the tufts of grey hair on his chest were exposed.

'I take it you've got planning permission for this?' Rebus asked, gazing at the surroundings.

'Is that what you're reduced to? Planning violations?'

Cafferty laughed and handed them their drinks, nodding towards a table. They sat down.

'Cheers,' he said, raising his glass of whisky.

'Good health,' Rebus said, his face set like stone.

Cafferty swallowed a mouthful and exhaled. 'So what brings you out at this time of night?'

'Do you know anyone called Montrose?' Rebus asked, swirling his own drink around the inside of the glass.

'As in Château Montrose?' Cafferty asked.

'I wouldn't know.'

'It's one of the better Bordeaux reds,' Cafferty explained. 'But then you're not a wine man, are you?'

'So you don't know anyone called Montrose?' Rebus asked again.

'No, I don't.'

'And it's not a name you've used yourself?' As Cafferty shook his head, Rebus produced a notebook and pen. 'So you wouldn't mind writing it down?'

'I'm not so sure about that, Strawman. I have to be careful of entrapment, don't I?'

'Just to compare to a handwriting sample. You can make it a scrawl if you prefer . . .' Rebus pushed the notebook and pen across the table. Cafferty looked at him, then at Siobhan.

'Maybe if you were to explain . . .'

'There was someone calling themselves Montrose at the preview,' Siobhan told him. 'They signed the guest book.'

'Ahh . . .' Cafferty nodded. 'Well, as I know damned fine it wasn't me . . .' He turned the notebook round, opened it at a clean page, and wrote the word Montrose. It looked nothing like the signature on the guest book.

'Want me to have another go?' Cafferty didn't wait for an answer, writing the name a further four times, each one slightly different. Still none of them looked like the signature.

'Thank you.' Rebus took the notebook back. Cafferty

was about to pocket the pen until Rebus reminded him that it wasn't his.

'Am I off the hook?' Cafferty asked.

'Did you talk to a man at the party . . . slightly taller than you, maybe similar build . . . brown sports jacket, darkish hair?'

Cafferty seemed to ponder this. Claret had at last shut up. Maybe the bodyguard had dragged her off to her basket.

'I don't remember,' he said at last.

'Maybe you're not really trying,' Rebus said accusingly.

Cafferty tutted. 'And I was just about to offer you a spare pair of swimmming trunks . . .'

'Tell you what,' Rebus said, 'you jump in again, and I'll fetch the toaster from the kitchen.'

Cafferty looked at Siobhan. 'Do you think he means it, DS Clarke?'

'Hard to say with DI Rebus. Tell me, Mr Cafferty, you know Ellen Dempsey, don't you?'

'We've had this conversation before, I seem to remember.'

'Maybe, but back then I didn't know that she'd worked for you in Dundee.'

'Worked for me?'

'A stint in a sauna,' Siobhan explained. She was thinking of what Bain had told her . . . about how Cafferty's tentacles might stretch as far as Fife and Dundee. 'I think maybe you were the owner.'

Cafferty just shrugged.

'In which case,' Siobhan went on, 'you might have come into contact with a local CID officer, name of McCullough?'

Cafferty shrugged again. 'When you're a businessman,' he told her, 'a lot of palms seem to want crossing with silver.'

'Care to expand?'

Cafferty chuckled and shook his head.

Rebus shifted in his seat. 'Okay, here's another one for you to try. Any chance you can account for your whereabouts this past weekend?'

Siobhan couldn't mask her surprise at the question.

'The whole forty-eight hours?' Cafferty asked. 'If I put my mind to it. But you'd probably just be jealous.'

'Try me,' Rebus said.

Cafferty sat back in his wicker chair. 'Saturday morning: I test-drove a new car. An Aston Martin. I'm still thinking about it . . . Lunch here, then a round of golf over at Prestonfield. Evening I was at a party . . . the neighbours two doors along. Lovely couple, both lawyers. That was me till around midnight. Sunday we took Claret for a walk around Blackford Hill and the Hermitage. Then I had to go to Glasgow to lunch with an old friend – I can't mention her name, she's still married. Hubbie's in Brussels on business, so we booked one of the rooms above the restaurant.' He winked at Siobhan, who was concentrating on her drink. 'Got back here about eight . . . watched some telly. Joe had to wake me up around midnight and tell me to go to bed.' He offered a thoughtful smile. 'I think I *will* buy that Aston, you know . . .'

'Not much room for the Weasel in the back,' Rebus stated blithely.

'That hardly matters, as he no longer works for me.'

'Had a falling-out?' Siobhan couldn't help but be curious.

'A business matter,' Cafferty said, the glass to his lips, eyes staring above the rim and straight into Rebus's.

'Care to tell us which loch we can expect to fish him out of?' Rebus asked.

Cafferty tutted again. 'Now you're *definitely* not getting that swim.'

'Just as well . . .' Rebus was putting down his glass, getting to his feet. 'I'd only go and pee in your pool.'

'I'd be disappointed if you didn't, Strawman.' Cafferty rose as if to see them out, but then called his bodyguard's name. Buckley must have been standing right behind the door. It opened immediately.

'Our visitors are leaving, Joe,' Cafferty instructed.

Rebus stood his ground a moment longer. 'You haven't asked why I was interested in your weekend.'

'So go ahead and tell me.'

Rebus shook his head slowly. 'Doesn't matter,' he said.

'Always playing your little games, Strawman,' Cafferty chuckled. As they left, he was back at the bar, throwing more ice into his glass.

Outside, bathed once more in halogen as they walked down the path, Siobhan had a question.

'What's all this about last weekend?'

'Not your problem.'

'It is if we're working as a team.'

'Since when have I been a team-player, Siobhan?'

'I thought that was what Tulliallan was for.'

Rebus just snorted, opened the gate. 'Claret's a funny name for a brown and white spaniel,' he commented.

'Maybe it's because too much of it gives you a bitch of a hangover.'

He smiled with half his mouth. 'Maybe,' he echoed, but she could tell he was thinking otherwise.

'Bit late to go dropping in on Miss Meikle, isn't it?' Siobhan said, angling her watch towards the intruder-lights.

'You don't think she's a night-owl?'

'Cocoa and a bedside radio,' Siobhan predicted. 'When do I get to know what you were doing in your flat?'

'When we see Miss Meikle.'

'Then let's go see her.'

'I was planning on doing just that . . .'

30

Jan Meikle lived in the top half of a house conversion facing Leith Links. Siobhan liked the area. When they'd turned an old bonded warehouse nearby into flats, she'd visited a couple of times, and the only thing that had stopped her buying was the thought of moving all her stuff. She was reminded of Cynthia Bessant, Edward Marber's closest friend, and the warehouse she lived in not more than a third of a mile from here. Would Bessant have known if Marber was thinking of a move to Tuscany? Probably. Yet she hadn't said anything – no doubt mindful of his good name. She would probably have known he was wanting to take Laura Stafford with him, too – he confided in her, trusted her. It was a plan Bessant would not have been able to agree with.

Siobhan thought of sharing her ideas with Rebus, but didn't want him to think she was showing off. He would ask her how she knew, and she'd have to shrug and tell him: 'intuition'. He'd smile at that and understand, having relied on his own instincts many a time in the past.

'No lights on,' he was saying. But he pressed the buzzer anyway. A face appeared at an upstairs window, and Siobhan waved.

'She's in,' she said.

The next moment, the intercom crackled into life. 'Yes?'

'DI Rebus and DS Clarke.' Rebus spoke into the grille. 'There's one thing we forgot to ask earlier.'

'Yes . . . ?'

'I need to show you something first. Can we come up?'

'I'm not dressed.'

'We won't be staying, Miss Meikle. Two minutes will do it . . .'

There was a pause, then another crackle. 'Very well,' the tinny voice said. The door buzzed to let them know the lock was off. They walked into the reception hall, then had to wait for Jan Meikle to unlock her door and lead them up a narrow flight of stairs. She was wearing a baggy yellow jumper over grey leggings. With her hair untied and falling in straggles either side of her face she seemed younger. She'd applied a layer of night cream, making her cheeks and forehead glow. The upstairs was cluttered. Meikle was obviously something of a collector herself. Rebus could imagine her spending long hours rummaging in junk shops and haunting car-boot sales, buying eclectic pieces which appealed to her. There was no particular style or period on display – just masses of stuff. Rebus stubbed his toe on a plinth, atop which sat a large carved bird of prey. Lighting was provided only by a series of wall-mounted lamps, throwing long shadows in odd directions.

'It's the Bates Motel,' Rebus muttered to Siobhan, who had to stifle a snort of laughter as Miss Meikle turned towards her.

'Just admiring your collection,' she managed to say.

'A few gewgaws,' Meikle answered. Rebus and Siobhan looked at one another, each wondering if the other knew what the word meant.

The living room was three parts Edwardian parlour to one part sixties kitsch and one part contemporary Scandinavian. Siobhan recognised the sofa as Ikea, but was that a lava lamp sitting in the ornately tiled fireplace? There was no carpet as such, just eight or nine rugs of different sizes and designs, causing bumps in the floor where they intersected.

Rebus walked over to the window, which had neither curtains nor shutters. All he could see was the darkened expanse of the links, a drunk meandering home, hands in pockets, stiff-legged.

'What is it you have to show me?' Meikle was asking. Good question, Siobhan thought. She, too, was keen to know. Rebus reached into his pocket and produced five photographs. They were passport-sized head-and-shoulders shots. Men unused to smiling were trying hard. Siobhan recognised them.

Francis Gray.

Jazz McCullough.

Allan Ward.

Stu Sutherland.

Tam Barclay.

They'd been cut from larger sheets, probably handed out at the start of the Tulliallan course. She knew now what Rebus had been doing during the Arden Street stopover. He'd been busy with a pair of scissors.

Rebus laid the five photos out on a round three-legged table, the kind their ancestors might have played a hand of cards at. There was a crystal fruit bowl there now, sitting on a white lace doily, but still room for the tiny photos. Miss Meikle peered at them closely.

'Ever seen any of these men?' Rebus was asking. 'Take your time.'

Meikle showed every sign of taking him at his word. She studied each face as though this were an examination she must not only pass, but score high marks in. Siobhan had lost interest in the room now. She could see all of a sudden where Rebus had been leading her. How much of it he'd known and how much was intuitive she couldn't say. But he'd obviously felt for some time that the crew from Tulliallan were somehow connected to Edward Marber's murder. And she got the feeling it went further than McCullough and Ellen Dempsey: Rebus had hinted as much. McCullough and Dempsey weren't Bonnie and Clyde . . . so there had to be some other explanation.

'He was at the gallery that night,' Miss Meikle stated. She was touching the edge of one of the photos.

'Brown jacket?' Rebus guessed.

'I'm not sure what he was wearing, but I remember his face. He spent most of the time looking at the paintings. He had this smile on his face, but I got the feeling he didn't really like any of them. He definitely wasn't going to be buying . . .'

Siobhan leaned closer. It was DI Francis Gray. Similar in build and hairstyle to Big Ger Cafferty, but taller. Gray had managed more of a smile for the camera than his colleagues, pretending he hadn't a care in the world. Siobhan looked at Rebus. The look on his face was one of grim satisfaction.

'Thank you, Miss Meikle,' he said, beginning to gather up the photos.

'Wait,' she ordered. Then she pointed to Jazz McCullough. 'He's been to the gallery, too. A very pleasant gentleman. I remember him well.'

'When did you last see him?'

She considered his question with the same amount of care she'd given to the photographs. 'Probably a year ago.'

'Around the time Mr Montrose was selling his collection?' Rebus guessed.

'I'm not sure . . . I suppose, yes, it would have been around the same time . . .'

'McCullough is Montrose?' Siobhan said, when they got back outside.

'Montrose is all three of them.'

'Three?'

'Gray, McCullough, Ward.' He paused. 'Though how much Ward has had to do with any of it I'm not sure . . .'

'The money from Bernie Johns bought all those paintings?'

Rebus nodded. 'Hellish hard to prove it, though.'

'And Gray killed Marber?'

Rebus shook his head. 'That wasn't Gray's job. All he had to do was keep an eye on Marber, see what his plans were after the show. When Marber said he needed a taxi, Gray called one for him . . .'

'Making sure it was an MG cab?'

Rebus nodded. 'Then all Ellen Dempsey had to do was dispatch one of her drivers and let someone else know Marber was on his way home.'

Siobhan had it now. 'McCullough was waiting for him?'

'Yes . . . Jazz McCullough.' Rebus tried to visualise it. Marber at the front door. Jazz calling to him. Marber recognising both face and voice, relaxing. Maybe he'd been expecting a visit, because Jazz had some money for him. What had McCullough used? A rock? An implement of some kind? He would have got rid of it afterwards, knowing how to dispose of a weapon in such a way that it would very likely never be found. But before that, he had taken Marber's keys, unlocked the door and turned off the alarm long enough to take the Vettriano. A matter of principle with him . . .

'Where do we begin?' Siobhan was asking.

'I've always favoured the direct approach.'

She wasn't sure she agreed, but she got in the car anyway.

At quarter to midnight, Francis Gray got a call on his mobile. He was in the bar at the police college. His tie was off, the top two buttons of his shirt undone. And he was smoking. He still had the cigarette in his mouth when he walked along the corridor and climbed the single flight of stairs to the mock-up courtroom. This was where fledgling officers learned how to present evidence and deal with hostile questions. It was scaled-down, but correct in every detail. Rebus was sitting alone on the public benches.

'Bit melodramatic, John. You could have come and had a drink.'

'I tend not to mix with murderers if I can avoid it.'

'Jesus, not back to all that again . . .' Gray turned as if to leave.

'I don't mean Dickie Diamond,' Rebus said coldly. The door opened and Jazz McCullough came in. 'Not sleeping over at North Queensferry tonight?' Rebus asked him.

'No.' McCullough had the look of a man who'd been roused from bed, dressing quickly. He walked over to the desk beneath which sat the room's recording apparatus – controls for video cameras and microphones.

'None of it's switched on,' Rebus assured him.

'Nobody hiding under the benches?' McCullough said. Gray bent down to look.

'Clean,' he reported.

'You're smoking again, Francis,' Rebus noticed.

'It's all the stress,' Gray answered. 'Are you here to divvy up your little drugs heist with us?'

'Wasn't me.' Rebus paused. 'Don't worry, I don't think it was you now either.'

'Well, that's a relief.' McCullough was doing a circuit of the room, as though unconvinced that Rebus didn't possess back-up of some kind.

'You've got bigger things to worry about, Jazz,' Rebus informed him.

'John here,' Gray explained, 'has another murder he wants to accuse us of.'

'You're a single-minded little bastard, aren't you?' McCullough said.

'I like to think so. I find it gets results.' Rebus was sitting very still, hands on knees.

'Tell me, John . . .' McCullough was close to him now, stopped three feet in front of him. 'How many times have you stretched the truth a little in a place like this?' His eyes surveyed the courtroom.

'A few,' Rebus admitted.

McCullough nodded. 'Ever gone further? Fabricated a

461

case to put away someone you knew was guilty of something else?'

'No comment.'

McCullough smiled. Rebus gazed at him.

'You killed Edward Marber,' he stated quietly.

Gray snorted. 'The accusations just get wilder and wilder . . .'

Rebus turned to him. 'You were at the preview, Francis. It was you who phoned Marber the cab. That way, Ellen Dempsey could let Jazz here know it was on its way. I've got witnesses who can identify you. The call to MG Cabs will be listed on your phone account. Maybe that squiggle you used when you signed the guest book can be identified – amazing what these handwriting experts can do. Juries love all that stuff . . .'

'Maybe I needed a taxi for myself,' Gray speculated.

'But you signed yourself "Montrose", and that was a mistake. Because I have all the records of Mr Montrose's various purchases and sales. A third of a million at the last count. What happened to the rest of Bernie Johns's millions?'

Gray snorted again. 'There *weren't* any millions!'

'I think you've said enough, Francis,' McCullough warned. 'I don't think John's in any position to—'

'I'm just here to piece it together, for my own satisfaction. From what Francis has just said, I'm presuming Bernie Johns didn't have as much salted away as expected? So much for the mythical millions. There was enough to give you an initial lump sum – not enough to arouse suspicion.' Rebus's eyes met McCullough's. 'Did you use your share to help Ellen Dempsey set herself up in Edinburgh? No other way she could have gone from two cars to a fleet . . . had to be some kind of down-payment.' He turned to Gray. 'What about you, Francis? A new car every year . . . ?'

Gray said nothing.

'And the rest you invested in modern art. Whose idea

was that?' Neither man spoke. Rebus kept his eyes on McCullough. 'Had to be yours, Jazz. How about this as a theory: Marber happened to be in that sauna in Dundee the night you raided it. I reckon if I dug deep enough into the records, his name might pop up. Here's another theory: Bernie Johns's stash was hidden in or near the town of Montrose. Nice little joke there . . .' He paused. 'How am I doing?'

'You're not in a position to threaten us, John,' McCullough said quietly. He'd lowered himself on to one of the other benches. Gray had hefted himself on to the table used by the prosecuting counsel and was swinging his legs, looking desperate for his feet to connect with Rebus's face.

'Diamond told us all about you,' Gray snarled. 'The manse rapist . . . how Rico Lomax had hidden him away at the caravan, but by the time you got there it was too late. He'd scarpered. So you took it out on Lomax and told Diamond to vanish. You didn't *want* to help those two cops when they came to Edinburgh looking for Diamond.' Gray laughed. 'If we solved the Lomax case, it was *your* name we'd have in the frame!'

'He told you all that, and you still killed him?'

'Bastard drew a gun on me,' Gray complained. 'I was just trying to stop him shooting the pair of us.'

'It was an accident, John,' McCullough drawled. 'Not something that can be said of Rico Lomax's fate.'

'I didn't kill Rico Lomax.'

McCullough smiled benignly. 'And we didn't kill Edward Marber. You talk a good game, John, but I'm not seeing any evidence. So what if you can place Francis at the party? So what if he did phone MG Cabs?'

'Marber wanted money from you, didn't he?' Rebus persisted. 'He'd already had his cut – bought that painting with it. But now you'd sold all your paintings and taken your money elsewhere . . .' He broke off, realising that Marber had concocted *his* scheme because of the way he

463

himself felt he was being squeezed by Malcolm Neilson. 'What was the plan? Keep it invested quietly till you and Francis reached retirement? That's less than a year away . . . Ward still young enough to enjoy his share . . .'

'Problem was,' McCullough said, picking a thread from his trousers, 'we got greedy, decided to play the stock market. New technologies . . .'

Rebus saw Gray's face sag. 'You lost the lot?' he guessed. Now he knew why they'd been so keen on the idea of the heist. And something else . . . 'Bothered to tell Allan yet?'

Nobody said anything, and Rebus had his answer.

'We can't *prove*,' McCullough said at last, 'that you killed Rico Lomax. But that needn't stop us circulating the story. Just as *you* can't prove any connection between us and Edward Marber.'

'So where does that leave us?' Gray asked. McCullough locked eyes with Rebus and shrugged his response.

'I think some tombs are best left undisturbed,' he said in the same quiet voice. Rebus knew what he was referring to: resurrection. 'Don't you, John? What do you say? Do we call it a draw?'

Rebus took a deep breath, then checked his watch. 'I have to make a call.' Gray and McCullough were like statues as he pushed the buttons.

'Siobhan? It's me.' He watched some of the tension leave either man. 'Out in five.' Rebus ended the call.

McCullough patted his hands together in muffled applause. 'She's waiting for you in the car?' he guessed. 'An insurance policy.'

'If I don't walk out of here,' Rebus acknowledged, 'she runs straight to the Chief Constable.'

'If we were chess players, we'd be shaking hands right now, happy to share a result.'

'But we're not,' Rebus stated. 'I'm a cop and you've killed two men.' He stood up, started to walk out. 'See you in court,' he said.

He closed the door after him, but didn't make straight for the car. He walked briskly along the corridor, punching Siobhan's number back into his phone. 'I might need a couple more minutes,' he warned her, turning into the accommodation block. He thumped hard on one of the doors, eyes darting back along the corridor, in case either McCullough or Gray was following.

The door opened a crack and a pair of eyes, slitted against the light, appeared. 'What the fuck do you want?' Allan Ward asked, his voice dry and rasping.

Rebus pushed him into the room, closed the door behind them. 'We need to talk,' he said. 'Or rather, I need to talk, you need to listen.'

'Get the hell out of here!'

Rebus shook his head. 'Your pals have blown the money,' he said.

Ward's eyes opened a fraction wider. 'Look, I don't know what you think you're trying to pull . . .'

'Have they told you about Marber? I don't suppose they have. Shows how much they trust you, Allan. Who was it asked you to pump Phyllida Hawes for information? Was it Jazz? Did he say it was because he's been slipping one to Ellen Dempsey?' Rebus shook his head slowly. 'He killed Marber. Marber's the dealer who bought and sold all those paintings for you, building the investment . . . Only Jazz decided you could make faster money playing the market. I'm sorry to be the one to tell you, Allan, but the whole lot's gone.'

'Fuck off.' But some of the force had left Ward's voice.

'Marber decided he wanted another cut, and they didn't have the money to pay him. They were worried he'd blab, so they killed him. And whether you like it or not, *you're* implicated.'

Ward looked at him unblinking, then sat down on his unmade bed. He was dressed in a Travis T-shirt and boxer shorts. He rubbed both hands through his hair.

'I don't know what they told you about the plan at the

warehouse,' Rebus went on. 'Maybe they said it would be easy money . . . But they needed it, because in under a year from now, when they started taking retirement, you were going to find out that there were no shares to divvy out. You could put all those dreams of yours on hold . . .'

Ward started shaking his head. 'No,' he said. 'No, no, no . . .'

Rebus opened the door an inch. 'Talk to them, Allan. They'll lie to you. Ask to see the money.' He nodded slowly. 'Ask to see it . . . and look into their eyes when you do. There's no money, Allan. Just a couple of corpses and some cops gone very, very bad.' He opened the door wider, but paused again on the threshold. 'You want to talk to me, you've got my number . . .'

He walked outside, expecting at any second to be grabbed, stabbed or bludgeoned. Saw that Siobhan was still in the car, and felt the first wave of relief. She slid over from the driver's seat to the passenger side, and he opened the door and got in behind the wheel.

'So?' she asked, still sounding frustrated that she'd been left out.

He shrugged. 'I don't know,' he said. 'I suppose all we can do now is wait and see.' He turned the ignition.

'You mean see if they try to kill us too?'

'We write up everything we know . . . every step we've just taken. Copies to be kept in safe places.'

'Tonight?' she frowned.

'Has to be,' Rebus said, sliding the gear-stick into first. 'Your place or mine?'

'Mine,' she sighed. 'And you can keep me awake on the drive by telling me a story.'

'What kind would you like?'

'The kind where you walk into Tulliallan leaving me outside in the cold.'

He smiled. 'You mean a courtroom drama then? So be it . . .'

31

Tuesday morning, Morris Gerald Cafferty was enjoying breakfast at his kitchen table, feeding pieces of glistening sausage to an attentive Claret. Rebus sat opposite him, nursing his second glass of orange juice. He'd managed four hours' sleep on Siobhan's sofa, tiptoeing out without waking her. At quarter to seven, he was at Tulliallan, and now, just over an hour later, he was having to endure the smell of Cafferty's fry-up. A bustling middle-aged woman had cooked it, and, Rebus refusing the offer of a helping, looked ready to start on the washing-up until Cafferty told her to come back later.

'See if you can hoover some of Claret's hair off the sofa, will you, Mrs Prentice?' Cafferty asked. She nodded brusquely and left them alone.

'You don't get many like Mrs Prentice to the pound,' Cafferty commented, biting into a crisp half-slice of toast. 'Bring your cossie this time, Strawman?'

'I know it was you that hit the warehouse. Weasel told you about it, didn't he?'

Rebus had worked it out. Claverhouse hadn't just stumbled on the lorry – he'd been pointed in its direction by the Weasel, the man shopping his own son because otherwise Aly's life would have been short indeed. But having delivered him into police custody, he'd realised that Cafferty would still want blood when he found out. Rebus had offered short-term deliverance, but in the end there was only one way to save Aly: take Cafferty out of the picture. Which meant setting him up – telling him about the drugs in the hope that he would be tempted. But

Cafferty had plotted the hit without telling the Weasel, and the Weasel's hint to Rebus that night in the tenement garden hadn't clicked quite hard enough. The Weasel had been left out of the loop, and the heist had succeeded, leaving him – rather than his son – as the wanted man . . .

Cafferty was shaking his head. 'Don't you ever rest for a second? What about some coffee to go with that juice?'

'I even know how you did it.'

Cafferty dropped another chunk of sausage into Claret's mouth.

'I need a favour,' Rebus continued. He took out his notebook and wrote down an address, tearing out the page and sliding it across the table. 'If some of the merchandise found its way here, you might find the heat dissipating a bit.'

'I didn't know there was any heat,' Cafferty said with a smile.

Rebus lifted his glass. 'Want me to tell you something I know about claret?'

'The wine or the dog?'

'Both, I suppose. You can tell their quality by their good nose. When I saw your dog last night, nosing its way up and down the path and across the lawn, I knew.' Rebus's eyes shifted from Claret to her owner. 'She's a sniffer dog, isn't she?'

Cafferty's smile broadened, and he leaned down to pat Claret's side. 'Customs and Excise pensioned her off. I don't like my staff doing drugs, so I thought she might come in handy.'

Rebus nodded. He remembered the video footage: the van going into the warehouse . . . then a wait as they realised they didn't know where the consignment was. A quick call, and Claret had been driven there in another van. A few minutes later, it was mission accomplished.

'You didn't have time to steal another van,' Rebus said,

'so I'm guessing you used one of your own . . . that's why you blacked out the licence plate . . .'

Cafferty waved his fork at him. 'As it happens, one of my vans *was* stolen Saturday night . . . found it burnt out in Wester Hailes . . .' There was silence between them for a moment, then Cafferty sniffed and slid the piece of notepaper closer to himself, reading it upside down. '*Another* favour, eh?' His eyes gleamed. 'Made any progress on the Rico Lomax case, Strawman?'

'News travels.'

'It does in this city.'

Rebus thought back six years. Dickie Diamond telling him that the manse rapist was holed up in Lomax's caravan . . . Rebus getting there too late . . . At the end of his tether, he'd torched the caravan and paid a visit to Barlinnie, not to ask Cafferty a favour but merely to tell him the story, hoping Cafferty's contacts would succeed where he had failed. But that hadn't happened. Instead, his men had attacked Rico Lomax, beating him mercilessly and leaving him to die. Which hadn't been Rebus's plan at all. Not that Cafferty had believed him. When Rebus had returned to Barlinnie to rage at him, Cafferty had laughed, sitting with arms folded.

We should be careful what we wish for, Strawman . . . The words ringing in Rebus's ears all down the years . . .

'The Lomax case is closed,' he stated now.

Cafferty lifted the address, folded it into the pocket of his clean white shirt. 'Funny the way things sometimes turn out,' he said.

'And is the Weasel busy laughing as we speak?' Rebus asked.

'He's history,' Cafferty said, brushing toast-crumbs from his fingers. 'Think his son could have come up with a scheme like that? Weasel was about to make a move on me. Then he got cold feet, shopped Aly . . .' Cafferty made sure there were no crumbs on his shirt-front or trousers, then dabbed his mouth with a cotton serviette. He looked at Rebus and sighed. 'Always nice to do business with you, Strawman . . .'

Rebus stood up, fearing at first that his legs might not support him. His whole body felt like it was turning to dust . . . the dull sensation of ashes in his mouth.

I've made a pact with the devil, he thought as his hands gripped the edge of the breakfast table. Resurrection would only come to those who deserved it; Rebus knew he was not among them. He could find a church and pray all he liked, or offer up his confession to Strathern. Neither would make a jot of difference. *This* was how the jobs got done: with a tainted conscience, guilty deals, and complicity. With grubby motives and a spirit grown corrupt. His steps were so shallow as he walked towards the door, he could have been wearing shackles.

'I'll be seeing you in court one of these days, Cafferty,' he said, his words failing to have any effect. It was as though Cafferty had ceased to see him, his annihilation complete.

'One of these days,' he repeated under his breath, hoping to God that he meant it . . .

Allan Ward woke up late that morning. He was making his way to the dining room when Stu Sutherland, looking sprightly as the course neared its end, told him there was a 'mysterious envelope' waiting for him at reception. Ward passed the dining room and opened the connecting door to the original baronial-style building, where a uniformed receptionist handed him a thick A4 packet. He opened it in front of her, knew at once what it was. A typed report of Rebus's findings. Deciding to skip breakfast for once, Allan Ward headed back to his room. He had some reading to do . . .

32

Rebus spent the morning at St Leonard's, where nothing was happening. Siobhan had argued that they should talk to Gill Templer, persuade her to at least get Malcolm Neilson out on bail.

'Just a bit longer,' Rebus told her, shaking his head.

'Why?'

'I want to see what Allan Ward will do.'

He got his answer at midday when, about to pop out for some lunch, his mobile sounded. Caller ID: Allan Ward.

'Hello there, Allan,' Rebus said. 'Had a chance to speak to your mates?'

'I've been too busy reading.' There was a lot of background noise: Ward was in his car.

'And?'

'And I don't think I've really got anything to say to them. It's you I want to talk to.'

'On the record?'

'If you like.'

'Do you want to come here?'

'Where are you?'

'St Leonard's.'

'No, not there. How about somewhere else? I want to get everything straight first, talk it through with you. Would your flat be all right? I'm just west of the city.'

'I'll have the beers waiting.'

'Better make it soft drinks only. I've got a lot of talking to do . . . want to make sure it comes out right.'

'The Irn-Brus are on me,' Rebus said, ending the call.

He didn't see Siobhan. Maybe she'd headed out to lunch

already, or was networking with the uniforms in the toilets. There was no sign of Derek Linford either. Word was, with the case wrapped up he'd high-tailed it back to HQ, to keep tabs on the future of his one-time mentor. Davie Hynds had sidled up to Rebus earlier, complaining that he felt Siobhan was freezing him out.

'Get used to it,' Rebus had advised coldly. 'That's the kind of cop she is.'

'I begin to see where she gets it from,' Hynds had muttered.

Rebus stopped at a corner shop, bought six cans of Irn-Bru and four of Fanta. Tuna mayonnaise roll for himself. He took two bites of it as he drove, but realised he wasn't hungry. He thought of Siobhan. More and more, she reminded him of himself. He wasn't sure it was necessarily a good thing, but was glad of it all the same . . .

There was a parking space outside his tenement: the rest of the day was going to be good to him. Red cone on the pavement, which might mean they were going to start laying cables or something. The council always seemed to be digging up Marchmont . . . He was just about to close his driver's-side door when feet shuffled up behind him.

'You got here quick,' Allan Ward's voice said.

'You too . . .' He had his head half turned, saw that Ward had brought some friends with him. Next thing, the doors to the Saab were open again and he was being bundled into the back, a knife pressing into his side with enough force to let him know Francis Gray wouldn't need much of an excuse to use it.

Now the cone made sense: they'd used it to keep the parking-bay free until he arrived.

Which didn't exactly help the situation any.

The car was reversing at speed, McCullough turning the steering-wheel hard. Allan Ward was in the front beside him, leaving Rebus in the back with Francis Gray. It was an evil-looking knife with a long black handle and a shining serrated edge.

'Christmas present, Francis?' Rebus asked.

'I could kill you now, save us some fucking hassle,' Gray spat, showing his teeth. A dull throb of pain told Rebus that the tip of the knife had already pierced his skin. When he dabbed with a finger, he found a large droplet of blood. Shock and adrenalin were doing their work, otherwise he'd be feeling it more than he was.

'Made your peace then, Allan?' he called out. Ward didn't reply. 'This is insane, you must know that.'

'It doesn't matter any more, John,' McCullough said softly. 'Hasn't that struck home yet?'

'Francis *has* tried making the point . . .' He caught McCullough's eyes in the mirror. They seemed to be smiling. 'Where are we heading?'

'If this was Glasgow,' Gray answered, 'we'd be going for what we call a "short walk in the Campsies".'

Rebus took his meaning. The Campsie Fells was a hill range outside the city.

'I'm sure we can find a suitable spot somewhere on Edinburgh's equivalent,' McCullough added. 'Somewhere a shallow grave won't be disturbed . . .'

'You've got to get me there first,' Rebus said. He knew they'd be heading south out of the city, making for the wild expanse of the Pentland Hills.

'Alive or dead, makes no odds to me,' Gray hissed.

'That go for you too, Allan?' Rebus asked. 'This'll be the first killing you've actually participated in. Got to break your cherry sometime, I suppose . . .'

Gray was holding the knife at stomach-level, so it wouldn't be seen from passing cars. Rebus doubted there was any way he could escape from the Saab without Gray doing him some serious damage before he got out. There was a mad gleam to the man's eyes. Maybe that was what McCullough had meant: it didn't matter any more . . . they'd crossed the line permanently. With Rebus out of the way, suspicion would fall on them, but still with no concrete proof they'd done anything. Strathern and his colleagues had suspected them for years, and nothing had come of it. Maybe they really believed they could take Rebus out of the game with impunity . . .

And maybe they were right.

'I had a wee look at the notes you sent Allan,' McCullough was saying, as though following Rebus's train of thought. 'I don't see that you've got much of a case.'

'Then why take the risk of killing me?'

'Because it'll be fun,' Gray replied.

'For you maybe,' Rebus told him, 'but I still don't see what Jazz and Allan get out of it. Except that it binds you all together, makes sure one of you can never grass the others . . .' He was staring at the back of Allan Ward's head, willing him to turn round, make eye contact. Finally, Ward did turn, but only to speak to Gray.

'Do me a favour, will you, Francis? Kill him now so we don't have to listen to any more of his squawking.'

Gray chuckled. 'Nice to have friends, eh, Rebus? Speaking of which, maybe it'll be your pal DS Clarke next. Three murders . . . four . . . stops making any difference after a while.'

'I know who's got the stuff from the warehouse,' Rebus said, holding his side as the pain increased. 'We could take it from him.'

'Who?' McCullough asked.

'Big Ger Cafferty.'

Gray snorted. 'I like *this* game better.'

Rebus looked at him. 'The one where you end up no better off, but with a few corpses littered across your conscience?'

'Bingo,' Gray said with a grin.

They'd left Marchmont and Mayfield behind. A few more minutes and they'd be within reach of the Pentlands.

'I seem to remember there's a pub car park with a golf course behind it,' McCullough was saying. Rebus looked out at the weather. Rain had started falling about an hour ago, and was turning heavy. 'Probably pretty quiet this time of year. Lots of people go walking there . . . not so unusual to see four men out for a hike.'

'In suits? In the rain?'

McCullough stared at him in the mirror. 'If it isn't quiet enough, we'll go someplace else.' He paused. 'But thanks for your concern.'

Gray let out a cold chuckle, shoulders shaking. Rebus was running out of ploys. It was hard to think beyond the pain in his side. His whole palm was damp with blood now. He'd taken a handkerchief out, but the blood had seeped through its folded layers, too.

'A nice slow death,' Gray assured him. Rebus leaned back against the head-rest. This is ridiculous, he thought. Any second now, I'll be unconscious. There was sweat on the back of his neck, but his arms felt icy. His knees ached, too: there never had been enough room for passengers in the back of the Saab . . .

'Could you slide your chair forward?' he asked Ward.

'Fuck you,' Ward replied, not turning round.

'Could be his last request,' Gray commented. After a minute or two, Ward found the lever and suddenly Rebus had a few more inches in which to stretch his legs.

Then he drifted away . . .

'This is the place.'

McCullough was signalling, making a hard turn into a gravel car park. Rebus knew the pub – he'd brought Jean here, the place got busy at weekends. But this was a midweek afternoon with rain falling. The car park was deserted.

'Thought we'd lost you there,' Gray said, pushing his face close to Rebus's. McCullough was directing them to a spot at the far corner of the car park, next to a grassy slope. A public footpath wound its way around the playing area of the golf course and up into the hills.

They'd walked off their lunch, Jean and him, until the climb had started making them breathless and they'd turned to start their descent . . .

It was only as Ward was climbing out that Rebus noticed he was carrying something. It was a small spade, folded into two or three. Rebus had seen them in camping shops . . . maybe the same sort of place which had furnished Gray with the hunting-knife.

'Going to take a while to dig a hole big enough for me,' Rebus said to no one in particular. He made to slap his stomach, but found his shirt-front sticky with blood. Gray had taken off his own jacket and was wrapping it around Rebus.

'Don't want people to see you in that state,' he said. Rebus felt ready to agree.

Then they were out of the car, hands grabbing his arms to help him up the slope. Pain seared down his side with every step he took.

'How far?' Ward was asking.

'Need to get off the beaten track,' McCullough advised. He was looking around to ensure they were alone. Rebus's blurred vision told him they were . . .

Quite, quite alone.

'Here, drink this . . .' Someone was tipping a hip-flask into his mouth. Whisky. Rebus swallowed, but McCullough wanted him to drink more. 'Come on, John, finish it off. Eases the aches and pains.'

Yes, Rebus thought, and makes me even easier to deal with. But he swallowed anyway, coughing some of it down his shirt, more dribbling from his nose. His eyes were growing so tearful, nothing was staying in focus. They were having to hold him upright now, almost dragging him . . . One of his shoes came off, and Ward stooped to pick it up, carrying it with him.

One shoe off and one shoe on, diddle-diddle-dumpling, my son John . . .

Could he really remember his mother reading out

nursery rhymes at his bedside? The rain was dripping down from his hair, stinging his eyes, running down into his shirt-front. Cold, cold rain. Dozens of songs about rain . . . hundreds . . . he couldn't recall a single one . . .

'What were you doing at Tulliallan, John?' McCullough was asking.

'I threw a mug of tea . . .'

'No . . . that was just your story. Someone put you there to spy on us, didn't they?'

'Is that why you broke into my flat?' Rebus took a deep, painful breath. 'Didn't find anything, did you?'

'You were too good for us, John. Who was it put you up to it?'

Rebus shook his head slowly.

'You want to take it to the grave, that's fine. But just remember: it was no accident they had us working the Lomax case. So don't think you owe them anything.'

'I know,' Rebus said. He'd already worked it out. There must have been something in the files, something pointing to his involvement in the murder of Rico Lomax, the disappearance of Dickie Diamond. Gray had said it himself: Tennant always used the same case, a murder in Rosyth, solved years back. There had to be some reason for the use of the Lomax case, and Rebus was that reason. The High Hiedyins had nothing to lose after all, and at best they'd be killing two birds with one stone: Rebus might solve *his* puzzle; the Wild Bunch might solve theirs . . .

'How much further?' he could hear Ward complaining.

'This'll do,' McCullough said.

'Allan,' Rebus spluttered. 'I feel really sorry for you.'

'Don't,' Ward snapped back. He'd taken the spade from its plastic sleeve and was straightening it out, tightening the connecting nuts. 'Who wants to start?' he asked.

'I wish you could have been spared this, Allan,' Rebus persisted.

'You're a lazy bastard sometimes, Allan,' Gray snarled.

'Correction: I'm a lazy bastard *all* the time.' Ward grinned and handed the spade to Gray, who snatched hold of it.

'Give me the knife,' Ward said. Gray gave it to him. Rebus noticed that it looked clean. Either Gray had wiped it on Rebus's shirt, or else the rain had washed his blood away. Gray pushed the spade into the earth and pressed down with his foot.

Next thing, the knife was sticking out of his neck, embedded in the top of his spine. Gray gave a high-pitched squeal and brought a suddenly shaking hand around to find the knife. But all he did was flap at its handle before dropping to his knees.

Ward had picked up the spade and was swinging it at McCullough. 'Lost my cherry now, eh, Jazz?' he was yelling. 'You cheating bastard!' Rebus was working hard at staying upright, watching it all happen in a hazy slow motion, realising that Allan Ward had been brooding and stewing these past hours. The spade was slicing into McCullough's cheek, bringing with it a spume of blood. McCullough staggered backwards, stumbling and falling. Gray had keeled over on to his side and was shuddering like a wasp hit with a blast of insecticide.

'Allan, for Christ's sake . . .' Blood gurgled in McCullough's mouth.

'It was always you two against me,' Ward was explaining, voice shaking. There were flecks of white at the corners of his mouth. 'Right down the line.'

'Kept you out of it to protect you.'

'Like hell you did!' Ward raised the spade again, towering over McCullough, but Rebus, standing next to the young man now, placed a hand on his arm.

'Enough, Allan. No need to take it further . . .'

Ward paused, then blinked, and his shoulders dropped. 'Call it in,' he said quietly. Rebus nodded. He already had the phone in his hand.

'When did you decide?' he asked, pushing the buttons.

'Decide what?'

'To let me live.'

Ward looked at him. 'Five, ten minutes ago.'

Rebus raised the phone to his ear. 'Thanks,' he said.

Allan Ward slumped down on to the wet grass. Rebus felt like joining him, maybe laying down and going back to sleep.

In a minute, he told himself. In a minute . . .

33

With Allan Ward's confession, there was no real necessity for the kilo of heroin which Claverhouse – recipient of an anonymous tip-off – found in Jazz McCullough's rented flat. But Rebus hadn't known that at the time. As it was, the fact that the heroin came from the stolen consignment meant that Claverhouse might salvage something of his career at the SDEA, though demotion remained a near cert. Rebus was curious to find out how Claverhouse would cope, serving under Ormiston, for so long his junior . . .

Rebus required a blood transfusion and seven stitches. As the blood from the anonymous donors dripped into him, Rebus felt he should repay them in some way for his gift of renewed life. He wondered who they were: adulterers, misfits, Christians, racists . . . ? It was the deed that mattered, not the individual. He was up and about soon afterwards. Rain was still falling on the city. On the route to the cemetery, Rebus's taxi-driver commented that it seemed it would never stop.

'And sometimes I don't want it to,' he admitted. 'Makes everything smell clean, doesn't it?'

Rebus agreed that it did. He told the driver to keep the meter running, he'd only be five minutes. The newest headstones were closest to the gate. Dickie Diamond's was no longer the latest addition. Rebus didn't feel bad that he'd missed the funeral. He had no flowers for the Diamond Dog, even though he was carrying a small posy. He didn't think Dickie would mind . . .

Further into the cemetery were the older graves, some

well tended, others seemingly forgotten. Louise Hodd's husband was still alive, though no longer a Church of Scotland minister. He'd gone to pieces after her rape and suicide, picking himself up again only slowly. There were fresh flowers by her headstone, to which Rebus added his posy, staying on his knees for a minute. It was as close as he came these days to prayer. He'd memorised the inscription, her dates of birth and death. Her maiden name had been Fielding. Six years since she took her life. Six years since Rico Lomax had died as a kind of retribution. Her attacker, Michael Veitch, was dead also, stabbed in jail by someone who'd known nothing of this particular crime. No one had planned it, or asked for it to happen. But it had happened anyway.

A complete and utter waste. Rebus could feel his stitches tingling, reminding him that *he* was still alive. All because Allan Ward had changed his mind. He rose to his feet again, brushing the earth from his trousers and hands.

Sometimes that was all it took to effect a kind of resurrection. Maybe Allan Ward, plenty of jail time ahead of him for contemplation, would come to realise that.

34

'Then why are you here?' Andrea Thomson pressed her hands together, resting her chin on her fingertips. For this meeting, she had borrowed an office at Fettes HQ. It was the same office she always used when there were officers in Edinburgh with a need for counselling. 'Is it because you feel cheated of some sort of victory?'

'Did I say that?'

'I felt it was what you were trying to say. Did I misunderstand?'

'I don't know ... I used to think policing was about upholding the law ... all that stuff they taught you at Tulliallan.'

'And now?' Thomson had picked up her pen, but only as a prop. She didn't write anything down until after the sessions.

'Now?' A shrug. 'I'm not sure those laws necessarily work.'

'Even when you achieve a successful result?'

'Is that what's been achieved?'

'You solved the case, didn't you? An innocent man has been released from custody. Doesn't sound like a bad result to me.'

'Maybe not.'

'Is it the means of achieving the end? You think that's where the system's at fault?'

'Maybe the fault lies with me. Maybe I'm just not cut out to ...'

'To what?'

Another shrug. 'Play the game, perhaps.'

Thomson studied her pen. 'You've seen someone die. It's bound to have affected you.'

'Only because I let it.'

'Because you're *human*.'

'I don't know where any of this is going,' Siobhan said with a shake of her head.

'No one's blaming you, DS Clarke. Quite the reverse.'

'And I don't deserve it.'

'We all get things we feel we don't deserve,' Thomson said with a smile. 'Most of us treat them as windfalls. Your career so far has been a success. Is that the problem perhaps? You don't *want* that easy success? You want to be an outsider, someone who breaks the rules with only a measure of impunity?' She paused. 'Maybe you want to be like DI Rebus?'

'I'm well aware that there's not the room for more than one of him.'

'But all the same . . . ?'

Siobhan thought about it, but ended up offering only a shrug.

'So tell me what you *like* about the job.' Andrea Thomson leaned forward in her chair, trying to appear genuinely interested.

Siobhan shrugged again. Thomson looked disappointed. 'What about outside work? Are there any keen interests you have?'

Siobhan thought for a long time. 'Music, chocolate, football, drink.' She looked at her watch. 'With any luck, I'll have time to indulge in at least three of them after this.'

Thomson's professional smile faded perceptibly.

'I also like long drives and home-delivery pizza,' Siobhan added, warming to the subject.

'What about relationships?' Thomson asked.

'What about them?'

'Is there some special relationship you're in just now?'

'Only with the job, Ms Thomson ... And I'm not absolutely sure it loves me any more.'

'What do you plan to do about that, DS Clarke?'

'I don't know ... maybe I could take it to bed with me and feed it Cadbury's Whole Nut. That's always worked for me in the past.'

When Thomson looked up from her cheap blue biro, she saw that Siobhan was grinning.

'I think that's probably enough for today,' the counsellor said.

'Probably,' Siobhan said, getting to her feet. 'And thank you ... I feel heaps better.'

'And I feel like a large bar of chocolate,' Andrea Thomson said.

'The canteen should still be open.'

Thomson put her unblemished A4 pad into her bag. 'Then what are we waiting for?' she asked.